ONE OF US IS DEAD

WANT YOU DEAD

Who knew online dating could be so deadly?

YOU ARE DEAD

Brighton falls victim to its first serial killer in eighty years.

LOVE YOU DEAD

A deadly black widow is on the hunt for
her next husband.

NEED YOU DEAD

Every killer makes a mistake somewhere.
You just have to find it.

DEAD IF YOU DON'T

A kidnapping triggers a parent's worst nightmare
and a race against time for Roy Grace.

DEAD AT FIRST SIGHT

Roy Grace exposes the lethal side
of online identity fraud.

FIND THEM DEAD

A ruthless Brighton gangster is on trial and will
do anything to walk free.

LEFT YOU DEAD

When a woman in Brighton vanishes without a trace,
Roy Grace is called in to investigate.

PICTURE YOU DEAD

Not all windfalls are lucky. Some can
lead to murder.

STOP THEM DEAD

A senseless murder hides a multitude of other crimes.

ONE OF US IS DEAD

Roy Grace is about to find out just how dangerous
a dead man can be.

ONE OF US IS DEAD

PETER JAMES

MACMILLAN

First published 2024 by Macmillan
an imprint of Pan Macmillan
The Smithson, 6 Briset Street, London EC1M 5NR
EU representative: Macmillan Publishers Ireland Ltd, 1st Floor,
The Liffey Trust Centre, 117–126 Sheriff Street Upper,
Dublin 1, D01 YC43
Associated companies throughout the world
www.panmacmillan.com

ISBN 978-1-5290-9001-7 HB
ISBN 978-1-5290-9002-4 TPB

1 3 5 7 9 8 6 4 2

A CIP catalogue record for this book is available from the British Library.

Map artwork by ML Design
Contains OS data © Crown copyright and database right (2024)

Typeset by Palimpsest Book Production Ltd, Falkirk, Stirlingshire
Printed and bound by CPI Group (UK) Ltd, Croydon, CR0 4YY

Visit **www.panmacmillan.com** to read more about all our books
and to buy them. You will also find features, author interviews and
news of any author events, and you can sign up for e-newsletters
so that you're always first to hear about our new releases.

TO LYN GAYLOR

VERY DEAR FRIEND, INVALUABLE CRITIC
AND ALL-ROUND GREAT TROOPER!

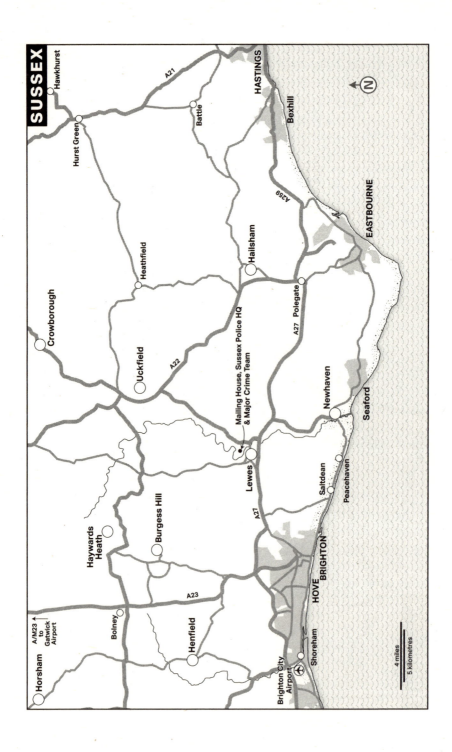

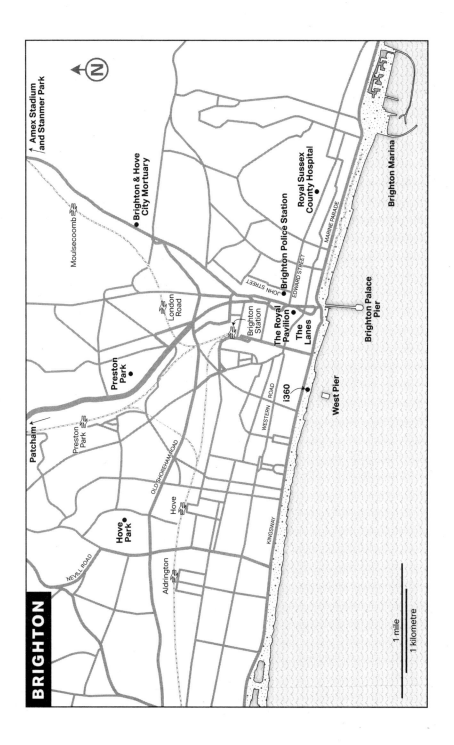

BRIGHTON

N

Amex Stadium
and Stanmer Park

Patcham

Preston Park

Moulsecoomb

Brighton & Hove
City Mortuary

NEVILL ROAD

Hove
Park

Aldrington

OLD SHOREHAM ROAD

Hove

Preston
Park

London
Road

Brighton
Station

The Royal
Pavilion

The
Lanes

Brighton Police Station

JOHN STREET

EDWARD STREET

Royal Sussex
County Hospital

MARINE PARADE

WESTERN ROAD

i360

KINGSWAY

West Pier

Brighton Palace
Pier

Brighton Marina

1 mile

1 kilometre

1

Friday 23 September 2022

The small village church was packed, and Taylor, who had arrived at the funeral late, just as the service was beginning, had to stand at the back, dripping wet from the pelting rain outside. But he wasn't looking at the coffin, nor at the cleric, the almost overbearingly pious Reverend Ian Parry-Jones with his pristine cassock, zealot's eyes and mad white hair, who was giving a good impression of genuine sincerity – but a less convincing one of having actually known the unfortunate star of the show.

Instead, Taylor was staring at the back of the head of a man sitting six rows in front of him. Transfixed.

Even though he hadn't yet had a chance to see the man's face clearly – the man was wearing dark glasses, a scarf and a baseball cap – Taylor was certain it was Rufus Rorke. His old school friend. Except it couldn't be. It wasn't possible.

The man inclined his head slightly to the left, as if resting it on his shoulder – the quirky way Rufus had always done when he was composing a reply to something someone had just said. And now Taylor was even more sure. It was Rufus, it absolutely was!

Except it could not be. Rufus Rorke had been dead for two years. Taylor had given the eulogy at his funeral.

2

WTF???

Taylor could not take his eyes off the man as the service proceeded, interminably. There were two cheesy poetry readings by – according to the service sheet – Barnie's nieces, and another that Taylor liked, about not being dead but just in the next room, which was read by a woman in a veil, Barnie's ex-wife, Debbie Martin (she'd kept her maiden name even when they were married), though several lines were drowned out by a baby screaming.

These were followed by a tribute given by a dapper man of around forty, who in a virtuoso performance of pure fiction, interrupted again by the baby, portrayed the deceased as pretty much just one miracle short of sainthood. The sun had come out and its rays shone through the stained-glass window behind the pulpit, creating a halo effect around the man's head.

Maybe Barnie would be canonized one day, Taylor thought wryly. He could be the patron saint of losers.

Taylor had only come to the funeral out of a sense of duty – he'd not seen Barnie for years, other than briefly at Rufus's funeral two years ago. But the three of them had been tight at school – Taylor, Rufus and Barnie. The Three Musketeers, they called themselves. And, for a while after leaving, they'd continued meeting up for lunch or for an evening at a boozer close to one of them. They'd vowed they would always stay in touch, but of course life had other plans.

The more time passed, the more they'd gone their own, very different ways. None of them had really had anything in common – beyond a shared dislike of their school – to bind them together. Rufus, the boisterous, loudmouth charmer, had bragged that he'd be a millionaire by the age of thirty. And maybe he had been, not that it had done him much good. He was dead at thirty-nine.

Well, so it had seemed.

And now poor Barnie, the eternal dreamer of fame and fortune, who had changed addresses more times than Taylor could count, was about to move to his forever home, Plot PY136, Woodvale Cemetery.

But at least poor Barnie was finally having his day in the sun, Taylor thought, the attention he had always craved. The coffin was far grander than its poor occupant had ever been, sitting centre stage on the catafalque, brass handles gleaming in the stained-glass sunlight. It looked magnificent enough to house the Pope.

Taylor wondered who had paid for it. Not that he really cared.

He only cared about one thing in that moment: the identity of the man sitting six rows in front of him.

Could it be Rufus?

Of course not.

And yet . . .

He continued to stare, totally fixated. Every move the man made further convinced Taylor that it was him. It was all he could do to restrain himself from walking down the aisle, reaching across and tapping the man on the shoulder, but with the church this rammed, that was not an option.

Then, suddenly, inexplicably, the man turned around, a full 180 degrees, and, for a few seconds, stared directly at him as if sensing his presence.

Although his face was almost completely obscured by the scarf and the peak of his cap, Taylor shivered, chilled to the core.

Then the man turned away again.

All kinds of thoughts rushed through his mind. Did Rufus have a brother? A twin? But never, ever, in all the years that they'd known each other, had Rufus given any indication that he had a sibling.

Shit. This was insane. Maybe, Taylor thought, he was going crazy?

Normally scrupulously punctual, he was cursing the circumstances that had conspired to cause his late arrival here, starting with a flat tyre after dropping off his son, who was staying with him this week, at school. And then, having changed the tyre, getting stopped in a speed trap. Not the best of days, but at least a better one than Barnie was having.

Had he arrived earlier, perhaps he could have seen who this man really was. He had to be imagining it was Rufus. Had to be.

But he could not stop staring at him. And he was feeling a deep prickle of unease.

There must be well over 150 people in here, he thought, and so far, other than Debbie and potentially Rufus, he didn't recognize any of them. He wondered sardonically if all of them – like himself – were owed money by Barnie.

Always the loser, Barnie had constantly been in debt at school – gambling away his pocket money – and nothing had changed. Every few years, in those early days after they had left, Taylor used to get calls from Barnie asking if he could loan him a few bob, promising to pay it back. And sometimes Taylor had reluctantly ponied up, because he felt sorry for him. Barnie seemed to have been born with a big 'L' tattooed on his forehead.

Rufus had once cruelly told Barnie, to his face, that he was the kind of man who would come second in an election, even if no one was running against him.

And yet, for as long as they had known each other, Barnie had always craved the limelight. Today he sure had it. Too bad he wasn't able to enjoy it, Taylor thought.

He took his eyes off the back of the head of the man six rows in front of him just for a moment, to glance at the order of service sheet he'd been handed. He looked from the photo on the back – angelic little Barnie, aged four, with blond curls, baggy shorts and mischief in his eyes – to the photo on the front: a balding, overweight and older-than-his years Barnie, with haunted eyes peering out from their hidey-holes in his flesh, as if trying to spot where all of life's promise had gone. Even the smudged funeral service sheets looked like rejects. Poor Barnie Wallace: failed musician, failed chef, failed husband, failed everything – including, fatally, failed forager.

The story Taylor had heard was that Barnie had been felled by mushrooms he was cooking as a starter at a dinner party, though fortunately his group of friends never got to eat them. According to Debbie, who had notified Taylor of the funeral, Barnie had mistaken death cap mushrooms for field mushrooms – apparently an easy error. Luckily for his intended guests, Barnie had prepped the meal a day in advance to do a photo shoot for his Instagram account. He'd eaten the leftover mushrooms for his dinner that night and been hospitalized twelve hours later, subsequently dying from multiple organ failure.

Taylor looked around the congregation again, but couldn't spot anyone else he knew. He was a little surprised that there were no familiar faces from school. Mind you, the trio had left over twenty years ago.

The tributes were followed by the eternally rousing hymn 'Jerusalem'. As the last strains of 'in England's green and pleasant land' faded, a man staggered up to the pulpit to deliver the eulogy. His name was Geoffrey Letts – a total tosser by any standards, Taylor thought. Geoffrey began by professing to be a drinking companion of Barnie at some pub (and he already appeared worse for wear at this hour). He told the congregation, slurring his words, that Barnie had once beaten the Belgian burping champion in a contest, played in tennis sets, that was, according to this chap, pretty much the sum total of Barnie's life achievements. Then he staggered back to his place unsteadily, holding on to each pew in turn, grinning like an ape.

That really pissed Taylor off. Whatever dark cloud of bad luck had hovered over poor Barnie throughout his life, he deserved a better finale than this.

A collection bag went around. The smallest note Taylor had was a fiver and he stuffed that into the crimson purse. After the closing prayers, the vicar told the mourners that there would be a private family committal. He asked everyone to leave in peace and continue to remember Barnie in their prayers and thoughts, reminding the congregation that they were invited to share further memories of Barnie over drinks and bites in the village hall.

Then – and credit to the Rev, Taylor thought, for forewarning everyone that what followed was on the explicit instructions of the deceased – the most ludicrous song began to play. It started with a plinkety-plink on the piano, followed by lyrics sung in a staccato voice.

They're coming to take me away, ha-ha, they're coming to take me away.

The mourners were looking around, bemused. Was this Barnie's final jibe at a world he'd never quite got to grips with?

People began filing out, starting from the front. Taylor, keeping his eyes on the back of the man's head as best he could, tried to squeeze his way along the aisle to catch up with him, but it was impossible. A tall woman in a ridiculous black hat was now blocking his view.

Meanwhile, the song kept playing.

It was several minutes before he reached the door where the Rev stood. A woman in front of Taylor was thanking the vicar effusively for such a wonderful service. Taylor gave the cleric a shake of the hand and lunged out into the torrential rain that was coming down again, searching every way for Rufus. Clusters of mourners were standing around, chatting beneath umbrellas. He hurried past them, until he reached the busy high street and looked up and down it.

There was no sign of him.

3

'Trying to improve your culinary skills, Roy, to impress young Cleo? Or have you taken up foraging? Searching for your inner caveman?'

Grace looked up with a start. He'd been concentrating so hard on his computer screen he'd not heard the DI enter his office. He grinned and gave him the bird.

Glenn Branson was wearing an electric-blue suit that would have been more appropriate for a games-show host than a detective inspector in Major Crime, Grace thought, but he said nothing. He'd long given up trying to explain to his best mate – and protégé – that the reason detectives wore conservative suits was to appear respectful when visiting the families of the victims of crimes. But Glenn, being one of life's natural peacocks, had his own definition of *conservative*.

And, as for his tie, Grace thought, *don't even go there*. It could rank, along with Perth, Australia, as one of the few things that would be identifiable from space. 'Culinary skills?' he asked.

Branson nodded at the book lying on Grace's desk, titled *The Complete Mushroom Hunter*.

'Ha!'

The DI gave him a sideways look, turned the book around, opened it and flicked through a few pages, barely glancing at them. 'Heard the one about the guy who walked into a pub, puts a mushroom down on the bar and orders a pint for it?'

8

Grace winced. 'No, but I'm clearly about to.'

'The landlord asks why he's brought the mushroom into the pub. And he replies, "Because he's a real fun guy!" Geddit?'

'Fungi,' he said flatly.

'Good to see you haven't lost your touch, despite your age.'

Roy Grace had turned forty-five a few weeks ago and Branson, who was thirty-eight, never missed an opportunity to rib him about it.

'And sad to see, despite your own advancing years, matey, your humour never improves. So can I do anything for you, or have you just come in here to annoy me?'

Branson pulled up one of the two chairs in front of Grace's desk, turned it around and straddled it with his powerful frame. 'I wanted to have a chat. Since being promoted to DI I've not had a really challenging investigation. Not that I'm wishing anyone dead, but I'd like a real complex murder to get my teeth into – know what I'm saying?'

Grace knew exactly. While every murder was investigated thoroughly and without prejudice, the vast majority of the twenty-five or so annual murders in the counties of Sussex and Surrey were domestics or involved drugs, drunks and petty feuds. There was also the worrying trend of the increasing use of knives – an unwelcome import from gangland London and other cities.

All murders were tragic in their own way, and left devastated loved ones behind who would never get over it. But they were not the cases you were ever going to put in your memoirs. What every homicide detective secretly hoped for – and Grace himself was no exception – was a high-profile and intriguing murder that would challenge their skills and, as a bonus, ultimately impress both their superiors and the media, as well as being part of their legacy.

'What do you know about mushrooms, Glenn? Apart from rubbish jokes.'

'I know Paris browns get their name from being grown in the catacombs under Paris, back in the eighteenth century. And they're one of the few that taste good raw. Love them thinly sliced on a salad.'

'And normal field mushrooms – the type you can buy in any greengrocer or supermarket?'

Branson nodded. 'Yeah, I like them too. Delicious on toast with a fried egg.'

'Ever picked any yourself?'

He shook his head. 'No, I don't trust my skills – I wouldn't know an edible one from a poisonous specimen.'

'What about the death cap?' Grace asked.

'Yeah, a mate of mine who's into the whole foraging thing warned me about them. Said they look quite like a field mushroom. That's one of the reasons I wouldn't trust myself to pick anything.'

'From what I'm reading on Google, the death cap is not a pleasant death.'

'Who you planning to despatch?' Branson quipped.

'Funny.' Grace grimaced at his friend. 'We try not to talk shop at home, but something happened at the mortuary that Cleo thought I should know about. There's not been a recorded death from mushroom poisoning in the city of Brighton and Hove for over twenty years, if not longer, but she told me over dinner that a fortnight ago they had a thirty-nine-year-old male who died from liver and kidney failure seventy-two hours after eating mushrooms he'd prepared for a dinner party – which he is believed to have bought in a local supermarket. Fortunately for the guests, he had to cancel the dinner party as he was so ill. Then two days ago there was another death from suspected poisoning by death cap mushroom – a man of fifty-nine.'

'For real?'

'The victim fell ill within a few hours of eating mushrooms his wife had picked while playing golf. She's critically ill too, in

Intensive Care but expected to survive. The pathologist rang Cleo this morning to say the lab results indicate death cap mushroom poisoning again.'

Branson frowned. 'Is this a massive coincidence, or is something else going on?'

'Funny you should say that. I had a call from the coroner earlier this morning, asking exactly the same question. I sent Will Glover off to Brighton Library to see what he could find on poisonous mushrooms and he came back with this book.'

'None for twenty years and then two in a fortnight?' Branson ruminated. 'Not great optics – if the press get hold of that.'

'And they won't, will they?' Roy Grace stared at him levelly. 'Not until we are ready.'

Branson was married to the senior crime reporter of the local newspaper, the *Argus*. He smiled, then ran his forefinger and thumb across his lips, zipping them shut.

'Good man. So here's your challenge for the day – go see if there's any link between the two people who died. On behalf of the coroner, we need to rule out foul play – or not.'

'Mushroom poisoning's not exactly the multi-layered investigation I'm hoping for.'

'Well maybe you just need to unearth some mould-breaking clues?'

'Funny,' Branson said, then grinned, shaking his head. 'Don't give up the day job.'

'I'm making you my deputy fungi.'

4

Because of the rain coming down even harder now, the mourners were dispersing rapidly. Taylor, holding up his umbrella, followed another group from the funeral along the High Street, which would have looked a lot prettier in sunshine, he thought.

After a couple of hundred yards they turned left towards a large municipal car park, and for a moment he wondered if he'd made a mistake following them, but then they hurried into a characterless, single-storey modern building, totally out of keeping with the mostly Georgian facades of the rest of the village.

If the outside was lacking charm, the interior, he thought, was even more bland. Trestle tables laid out with a buffet that only the British could do quite so badly. White bread sandwiches with the ends curling up, drab quiches, sausage rolls that looked like they were still defrosting, a platter of cheese and pineapple cubes pierced with cocktail sticks, and bowls of crisps, cheese straws, and mixed nuts and raisins. There were glasses and bottles of cheap red and white wine on another table, with no indication that the white wine was at anything other than room temperature.

Fifty or so people were already in the room, some awkwardly holding laden paper plates in one hand and glasses in the other, and many of them glancing around with an air of desperation, as if looking for someone they knew to go and talk to.

Taylor, whose sole interest in being here was to see if he could spot the man in the baseball cap and scarf, recognized none of them. Single himself once more, after a long and challenging divorce from his wife, Marianne, and custody fight for his ten-year-old son, Harrison, he was just getting back to feeling himself again after a difficult time. He knew it wasn't really appropriate, but he couldn't help casting a glance around at the women in the room – it had been at a funeral that he met Marianne. But none of them that he could see were his type. Not that he was really sure any more who was his *type*.

'Hello, James!'

He turned sharply to see Barnie's ex-wife, her veil gone now, smiling at him beneath stylish fair hair, holding a glass of red wine. A confident and very good-looking woman in her mid-thirties, with the faintly husky voice of a smoker. She smelled of smoke now – no doubt she'd had a quick fag after the service. Taylor, who had quit some years ago, still had the occasional craving, and he had one now. Badly.

'Debbie!' he replied. 'I'm so sorry about Barnie.'

She gave him a wan smile. 'Thanks.' She hesitated. 'I guess he was someone who was never going to make old bones. But I didn't think he'd go this young.' She shrugged.

'It's good to see you,' he said. And it was, really good. Taylor had always liked her, although they barely knew each other. One of the few times he'd met her before had been at Rufus Rorke's funeral.

'It's lovely of you to come. Really, I do appreciate it and it's nice to see your face again.'

He shrugged. 'Of course. Barnie and I go back a long way. How are you doing?'

'I'm fine,' she said. 'Although I'm sad. We became much better friends after we separated than when we were married. I'm really fine.'

And she looked it. Totally fine. Handsome, classy and even more attractive than when he'd last seen her two years ago.

He'd always thought that Barnie had been punching above his weight when he and Debbie married. But there was no rationalizing attraction.

'Of course I'm sorry he's dead,' she added. 'And I'm sorry it never worked out for Barnie and me. He is . . . was,' she corrected herself, 'a lovely guy. But a dreamer. With a temper.'

Taylor frowned. 'He had a temper? I never saw that at school.'

She tilted her head. 'You never saw it?'

'Nope! Honestly!'

She gave him a disbelieving frown.

He shook his head. 'I was shy as hell – still am. Barnie always wanted to be the centre of attention. He made sure he got a part in every school play, but unfortunately the drama teacher always gave him the smallest role, usually with just one line or no speaking part at all. Barnie always accepted it. He told me he would be an A-list movie star one day. Or a rock star. I remember he started a school band, but the others kicked him out after a year because they said he was tone deaf. As well as being completely unreliable.'

'That's Barnie,' she said with a wistful smile. 'He tried hard to get into a drama school but none of them would take him – partly because he couldn't sing. When we married, he was on the books of a film extras agency, hoping to get discovered in a walk-on part. But that never happened. He did once have a small speaking part in an episode of *Endeavour* – as a copper. He got to say "good morning, sir" to the actor playing the lead, Shaun Evans. But most of it was cut, so when he appeared he was like a tiny ant in the background!'

He grinned. 'The old cutting-room floor, eh?'

'Exactly. Then he lost his job as a chef at a pub when one evening all the diners went down with salmonella. He ended up doing telesales for a company in Newhaven that sold advertising space in the Network Rail staff bulletin and *The International*

Review of the Red Cross journal. He'd come home all excited, telling me he'd sold a quarter-page, a half-page or a whole page! Then a week later, crestfallen, he'd tell me they'd cancelled.'

'He was a nice guy, though,' Taylor said.

She shook her head. 'No, James, that's what everyone thought, including me when I first met him. I don't want to speak ill of the dead, but he turned into a total bastard, angry and bitter at a world that did not appreciate him. And he got increasingly desperate for success and recognition – to the point where he scared me.'

'Scared you? In what way?'

She shrugged. 'I can't explain it very well. I just got the feeling, during that last year we were still together, he would have killed to get what he craved – that elusive success. I did my best but it was never enough.'

'Instead he was felled by a mushroom.'

That made her smile. And when she did so, he knew again, after a long time, what his *type* was.

'Let's have lunch sometime,' he said.

'I'd like that, James. I'd like that a lot.'

'So would I. A lot.' He wondered about asking her if she fancied a cigarette, then he could cadge one from her, but first he asked, 'Do you remember Rufus?'

'Rufus Rorke?'

'Yep.'

'I do,' she said, hesitantly. 'I'm afraid I never liked him – the few times we met. But you, he and Barnie were tight, you were the Three Musketeers, right? Athos, Porthos and Aramis?'

'We were.'

'I always thought there was something of the night about him.'

'Something of the night?' Taylor frowned. 'About Rufus?'

'He had a dark side, I can't explain – he made me feel uncomfortable. I went to his funeral with Barnie – you gave a great eulogy. Too bad you didn't do the one today instead of that total twat,' she added. 'But I have always wondered just how heartfelt your eulogy really was?' She questioned him with her eyebrows.

'Heartfelt?'

'Uh-huh.'

He looked at her, wondering how to reply. The truth was (not that he would ever have admitted it): Rufus had intimidated both him and Barnie. He had been a control freak, and part of the reason Taylor had delivered such a gushing eulogy was that, even though Rufus was dead, he was still a little in awe of him. Worried about upsetting him if he'd said anything Rufus didn't approve of – upsetting him even beyond the grave.

Maybe in view of what he thought he'd seen in church, he had been smart to worry about that.

He looked her back in the eye. 'Now there was someone with a big temper. Did you know Rufus had to go to anger management therapy due to awful road rage? It was terrifying if you were ever in the car with him, it was like a switch had flipped. We grew apart for sure, but we couldn't change the fact we were very old mates. Boarding school at a young age bonds you with people – even those you're not that keen on. It was like a glue that held us together despite us all growing up and changing, some for the better, some for the worse. I guess, as you say, we were the Three Musketeers, that's why I did his eulogy. In all honesty I don't think there was anyone else lining up to do it.'

'*All for one and one for all.*'

He smiled. 'Exactly!'

'Do you really think Rufus would have given a toss about either you or Barnie, when the chips were down?' she said, her voice suddenly laced with venom. '*One for all*? No way. Rufus was for Rufus and hang the world. You were generous to Barnie, I know you loaned him money a number of times. But Rufus never did – he'd made a fortune and he could have helped Barnie, it would have cost him relative peanuts. I'm not saying he deserved to die, but he was a shit, a total shit.'

'You know, this is going to sound strange,' Taylor said, 'but I could have sworn I saw him in the church today, just now, sitting a few rows in front of me.'

She gave him an odd look. 'Rufus?'

Taylor nodded.

'At the funeral?'

'Yes.'

'What do you mean *saw* him? Like, you saw his ghost?'

'No, not his ghost. I saw him. Rufus – or someone who looks very like him.'

She frowned. 'Does he have a brother, perhaps – a twin?'

'I'm certain he doesn't. We were close enough friends at school for me to have known that. Maybe he has a doppelganger. I don't know. They say we all have one. I just felt a shiver go through me when I saw him.'

'Did you talk to him – this chap?'

'I tried really hard to get to him at the end of the service, but there were dozens of people in the way. By the time I reached the door he'd vanished. I hoped maybe he'd be here.'

'As far as I'm aware there was only one dead man in that church today,' she said irreverently, and smiled.

Smiling back, he studied her face carefully. He saw no hint of disingenuity. If it really had been Rufus in the church, she genuinely had not seen him.

Then the drunk who'd delivered the eulogy tottered over, holding an open bottle in his hand, and put an arm around Debbie. 'Think I messed it up a bit,' he slurred.

5

October 2021, eleven months earlier

Pelting rain, howling wind and darkness. The forecast had delivered its promise of foul weather, with bells on – and it had been well worth the wait. Ten days of repeatedly returning to this spot on London's Bond Street at the same time every weekday evening – 6.16 p.m. – watching, learning and then waiting for the right conditions.

A tall man, he wore a dark tracksuit with the hood up, and clutched a small, weighty black velvet bag. Weighty because it housed a brass knuckle duster. He had long ago named this bag and its contents Uncle Johnny. And Uncle Johnny often served him discreetly and well.

Unseen in this maelstrom of weather, he waited a few yards down the pavement from the doorway between a dress shop and a shoe shop, from which Darius Sacher would emerge more or less any time now, as he did every weekday when he wasn't away on business or holiday, and he wasn't away at the moment.

The rag-trade tycoon had made his small fortune from copying the latest fashions at the Paris and Milan shows and getting them made in factories in China and out across the UK's major low-cost fashion retailers within weeks. He had a personal wealth in excess of £7 million, yet every weekday night the tight bastard caught the bus to Trafalgar Square, then hurried to Charing Cross station to catch the 18.46 train to Tunbridge Wells with his season ticket.

Tightwad Sacher could have afforded a taxi, or even a chauffeured limousine, for God's sake! A crowded bus and a rammed train every night – what was that about? Sacher didn't know it, but he had made a big mistake. He had gifted his son, Zach, £250,000 on his recent twenty-first birthday. The money had been to set him up for life and give him a head start. But not content with that chunk of cash, Zach was angry that there would be no further inheritance from his father, who was now engaged to be married next year. Married to a woman Zach despised. His father had made it clear that she would be the sole beneficiary in his will once they were married. Hardly surprising that Zach, who had hired him, was hacked off. Anyone would be.

Oh yes, it was just such a perfect evening! All the pedestrians had their heads bowed against the rain or were fighting the elements with their umbrellas – and mostly losing. None of them hurrying past, thinking about a pint in a pub or their centrally heated living room or cosy kitchen, even cast a glance at the figure sheltering in the doorway of a fashion brand emporium.

Darius Sacher was coming out now! Yes! There he was, caught in the street lighting and in the passing headlights of a black cab, shaven head and bright red spectacle frames, wearing a natty overcoat with a velour collar, battling the elements to open his brolly, then turning right and heading up Bond Street in the direction of Oxford Circus, towards the bus stop.

He began to follow, quickening his pace, so that within a few yards he was right behind him, unseen and unheard. Waiting for the right moment.

And as if the same god that had answered his prayers about the weather tonight had now arranged for the right bus to come along, he saw a blare of headlights and the hulking shape of a double-decker looming out of the rain and wind-lashed darkness, travelling down the street at a pace.

He drew towards Darius Sacher and then, just seconds before the bus was level, he ducked under Sacher's umbrella and whacked him hard on the right side of his head with Uncle Johnny. Hard enough to have killed him, although that wasn't necessary – just a precaution. The massive sideways push he gave the already unconscious man, straight off the pavement and directly in front of the bus, was actually all he needed to have done. But he liked to make sure.

He heard the slither of the bus's locked tyres on the wet tarmac. Heard someone scream. Then someone else.

He briefly looked at what was left of Darius Sacher, lying on the wet, black, glistening surface, half his entrails spread around him. Then he broke into a jog. Jogging was good. It was just under three miles to the Airbnb in Westbourne Grove where he was staying. But he ran a further three miles once he was there. It felt so good to be out running, and with a job done!

But not as good as it would feel tomorrow when the second payment of £50,000 from Zach Sacher landed in his Panamanian bank account. He had no doubt it would. For insurance he had recorded all of Zach Sacher's instructions about killing his father.

Or – as the man in the hoodie, jogging happily through the foul night, preferred to call it – simply facilitating a very tragic *accidental* death.

6

Shannon Kendall was twenty-four. She was looking good right now and she knew it, but that hadn't always been the case. She had come on a long personal journey since her dark university days that had, on the one hand, given her a first-class honours degree, but on the other hand stripped her of so much.

During the few years between finishing university and meeting Paul, she had had very few friendships and no other boyfriends. She lived in a small flat close to Hove seafront, never accepting invites to parties, and with just her cat for company. A stray, ginger moggie, a chunk of its fur missing down one side, along with half of its left ear, who two years ago had walked in through the cat-flap left by the previous tenant and decided to stay for a while, until he'd eventually moved on.

She'd called him Chancer, because it felt like he'd taken a chance on her. Sometimes she looked into his eyes and asked him how he had got hurt. 'Have you been in a fight? Did you win or lose?'

He'd always just look back at her, and she could swear he had a smug grin on his face, as if replying, *I'm not telling.*

She liked that. She was the same, she wasn't telling either. Not even her best friend Tara knew the story – not the full story, not the bit that actually mattered. She had told no one that she was damaged goods. Vulnerable. Afraid. Angry.

Maybe she'd have confided in her father, Don. He would have listened and understood and kept the secret. But he was dead. He'd been dead for four years, killed in a stupid avalanche while climbing a stupid mountain in stupid Switzerland.

She had not spoken to her mother, Holly, for seven years, not since the day she had left her father, breaking his heart. She had vowed never to speak to her again, and so far had resisted replying to any of the endless barrage of texts, emails and Facebook messages from her.

For her primary job, she was buried away in a computer research laboratory, called SQLMT Ltd, on an industrial estate near Shoreham Harbour. She loved the work but hated the workplace, where all her colleagues were assholes, most of all her line manager, Derek Northrup. He was the computer geek equivalent of Ricky Gervais in *The Office*. The groups of programmers working in silos with dimmed lighting were discouraged from socializing with each other, and even from chatting – not that there were any she remotely fancied socializing with.

No one knew what SQLMT stood for. There was a rumour the lab was funded by Microsoft. But another rumour that it was funded by Elon Musk. A geeky guy, with a furtive voice and a stupid man bun, who Shannon had met at a watercooler, told her with a wink that it was the Chinese government who secretly owned the company.

That kind of fitted, she thought. The CEO was a smart Chinese-English woman. Not that it mattered to Shannon who owned it. She only stayed there for three reasons. Firstly, because she liked the anonymity of the job: no one apart from Derek Northrup ever attempted to engage her in conversation and she'd long developed the art of dismissing him quickly.

Secondly, being a part-time post, the job allowed her to take on other freelance work as she pleased, and she'd helped a few clients selling merchandise through the dark web – mostly cannabis and cocaine, but also, on a couple of occasions, high-profile stolen works of art that were too well known to ever be sold on the open market. She'd found homes for them in China and Russia.

But the main reason she stayed – quite apart from the big monthly paycheque – was that she was genuinely intrigued by the work she and everyone there was doing. It was cutting-edge computing science, creating artificial intelligence algorithms to spy on people and companies operating on the dark web. At times her role totally consumed her, often working long hours into the night. It enabled her, if not to forget, to at least park for a while what had happened over three years ago, refusing to recede into a past where everything else in her life had faded like a photograph left in the sun.

But not this.

It would never fade.

She'd been encouraged – after much reluctance – to register on a couple of dating apps by Tara, who was concerned about the way she'd retreated into her shell since leaving university, turning almost into a recluse. Tara and the others in her friendship group were having fun; two were now engaged, with weddings on the horizon next summer. And she had been just so damned lonely. But not any more. She had struck lucky after swiping right on her fifth attempt, after she'd gingerly put a toe in the water of online dating. Paul Anthony had used one of his privileged *swipe ups* to indicate he was super keen. He was sitting opposite her now.

Being with him had awoken something inside her that she had thought was gone for ever, and since meeting him she had felt secure and safe in a relationship like never before. She was completely enamoured and had actually come really close to telling him her secret, but so far had protectively held back. She planned to tell him someday soon. If there was one person in the world she would share this with, it would be him.

There were so many things about this charismatic man that

captivated her. He was tall and good-looking if not exactly hand-some. He was damaged goods, like herself, but in a different way. Her damage was psychological, his was physical and a lot more superficial. A big scar above and below his right eye from a car crash in his teens, leaving his eye slightly misaligned, gave him a raffish look, accentuated by his straight, dark hair that hung at a slant across his forehead. Dead sexy, actually, she thought. As was his very slight limp.

He was strictly pescatarian, borderline vegetarian, borderline vegan. Another box ticked.

She felt seen by him, like he really understood her. A rare tick.

He was intensely interested in her and curious about her. A big tick.

It took him three dates before he'd made any sexual advances towards her. Biggest tick of all.

Right here, right now, after those three years of being single, she felt she could be falling head over heels in love with Paul Anthony.

But there was a negative. Of course there was.

7

December 2021

'Cheers, my gorgeous! To us.' He clinked his Champagne glass against hers.

'Cheers,' Shannon replied, smiling at him.

'Eight weeks to the day since our first date – not bad, eh?' Paul Anthony tilted his head and grinned.

She grinned too. 'Eight weeks!' she replied. 'Sort of flown by! We'd make a good team,' she said, and immediately wondered why she'd used those words.

'More than just a *team*, right?' he urged. 'Kindred spirits. It really feels like we're soulmates. I'm falling in love with you, Shannon. Actually, strike that.' He grinned at her again, over the top of his glass. 'I am in love with you. I love you.'

'I love you too,' she replied. But she didn't say it with her entire heart and soul. She was in thrall to him, and yet there was something, some part of him that she didn't know – yet, at any rate – which she felt he was holding back from her.

Or maybe it was just that negative. Because it was a big one.

That *negative* was the business Paul Anthony ran. During those first magical two months when they had begun dating, she could not get out of him exactly what it was that he did for a living. From the way he dressed, in stylish jackets, smart shirts, neat jeans and classy shoes, and the fact that he collected her in a chauffeured Mercedes, she figured he had to be well off. He'd told her, somewhat evasively, that he was involved in a number of businesses, but never said what they actually were.

She'd used all her skills in navigating the internet to see what she could find out about him, and had come up with absolutely nothing. It was as if he did not exist.

It was on a date a month or so into their relationship, over a monkfish stew in Tosca, a riverside restaurant in Shoreham, to the west of Brighton, when Paul and she had drunk more than they had together previously, that he finally explained a little about his work. Or at least one part of it: 3D printed handguns.

Up until then, while she had heard about 3D printed guns, she assumed they were just toys, harmless replicas. Far from it, he had explained, and had shown her photos on his phone of examples he had produced. Some did look very plastic, more like water pistols, but some looked chillingly realistic. All of them, he told her, he had made from raw materials – mostly easily obtainable – on his 3D printing equipment in his workshop. Even the bullets. And each of the guns she looked at, he told her, almost boastfully, was capable of firing live rounds of ammunition that would be lethal at varying distances.

It had shocked her. But, she had to admit, it had also thrilled her.

To be fair to Paul, since they had first met, she had always been quite cagey about her career, so neither could quite extract specifics from the other, but they each recognized that they spoke the same techy, somewhat underground language. As the boozy evening went on they asked each other more and more revealing questions, testing the water, pushing the boundaries, playfully. By what they each interpreted as a bizarre alignment in the stars, they soon realized that some of their work overlapped.

Both of them operated on the so-called dark web, via Tor – a network also known by the less sinister name of The Onion Router, partly because accessing it was like peeling back the layers of an onion. And that night each of them peeled off a few layers of themselves, including their clothes. She confided in him that she worked for a number of agencies, monitoring the dark web for a variety of objectives.

'Shannon Kendall,' he had said flirtatiously, back in Tosca that night. 'I'd like to formally offer you the position of Business Development Officer. If you should choose to accept what will be a very generous offer, you will be the discreet face of my 3D gun printing business. You can start part-time to dip a toe in, as it were, and you'll be the one to get the sales transactions, deal with manufacturing process and sort the Bitcoin payments and the despatching. It would relieve me of a load of work and free me up to focus on other aspects of my business. What do you think?'

At that moment, Shannon had the strange sense it was destiny. Paul made light of that, merely calling it a *favourable circumstance*. But it clearly excited them both. She liked that it was completely different to her work at SQLMT, and she knew her skill set was a perfect complement to his. But one thing concerned her.

'You and me in the business of printing 3D guns, Paul, it's not quite what I had in my thoughts for my next career move. Before I accept, you need to convince me that my morals haven't gone AWOL.'

'Look, babe,' he'd replied. 'You know how it is. People who want guns, want guns. They are going to get them whatever anyone does to try to stop them. You and I may as well benefit from the purchase. There's a lot of money in this. I mean a bucket load of money. It will make both of us very rich. We don't have to do this for ever. We don't know or care what they use them for. We don't ask any questions, so there's no guilt. Supplying the guns is our business, what our customers do with the products they buy is not our concern. If we don't do it someone else will. Right?'

'I suppose so,' she said somewhat hesitantly.

'Are you in?'

She shut her eyes, leant back in her chair, took a deep breath and smiled seductively. This guy was dangerous. Dangerously attractive. And, what the hell, she felt dangerous!

'I'm in.'

8

Friday 23 September 2022

Paul Anthony, Shannon had come to realize over the past year, was a man of habit, and some of those habits a little unfathomable. Such as why, when he lived in Kemp Town, to the east of Brighton, a mecca for eateries, did he prefer to dine in the same restaurant, Tosca, several miles by car to the west of the city, and always at the same corner table, with his back to all the other diners.

Tonight she arrived fifteen minutes late and sat down opposite him, with her back to the river, without saying a word, looking and feeling really pissed off and flustered. She gulped down most of the glass of wine he'd poured for her.

'You OK, babes?' he asked.

'Not really, Paul, no.'

'What's the matter?'

She pulled out a sheet of newspaper from her handbag, turned it to face him and pointed at the headline. 'Have you seen this?'

It was a page of the *Daily Mail*.

3D PRINTED GUN SERIOUSLY WOUNDS SCHOOLBOY

Beneath was a photograph of the gun, which had been seized by the police. Beneath that was the story of a 3D printed handgun, a facsimile of a Glock pistol, that had got into the hands of a fourteen-year-old boy, who had used it to shoot a fifteen-year-old in a suspected Hoxton gang turf war. According to the article, the bullet had missed the boy's heart by the narrowest of margins. The article then went on to point out just how easy it was for anyone with the right equipment and technical know-how to create such a weapon through the latest advances in 3D printing technology.

'Wow!' Paul Anthony said, looking animated. 'That's one of ours – I can tell from the colour combination.'

'You look excited, Paul. This is awful. A kid has been shot and might have been killed. And you are excited? Don't you feel any responsibility?'

'No. No I don't. You know exactly what I feel about this. These people will get guns somehow. It's not our business what they do with them.'

She was silent. She did know what he felt about this. But that didn't make it any better.

'Babes, listen,' he replied. 'You don't know these kids, they're just gangland scumbags, county lines drug dealers or whatever, just vermin. Why do you care?'

He gave her a really strange look that she'd not seen before. And she saw something in him that she'd not seen before, this previously tough, confident guy squirming, almost weaselly. She felt as if all her trust in him had spilled out of a bottle onto the floor. Had she badly misjudged him?

As if sensing this, he said, 'Babes, listen, I love you more than anything. It's you and me versus the world, that's what being in love means. We're good together, we're strong, we get that we're in a morally questionable business, but, hey, we're in it with our eyes open. Love is like a wagon-train circle. We make that circle and we sit inside it – with the rest of the world outside. Understand?'

She frowned. 'Yes, but—'

'You make me so happy, I've never felt like this in all my life. It's like – you make me complete.'

'I love you too, Paul. I just find it hard to be a part of this sometimes. Like now.'

He filled her glass, then drained his, picked up the bottle – their second – or maybe their third – to refill his, and it was empty. He put it down. 'Well, you're kind of in it now, hun, it's a bit late to be preachy. That horse has bolted. Just think of all the money we're making – much of it, credit to you.'

She smiled, uneasily. 'Maybe I need to stop reading the news.'

'No more news!' Paul said. 'Good plan! OK. Let's change the subject. Tell me some more about you before we met. Your uni days, what were they like?'

He was feeling a little smashed now but it didn't stop him reaching for the complimentary amaretto they'd each been given after they'd finished their meal.

'Really? What do you want to know? I wasn't all that happy.' She was trying to buy herself a bit of time to think more clearly and decide how to answer him. Should she tell him tonight? The glasses of wine she had lost count of were making her reckless. She told Paul about her course and about the university.

'So in your third year you were told by your professor, Bill Llewellyn, that you were on track for a First – but then you quit the university and had to come back and retake a year later? I'm trying to make sense of that. Why?'

The booze had really gone to her head, and she was feeling quite drunk now.

'What's up? Did something happen?' he pressed.

She was silent for some moments, thinking. There was something about this evening and the drink that made her feel that she could speak up and confide in him.

She said the four words she had not said to anyone else, ever.

'Professor Llewellyn raped me.'

9

Paul Anthony acknowledged this bombshell with a widening of his eyes, and then a toss of his head in which he shook away the forelock over his eyes. 'That's a pretty big ticket,' he said.

'One way of describing it.'

She felt a burden had lifted in telling him. And he wasn't judging her like she feared he might.

'Do you want to talk about the circumstances?'

She shrugged. 'Not really. I – he seemed very charming when I first knew him, in a bit of a boffin kind of way, if you know what I mean? Almost the classic absent-minded professor. He even looked it, you know, bald at the front, tangled hair, a little shambolic, but he wore the kind of glasses that shout, *I am cool!* Big, round black rims.'

He nodded. 'Don't tell me he has leather patches on his sleeves.'

'He has leather patches on his sleeves.'

'Part shabby-shabby, like a down-at-heel teacher, part shabby-genius, like Einstein, and part vain cockerel?'

'That sums him up pretty well. His nickname was Lechy Lew.'

'You didn't go to the police?'

'I should have done, I know.' And she felt that more than ever at this moment. 'I'm sure there would have been evidence. I know he took the underwear I was wearing, the dirty pervert, so that would be somewhere. Pink, it was. Isn't it strange the stuff you remember? But – I was in such a messed-up state. I needed my degree, I just couldn't think straight. It was the brutality of his attack – I realized he was a freaky Jekyll and Hyde character. I couldn't go back to my tuition that year because I was scared it would happen again. In the end I had to request a change of tutor and go back a year later to complete it, at further expense. I never told anyone what he'd done. This is the first time I've told anyone.' She shrugged. 'I guess it's because I totally trust you not to judge me.'

'I'd never judge you.' He twisted his glass of amaretto around in his elegant hand. 'I could get rid of him for you,' he said, with a casual, cheeky grin.

She looked back at him. 'Oh yeah? Pop, pop, gone? One of our 3D guns? Um, small problem there, Paul, you'd get caught!'

'No, I wouldn't get caught. I would set it up like an accident. Simples.'

She shrugged. 'Nice idea, Paul.' She paused. 'But, I'm not a murderer, are you?' she said sarcastically.

'Do you think I look like one?'

'Do I think you look like a murderer?' She saw a waiter hovering nearby, asked for another amaretto and turned back to Paul. 'I don't know, I've no idea what a murderer looks like.'

He gave her an intense gaze. 'Did you ever see the Hitchcock movie *Strangers on a Train*?'

She had but a long time ago. Trying to recall it, she had a faint black and white image in her mind of two men, in business suits, in a railway carriage. 'I did, I've always loved Hitchcock. I can't remember who the actors were – but from memory they agreed to *swap* murders. One stranger kills his new friend's wife, and the other his new friend's father, so there would be no apparent motive for either murder, right?'

He nodded approval. 'Pretty much spot on!' He was silent for a moment then gave her a strange smile. 'You just said you have no idea what a murderer looks like, right?'

She nodded.

'In the book that film was based on, Guy says to Owen, "Nobody knows what a murderer looks like. A murderer looks like anybody!".'

She sat in silence, absorbing this. After a moment she said, 'Ha-ha, nice one. OK, go on then, see ya later, Llewellyn. Night night!'

He tilted his head so that his damaged eye was looking at her, almost piercingly, like the eye of a bird of prey.

'I'm going to sort it out. Payback time. You don't need to say anything else.'

She glanced around, checking that the diners on the tables either side of them and behind them had left.

'Am I dating a murderer?' She was playing with him but quite enjoying it.

'I wouldn't call it that, Shannon. Let's just say you're dating a *facilitator.*'

'Facilitator? Meaning what, exactly?'

'You keep asking me more about my businesses,' he said and downed most of the liqueur in one tip of the glass. 'Do you want to know where I make most of my money?'

'I do, I'm intrigued.'

'I've another business I operate on the dark web.'

He fell silent as her second amaretto was delivered, then continued. 'How much do you really know about the dark web – and The Onion Router?'

Letting her guard down, she said, 'Probably a lot more than you realize. I prefer using the acronym Tor myself. So your other business on the dark web is what?'

'It's also in facilitating,' he replied, but this time more cagily.

'Facilitating what?'

'It's your turn first to tell me what exactly you do at SQLMT.'

She gave him a teasing smile. 'I'm not allowed to tell you. I've already said more than I'm allowed under the terms of my non-disclosure contract, which is why I've never talked about it. You know this, Paul.'

He didn't return the smile. 'Let me guess – the company you are working for is developing systems to crack the different onion layers of the dark web, and it could only be doing that for one of three clients – the police, the military intelligence services or the members of the British Bankers' Association, right?'

After a brief hesitation she said, 'It's two of those, actually.'

'Of course it is. So what else do you do for them?'

'I program bots to dig deep into it, learning as they go. Every now and then, in my down time, I take a trawl around the dark web out of curiosity – I see a lot more shocking stuff than what we're doing.'

He stared back at her for a long while. Finally he said, 'So you could tell the police or MI5 or MI6 everything about my business, in theory?'

'It will be a while before we're that smart and sophisticated but, yes, that's the aim of the team I'm working with. To stop people like you being able to hide what you do.'

He shook his head. 'That will never happen. We'll always be one step ahead. We always have been. Criminals don't get locked up because the police have caught up with their technology, they only get locked up when they make a mistake.'

'Have you ever made a mistake?'

'I don't make mistakes.' He said it as a flat, bald statement. 'Well – one, once, but that's another story.'

'OK.' She shrugged and smiled then asked, 'So we know we could get a gun, one of our untraceable 3D printed handguns, but could you actually shoot it at someone? Could you shoot that bastard Llewellyn? I'm not sure I could, however much I would like to.'

He looked at her, hard. 'What if I could produce someone who could?'

Lowering her voice she said, 'You mean a hitman?'

'Exactly.'

She stared at him, surprised by how disturbed his words made her feel, despite her loathing of Llewellyn. 'I don't think so, no.' She shook her head. 'I guess that's not in my DNA. I don't think I could live with having paid someone to murder him, however much I hate him, however much I want him dead – or however much I'd like to cut his dick and balls off and shove them down his throat,' she said, vitriol rising in her voice.

Paul replied quietly. 'Shannon, how would you feel if Professor Bill Llewellyn were to die an accidental death?'

'I'd feel the world had been rid of one piece of vermin.'

He smiled. 'OK, now we're on the same page. You are starting to understand my business more.'

She stared back at him hard. 'You arrange accidental deaths?'

He looked back at her dubiously. 'Does that shock you?'

'I . . .' She hesitated, wondering, *Is this guy for real? Is this conversation actually happening with my boyfriend of nearly a year?* 'If you're telling the truth then, no, well, sort of, I suppose. I'm up for him getting a lesson, not an accidental death, of course, but a wake-up call. A taste of his own bitter pill, perhaps.'

And he could see in her eyes that she really meant it.

'I guess,' she went on, 'I guess I've always believed that things happen for a reason. That people meet for a reason. Maybe that's why we're both sitting here.' She shrugged.

'Maybe,' he said, searching her face with his eyes. 'OK, for this *wake-up call*, there are two things I'm going to need from you. The first is your absolute trust.'

'And the second?'

'You're going to tell me everything you know about the professor, Shannon. What his habits and hobbies are. Things he likes and dislikes. Does he support a football team? What does he like to eat, drink?'

'Well, he's a functioning alcoholic for certain, and he's a Diet Coke freak. I'd call him an alco-coke-oholic! He drinks continuously throughout the day. If he's not drinking whisky, he's drinking cans of Coke. Honestly, I've never seen someone drink so much Coke.'

Paul nodded. 'OK, he's a Coke-oholic,' he said slowly. 'Interesting. Does he have any allergies?'

'Allergies? You mean any kind of allergy?'

'Any kind.'

She thought for a moment, then, despite herself, smiled. 'Yes, yes he does, actually. A bad one. There's something he's petrified of.'

He leaned in over the table and lowered his voice even more. 'Tell me about it.'

10

Roy Grace had been reluctant to go in to work today, wishing he could spend the whole of what promised to be a glorious weekend at home instead with his family. The weather forecast was brilliant, and he was planning to barbecue tomorrow. There were few things that brought a bigger smile to his five-year-old son Noah's face than a barbecued sausage smothered in ketchup. Although actually pretty much anything that had ketchup on it made Noah very happy. He looked at the photo on his desk, of Cleo, Noah and Molly, who was coming up to her third birthday, and Humphrey, their dog, and just wanted to be home with them all.

But a major and complex trial was looming. Three particularly unpleasant specimens of the human race – members of a Sussex crime family, currently on remand in prison. They faced charges of murder, attempted murder and worst of all – from Grace's perspective as a dog lover – conspiracy charges relating to illegal breeding and importation of puppies. Which was why, at 8 a.m. on this fine Saturday morning, he was sitting at his desk in his office in the Major Crime suite at Sussex House, staring at his computer screen, and surrounded by piles of paperwork he had to read through, and check word by word.

The public mostly only ever saw the headlines. The first announcing the bust and arrest of a criminal or a whole gang. Sometimes, the second, much later on, announcing their sentences. Guidelines stated that suspects should be brought to trial within eight months of their arrest, but in practice that time was often much longer.

What the public never saw was the tidal wave of paperwork that an arrest created, in building the case for the prosecution. It all ultimately landed on the Senior Investigating Officer's shoulders. This paperwork contained minefield after minefield, which Roy had to navigate with great caution. He had to ensure every step of the way that there was nothing in the police prosecution case that a smart defence barrister could drive a coach and horses through. Timelines that matched the events. Chains of evidence that had no gaps that could be challenged. The correct cautions given to arrested suspects. The procedures followed at the labs. And much more.

Although some of the trial paperwork was now digitized, there were still a good eight piles of documents lined up on his office floor, each tied with a different-coloured tape to signify their relevance.

At this moment he was reviewing, on his screen, the process of obtaining search warrants for two farms, and the legality of the raids that were subsequently carried out, resulting in over eight arrests, including the two men and one woman currently in prison, when he was interrupted by a phone call. It was a DC he had worked with in the past, Jamie Carruthers, attached to the Digital Forensics Unit but working in the field, undercover, as part of a small team looking at criminal activity on the internet and particularly the dark web.

After a brief exchange of pleasantries, Carruthers came to the point. 'Sir, we've become aware of some criminal activity where we believe the offenders to be based in Sussex, possibly in Brighton and Hove – relating to the supply of 3D printed handguns. We believe there may also be links to an individual offering their services as a contract killer with a guarantee that the death will be seen by the authorities as an accident or misadventure.'

'How much hard information do you have at this stage, Jamie?' Grace asked.

'It's early doors with our research, sir, but we are monitoring a number of sites. I wanted to give you a heads-up as this is an active investigation, and we may need the involvement of the Major Crime Team if we make substantial progress. But in the meantime we need to keep this very confidential and treat it in a sensitive manner.'

'OK,' Grace said. 'I'll have Polly Sweeney act as liaison with you, and all contact should be either through her or to me directly.'

As he ended the call, he heard the sound of his door opening, followed by Glenn Branson's voice, far too breezy for this hour.

'Hey, fun guy!' Branson said.

Grace, dressed casually in jeans and a polo shirt, narrowed his eyes, looking suspiciously at his friend, who was fully suited and booted as ever. 'What are you so damned perky about at this hour? And what are you doing in here on a Saturday instead of cherishing your wife?'

'This!' Branson fished in his pocket and produced a shiny USB memory stick, which he laid on the detective superintendent's desk as delicately as if it were a priceless Fabergé egg.

'What is it?'

'Our ticket to that headline murder investigation I've been after. Perhaps?'

'Seriously?'

'Seriously. Take a look.'

Grace inserted the memory stick into the side of his computer, then opened the folder that appeared after a few moments on his desktop. It contained three files. He double-clicked on the first one, labelled Organica Exhibit 1 and it began to play; a digital time display in the top right-hand corner read: *3.25 p.m., Saturday 3 September.*

He saw an overhead view of a supermarket checkout till. A young woman, distracted by a bawling baby in her trolley, was lifting various items from the trolley onto the conveyor, finishing with a bagged bunch of bananas. She put the 'next customer' board up and wheeled a buggy and her trolley forward, in front of the cashier.

A rather shapeless man, in his late thirties, with fair, threadbare hair, chinos, a big jumper and poor posture was queuing behind her, his back to the camera.

'That's Barnie Wallace,' Branson said. 'His partner's confirmed it.'

Behind Wallace was a tall figure in a bulky black jacket, hoodie, jeans and trainers, with a very confident, erect posture. As Wallace began placing items from his heavily stacked trolley onto the conveyor, the hooded person behind him glanced around, shiftily, his face further obscured by a scarf and dark glasses, then lifted a pack of what looked like mushrooms out of Wallace's trolley and replaced them with an apparently identical, shrink-wrapped pack. Wallace had not noticed.

The hooded person dropped the pack into his own trolley, which contained just a handful of items.

'What's going on?' Grace said. 'Does hoodie think the other pack of mushrooms looks better?'

'I don't think so, boss.' Branson paused the recording. 'This is the supermarket Organica, where Barnie Wallace's ex, Angi Colman, who was still friends with him at the time, said he may have bought the mushrooms. She also said he likes to forage for mushrooms because he's too mean to buy them. Organica is a new all-organic place in Western Road. Doing a roaring trade, apparently.'

'This Angi didn't eat any of the mushrooms herself?'

Branson shook his head. 'She's allergic to them.'

'So, it seems, was Barnie Wallace.'

'Hummm,' the DI said softly.

Grace gave a thin smile, then indicated for him to continue.

'There's not much else worth seeing.' Branson ran the rest of the recording, which showed the hooded man paying cash for his items after Barnie Wallace had left, and exiting into the busy street. They watched two more short clips, marked Exhibit 2 and Exhibit 3, showing the hooded man, face always obscured by the scarf and dark glasses, in a couple of aisles of the supermarket, always closely following Barnie Wallace.

'OK,' Roy Grace said. 'We know there are a lot of CCTV cameras in that area – both our own and the ones owned by the shops.'

'I'm on it,' Branson said. 'I've got an outside inquiry team collecting all the footage to see if we can plot our hooded friend's movements after leaving the place.'

'Creepy-looking – he's like a crow,' Grace said. Then he frowned. 'So, whoever the Crow is, he seemingly swapped the harmless, edible field mushrooms that Barnie Wallace bought in the supermarket for the highly toxic death cap mushrooms, in identical packaging. Which gives me a number of questions. The first is, if the Crow did this swap deliberately, and I think we hypothesize that he did, was he targeting Barnie Wallace, or did he have another agenda?'

'Another agenda? It's been over two weeks since he died, boss. Don't you think if there was going to be a ransom demand to Organica it would have happened by now? And we've checked back with the supermarket and they've had no other issues with any of their mushrooms at the time or since.'

Grace nodded. 'Yes, it makes it unlikely. But, if he was targeting Barnie Wallace, how did he know he was going to be at this supermarket, at this exact time, and buying field mushrooms? We could just be dealing with a random nutter.'

'I can answer that, boss.' He held up his phone, opened Instagram and took them to @barniewallacegourmetdinners.

Grace was surprised to see he had 12,500 followers.

'It looks like he's been posting a recipe every day, and where he's going to buy his ingredients. His last post was Saturday, September the third.'

'The night he died?' Grace quizzed.

'Technically he didn't die until the early hours of the sixth, never having regained consciousness, but I'll give you that one.'

'You're all heart.'

Branson raised a finger. 'You learned me, boss, that every detail counts.'

'I did, yadda, yadda. Can we move on? It's the weekend and I'd quite like to get home to my family and show them I'm capable of having a life. Just like you should be going home.'

'Even though we're in a murder inquiry?'

'We're in slow time, matey – if we have a murder at all. We've just watched a man swap a box of mushrooms in a supermarket. We don't have enough yet to launch a full-on inquiry – we're not yet at that level you're hot to trot for. This is a suspicious death at best, so let's continue with our enquiries first.'

Branson shrugged. 'Siobhan's off up in Birmingham chasing a story.'

'And your kids?'

'My sister's with them. I'm taking them to the skate park this afternoon.'

'OK.'

'Trust me, Roy, Barnie Wallace was murdered.'

'That's what you really think?'

Branson touched the side of his nose. 'Copper's nose!'

Grace grinned, and scanned the recent Instagram posts from Barnie Wallace. 'So, if our Crow followed Barnie Wallace on Instagram, he would have seen the post that he would be buying his mushrooms at Organica on Western Road, Brighton. That post was on Thursday, September the first. The footage of him buying them is at 3.25 p.m. Saturday, September the third. That gives our killer, if he is a killer at all, very little time to pick the death cap mushrooms and then put them into identical packaging to the ones on display in Organica. That's a pretty big ask, don't you think?'

Branson nodded pensively. 'You've a point.'

'And here's another point. Wallace, a professional chef, cooked these mushrooms as part of his menu for a dinner for a group of friends. If he was a trained chef, how on earth did he not realize these were deadly? Was he a total idiot?'

'I've done a bit of digging into Barnie Wallace's background,' Branson said. 'He wasn't a trained *anything*, he was what you'd call a proper dilettante. Seems like he has gone from one career to another. He started out as a failed actor, then got sacked as a chef in a gastropub – the Three Horseshoes in Rottingdean – after a whole bunch of diners went down with salmonella poisoning. At the time of his death he was working in telesales for a company in Newhaven, but trying to build up his following as a cookery expert on social media in the hope of monetizing it.'

Grace nodded. 'OK, so let's go for a moment with Barnie Wallace being a total plonker who *thinks* he's a chef. Who is this guy who is switching the mushrooms and why?'

'You've still got all three lifelines left, boss. Want to ask the audience, phone a friend or go fifty-fifty?'

'I'll go fifty-fifty. Did the Crow target Barnie Wallace because he wanted to harm – or maybe kill – him, or, as I said, are we dealing with a highly dangerous nutter who is randomly targeting people?'

'I'm going with the first part of your question,' Branson said. 'EJ and Norman interviewed the golfer, Susie Pfeiffer, who is still in a bad way but lucid enough to talk. She said she often picks mushrooms when she's on the golf course. She did think these particular ones looked a little different to the normal field mushrooms, but she checked them on an app on her phone and decided they were OK to eat.'

'They were in her possession all the time, from the moment she picked them to when she cooked them?' Grace asked beadily.

'So it would appear, boss.'

'OK, let's park her for now and focus on Barnie Wallace. Have you done an association chart on him?'

'It's on a whiteboard in the conference room. He's got a pretty wide circle of friends or acquaintances. We're working through them. He's divorced with a long trail of people he owes money to. We've interviewed this ex-girlfriend of his, Angi Colman. She said that in the weeks before he died, Barnie was acting a bit mysteriously. Said he told her he had a deal brewing that was about to make him a great amount of money.'

'Did he tell her what that was?'

Branson shook his head. 'But then we interviewed Barnie's ex-wife, Debbie Martin, and it gets more interesting. She said Barnie was making a hard play to try to win her back. She said part of the reason they'd broken up in the first place was Barnie never sticking to anything, and always in debt, always promising the next thing would work out. He told her this time that he really was on the verge of making a fortune. That he had the goods on someone – an old school friend or former work colleague, possibly, she thought. She said it sounded like some kind of blackmail.'

'Sexual blackmail?'

He shook his head. 'I didn't get that impression.'

'Did she speculate who it might be?' Grace pressed.

'No. But Barnie Wallace's debts had mounted up significantly in the months before his death. We've requested copies of his bank statements from our financial investigators and should have them early next week.'

'What about his phone and computer?'

'The laptop's gone to Aiden Gilbert and the phone to Charlotte Mckee at Digital Forensics.'

'You're not letting the grass grow under your feet, are you?' Grace said, impressed. 'Any bones you can throw me for what I brief the ACC on this? Do you have a hypothesis?'

Branson nodded. 'Yeah, the butler did it.'

11

All Saints, Patcham, like many rural English parish churches, was a picture-postcard hodge-podge of architectural styles through the centuries. It had a Saxon doorway, a Norman interior, and nods to Gothic, Early English and Perpendicular. It was the kind of church that tourists ticked off their lists and that couples craved for the background to their wedding photos. Just as Roy and his first wife had twenty-four years ago.

Sandy was now, after many traumatic years, at peace. She lay in the graveyard close to the flint wall at the rear, beyond which sheep grazed on the soft contours of a hill. Their troubled son, Bruno, was buried just fifty feet away from his mother, in the nearest plot that had been available at the time of his death. Just eleven years old.

Despite his sadness about Sandy's death, in 2018, Grace had never quite been able to forgive her for running off, without a word, on his thirtieth birthday. He still carried some anger towards her. It had been the worst time of his life, following her disappearance, as he searched continuously for clues about what might have happened to her. Had she been murdered? Kidnapped? Run off with a lover? Had an accident? Taken her own life? Lost her memory?

It had turned out to be none of these. And it also turned out she had subsequently given birth to Bruno, less than nine months after leaving him. After her death, Bruno had come to live with him and Cleo.

47

He had been a challenging boy – hardly surprising considering all his mother had put him through, Grace always thought. Given time, he was confident he could have helped Bruno shake off all the traumas his erratic early years with Sandy had left him with. But a stupid accident, a moment of carelessness, had deprived Bruno of his life and Roy of that chance.

He was feeling guilty this Sunday afternoon because it had been over a month since he'd last visited Bruno's grave; he normally tried to come at least once a fortnight, to stand beside it and chat to him. He carried in his hand a small posy of blue and red flowers – the colours of Bruno's beloved Bayern Munich football club – to place on the grave, as he did each time he came.

But, as he walked around to the rear of the church and along the path, he saw in the distance a figure he thought he recognized. And as he drew closer, he realized who it was.

Seriously? What the hell was he doing here?

The man had seen him, and was just standing there, immaculately dressed as ever in a Crombie coat with a velvet collar, and shiny brogues, his coiffed fair hair barely ruffled by the wind.

Standing, Grace realized as he drew nearer, right by Bruno's grave.

What?

Throughout his life, Roy Grace had always given people the benefit of the doubt. A Buddhist saying had long been part of his philosophy: *Everyone you meet is fighting a battle of their own that you know nothing about. Be kind, always.*

If there had been one exception to this it had been Cassian Pewe, the man he was looking at now with great curiosity. And he knew one thing. Whatever the reason this bastard was here, it wasn't going to be a good one.

A few years back he had risked his own life saving Pewe's, when the front part of the former senior police officer's car had gone over the edge of a cliff. How had Pewe rewarded him?

Firstly by trying to establish that Roy Grace had murdered his then missing wife, Sandy. Then secondly, after being promoted to the role of assistant chief constable, above him, by doing his best to make Roy's life hell for two years.

But, as proof there really was a God, Grace liked to joke, Pewe's career had crashed and burned after Grace had discovered – and subsequently proved – that the ACC was corrupt. He had been kicked out of the force and jailed for two years; the last Grace had heard, which had made him smile, was that the former very senior cop was now working selling advertising space.

So what the hell *was* he doing here?

As Grace strode towards him, memories were playing like old videos inside his head. Cassian Pewe, when he had been ACC, turning up to Sandy's funeral. That had surprised him, and then it had surprised him even more when he'd seen, at the wake, Pewe talking animatedly to Bruno in fluent German. Clearly on a charm offensive.

For what reason?

Grace, still some distance away, saw Pewe had clocked him. That old, unpleasantly familiar supercilious smile.

'Roy!' he said. 'How very good to see you!' He stretched out a hand.

Ignoring it and keeping one hand firmly in his pocket and the other holding the posy, Grace couldn't restrain himself after all these years of pent-up anger at this total bastard. 'How was prison, Cassian?'

'Pretty bearable actually, Roy.' He raised his hands in the air. 'Please don't think I'm bitter – you were just a humble copper doing your duty. I don't take it personally that you snitched on me.'

Grace stared at him levelly.

'I've no idea what you are talking about, Cassian,' he said. 'You were a corrupt copper who abused your position as an assistant

49

chief constable, using it to line your pockets. If I reported you and that made me a snitch, what would my not reporting you have made me?'

'You didn't have to report me. You could have spoken to me. But you wouldn't do that, would you, because you knew I was screwing your wife, didn't you?'

12

Roy Grace stared at Cassian Pewe for a long moment as the words sank in. He'd never been unfaithful to Sandy throughout the length of their marriage and it had never remotely occurred to him, back then, that she might have been cheating on him.

Of course, all bets were off now that he knew more about her and her erratic behaviour during and after leaving him. But it was more than likely, too, that this sewer rat standing in front of him was lying, being spiteful, winding him up in a way he thought would hurt Grace the most.

'Why are you here, Cassian?' he said calmly but coldly.

'I could ask you the same question, Roy,' Pewe said, with that smile again, flashing a set of perfect teeth, although Roy clocked that even they had yellowed a little. No teeth-whitening facilities in prison? How sad.

It was all Grace could do to restrain himself from punching the man in the mouth and bashing those teeth – which had always been far too white for his age – down his throat. 'I'm putting flowers on my son's grave,' he said tightly. 'And I'd appreciate some privacy.'

Pewe locked eyes with him. 'Ah, you see that's where you are mistaken I'm afraid, Roy. Bruno wasn't your son, he was mine. I was his father.'

The grass beneath Grace's feet suddenly felt unstable, as if it was tilting slightly. What Pewe was saying was absurd. Sandy had

51

confirmed that he was Bruno's father, he had her letter in which she said she'd had Bruno's DNA tested. But, all the same, for an instant he felt the cold wind of doubt chill his bones. Had she lied to him?

'No way, Cassian. No way in hell.'

Pewe was looking at him so confidently, winding Grace's mind back to the time when Pewe was his boss and seemed to take a sadistic delight in that superiority, giving Grace the feeling that no matter how much it angered him, there was nothing he could do about it; he was impotent. The police command structure was a hierarchy that operated like the military. You obeyed the orders from your senior officers without question and there was no appeal.

It felt to him at this fleeting moment that Pewe was back in his swanky office, in his crisp uniform, standing behind his massive desk. Holding all the aces.

'You may think you were his father, Roy. But I did the maths. The dates when I was having sex with Sandy correspond precisely with when Bruno was born.' He smiled that supercilious smile again. 'You only had to look at him to see he was nothing like you; he looked like me.'

Grace was staring back at him, incredulous, and thinking hard – and trying to hang on to the last fraying threads of his temper. 'I'm not taking this shit from a jailbird, a bent copper – sorry, ex-copper. I see your game exactly. How does selling advertising space pay? Not too great, I would imagine.'

Still smiling, Pewe said, 'Sandy had a birthmark, didn't she, Roy, or did you never get intimate enough with her to see it? You'll know the one I'm talking about if you did.'

Grace stared at him, saying nothing, feeling that chill wind in his bones again.

'Like a tiny starfish with two of its arms missing, yes? Just inside her right thigh, about three inches below her pudenda. It drove her wild when I kissed it.'

The wind turned into a gale of cold fury, roiling every cell in his body. No one could ever have seen that birthmark, not even if Sandy was in a bikini, unless they'd been with her close-up when she was naked. As he now realized Cassian Pewe must have been.

'It's very simple, Roy. Maybe you don't want to accept it, but I'm the father. I'll do whatever it takes to prove it – if I have to have Bruno's body exhumed, I'll do it.'

'You filthy, grubby bastard.' Grace almost spat the words at him. 'You'd dig an eleven-year-old boy's body out of his grave? Let me tell you straight, Cassian. Sandy confirmed in writing that I'm the father and, in any case, you'd never get approval for an exhumation.'

Pewe shook his head and gave another smile that angered Grace even more. More threads were fraying and he was close to losing it. 'Really, Roy? Sandy was hardly going to tell you that we were having an affair, was she? She obviously felt sorry for you.' He shrugged.

'You really are an even bigger tosser than I ever thought, Cassian. You have no place here. Just fucking walk away now and do something to try to prove you exist as more than just a scumbag.'

Pewe covered the five feet separating them in two strides, attempting a punch straight at Roy's face. The punch fell short and Roy sprang forward in self-defence.

Police officers were prime targets of hate in prison, ranking only just below paedophiles and rapists. Cassian Pewe's two years behind bars had sharpened up both his reflexes and his fighting skills. He ducked as Grace's fist caught his right ear a glancing blow, then he threw a sharp left back at Grace's nose. But Grace saw it coming, side-stepped, grabbed Pewe's arm and, in a classic ju-jitsu movement, threw him onto his back on the ground between two graves, but fell down with him.

Pewe held one of his hands to Grace's windpipe. It had been many years since Grace's time as a beat copper, when getting into a bundle in the centre of Brighton on a Thursday, Friday or Saturday night was commonplace, but he still retained that muscle memory – as he knew, no doubt, Pewe would have too. He knew instinctively that even though Pewe was trying to choke him, his outstretched arm made him vulnerable.

Grabbing Pewe's right elbow and using the leverage to spin away, he threw his weight back and drove his hips upwards, hyperextending his elbow. He heard a yelp of pain, as the man's arm twisted desperately to avoid being snapped.

Grace scrambled to maintain his position on top of his foe and held him there long enough for Pewe to gain the composure to speak.

'You know, Roy, as Bruno's father I will inherit his trust fund, don't you?'

'Oh, fuck you, Cassian. You won't get away with pretending you slept with Sandy to get your hands on that. You really are way below the lowest of the low, aren't you? Sandy had her standards, and she'd never have slept with a pile of filth like you.'

Grace let go of him, staggered to his feet, thinking it was game over, and took a step back, his hand hurting badly. But Pewe, much stronger than he had imagined him to be, came hurtling up at him again, landing an agonizing punch straight to his nose. Grace punched blindly back despite his hand hurting more and more, then took another hammer punch to the eye, dazing him and blurring his vision further.

Stumbling to the ground, Grace desperately wiped his eyes clear only to see Pewe right on top of him, cutting off his oxygen again. He couldn't move his head properly because his balance was still messed up; all he could do for a moment was cover his face defensively with his forearms and try to find some release.

He could hear Pewe hissing in his ear, 'This is where you join them, Roy, they're both right beneath you, just a few feet below you.'

And for an instant, he believed it. The choke was tightening and it was getting harder and harder to breathe at all. Pewe wasn't stopping. Everything started going dark; he felt his head was being squeezed off his neck. Everything was going quiet and the ringing in his ears was becoming louder. He knew these were signs that he was on the brink of passing out.

No, not here, not like this. Not Pewe winning.

He flailed and kicked. Was this where it ended? Dying where Sandy and Bruno were buried? He tried desperately to think what to do, but then heard Cassian Pewe's voice, faint, in his ear.

'Die with them, Roy, I'm going to take it all.'

Then he heard the words again.

Somehow, finding strength in his desperation, he wrenched free his left hand and clamped onto the side of Pewe's head, pushing as hard as he could into his temple. He heard a faint, almost distant scream, but he continued pressing down, his life depending on it, as Pewe's scream got louder. The choke was loosening but not enough, his head was still pulsing. He sucked down a little air as Pewe, howling in agony now, released his choke hold. Finally, before Pewe had a chance to retaliate, Grace stood, shaking with both rage and adrenaline and took a step backward. He had his balance back but he was still breathing heavily and his vision was still blurred.

He looked down at the disgraced former assistant chief constable and his long-time nemesis with grim satisfaction. Pewe's coat was ripped and his white shirt collar and front stained with blood and mud. The bottom of it had untucked from his trousers, exposing some of the pale, bare flesh of his stomach, which looked more paunchy than he imagined it would. His legs were spread-eagled, one shoe off.

'You bastard!' Pewe screamed as he scrambled to his knees. Grace, still weakened, could see him coming at him again. He knew he had one last shot at this. As if preparing to drop kick a rugby ball over the goal post he swung his right leg back, then drove it forward with every ounce of strength he had in his body, straight up between Pewe's legs.

Like some marionette on which the strings had been brutally jerked, Pewe momentarily sat bolt upright with a gasp of agony. Then, clasping his hands to his groin, eyes rolling, he writhed on the ground, moaning.

'That, Cassian, was for disrespecting me after I risked my life saving yours, for all the years you were a complete and utter arrogant shit to me. And, Cassian,' Grace said, 'it was for sleeping with my wife.' He glared down at him. 'You're a ghoul. Why don't you get her body exhumed at the same time as Bruno's – she's just over there.' He pointed his finger in the direction of Sandy's grave. 'Then you can shag her again.'

13

Paul lived with his black Labrador, Montmorency, in a sixth-floor penthouse duplex on the top two floors of a handsome nineteenth-century Regency terrace house in the Kemp Town district of Brighton. It was leased to him as Mr Paul Anthony, which was the name the world outside of the dark web knew him by, these days.

He owned a second property in the city, a row of ten lock-up garages behind an industrial estate near Shoreham Harbour. He'd bought the lot anonymously, through a lawyer and a shell company, eighteen months ago and referred to them privately as his *office*. He only used four of the garages. One, his actual office, where he kept his computers, servers and his burner phones; one used as a workshop, where he kept his 3D printing apparatus; one he had converted into an emergency hideout bathroom and bedroom; and the other for concealing his car – a grey, five-year-old Honda Jazz, the kind of car nobody would notice, the automotive equivalent of a man in a hi-vis jacket holding a clipboard.

He owned the other six garages purely to guard his privacy. He didn't want neighbours.

The name he used as his alias on the dark web was Mr Oswald. This amused him. It was taken from the man who allegedly shot dead President John F. Kennedy. It was good to have a name that people remembered – well, for the right reasons, anyhow. And it had led to several referrals. Quality ones.

He was all about quality. Aristotle said, *Quality is not an act, it is a habit.* That was his motto. And quality began with his residence, which he kept spotless.

The subtle alterations to his appearance were quality too. His hair transplant. Before his disappearance he had been going bald. Now he had a thick head of dark brown hair. It had been a top-quality transplant. His goatee and new specs made him look a changed, perfectly groomed man versus his rugged old looks.

His dog was quality too. A pedigree Labrador retriever. He'd named him from a book he'd read as a kid and had enjoyed, called *Three Men in a Boat.* It had actually been three men and a dog called Montmorency.

Montmorency had a grandmother who had been a winner in class at Crufts. He was docile, streetwise, in the sense that after elaborate training, he would never let his master cross a main road other than on a green light. Paul Anthony could understand why Labrador retrievers like Montmorency made such good guide dogs for the blind. And there were occasions when he employed Montmorency's services for just that. He kept a harness, an exaggeratedly large pair of dark sunglasses, and a white stick in a closet close to the front door. Out of sight of visitors. Not that he had many visitors.

There was nothing actually wrong with his eyesight. And on fine days, like this one, he had a majestic view out across the Channel to the hazy white spindles of the Rampion wind farm, some fifteen miles to the south, like a spectral town rising out of the sea. He had another equally grand view to the west of the Palace Pier, less than a mile away, and a somewhat less attractive view, unless it had been his thing (which naked bottoms, limp appendages and hard pebbles really weren't), of the nudist beach a few hundred yards to the east.

He would miss this view when he moved, which he would be

doing soon. You could only hide in plain sight in one place for so long. But all the time he was in England he would have to keep on the move. At some point, he would quietly slip away to one of his bolt-holes abroad with Shannon. His apartment in Puerto Banús or his house on Mykonos. He would do that the moment he felt they were in danger. And he was starting to feel that now, owing to Barnie's meddling. Thanks, pal.

For the past two years he had lived alone with his dog, anonymous and invisible. He was more than comfortable in his own company, and he liked that he and Shannon lived separately, for now, at least. They could link up for work and for pleasure when it suited him. But meeting and falling in love with her had given him back desires he had forgotten existed, and she was proving very, very useful to his business. He had felt for a long time after his *death* that he had too much baggage, too much history, and too much to risk to share his life with anyone.

But Shannon was different. Damaged goods, like himself, in some ways, and he trusted her. And he had a plan to make sure of that. To win her eternal trust. Not that he necessarily wanted to co-habit with her all the time.

Living on his own had its compensations. The first of which was being able to smoke a cigar indoors without anyone complaining – especially his wife – former wife – estranged wife – non-wife? Whatever.

He missed the boys though. The twins. They'd be eight now. They would never know him and, likewise, he would never see them growing up, and that made him sad. Well, a little sad. He knew guys from the squash club and the golf club who went all doolally over their kids. He'd never really felt that way but he did love them.

Well, OK, just occasionally he did miss them. He did have a yearning to see them more than from a distance, through binoculars, on their school playing fields, when they were playing football or rugby or cricket matches. Financially they were fine – well, actually, way more than fine. Their mother was a very wealthy lady. The boys would want for nothing. He'd seen to that. Conscience clear. He knew where to find his boys if he ever wanted to. He could always check up on them – again, if he *wanted* to.

And why would he *want* to when he had all this freedom? To do whatever the hell he wanted, he kidded himself.

Paul Anthony wrinkled his eyes. He smiled. He was doing exactly what he wanted to do. And part of that right now was smoking this cigar.

Montmorency seemed to like the smell and snuggled up to him on the sofa whenever he lit up. God, how Fiona used to moan about it stinking out the house the next morning and making his clothes smell.

The second compensation was being able to slob about all day in his silk dressing gown without having to shave or get dressed if he didn't feel like it. And the third was having breakfast in proper French cafe style – an almond croissant, an exquisite double espresso from beans he had ground, freshly obtained each day from a local specialist purveyor here in Kemp Town, and a fine Armagnac, in a perfect small round breakfast-sized glass, like he'd seen contented-looking old men drinking from in France. Just a nip. Just enough to take the edge off the day.

Just enough to raise his glass in his daily toast to whoever it was who said: *I feel sorry for people who don't drink, because when they wake up in the morning, that's as good as they're going to feel all day.*

And could it get much better than starting his day with a long walk with Montmorency, then sitting out on this terrace, with a forty-year-old Dartigalongue Armagnac, accompanied by a very fine thirty-year-old Cohiba Coronas Especiales cigar, the morning's newspapers and his dog at his side? Particularly when it was such a fine summer day in so many ways?

Being dead definitely had its compensations.

Although perhaps not for his next victim, Dermot Quince Bryson. The man, who Shannon had already '*met*' and sold a 3D printed handgun to, was an even bigger asshole than his name suggested. But it wasn't just the thought of the pleasure of killing him nor the glorious late September sunshine that was putting him in such a good mood. It was the challenge Shannon Kendall had – perhaps inadvertently – set him.

He was rising to that challenge, one with a lot of upside. It would buy him the eternal loyalty of his attractive, super-smart accomplice and soulmate. He'd spent much of the weekend thinking, planning, and poking around the dark web for the tools he needed.

He took another sip of his brandy, pulled out the local newspaper, the *Argus*, from under the fresh copy of *The Times*. He always liked to begin with the local news. But, as he stared at the front page, his mood instantly clouded over.

CONCERN AFTER SECOND SUSSEX MUSHROOM DEATH

He put the cigar down in the ashtray he'd stolen some years ago from the Hermitage hotel in Monaco.

Shit! What? What the fuck?????

He read the words beneath with rising fury, the rage growing inside him with every word.

Almost three weeks after Brighton-born actor Barnie Wallace died after mistaking lethal death cap mushrooms for common field mushrooms, in a scenario that could have come from the hit ITV series *Endeavour*, in an episode of which Wallace had once played a police officer, in an unrelated incident, a second member of the public has also died after eating death cap mushrooms.

Nice of them to big up Barnie up by calling him an *actor*, he thought acidly. That role was about the only television part he'd ever had, in a short-lived career as a mostly *resting* actor. Although of course, at school, all three of them, the Three Musketeers, had been part of the school thespian group. Barnie was a pretty wooden performer. James Taylor had some talent, for sure, and had once played a very convincing Polonius in *Hamlet*. And he himself always loved performing, being someone other than himself. Dressing up. He knew he was particularly talented at playing female roles, his favourite being Becky Sharpe in *Vanity Fair*. But he could be anyone, anyone at all. That was the beauty of being dead.

He read on.

Barnie Wallace, 39, died from ingesting mushrooms that he was preparing for a dinner party that never went ahead.

That was fine, Mr Oswald had thought when he'd originally read this news.

A simple mistake over mushrooms had been his intention and, he thought, pretty much the perfect murder. No one would pay it much attention. Barnie had been an internet chef at the time of his death. A pretty dumb chef. Just a tragic accident. Nothing to trouble the local plod, and all nicely teed-up for a coroner's verdict of death by misadventure. End of story.

Until this stupid sodding woman.

You cretin, Susie Pfeiffer!

Reading on, he learned that Susie Pfeiffer, fifty-seven, Ladies Captain of the Dyke Golf Club, had picked what she thought were edible field mushrooms on a round of golf, and had later cooked them for supper for her and her husband, along with two poached eggs each. Within hours, both of them had been taken ill. Her husband had subsequently died and she was in hospital with acute kidney failure.

And now some nosy parker of a copper, a Detective Super-intendent Grace, had told an *Argus* reporter the police were investigating both deaths. If that stupid golfer hadn't died, no one would have paid Barnie Wallace's death any attention at all. Sodding Susie Pfeiffer was putting his very clever plan in jeopardy.

And just to add fuel to the fire, the editor of the *Argus*, someone called Arron Hendy, had launched an appeal to all foragers in the county of Sussex to bring any mushrooms that they believed to be edible along to the *Argus* offices to be inspected by a mycol-ogist called Merilee Williams. Prompted by these two deaths, Merilee Williams would be giving a lecture this coming Thursday in the Friends Meeting House, Ship Street, on mushroom taxonomy, biology, ecology and the medicinal or culinary uses of different mushroom species.

Barnie Wallace had been an asshole. Worse than that, a greedy asshole. And a desperate one.

Desperate people were always dangerous.

It had been necessary to dispense with Barnie; besides, he wasn't going to be any big loss to the world. It wasn't exactly like killing Einstein or Bill Gates or any of the other select few who had actually added value to the sum total of humanity. Barnie was a twat, he'd been a living twat and now he was a dead twat.

End of.

Or it should have been.

He stood up in utter blind fury, banging his fists together, and yelled, out at the sea, at the top of his voice, 'Susie Pfeiffer you moron, you stupid stupid stupid MORON!' Then he banged his fist so hard on the table his coffee cup fell over and broke.

Jesus. Calm down.

Calm down.

He tried. Took several deep breaths, eight in through his nose and eight out through his mouth, as his therapist had told him. Then focused his mind, hard. Had he pushed his luck too far attending Barnie's funeral? He thought it would be exhilarating to be among the mourners and no one knowing he was there. He hadn't imagined anyone would have recognized him. No one would have been looking out for him – why would they? Who would be looking out for a dead man?

James Taylor?

Had James recognized him? No way he could have been sure it was him, no way at all. But, he reminded himself . . .

Be aware of your weaknesses.

It was his mantra. Every morning as he stared in the mirror, brushing his teeth, he would repeat this over and over for the boring two minutes his electric toothbrush took to complete its cycles.

And he knew his biggest weakness was being unable to control his temper. But Barnie had so much pissed him off. That pathetic loser. How had Barnie tracked him down after his quite magnificent and convincing funeral? Then figured he could blackmail him for big money?

Barnie had had to go.

James Taylor was someone he was grateful to. Jamesy had given him a sensational eulogy. Tears shed all around the church, and no one had spotted him, sitting near the back. Well, no way anyone would have done – he was attired all in black in widow's weeds, and a black veil. And that had been fun. Hey, how many people got to attend their own funeral?

But then he'd been really pissed off by Barnie poking his nose in.

Don't you start sniffing around too, James Taylor. You have one credit, thanks to your eulogy. Use it wisely. You won't get a second one. Dead men can be very angry and very dangerous.

Suddenly, the Nest app on his phone chimed, and he looked at it. A figure, slightly distorted in the wide-angle camera lens, stood at the front door, downstairs, holding a package.

'Hello?' he answered.

'Package for Mr Oswald?'

He smiled. It would be one of several items he had ordered off sites on the dark web. Items that might help make Shannon Kendall even more beholden to him.

Not bothering with the painfully slow lift, he bounded down the long, steep staircase with a big smile on his face. His morning was back on track.

14

Tuesday 27 September 2022

James Taylor, still shaken by what he had seen at the wake, had been unable to follow up on his sighting – or rather *possible sighting* – of Rufus Rorke at the funeral, over the weekend. On Saturday he'd had to fly his employer's Pilatus to the Aéroport du Golfe de Saint-Tropez, in the South of France, to collect Mr and Mrs Towne from one of their many summer sojourns at their villa in Gassin, in the hills above Saint-Tropez, and drop them back at Jersey airport, before flying on to Shoreham in Sussex, where the Pilatus had a hangar.

Sunday, he knew, was not a good day to trouble a God-botherer, and then yesterday he'd had to fly the Pilatus to Biggin Hill for its annual service and check. Finally, at what he considered a respectable time, 9.30 a.m. on this Tuesday morning, he parked his cherished black MGB GT in the street, and presented himself at the handsome – if a little in need of some TLC – rural vicarage, a Georgian house that was set back a short distance from the High Street, a few miles north-west of Brighton. He stood outside the porch and pressed the doorbell. And heard no sound. After a few moments he pressed again. And again heard no sound. He then rapped the corroded brass lion-head knocker.

Almost before he had finished striking, the door flew open and the tall Reverend Ian Parry-Jones was standing in front of him, wearing a dog collar partially visible beneath the neck of a ragged jumper, black trousers and leather slippers. Unlike at the funeral, his expression was now more of irritation than piety, his hair looking as bad tempered as he was. 'Yes?' he said.

'I'm sorry to trouble you,' Taylor said. 'I was at Barnie Wallace's funeral on Friday. We were at school together.'

The vicar's expression softened a little but not much. 'Ah yes, so sad, taken so young. He was clearly a popular fellow – it's not often I see our church so packed these days. Very comforting for his loved ones.' Then he gave Taylor a hard stare. After a few moments of awkward silence he asked, 'What exactly can I do for you?'

Taylor, who had been expecting a somewhat warmer greeting, hesitated before ploughing on. 'This may seem an odd request. Do you happen to have CCTV cameras at the church? I looked around as I was leaving but couldn't spot any.'

Parry-Jones frowned. 'No, you wouldn't, because they are concealed. Unfortunately we do. Why are you asking?'

'It's a bit of a long story. Do you have a few minutes or can we arrange another time?'

'Now's fine. Come in – can I offer you some tea or coffee?'

'A coffee would be very welcome, thank you.'

Taylor entered a hallway that was more spartan and shabby than the rather grand exterior had indicated, and followed the vicar through into an even more spartan room, badly in need of redecoration and with mismatched furniture that all looked tired. He perched on a busted sofa and the vicar went out. Taylor looked around. There were some invitations on the mantelpiece, one from the Bishop of Chichester, a photograph of a young man in a graduation gown, wearing a mortar board, and another of a young woman, similarly attired. Hanging above was a cheaply framed, poor-quality print of the famous El Greco painting *Christ Carrying the Cross*. A window looked out onto a lawn that looked as though it was still waiting for its first cut of the year; in contrast it was lined by well-tended flower beds.

The vicar returned with a tray on which were two cups of coffee and a plate of chocolate digestive biscuits, setting them down on a nondescript coffee table that was too young to be an antique and too old to be IKEA.

'So what exactly is your interest in our CCTV, Mr . . . ?'

'Taylor. James Taylor.' He took a cup and, out of politeness, a biscuit, although, borderline fanatical about keeping in shape, he didn't really want one.

'You've got a friend, have you?' The vicar said it with a cheeky smile, perching himself on the battered leather armchair opposite.

Taylor grinned.

'My wife's a big fan of James Taylor,' the vicar said, becoming a tad more jovial. 'She loves all his work. *You've got a friend.* Amazing, right? I'm assuming you are not him?'

Taylor nodded. 'I wish I could claim to be him, but I'm not – and, besides, he's in his seventies. No, I'm just a humble pilot.'

'Ah, who do you fly for?'

'Well, it used to be easyJet but I got made redundant early on during Covid lockdown. But I was lucky, I got a job flying a private jet for a wealthy man in Jersey.'

'Is that better than working for an airline? It sounds like it might be?'

'I miss the camaraderie – it's just me – but on the plus side, most of the time he only ever uses the plane once every couple of weeks.'

'Which gives you more time at home with your family?' The vicar, clocking his wedding ring, looked at him expectantly.

Taylor did not want to go there. So he nodded and smiled politely. 'Indeed.'

There was a moment of awkward silence. The vicar stirred his coffee noisily, a distant, beatific smile on his face, the spoon making a ting-ting-ting of which he seemed unaware. Taylor ate some of the biscuit, trying to stop any crumbs from falling onto the threadbare carpet. A grey Burmese cat wandered in, made a screeching miaow sound and walked back out.

'We call him Willy-Two-Breakfasts,' Parry-Jones said. 'He's telling me it's time for his second one.' He smiled again and stirred his coffee once more. Ting-ting-ting. 'So – um – ah – how exactly can I help you, Mr Taylor?' He wrung his hands together as if unsure what else he might do with them.

'Well, the thing is, at the funeral on Friday I saw someone I was sure I knew, sitting a few rows in front of me, and have lost contact with. I really wanted to catch him, but by the time I got to the door of the church at the end of the funeral, he had gone. I just wondered if there was any possibility I could view the CCTV footage, if you had any, to see if it was actually him?'

The vicar was looking at him strangely. 'Did you attend the wake?'

'I did, yes. But he wasn't there.'

'Can you describe him? I was at the door, shaking hands with everyone – with the collection plate, of course. I might remember him.'

'He's tall, over six foot. He was wearing glasses, a black base-ball cap and a scarf covering his face.'

The vicar frowned. 'A baseball cap, in my church, during the service?'

'Yes, he had it on the whole time.'

He shook his head. 'Are you quite sure? I would have noticed. I don't approve of men wearing hats in my church – unless it's for their own religion.'

Taylor hesitated for a moment. Was he *quite* sure? Could this all have been a figment of his imagination? He pressed on. 'I'm sure your CCTV would show us.'

Parry-Jones frowned, took a sip of his coffee then set the cup down in the saucer. 'I'm not really sure under all these new GDPR regulations I can show you the footage, I'm afraid. I think it might be a breach of the Data Protection Act.'

'It's only for my personal interest,' Taylor said. 'It won't go beyond me.'

The vicar looked pensive. 'I really don't know.'

'I saw you have an appeal for repairs to your church roof,' Taylor said.

'We do indeed. It's a desperate situation – and hard to raise money in these current times.'

'If I were to pledge a hundred pounds – might that ease your way to letting me see that CCTV footage?'

The vicar looked at him, then swept his hands through his mane of hair. 'One hundred pounds?'

Taylor nodded.

'That's a very generous offer. I think we could come to an arrangement on that. An equitable one. So long as I have your assurance that what you see would go no further?'

'It will go no further.' Taylor pulled out his wallet.

15

'Shit!' Glenn Branson said.

Grace squinted at him.

'Don't tell me, you walked into a door, right? Or you went five rounds with Eubank Junior?'

'It was a door. A Cassian Pewe shaped one.'

Branson stopped in his tracks. 'What?'

Grace shrugged, and immediately winced.

'Man, you look like shit. You look like you walked into five different doors then fell down a staircase and hit a post at the bottom.'

'Thanks, I feel like shit.' He gave his friend a brief download of the fight in the graveyard.

Branson shook his head. 'You might need to brush up your boxing skills.'

Grace cocked his head. 'It's ju-jitsu actually. Any more advice?'

'Plenty, but you won't listen, so what's the point?'

Grace said nothing.

'Are you OK? I mean, like seriously, are you OK? Have you been checked out by any medic?'

He grinned – and even that hurt. 'You should see the other guy.'

'I'd pay good money for that!' Then he shook his head. 'You really had fisticuffs – like proper fisticuffs?'

'Long overdue.'

'And you gave him a beating, right? You should have belled me, I'd have come over and given him a few kicks in the nuts, too, for old times' sake.' He shook his head again. 'It must have been a big one if the most level-headed man I know threw punches. You really should go to hospital to get checked out – I'll take you there.'

'I'm fine, I'll be OK, enough nagging. I've had it up to here from Cleo wanting me to go and sit for six hours in the A&E waiting room. But she cleaned me up well. Trust me, this is me looking good! Come on, we need to get out to the briefing. Would you please go in first and tell the team to ask no questions about this, we need to crack on with the investigation.'

Branson left Roy's office and addressed the team. As Roy appeared, the room went embarrassingly quiet, with most trying to take a discreet look. It took Norman Potting to break the awkwardness. 'The Phantom Mushroom Switcher strikes again,' he announced.

Jack Alexander grinned and Roy Grace was grateful for the playful humour. Glenn Branson, who was now sitting centre stage at the oval table in the Major Crime suite conference room, didn't react for some moments. He was focusing on his notes for his first briefing for what was now Operation Meadow. And on his desk was a copy of this morning's *Argus* with an alarmist headline.

On the wide screen behind Roy Grace's head was a photograph of a mushroom. It rose on a long stalk out of what seemed to be woodland brambles and had a flat top.

'*Amanita phalloides*,' Branson announced. 'Otherwise known as the death cap mushroom, is the deadliest of all poisonous mushrooms. After consuming one, there's a latency period of six to twenty-four hours with no symptoms. This is followed by severe abdominal pain, vomiting and diarrhoea. Signs of liver failure follow, such as jaundice, confusion and internal bleeding.

Kidney damage also occurs concurrently. Without major medical intervention, anyone poisoned will fall into a coma and die – normally within a week but can be quicker.'

'Well, I know what to cook the missus for dinner tonight!' quipped Norman Potting.

Several of the team laughed.

Although Roy Grace was the overall SIO, he was letting Glenn Branson head the investigation, giving him much more responsibility as his deputy.

So far it was just a small group: DS Potting; DS Alexander, who was acting as office manager; DCs Nick Nicholl, Emma-Jane Boutwood, Velvet Wilde, Polly Sweeney and Will Glover (the most recent and youngest member of the team); a researcher, Luke Stanstead; financial investigator Emily Denyer; an indexer; and a computer supervisor for HOLMES – the Home Office Large Major Crime Enquiry System.

They had all just watched the replay of the three recordings of Barnie Wallace in the Organica supermarket on the large wall-mounted screen behind Roy Grace.

'We don't know that this person has struck before, Norman,' Branson cautioned. 'We need to establish whether there is any link between Barnie Wallace, who died nearly three weeks ago from poisoning by death cap mushroom, and a Stephan Pfeiffer, who died from death cap mushroom poisoning last Thursday. On the surface they appear very different circumstances – from the CCTV evidence we have seen, Barnie Wallace was targeted, but from the information I have currently available, Stephan Pfeiffer was poisoned by his wife, who it seems innocently mistook poison cap – or death cap as they are better known – for common edible field mushrooms.'

Potting raised an eyebrow. 'How long had the Pfeiffers been married, boss?'

'I don't have that information, yet.'

'Could be relevant,' Potting said and gave a sly tap on his nose. 'The longer people are married, the more likely one of them is to want to off the other.'

There were several sniggers. 'Speaking from experience are we, Norman?' Velvet Wilde asked in her rich Belfast accent.

'Exactly that, young lady,' he replied. 'Any one of my ex-wives would have murdered me if they'd had the chance.'

Cutting through the frivolity, Roy Grace interjected. 'It's highly unlikely this is a murder–suicide by mushroom poisoning, Norman. I think we can discount that completely.'

'I agree,' Branson said. 'Norman and Velvet, I'll still give you the action of doing the victimology on the Pfeiffers. She's currently Lady Captain at the Dyke Golf Club. I gather she's still in the High Dependency Unit and the staff are reluctant to let us speak to her for too long, so while we wait for her to recover, go to the golf club and see what people have to say about her and about their relationship – and if there are any innuendos about any kind of animosity between them or chinks in their marriage. Anything that might give her reason to have, as Norman so elegantly puts it, *offed* her hubby.'

Then he addressed the team again. 'Something we need to establish, which is very important for this investigation, is just how easy – or difficult – it is to mistake a death cap mushroom for an ordinary edible field mushroom. From the limited research I've done so far on the internet it seems they are dangerously similar. Anyone here a forager?'

They all shook their heads. No one was.

'Wouldn't it be part of a professional chef's training, boss?' DC Nick Nicholl asked.

'I'd like to think so, Nick,' Branson replied.

'On the briefing notes it says that Barnie Wallace worked as a chef for eighteen months at the Three Horseshoes pub in Rottingdean,' Nicholl continued. 'I've been there a few times – it's a proper decent gastropub with a good local reputation. Barnie Wallace can't have been a totally rubbish chef to have survived there that long.'

'Go and have a word with the landlord and see what he has to say about Wallace, Nick,' the DI said. Then he turned to Stanstead. 'Luke, I need you to work on association charts for Barnie Wallace and for the Pfeiffers – see if we can either find anything that links them, or establish conclusively there is no connection between them at all.'

'Yes, boss,' Stanstead acknowledged.

'Nick,' Branson said, addressing the detective. 'I need you to run mushroom poisoning, all types of mushrooms, on national crime databases – see what other recorded instances there have been in the past couple of years.'

'Yes, sir.'

Branson then held up the newspaper, showing everyone in the room the front page. The splash headline read: SHOULD ALL MUSHROOMS BE WITHDRAWN FROM SALE IN THE CITY?

The only good news Roy Grace could take from it was that the by-line for the piece was Patrick Barlow and not Siobhan Sheldrake – Branson's wife. He interjected. 'We will be holding a press conference later this morning, at the request of ACC Downing, to reassure the public that we believe these two instances of mushroom poisoning are isolated.'

'Are you confident, chief?' Potting asked.

'I am, Norman, yes,' Grace replied.

Branson continued. 'We have every supermarket, every greengrocer and every market stall in the city, not to mention all the local mushroom farmers, looking at us to provide reassurance to the public, particularly as we are just coming into peak mushroom season,' he said.

'That headline puts a new meaning on the word *fungicide*,' Potting quipped.

'Thanks, Norman, I think we're done with all the mushroom jokes,' Branson said.

He continued. 'We need to establish extremely quickly if this is a one-off – an enemy of Barnie Wallace who wanted him dead – or a random, very dangerous nutter with an axe to grind against God knows what. Organic produce? Vegetarians or vegans? Supermarkets? Or society in general?'

He addressed DC Boutwood. 'EJ, I'd like you and Will Glover to check all the premises either side of the Organica supermarket and across the road, for any CCTV they may have that would show us our hooded friend. We need to try to establish where he came from and where he was heading.' He smiled wryly at Potting. 'I sent this footage over to the Control Room CCTV yesterday to see if they can get any sightings of either Barnie Wallace or our hooded friend, the Phantom Mushroom Switcher.' He looked around the table. 'Any other considerations?'

Jack Alexander raised his hand. 'Just a thought, boss – to make sure we're not missing anything. These two poisonings have come to our attention because they were fatal. Would it be worth doing a trawl of hospital Emergency Departments for any mushroom poisonings they've had where the victims survived?'

'Good point,' Branson said. 'Will, I'll give you that as a further action.'

'Yes, sir!' The young officer, who had been ambitious to join the Major Crime Team and was now in his first week with them, looked delighted to be given sole responsibility for this task. 'I'll be on it, sir!'

'Any other thoughts at this stage?' Branson asked the team.

Grace said, 'I remember we had a charmer some years ago trying to extort money from supermarkets around Sussex – he was swapping tins of tuna with identically branded ones he'd poisoned with botulism. He thought by targeting all the different major supermarkets he'd make a fortune. Fortunately he got potted before anyone died, but several people were extremely ill.'

'Bruce Knaggs,' Potting said. 'That was his name. Caused a lot of panic at the time. I think it was Nick May who caught him.'

'Do you remember how long he got, Norman?' Grace asked.

'I'm pretty sure it was seven years, boss. I remember thinking it wasn't nearly enough for what was effectively attempted murder.'

'Does anyone get long enough?' Grace retorted, with a trace of bitterness.

'Only Russell Bishop,' Potting replied, 'then he went and cheated the system.'

He was referring to a double child killer who received one of the longest sentences ever handed out. But within three years he was dead, still in his fifties, from cancer.

'So,' Grace said pensively, 'Knaggs will almost certainly be out by now.' He turned to Stanstead. 'Can you check?'

The researcher immediately tapped on his keyboard. While he was doing so, DC Boutwood raised a hand. 'Sir, are you thinking it could be the same person?'

'Offenders have a habit of sticking to their tradecraft, EJ.'

'Bruce Knaggs has been out nearly four years, boss,' Stanstead announced. 'Released from Ford in December 2018. Last I heard, he moved to London straight after release.'

'Can you pull up his mugshots?' Grace asked him.

They all watched as, a minute later, the face of a sly-looking man in his late fifties, with lank grey hair a little too long, appeared on the monitor. His left arm was in a cast.

'Bet his mother said he never did anyone any 'arm,' Nick Nicholl quipped. There were several laughs.

Grace studied the screen. 'He bears a resemblance to our suspect in the supermarket footage we've just seen. There must have been quite a lot of CCTV history of Knaggs from the supermarkets. They'll be in the Archives somewhere. Nick May retired a few years ago but I meet up with him from time to time – I can ask him if we can't find anything.'

'Operation Newtimber,' Potting supplied, helpfully.

'You should go on *Mastermind*, Norman,' Velvet Wilde said.

He turned to her with a conceited look. 'Nah, I wouldn't want to ruin it for the other contestants.'

Grace looked at Branson, as if to cue him, but Branson merely frowned back a *what?*

'OK, Norman,' Grace temporarily taking over. 'Since you're our resident Memory Man, I'll give you the action of, as quickly as possible, retrieving CCTV footage of Knaggs. Then ping it, together with what we've just seen, to DS Jonathan Jackson at the Met's Central Image Investigation Unit. I'm not convinced we will get a warrant for him based on the footage and the old custody image. Get JJ to circulate the image and moving footage onto the Met's Forensic Image Management System and see if anyone has dealt with Knaggs recently while he's been living in London.' Jonathan Jackson was formerly a detective on Grace's Major Crime Team before moving to the Metropolitan Police in London. 'I'll alert JJ.'

'Yes, guv.'

Will Glover raised his arm. 'Sir, I'm happy to help.'

Grace smiled, remembering first coming across this sparky detective a number of years ago when he'd been a PC and had told Grace his ambition in life was to be a detective. 'I'll leave it to DI Branson to make that call, Will.' He glanced back at the DI.

'That would be very helpful, I'm sure,' Branson said.

As soon as Branson ended the meeting, Grace headed back to his office. The DI followed him in. 'How did I do?' he asked anxiously.

'You were complete crap.'

Branson looked crestfallen. 'Seriously?'

Grace grinned. 'Nope! You did OK, but you forgot a few things I've always found important.'

'Like?'

'Right from the get-go on every investigation, I want to see whiteboards up with photographs of the victims. It gives the team an instant focus and connection.'

'I was going to do that – for this evening's briefing,' he said defensively. 'What else?'

Grace shook his head. 'Photographs always from the very start. But nothing else, you did good, you were word perfect.'

'Really?'

'You don't believe me? Ask the audience or phone a friend?'

16

The office, tucked away behind the vestry of the Church of the Good Shepherd, had none of the grandeur or beauty of the church's Perpendicular exterior. It was chilly, with a window that was little more than a slit in the thick wall, and spartan furnishing. There was a basic desk, a row of filing cabinets, clutter everywhere, a rather severe-looking crucifix hung on the wall, and an elderly wall-mounted monitor, on which Taylor was watching the CCTV replay, camera by camera – three in total – of Barnie Wallace's funeral.

The cameras had been installed a few years back, the vicar informed him, after a spate of vandalism, with graves desecrated, graffiti daubed on the church walls, and, separately, an incident when lead had been stolen from the church roof.

There were two cameras outside the church. The third was sited in the ceiling of the entrance portico, facing directly down, capturing a bird's-eye view of the faces of everyone entering or leaving the vestibule. Due to the near torrential rain as the mourners were both arriving and later departing, the images from the exterior cameras were so blurred they were useless.

But the one in the vestibule roof was pin sharp. The service had kicked off at 11.45 a.m. and the vicar had obligingly started the footage thirty minutes earlier, shortly before the first people came in. Just as the digital time on the screen showed 11.50, he watched himself enter.

Strange, he thought, he didn't often see an overhead shot of himself. The bald patch on the crown of his head seemed much bigger than the last time he'd looked. And his physique, which he prided on being muscular, looked distinctly stocky from this angle. He watched himself collapse his umbrella, dump it in a receptacle and hurry through into the nave.

The one person he had not seen enter was Rufus Rorke. Had he missed him?

He asked the vicar if he could jump to the point on the CCTV around forty minutes on, when the mourners were leaving. From the irritated glare he received, he had a feeling he was about to be stung for an increased donation to the church roof fund. But then the clergyman appeared to relent and hit the fast-forward icon.

The vicar came into view and positioned himself beside the collection plate, ready to shake hands with all the exiting mourners, with the plate sitting beside him like a wagging finger. Then, moments before the long procession of people began, Taylor saw the vicar slip a handful of banknotes onto the plate.

You wily bugger! he thought.

He was waiting impatiently for that man in the baseball cap and scarf. To see if he could get a good view of him and confirm, at least to himself, that it was Rufus. As well as having photographic evidence – not that he was sure what he might use that for, if anything.

The line was interminable. Handshake after handshake, but little engagement now. People retrieved their brollies and ducked out into the elements. But so far no sign of Rufus Rorke. He would have to appear soon.

But he didn't.

Taylor suddenly saw himself, tucking the service sheet under his arm and fleetingly shaking the vicar's hand, then looking anxious, grabbing his umbrella and hurrying out.

No Rufus.

How was that possible? Rufus was definitely well ahead of him.

He asked the vicar to pause the recording. 'Would it be possible for someone to come into the vestibule or leave without being picked up on the camera?'

'Yes, it would,' the vicar replied. 'There is one blind spot.'

Taylor thought about this for a moment. 'Is it likely that someone coming into the church, and leaving later, could do so through that blind spot?'

Parry-Jones shook his head. 'Most unlikely. They would have to press up hard against the wall where the parish magazine and the events flyers are kept in their little pigeon holes, and almost go sideways. It would need to be someone who really did not want to be seen.'

Someone who really did not want to be seen – or a ghost?

But Taylor didn't think the latter for one simple reason: he didn't believe in ghosts.

17

Six degrees of separation. Maybe that was true before the internet existed, Paul Anthony thought, but not now. And certainly not since the dark web, which scythed a bypass through several of these degrees, for most of the connections you might need. You could get pretty much anything you wanted there, if you knew how and where to look, and had the currency, such as Bitcoins, to pay for it.

The most pressing thing he had been separated from these past few days was a particular lanyard and the equally vital key card attached to it.

Students, generally, were separated from stuff they wanted by a lack of cash. Certainly, he figured, Ryan Glazier must have been. Which was how, late on this Tuesday afternoon, beneath a darkening sky, he was wearing a blue and white University of Brighton lanyard attached to an electronic pass card bearing his own photograph in the top right corner, a bar code and the name of the student who had no doubt sold it to the source he had acquired it from. He guessed Ryan Glazier had received £500 for his card and would later request a replacement, claiming he had lost it. He himself had paid a not unreasonable markup, all things considered, of £5,000, inclusive of doctored photograph. Quality, on the dark web, came at a price that was always worth paying.

It was Welcome Week, or Freshers', at the uni – the timing

could not be more perfect. Definitely a good omen, portent, whatever! A huge influx of new students, some young, some mature, and all kinds of support staff. All of them milling around the uber-modern campus, in the late afternoon sun, wearing the university's uniform – which was no uniform at all – just the lanyard and key card. Hardly anyone knew anyone, but if you had one of these hanging around your neck then you were a member, you were one of the gang. No one was going to challenge you, because you *belonged* here.

And he was feeling a big sense of belonging as he pedalled along in the cycle lane of the Lewes Road, approaching the imposing glass and steel edifice of the Cockcroft Building ahead to his left. To the casual passer-by it looked more like the high-rise headquarters of a multinational corporation than the computing sciences department of the city of Brighton and Hove's university.

Dismounting from the serviceable second-hand bicycle he'd bought earlier today, he wheeled it up to a long, rammed bike rack beneath an artistically curved glass roof, and found a free slot. He padlocked it, not that he gave a flying toss if it got stolen, but just in case anyone was watching he wanted to ensure he did what any sensible university person would do. All part of blending in like a chameleon.

Just like he blended in with his clothes. And he honestly couldn't have looked more like he belonged in a university setting if he'd tried. Then, with a big smile, he reminded himself that he had tried, so hard, as always. The Devil always skulked around inside the details.

Skinny jeans, beat-up trainers, a black fleece over an Iron Maiden T-shirt, reflective rucksack and bike helmet. And that lanyard and card – the passport to invisibility!

Paul Anthony, or to his customers Mr Oswald, the chameleon, the invisible, the Great Warrior, swapped over his helmet for a

Chicago Bears baseball cap, removed a black and yellow voltage tester from his rucksack, and strapped it back on. Then he strode from the bike rack along the front facade of the Cockcroft Building. He felt confident. As ever his research was everything. It was the thoroughness of his research that had enabled him to operate his businesses for over ten years now without attracting unwelcome attention.

Well, almost. Apart from what euphemistically might be described as a close call. Kind of an *Apart from that, Mrs Kennedy, how did you like Dallas?* moment.

Which was why he'd been lying pretty damned low. And starting to get pretty damned bored. And restless.

His two businesses were highly lucrative, but operating them had given him something much more important, something money could not buy. He might have made massive profits, but what mattered more was the even bigger pleasure that what he did gave him. The sheer sense of satisfaction. The knowledge of just how much power he had. The way he deployed his brilliant skills and cunning mind to give him power over the life of anyone that he chose.

Although mostly it wasn't actually his choice, it was someone else's. And the victims – well, it had always been their fault. Not that he was ever going to split hairs over moral dilemmas. He slept well at night, comfortable in his own skin. At least, he had done up until that little bit of a close call. That little hiccup.

The police were getting smarter in their digital forensics. He'd only made a small mistake, but, as he knew, there was no such thing as a *small* mistake. It was a big screw-up. Because he'd got complacent.

He had always liked to joke about experts, telling people to beware of them, that it was the experts who always got complacent and made the screw-ups. Many of the world's biggest air disasters had senior captains of the airline in the left seat of the cockpit when they'd happened. Most of the world's leading avalanche experts had been killed in avalanches. It was usually the senior orthopaedic surgeon who amputated the wrong limb. And so on. Maybe one day he would write a book. It would be titled *Beware of Experts*.

And now he had joined their ranks. The expert contract killer who got complacent and made a mistake. A stupid, damned avoidable mistake. And the consequences had been enormous and near catastrophic – for him.

He'd recently thought about taking on an employee, an accomplice, to watch his back and ensure that mistake never happened again, but then dismissed it. There was an old police adage: *Once a criminal has told one person, he's told the world.*

But that might just have changed. Now, with Shannon Kendall fully engaged in the 3D gun business, relieving him of some important tasks and driving sales. His soulmate. And once he had completed this job, they would be bound together for ever. Omertà, the Sicilians called it. The criminal code of silence.

And she had all the skills he needed to keep abreast of the technology that was advancing in ways he was struggling to keep up with. The technology that had tripped him up and hurled him flat on his face – as it were.

Ahead was a group of female students standing outside the sliding glass doors. Two of them were smoking and one was vaping. 'Hi,' he said pleasantly, as he approached them. 'Can any of you tell me where I can find Professor Bill Llewellyn's office?'

'Oh him? Sure. Fifth floor, room five twenty-seven,' one of them, a Goth, said insolently, without looking at him. She was holding a roll-up between her finger and thumb as if it was a dart.

He thanked her, held his card to the reader at the front entrance, and the glass doors slid open. He entered the vast atrium with a black and white floor that looked like a chessboard someone had tried to design while off their face on a psychotropic drug. Facing him was a large white-faced desk, with a Perspex wall and a row of bunting, and the words STUDENT INFORMATION DESK emblazoned in black. It was manned by a young woman busy helping a male student. There was a wide staircase, and corridors stretching away in both directions. From his recce earlier in the week, when he had simply followed two students in through the sliding doors and tried to get his bearings and to log the positions of any CCTV cameras, he knew where the lifts were, and that they required a pass card. But he preferred to take the stairs. The less people who saw him, the better.

Arriving on the fifth floor, he entered a long corridor, with a yellow wall on one side and windows giving a view across the sprawling Moulsecoomb housing estate on the other.

Unsure which direction to head in, he took a punt and turned left. He walked past a wall-mounted fire extinguisher and two drinking water fountains, then a long internal window onto a vast, empty room filled with rows and rows of computing equipment on flat worktops, each workstation delineated by a modern black stool on wheels.

Two women were approaching from the opposite direction. He stiffened as they both looked at him quizzically.

He had a brief moment of panic, then they passed, giving him a pleasant smile.

He reached 527. It had the same smart wooden door as all the other offices, but the windows were obscured with drawn blinds, giving the occupant total privacy. The name on the door plaque read: *Professor Bill Llewellyn. Faculty of Artificial Intelligence.*

He knocked. There was no answer. He glanced up and down the corridor and saw no sign of anyone. The lock was electronic, like most modern hotel locks – a black glass oval beneath the handle where you tapped your key card and waited for a green light.

He knocked again, louder this time, to be safe.

A moment later, he was startled by a voice coming from the other side. It was a strong Welsh accent and sounded irked. 'Who is it?'

Putting on a gruff voice he called back, 'Tech Support, come to check your broadband issue.'

'What do you mean? I don't have a broadband issue.'

'It's a line fault, Professor, we get automatic notification.'

He heard what sounded like breaking glass, followed by what might have been a curse, then the professor called out, 'You'll have to wait a moment.'

As the door opened, a good two minutes later, he saw the reason.

18

'Of course you can, James!' Tommy Towne said.

It was 5.20 p.m. The moonscape of fog below them, through the Pilatus cockpit windows, was proper dense pea soup. Taylor was in a holding pattern at three thousand feet. They'd been flying around and around, in the race-track holding pattern to the east of the nine-by-five-mile island of Jersey, for thirty minutes now, after flying down from Manchester, where his mercurial octogenarian employer had been at a board meeting. Towne was now anxious to get home for his granddaughter's twenty-first birthday tonight. Anxious and increasingly stroppy. 'You just need to descend a bit more, you'll find it won't be so bad. There'll be a pocket in it.'

'Jersey Tower says visibility on the ground is 300 metres, Tommy,' Taylor said, his voice authoritative and calm. 'When I flew for easyJet, they needed a minimum here of 450 metres RVR – runway visual range – at the touchdown point, and that's less than British Airways who required 550 metres. Today we need a minimum touchdown of 550 metres in order to make an approach.'

The Pilatus PC-12 had less than ten minutes of fuel reserve remaining before they would need to head to an alternative airport. Guernsey was still shrouded in fog, so unless they got a sudden window in the fog – and it sometimes happened that they got lucky and did – they would be flying back to mainland England or Dinard in neighbouring France, which was a regular splash-and-dash refuelling spot. Maybe put down at Shoreham, in case they had to overnight, and try again after refuelling.

Tommy – Sir Thomas – Towne, was short, bald as a coot, always bristling with restless energy and with a total can-do mindset. He sat on Taylor's right in the co-pilot's seat, peering down into the murk, opening and closing his pudgy fingers, which, Taylor had long noticed, he always did when he was agitated. 'I can definitely see the church tower, James.'

'You've got better eyesight than I have,' Taylor humoured him.

'They say in the flying club, if you can see the church tower, there's enough visibility to land, right?'

'If you can see the church tower from this level through thick cloud, you've probably noticed the number of pigs flying past us too?'

He grunted. 'I'm serious, James. We're good to go, you can get this crate down.'

Tommy Towne was like this every time bad visibility caused them a problem at any airport they were approaching. Towne had had a somewhat cavalier attitude towards his personal safety all his life, Taylor was well aware. He'd paid a fortune to be one of the first civilians to be blasted into space; a pilot himself before failing eyesight had lost him his licence, he'd taken part in air races in Second World War aircraft. And the fact that Tommy Towne had survived all these exploits, and countless more, made him a dangerous passenger. There had been a number of previous occasions where Taylor had had to put his foot down and remind his boss, as he did once again now. 'Tommy, how many times have I told you, there are no old bold pilots.'

Towne tapped his chest. 'Yes there are. Me.'

Grinning and shaking his head, Taylor looked at the fuel gauges and then down again. Then he blinked – was it his imagination or was the fog actually thinning a little?

'We'll go around once more and I'll ask for an update.'

Taylor hadn't told Towne, but he was equally anxious to land now if he could, drop him off and then fly back to England. He had a lunch date on Saturday and had been banking on a day off tomorrow to sort out a new suit that he planned to wear to the date. Well, maybe not exactly a date but . . . how did you define a date? He was having lunch with a beautiful woman, taking her to his current favourite restaurant, Wild Flor in Hove. It was because he had a hundred questions to ask her, that was the reason he'd asked Debbie out. And that was the real reason, wasn't it, and not because he fancied her? And she had looked pleased to see him, or had he just imagined it?

He was kidding himself, he knew. Just like Tommy was kidding himself he could see the church tower. But then suddenly, through a break in the clouds, he actually could see it. He radioed the approach controller. 'Request the latest RVR.'

'Roger, Golf Uniform Zulu, current RVRs are touchdown 600 metres, midpoint 550 metres, stopend 500 metres.'

Taylor responded, 'Roger, request approach to runway two-six.'

'Golf Uniform Zulu next time over the beacon you are cleared for the ILS approach runway two-six, report established.'

A short while later, Taylor confirmed.

There was a further series of exchanges between Taylor and the air traffic controller. Then after a further few minutes, with Tommy looking at him anxiously, Taylor transmitted, 'Jersey tower good afternoon, Golf Uniform Zulu, ILS established at 8 kilometres.'

Immediately the tower responded, 'Current RVRs are touchdown 550 metres, midpoint 450 metres, stopend 400 metres, you are cleared to land runway two-six, surface wind two one zero degrees nine knots.'

'Copy the RVRs, cleared to land two-six, Golf Uniform Zulu.'

Despite the assurances from the tower, as they descended

blindly and bumpily through the increasingly wispy cloud, Taylor realized he was holding his breath.

'Good boy!' Tommy Towne said, breezily.

Taylor didn't respond. He was still holding his breath.

19

Tuesday 27 September 2022

The reek of whisky hit Paul's nostrils the moment the door opened. Professor Llewellyn smelled like he had been marinated in the stuff. His sallow face, wiry hair, big lopsided glasses, untucked T-shirt, shabby chinos, and moccasins made him look like Woody Allen's younger, taller, scruffier brother.

Behind him on the floor was a pool of liquid, shards of broken glass and the neck of a bottle with part of the label visible. *JOHNNIE WALK*

Glaring at the supposed tech support, the academic demanded, his voice a little slurred, 'Had a little accident, the cleaners can sort it out. How long are you going to be?'

Holding up his voltage meter, Paul replied, disguising his voice with a mock Australian accent, 'Depends on the problem, mate, might be a quick fix, but could be rodents chewing the cables – we've had this in other offices here. Then I'd have to rewire – could be a couple of hours, mate.'

'Vermin? In a new building?'

Well, there is in your office, Paul Anthony thought, as Llewellyn slunk off, with a clumsily stuffed, battered leather briefcase, muttering, 'I'm off home, fill your boots.'

Anthony closed the door behind him, snapped on a pair of thin latex gloves, then took a good look around. The office was large, with one wall painted yellow, the rest white, and clutter everywhere. The furniture was mostly bland and functional, with the exception of an oversized sofa that seemed far too big for the room. Horizontal Venetian blinds were closed, which was odd as it was still full daylight outside. There was a faded Persian rug covering part of the floor. He also noticed an open can of Diet Coke on the desk, and that made him smile. There was no sign of a glass anywhere in the room. So the professor drank straight from the can? Or the bottle, he smirked, judgingly. Good. That was very helpful. Very helpful indeed. Quite obliging of him, in fact.

He opened each of the six drawers in the desk but saw nothing of interest, other than the expected liquor flask, which he checked. It was full. Curious, he thought, and wondered how badly addicted he was. Then he checked out the bin beside the desk. You could often learn quite a bit from what people threw away.

The bin contained seven discarded cans of Diet Coke. Shannon hadn't been exaggerating. He assumed in a place like this the bin would be emptied nightly, so this would likely be his daily consumption. Looking around he couldn't see a coffee machine or a kettle.

He saw a whiteboard on a metal easel next to a wall almost entirely lined with bookshelves, each shelf containing rows of books looking as dishevelled as the professor himself. He glanced at a few titles. *The Anthropic Cosmological Principle*; *AI: Its Nature and Future*; *Cognitive Behavioural Therapy*; *The AI Compass*.

Then he heard a sound outside. A distinct clump. He knelt, hurriedly, pulled his toolbox out of his rucksack, placed it on the floor and opened it, ready to look busy if anyone entered. But moments later there was the whine of a vacuum cleaner. It was accompanied by another clump . . . clump . . . clump . . . moving away.

He breathed out and continued looking around. So where did Professor Llewellyn keep his hoard of Diet Coke?

A phone warbled right behind him, making him start. It warbled again. He turned and saw a red light flashing on an elaborate-looking phone-intercom on the desk. Three more warbles and it stopped.

Then he saw what might be the fridge, or at least a concealed cupboard. It was cleverly camouflaged with a covering of fake books, seemingly to make it blend in with the shelves, and the only giveaway was that the fake rows were much neater than the real books. He strode over, got a purchase on the metal edge at the bottom, pulled the door open and felt the blast of cold air.

It was indeed a fridge. Why conceal it? For cosmetic reasons? But this wasn't exactly a room in the Ritz or the Four Seasons. It was just a functional office in a functional building. And the professor didn't exactly seem like an aesthete. He had more likely concealed it in order to hide something. What?

He looked at the three rows of shelves and counted eleven cans of Diet Coke on the middle shelf. He looked at the rest of the contents of the fridge. There were a few bars of Waitrose-branded dark chocolate, a tub of Greek yoghurt and a small carton of red grapes. Two of the slim shelves in the door were empty.

None of these items needed hiding, so what was he missing? He opened the freezer compartment at the top of the fridge, and was surprised it was no colder than the rest of the fridge. Inside were two racks of ice trays.

He removed the top one, and had his answer.

Exactly as Shannon had described them, he pulled out a pair of pink knickers in a plastic bag. What. A. Creep.

Paul Anthony was glad he had found the fridge and its evil contents. He liked to be able to have justification for what he did. And now with Professor Llewellyn, he had it in spades.

He was so happy about this he almost wished the professor would return to his office, so he could shake his hand and thank him in person, for making it so easy to plan his demise.

20

Roy and Cleo Grace had a tacit agreement with each other that, whenever possible, they would take it in turns to create their evening meal. This Friday it was Roy's turn. He loved cooking, always finding it immensely relaxing, and as he preferred to invent as he went along rather than following recipes, it was always a journey of surprises. Not all of them hit the high notes, but enough had done over the years for Cleo to have presented him with an apron emblazoned with the accolade 'Head Chef!'

They tried to eat healthily, often following the latest fads, and right now it was a high-protein diet. Tonight he was cooking Thai-style salmon fillets with quinoa, parmesan polenta, grilled broccoli with chilli, and a tomato, onion and cottage cheese salad. He had the two fillets laid out on foil and had just finished making a series of incisions down them. He was now busy infusing them first with teriyaki sauce, then ginger and garlic cloves, followed by a dab of a sherry from a bottle he'd won in an office charity raffle at Christmas, then a couple of shakes of soy, before curling the foil over each fillet, making them into parcels and placing them into the steamer.

Then, as he turned his attention to the broccoli, he wrinkled his nose and shook his head, as a vile, dense smell struck him, almost making him gag. Humphrey, their beloved rescue Labrador-cross, had silently blown off again. It smelled like the drain at the core of the earth.

'Yecchhhh!' Cleo, at the kitchen table, exclaimed, pinching her nose. Then she admonished, 'HUMPHREY!'

The dog, curled up in his wicker basket, barely lifted an eyelid.

'I think it was something he ate yesterday,' she said. 'When I was walking him on the hill. The little bugger stopped and began digging, totally ignoring me. Then I saw him chewing. I tried to get him to stop but he didn't want to know. By the time I got over to him he'd swallowed whatever it was, and looked pretty pleased with himself. I think it might have been a mole.' She turned and looked at the dog. 'You are soooooo gross!'

Humphrey wagged his tail.

They both grinned. They loved this damned ridiculously gangly-legged and soppy creature.

'The thing is,' Cleo said, looking puzzled, 'what I don't get is how a professional chef could mistake a death cap mushroom for an edible field mushroom. There must be distinguishing features, surely?'

'There are, but the differences are subtle. Nick Nicholl went to see the owner of the pub where Barnie Wallace worked in the kitchen for about eighteen months. He wasn't the senior chef there but an underling and was eventually fired for making constant mistakes, culminating in the salmonella incident. But it has happened before,' Roy said. 'There's a well-documented case – in 2012 in Australia. A Chinese chef, apparently brilliant with a big future, cooked some in error for a New Year's Eve dinner. The mushrooms killed him and another guest.' He shrugged. 'I'm no expert but apparently they're very easy to mistake for one another. Luke Stanstead's looked up the stats, and there are twelve thousand people every year around the world who die from the same error.'

She shook her head. 'That's putting me right off them!'

He nodded. 'Yep, I was planning a mushroom risotto tonight, saw loads in the field when I was out running with Humphrey this morning, but I decided it probably wasn't the best idea.'

He grinned as she gave him a very dubious look. But before he could say anything his job phone rang.

'Roy Grace,' he answered, waving his forever apologetic hand at Cleo, who returned her forever-wan, no-need-to-apologize smile.

'Sorry to disturb you at home, sir. I thought I should come directly to you on this.'

He recognized DC Carruthers' voice before he'd said his name. 'That's fine, Jamie. Tell me?'

'We've picked up chatter on the dark web about someone looking to hire a contract killer. It appears to be a wife who wants to off her husband. It sounds like there are local connections and it could be fairly soon. We're working on trying to get more infor-mation and when we do I'll get back to you. I wanted you to know straight away. And I apologize again for disturbing your evening.'

'I'm grateful for your call, Jamie,' Grace said. 'Do you have any more information at this stage? Anything we can act on?'

'Not at present, but it could well be very imminent, sir.'

Ending the call, Grace continued with his meal preparation. And after Cleo had cleaned her plate, he got a *sensational!* accolade.

Smiling, he took Humphrey out into the darkness for his walk before bedtime. As they ambled a short distance up the hill behind their cottage, he saw mushrooms in his torchlight every-where he looked. Field mushrooms or death cap? It seemed like they had all come out to taunt him. He thought about what Carruthers had just told him. It was a worrying development but nothing he could act on, and one he was going to keep to himself at this stage.

When he got home, after settling Humphrey in his basket with his nightly treat of a chew, he checked his email. There was a message in his inbox from DS Jackson of the Met's Central Image Investigation Unit. Could Grace please call him in the morning?

21

Saturday 1 October 2022

Pinch and a punch for the first of the month!

It was a sunny Saturday morning, and October couldn't start much better than this, Paul Anthony thought, remembering how his dad used to wake him on the first day of every month with that line. You had to say *grey hares* before going to sleep and *white rabbits* first thing in the morning if you wanted money that month, his dad always said.

Paul Anthony did not like to think he was superstitious. But on the last night of every month, before he fell asleep, he would always murmur *grey hares*, and if he forgot to say *white rabbits* first thing in the morning, he'd be in a bad mood and know for sure he was in for a meagre month. So he said it aloud and triumphantly now. 'White rabbits!'

Pathetic, he knew. But he'd remembered to say *grey hares* last night, so October was going to be a very rewarding month! Oh yes! And, as if on cue, his doorbell rang, out in the hallway and on his phone. He glanced at the app and saw a man on the doorstep holding a parcel.

'Hello?' he said.

'Delivery for Mr Paul Anthony.'

'I'll be right down!'

Oh yes, the *grey hares* and *white rabbits* had already worked a treat! The final bit of kit he needed for his little surprise to start – and hopefully end – Professor Llewellyn's week, on

Monday morning. Not bothering with the lift, he sprinted down the stairs, then hurried back up, clutching his square Amazon package. He opened it carefully on the kitchen table, lifted out the main content, removed some wrapping, then held it up like it was the Men's Singles trophy at Wimbledon.

Yes, oh yes, oh yes! Hard to believe he could be so excited over a red-and-white striped candyfloss spinning machine, which had cost a princely forty-five pounds. But he was, he really was very excited indeed.

It was still warm enough for him to have breakfast out on his balcony, and there was barely enough breeze to flap the pages of his newspapers. The Indian summer weather would break soon, but until then he would make the most of it. For someone who was dead he had a lot to smile about. Tonight he was having dinner with Shannon. And, he had to admit, he was looking forward to it rather a lot.

That put a very big smile on his face.

He finished the last bite of his almond croissant, and the last sip of his double espresso, then fired up his Cohiba Robusto with his Dunhill flamethrower of a lighter. He liked Cohibas. Fidel Castro, paranoid about assassination attempts by the CIA, even more so after they had attempted to kill him with the absurdly ill-fated exploding cigars, brought all the people he considered to be the finest cigar makers in Cuba to his private estate, to make cigars just for him. These cigars had evolved into the Cohiba brand. The cigars many considered to be still the finest in the world.

But, as he exhaled the rich, sweet blue-grey smoke, his mind was not on the taste of the cigars, but the contents of the four glass jars on the far side of his table, each of them half-full. Two with honey, one with strawberry jam and the other, raspberry jam.

What was really floating his boat right now was the contents of each jar – well, three of them. Large, fat, autumnal wasps. The lifespan of a wasp was twelve to twenty-two days. In his experience, those that were still alive at the end of summer became fat and lethargic, their venom building up to a toxic level. Just perfect – not – for anyone allergic to them.

And there were five of the creatures crawling around inside those three jars, all of them off their faces on the sugar hit!

'Oh yes, my little babies! Oh yes! Have you ever met a professor of artificial intelligence? One of you will, soon, you lucky chaps!'

His traps had worked a treat. As had his scientific research. He had learned that a wasp typically maintains 4–5 kilopascals of oxygen in their respiratory system, four to five times lower than the normal oxygen concentration in the atmosphere. In a normal oxygen-concentration environment, the insect breathes in and releases a burst of carbon dioxide.

Paul Anthony knew, from his chemistry studies at school, what carbon dioxide would dissolve. What he needed was to create, chemically, an environment containing oxygen in which a wasp could survive for a period of hours. The solution he had come up with was, in his opinion, nothing short of genius.

Happy days! Well, perhaps not so much for Professor Llewellyn.

22

Glenn Branson opened the 9 a.m. briefing of Operation Meadow with some news Roy Grace had received this morning from the forensic gait analyst, Haydn Kelly. He informed the team of the bad news that Kelly was certain the former supermarket black-mailer, Bruce Knaggs, was not the man on the CCTV in the Organica supermarket – the man to whom Norman Potting had given the moniker the Phantom Mushroom Switcher. Then he handed over to Roy Grace.

'The potential good news is . . .' Grace announced, somewhat cryptically, 'also bad news. Although it's a massive coincidence, Kelly swears that he has seen this man in another case, although he didn't have the file to hand, he was pretty sure his name was Rufus Rorke. I've also spoken at length to DS Jackson at the Met's Central Image Investigation Unit. His findings are much less conclusive, but they do possibly point to the same person.' He turned to the three whiteboards behind him.

One was pinned with photographs taken from the CCTV inside the Organica supermarket, as well as individual high-res blown-up photographs of both an edible field mushroom and a potentially fatal death cap mushroom.

The top of the second whiteboard was pinned with photographs of Barnie Wallace, with an association chart below. The largest image of Wallace was full length. Hands behind his back in a confrontational stance, he was dressed in baggy jeans, loafers, and a white, collarless, shapeless shirt. A bunch of gelled fair hair rose vertically from the top of his head, like a small clump of trees on a hill. His face was sallow and his eyes, small and piggy, seemed to be glaring at the world with anger.

A smaller photograph, from his Instagram account, showed him wearing a chef's tunic and white toque and smiling this time, arms outspread expansively, with pride, at his *création-du-jour* as he labelled it, a sumptuously laid-out lobster, avocado and mango salad.

The third whiteboard, a new association chart, begun earlier this morning, had photographs of Rufus Rorke at the top.

'The problem with Kelly's hypothesis is that the man in the CCTV – the prime suspect who he has identified from his gait, the person JJ Jackson at the Met's Central Image Investigation Unit has recognized – is dead and has been for over two years. So either they are both wrong or . . .'

'Or we have a killer ghost?' suggested Potting. 'Hamlet's father walking the aisles of a supermarket?'

'Is he definitely dead, sir?' Jack Alexander asked.

Branson replied. 'He was declared missing, presumed dead, after going overboard from a yacht, in shark-infested waters in the Caribbean, on September the twenty-third, 2020.'

'You're talking about someone called Rufus Rorke?' Potting asked.

'I am, yes,' Branson replied.

'I was on Op Stenographer,' Potting said. 'Detective Superintendent Sloane was the SIO. I interviewed Rorke under caution about a month before he died, with DI Branson, although he doesn't recall the exact details this far on. As you can see, Rorke had a funny right eye that always seemed to be looking at you – his skull got misshapen in a car accident back in his youth, I was told.'

Everyone turned to look at the photographs of Rorke. Potting continued. 'An arrogant bastard, that's what I remember most of all. One of those people who believe they hold all the cards. Well, he didn't this time, we were on the verge of arresting him, then he went and died on us.'

'What was Op Stenographer, Norman?' Jack Alexander asked.

'You never read about it?' Potting asked him.

'You forget that a lot of stuff you dealt with happened before I was born,' the young DS replied, only a tad cheekily.

'Don't push your luck, laddie,' Potting admonished. 'But, OK, for the benefit of those who arrived on this planet after the age of steam carriages, the invention of electricity and the telephone, and the first heavier-than-air flight, let me bring you up to date on Op Stenographer.'

He paused for some laughs to stop before continuing.

'It was a big story – made the front pages of the nation's tabloids. A fifty-five-year-old brewery worker – a drayman, name of Orville Ormonde – won over £160 million on the EuroMillions on a shared ticket with his wife, Pauline. We're not talking the fairy-tale *and they lived happily ever after* here. We're talking a heavy drinker, a big, ugly bloke who humped beer barrels for a living, with past form for GBH and a long history of violence towards his wife – who was also on the sauce. They lived on a rough estate in Worthing. After the amount was confirmed, they did everything they say you shouldn't if you win big – quit their jobs, went on a wild spree, splurged on a fuck-off mansion and a fleet of high-end wheels. They enjoyed showing off, letting themselves be splashed all over the national press lying together in a huge bathtub filled with Champagne – and it wasn't a pretty sight, I can tell you. He was not exactly Mr Universe and she was no Miss World.'

'Any pictures, Norman?' Jack Alexander asked.

'You do not want to see them, believe me. Not a tender youth like you.'

Several of the team grinned.

Potting nodded at the detective superintendent. 'The chief knows the whole story better than me.'

Grace nodded. 'Predictably,' he said, 'in less than a year it all started going wrong. Orville figured he'd trade Pauline in for a younger model, aged twenty-five – it's amazing what a hundred and fifty million or so quid can do to a man's sex appeal. Pauline was having none of it, and booted him out. Although she was a boozer too, she was a smart lady, and from the get-go had insisted on a joint bank account. Orville faced lengthy divorce proceedings, and meanwhile Pauline's living in the house and he's only been able to grab a couple of million for himself.'

'It's so tough for some people to get by,' Velvet Wilde said.

'Yeah, my heart bled for him,' Potting replied. 'Pauline was actually a nice person. I interviewed her several times and she told me – and her best friend – she'd had death threats from him.'

'You didn't find the money made her attractive, did you, Norm?' Luke Stanstead jested.

'It would take more than a hundred million, and then some, for me to go there, Luke,' he said, and carried on. 'So one night her eldest daughter, Sally Jane I think her name was, who spoke to her most days, was concerned when she couldn't get hold of her on the phone.' He turned to Grace. 'Right, chief?'

'Correct,' Grace said.

Potting continued. 'Sally Jane went to the house and found her mum at the bottom of the stairs with her head looking like it had been put on backwards. There was a broken glass and an upended bottle of whisky on the floor, and her two Westie dogs sitting faithfully beside her. The post-mortem showed a broken neck and other traumas to the body, commensurate with a fall down the stairs. And she had a blood alcohol of 220 – that's close to three times the legal limit for driving. And we all know how difficult it is to prove guilt in a fall down stairs,' he added.

'Exactly,' Grace said. 'Sometimes forensic evidence may support a push, as well as the type, severity and angle of injuries, but it usually needs pretty compelling circumstantial evidence.'

'Presumably the husband, Orville, was the prime suspect?' Velvet Wilde asked.

'He was,' Grace replied. 'But he had a cast-iron alibi. He was larging it in Marbella with his bimbo and a group of friends that night. We interviewed them all and obtained CCTV from the restaurant, confirming they were there. Which is where Rufus Rorke comes in.' He paused to check his notes before continuing.

'The National Crime Agency had him on their radar – they'd been monitoring the internet for links to serious criminals, and Rorke had popped up some while previously as a POI. Outwardly, he was a successful property developer, with a number of homes, one a palazzo near Florence in Italy, where the Italian police suspected he had links with organized crime there. He had both a fixed wing and chopper licences, and flew himself around in a five million quid Agusta helicopter. The National Crime Agency had been monitoring him because of his suspected links with international Organized Crime groups, which is what gave us our break.'

'How come?' Branson asked.

'The house Orville and Pauline bought was quite isolated, on the edge of a hamlet a few miles north of Brighton. Pauline was paranoid about security – neither of them had ever lived in the countryside before, and on her insistence they'd installed state-of-the-art CCTV. But when she'd kicked her old man out, she became worried that if he did come back, intending to hurt her – again – he would know where the cameras were and would be able to dodge them. So she had new, concealed ones installed. Footage from these, date-stamped the day before her daughter found her dead, showed someone walking up the lawn, keeping well to the side of the driveway, obviously confident that they were out of range of the cameras, but still keeping their face concealed.

'And that someone had a matching gait or facial image to Rufus Rorke?' Branson asked.

'Exactly, boss,' Potting replied. 'Kelly produced evidence, with over ninety per cent certainty, it was the same person the NCA had on their Persons of Interest list. DS Jackson's team came up with less certainty running the image through the Met's Facial Recognition System, but he says the team on the Met's Central Image Investigation Unit think it is a viable match.'

Grace turned to the financial investigator, Emily Denyer, a serious-looking, smartly dressed woman in her thirties. 'There's something else that may be of significance. Perhaps you'd like to explain, Emily?'

'Yes, sir. We had a look at Rufus Rorke's bank accounts – those that we could find. Ten days before Pauline Ormonde fell down those stairs to her death, Rorke cashed in a quantity of Bitcoins, which are pretty much untraceable. This was a substantial amount – approximately half a million pounds. Two days after she was found dead, he sold more Bitcoins – an identical amount.'

'Half now, half on completion,' Glenn Branson said. 'Classic high-end hitman rates.'

Grace gave him a sideways look. 'Been watching too many movies?'

Branson shook his head and with a cheeky grin said, 'Maybe not enough.'

'There's another possibly significant aspect to this,' Emily Denyer went on, ignoring the banter. 'With the help of the Spanish police, we learned that three weeks before Rorke cashed in the first half a million pounds of Bitcoins, Orville Ormonde, over a short period of time, gambled around one million pounds at a casino in Marbella. It appears he was canny, starting out with a million and ending up with a million.

We subsequently learned from the police there that while he was changing money into high denomination chips, he was actually playing with peanuts at the tables. A classic money-laundering ploy. I don't think he's the sharpest tack in the box, because I'm not sure what he thought it would achieve, but maybe he saw in some television programme on criminals that it was a smart thing to do.'

'So what did Mr Mastermind do with his freshly laundered million quid?' Glenn Branson asked. 'Wait, don't tell me, let me guess – he used it to purchase a million quid's worth of Bitcoins, right? And now he doesn't have them any more because he lost them gambling in the casino?'

'And might there just be a connection between the one million in Bitcoins Rufus Rorke received, the one million that Orville Ormonde lost in the casino, and a dead Mrs Orville Ormonde at the bottom of her stairs?' Nick Nicholl suggested.

'We're all cooking on gas this morning!' Grace said. 'We didn't have enough evidence on Ormonde at that stage, but we were closing in on Rufus Rorke – preparing to arrest him.'

'So what were the circumstances of his death, sir, because it sounds damned convenient?' Velvet Wilde asked.

'It did to me at the time, too,' Grace said. 'But there was an eyewitness and strong supporting evidence.'

'What happened?'

'It was a couple of weeks after Rorke had been interviewed,' Potting said. 'He and his wife, Fiona, chartered a yacht for a sailing trip around the Caribbean, as you do. Not just any old tub, this was an eighty-grand a week superyacht with a crew of ten.'

'Mostly underpaid, probably,' interjected Velvet Wilde.

'I can't comment on that,' Potting said dismissively. 'Anyhow, when I interviewed Fiona Rorke – incidentally, a very nice lady who I did really feel was grieving her husband – she told me that

Rufus had seemed very troubled in the weeks before he died, but wouldn't talk about why.'

'Perhaps he hadn't told her he was a POI in a murder case, and had been interviewed by the police under caution,' Grace said.

'No, he hadn't. It was a complete surprise to her when I told her. She said that could explain something. Apparently, shortly before his death he had started drinking a lot – which wasn't normal for him because he always wanted to be in control. On the night in question, the yacht, *Eloise III*, had just sailed from Barbados. According to the captain, they were five nautical miles out of Bridgetown, in quite a heavy sea, heading on a night passage to Grenada, when the man overboard alarm was given at 1.45 a.m.'

Potting paused to slurp some coffee, then continued. 'A crew member had gone to the stern of the ship for a fag at around 1.40 a.m. He said Rorke, who seemed very drunk, wearing a white tuxedo, had barged into him as the ship lurched in the swell. Rorke had then stood some distance from him, propped against the deck-rail, and lit a cigarette. At some point shortly after, Rorke leaned over the rail and began retching. The crew member turned away, then he heard a splash and a yell – a yell for help. He instantly threw a lifebelt into the sea, raised the alarm, and tried desperately to locate him with a flashlight. They turned the boat around and spent five hours searching. The Barbados coastguard sent a patrol boat, as well as a helicopter at first light, but nothing was found.'

'Where was his wife?' DC Nicholl asked.

'She was asleep. At around 2 a.m., she woke and noticed her husband wasn't in their suite; she was then visited by a crew member who told her what had happened,' he said.

'I can't imagine a scarier way to go,' EJ said. 'Pitch-dark sea, watching the lights of the ship sailing away from you – and thinking about sharks. Ever since I saw *Jaws* I've never felt the same about swimming in the sea!'

'Well, as a shark himself he'd have felt pretty at home,' Potting said.

'How does that saying go?' Luke Stanstead added. 'The lion may be king of the jungle, but throw him in the shark tank and he's just another lunch.'

Grace nodded. 'Seems like that's what happened, Luke. A couple of days later a fisherman in Barbados noticed something tangled around one of his net ropes. It was a white linen jacket with one arm and part of the shoulder ripped off, and bloodstains on it despite its immersion. Fiona identified the jacket as her husband's, from the label and from a Mont Blanc pen found within a zipped internal pocket. The jacket had a Savile Row label in it, upmarket – much like the tailors Glenn likes to frequent,' he added with a smile.

'You're the one who told me a detective should always look smart,' Branson retorted.

'True! So Barbados Police sent the jacket to us for forensic analysis. What they did state in their report was that examination by a marine biologist identified multiple bite marks on the jacket that were compatible with a tiger shark attack. Apparently, sharks have rows of successional teeth they continually replace during their lives. This was confirmed by a forensic orthodontist in Sussex who also examined the cloth. DNA obtained from the blood was identified as Rorke's along with further DNA obtained from Rorke's skin cells in the jacket. I remember a long and very detailed report from James Stather of the Surrey and Sussex Forensic Services leaving little doubt this was Rufus Rorke's – and his wife confirmed it was the jacket he had been wearing on the night he went overboard.'

DC Boutwood, frowning, asked Grace, 'This may sound a bit gruesome, sir. They obviously wouldn't be able to tell, from the blood on the jacket, whether he was taken by the shark when he was still alive or – hopefully – dead. Are we agreed?'

'I think after immersion in seawater for two days, they weren't able to tell that, mercifully, EJ.'

'Thank you, sir, as I thought. I mean, not that Rorke sounds exactly a saint. But I don't think I'd wish that on anyone.'

'Oh, I can think of a few people,' Norman Potting said, and chortled. 'One or two of them within Sussex Police.'

'So where does this leave us?' Glenn Branson asked, rhetorically. 'When we have a prime suspect who's been deceased for two years?'

'At a dead end?' Potting said, and chuckled again. Then he looked at Branson. 'Sorry, guv.'

'Maybe,' Grace suggested, 'we need to start considering just how dead you need to be, to not be a suspect.'

'Meaning what exactly, boss?' DS Alexander asked.

'Exactly that, Jack. In the absence of any other suspects, right now our best hope is a dead man. He was declared legally dead under the Presumption of Death Act. Now we have a ninety per cent positive sighting of this dead man, four weeks ago. No body or any human remains were ever found, we have just the word of a crew member on a yacht to go on, and the remains of a bloodstained jacket.' He looked around at the team. 'Anyone in this room who thinks that's enough, raise your hand, given what we know now.'

No one did.

'There's something else,' Grace said. He stood up and walked over to the whiteboards. 'If we look at the association chart for Barnie Wallace, we see that he attended Brighton College here in the city from 1994 to 2001. Then if we look at the association chart for the *late* Rufus Rorke, guess where he went to school? That's right, none other than Brighton College, and exactly the same years as Wallace. It could of course be just coincidence, and if it is, we need to eliminate this PDQ from our lines of enquiry. Glenn and I will formally interview both Wallace's former girlfriend Angi Colman and his ex-wife, Debbie Martin. I will also speak to the Barbados police inspector who was in charge of the search for Rorke, and who organized the analysis of the jacket remains by a marine biologist in Barbados before sending it on to us – he was a helpful guy, his name's Terry Stephens.'

He turned to DS Alexander. 'Jack, I need you to find out where the *Eloise III* is currently, and who the crew member was who raised the man overboard alarm. I want to talk first to the yacht's captain – from memory, his name was Richard Le Quesne – and then to the crew member.'

'If they're out in the Caribbean, shall I come with you, for protection, chief?' Potting offered.

'Thanks, Norman,' Grace said with a grin. 'Your altruism knows no bounds.'

23

They weren't quite the last people in the restaurant, there was one other couple. It was gone 4 p.m. and Taylor was conscious the staff would be wanting a break before their evening began, but their waiter at Wild Flor, a young Frenchman with a happy disposition, made no attempt to rush them.

Taylor had shared a seafood platter with Debbie, and rather more Champagne and white wine than he normally would have drunk, but it was fine; firstly because he was having just the best time with this perfect dining buddy; and secondly because his master and commander, Tommy Towne, did not need to fly anywhere until next Tuesday.

Debbie, seated across the wooden table, dressed in a trouser suit, with a thin silver necklace, looked the proverbial million dollars – and more. She was elegant, she was smart, she had poise, and she was extremely intelligent. And, most importantly of all, she genuinely seemed to like him – quite a lot. She'd taken his hand across the table some while ago and had not let go since, gently massaging his fingers and looking suggestively into his eyes.

'You really do look in great shape,' she said.

He grinned. 'For my age, you mean?'

'You're the same age as Barnie – was – thirty-nine?'

'Uh-huh.'

'You work out?'

Was she hitting on him? This had not been part of his plan when he'd invited her out this lunchtime. Well, it had always been a possibility lurking at the back of his mind and he felt no guilt about it. Barnie and Debbie had been separated a long time before he had died and he and Barnie had barely spoken in years. He realized he was letting his thoughts go there despite the other thoughts in his head telling him to prepare for disappointment. Surely Debbie was in a different league to him?

But then again, as he'd thought so often previously, Barnie sure as hell had been punching above his weight when he'd married her.

'I'm a runner,' he said. 'I've done eighteen marathons.'

'Impressive. When's your next?'

'Tomorrow week – Chicago. I shouldn't be drinking wine or any booze at the moment.' He grinned. 'I won't tell my trainer, Malcolm, if you don't.'

'The Chicago marathon. Seriously?'

'Yes, I'm trying to bag the Big Six – Chicago, Boston, New York, London, Berlin and Tokyo.'

'What happens when you've done that?'

'I get a medal.'

'Just a medal – that's all?'

'It's enough. It's a big medal!'

She laughed, and said, 'Respect!' Then she gave a slight toss of her head, flicking away some of her long blonde fringe that continually tumbled over her right eye. He found that toss – more just a casual flick – endearing. Sexy, even.

For most of the time so far they'd actually talked about everything except the thing Taylor had invited her out to talk about. He was about to broach it now when Debbie asked him, 'Tell me about your marriage? What happened?'

'How long do you have?'

'As long as it takes.' She smiled. And in that moment, if he could have chosen one image to look at in his final dying moments on earth, it would have been that smile.

'Another time,' he said. He was in a happy place right now and didn't want to go there. It hurt too much.

'Are you still in touch with Marianne?'

'I get to have my son for a few days once a month, kind of. When she's in the right mood, and not in one of her *do anything to piss off Taylor* moods again.'

'Harrison, right?'

He nodded. 'He's ten.'

'You miss him?'

'I miss everything about him, every moment of every day. Most of all, I miss being able to be part of his life, and to help him with choices – and just to kick a ball around with him, which he loves so much.' He shrugged. 'Marianne's manipulated things so that I'm pretty much a stranger to him.'

'Must be tough.'

'It is, very.'

'But you're the one who had the affair, right?'

From her smile, Taylor could see it wasn't a criticism. Just a fact. The raw and still painful truth. And she understood.

'I did, yes. But . . .'

'But?'

'I'm not making excuses, but things hadn't exactly been great for a very long time. She had a whole string of affairs, that I kept forgiving her for, long before I had mine.'

She smiled and the world seemed to grow brighter as she did. 'Does your affair make it OK?'

He shook his head and said, a tad wistfully, 'My bad.'

She smiled again. 'You must have loved her once.'

'Of course. A lot. Insanely!' Then, changing the subject, he asked, 'Did you and Barnie never want kids?'

She said nothing for some moments. Then she replied, 'At first, it was something I really did want.' She shrugged, looking sullen. 'I was pregnant twice, but sadly I miscarried each time.'

'That must have been hard.'

'At the time, yes. But then when I got to know the real Barnie, the Barnie with the dark underbelly, in a kind of way I was glad – about the miscarriages. Does that sound terrible?'

He shook his head. 'You told me at the wake he had a temper that scared you. I never saw that at Brighton College – well, no real sign of it anyway.'

'Maybe because his head was full of dreams at school. After we married, he told me repeatedly how important he felt it was to make it by the age of forty. He said that if someone didn't make it by forty they would never make it. And as he approached forty himself, he began to realize that all those dreams just weren't going to happen – to come true.'

She paused as the waiter refilled their glasses of white wine from the second bottle, emptying it. 'Another?' he asked, showing no sign of desperation for them to leave.

They looked at each other. 'I'd love an espresso – oh – and the bill,' Taylor said.

'I'll have a macchiato – and we'll split the bill,' she suggested.

'No way!' he retorted. Then, with a grin, he said, 'You can get the next one.'

Her eyes lingered on him for a moment longer than they needed before she spoke with a big smile, 'Deal!' Then she continued. 'I began to realize it too – that he had all these dreams but never a plan to make them actually happen. As each of his grand schemes fell over, one by one, I could see that he was changing, and not in a good way. It got worse when we ran short of money, when he began to rail at a world he felt owed him a living and did not appreciate him. Luckily, throughout that time I'd kept my job.'

'In PR?'

She nodded. 'If I hadn't, we'd have lost the house. Then he went and had an affair and that was it, as far as I was concerned. I kicked him out and he was fine with that for two years, until his new lady – Angi Bitchface – kicked him out too. And he came crawling, begging me to take him back. He had a cock-and-bull story about how he had the goods on an old school friend and was looking to get a massive pay-off to keep silent, which would make us rich.'

Taylor frowned. 'An old school friend? Did he elaborate?'

'To be honest, I didn't really listen. I told him that the day he proved to me he was actually capable of succeeding at something was the day I might start to think about taking him back. I knew that was never going to happen.' She was silent for a moment. 'This may sound crazy, but I did still sort of love him.' She shook her head.

He nodded. 'I get it. Barnie had a lot of charisma.'

'He did.'

'I'm interested in this *old school friend* he talked about. Did he say any more about him?'

'Not really, no.' She shrugged. 'Well, other than that he was someone everyone thought was dead – and Barnie had found out he wasn't.'

24

Taylor stared at Debbie Martin for some moments in stunned silence. 'Barnie didn't say who he was?'

She shook her head vigorously. 'No.'

Although he had downed more than he usually did, he wasn't so drunk that his mind was no longer functioning clearly. He was trying to piece the different parts of the puzzle together.

Barnie had the goods on an old school friend. Someone everyone thought was dead.

And now Barnie was dead.

'To get this right, Debbie, Barnie thought he could get a big pay-off, presumably by blackmailing this old school friend, and getting enough to make you both rich?'

'Yes.'

Taylor reflected for a moment. 'The only person Barnie and I were friends with who went on to become properly wealthy was Rufus.' He sipped the last drops of his wine. 'But if Rufus had faked his disappearance for whatever reason, and Barnie had recognized him and was threatening to expose him, then why would Rufus want to risk showing up at his funeral?'

'Isn't that something murderers often do? You see it in the true crime stuff on television, it seems to happen a lot. They turn up out of macabre curiosity, or maybe just to gloat, right?'

'*Murderers?* Are you suggesting Rufus killed Barnie? I thought he died from mushroom poisoning?'

Debbie said nothing for a moment, waiting while their coffees were served, along with the bill, which Taylor moved to his side plate.

'It *was* mushroom poisoning – death cap mushrooms.' She began rolling her necklace between her forefinger and thumb, and looking a little uneasy. 'Barnie had formerly been a chef. Recently he'd been trying to build up a following on Instagram showing cheat recipes to impress your friends with. Sure he was a dreamer and a loser, but he wasn't a total idiot. Maybe he did make a genuine mistake – I've read that mistaking death caps for edible mushrooms is easily done. But what if – and I'm just speculating now – Rufus had something to do with it? I get the very distinct feeling the police are viewing his death as suspicious – they've interviewed me twice.'

'They don't suspect you, surely?'

She shook her head, smiling. 'No – but isn't it true that most people who are murdered are killed by a member of their family, or by someone they know? Anyhow, what motive could I have for killing him? He didn't have any money and we were already happily apart.'

He frowned. 'Are you suggesting that, if Rufus was the one Barnie was trying to blackmail, Rufus poisoned him to get him off his back? Then turned up to the funeral to – as you said – *gloat*?'

'On the very big assumption Rufus is still alive?'

Taylor widened his eyes. 'Maybe not such a big assumption.'

'A great shame if that eulogy you did was all for nothing!'

He gave a wry grimace. 'You could say that . . .'

She sipped her coffee and continued. 'I barely knew Rufus, but Barnie always used to say that he was dangerous. He once told me he thought Rufus was a psychopath, and that he was the only person he knew who he thought could actually be capable of murdering someone.' She glanced down for a few moments, then stared directly at Taylor. 'Do you share that view?'

This was a moment when Taylor would have loved a cigarette. If Debbie had suggesting stepping outside for one, he'd have joined her in a shot. But she showed no sign of doing that and he didn't want to ask. 'How much did Barnie ever tell you about our schooldays?'

'Very little – other than that you, he and Rufus were tight. Whenever I tried to get him to talk about those days, it was like a shutter came down. I could see it in his eyes.' She looked at him almost a little sharply. 'Was there some scandal you three were involved in back then? Something you all did that you can never talk about?'

He shook his head. 'Not a scandal. But there was something.'

'Something?'

Taylor hesitated for a moment. 'You said at Barnie's funeral that you always felt Rufus had a dark side – that he had *something of the night* about him, right?'

She nodded. 'Yes.'

'I always felt that too.'

'Tell me more.'

'How much time do you have?'

'More than enough for another glass of wine.'

'You're going to need it,' he said.

The waiter, still smiling, happily brought them over two fresh, large glasses of white wine. Never normally a big drinker, Taylor was surprised how sober he still felt. Sober, but wanting to tell her. To tell her something he'd not talked about in years. The thing he'd never even told his wife. The trauma that in a strange kind of way – and not a good way – had bound the three of them together since the day it happened.

He picked up his glass and put it down again without drinking. 'The three of us met when we were eleven. At school we had to do a half-day of some kind of military service every week – it was called CCF, Combined Cadet Force.'

She nodded. 'I'm familiar with it.'

'You could choose whether you wanted to do Army, Navy or Air Force. Rufus, Barnie and I all had an interest in aviation. Right back then all three of us had ambitions to be pilots. It was all I'd ever wanted to do since as far back as I could remember. My dad was senior partner of a sizeable family law firm and he'd hoped I would go into that, but I wasn't interested. I'd set my heart on becoming a pilot. So in my first week at boarding school I enrolled in the RAF section of the Corps, which is where I met Rufus and Barnie.' He sipped some wine then went on.

'Barnie was a nice guy, but I always felt he was a bit of a dreamer, I know you feel that too. He once told me very seriously that he believed he'd been a Spitfire pilot in a former life, who'd been shot down and killed in the Battle of Britain, and that it was his destiny to fly again. That was before he told me, some while later, that he'd been an actor in a past life, in the Victorian age, and he realized it was now his destiny to be an actor again.'

She smiled. 'Sounds like Barnie all over!'

'I did genuinely like him – I felt I almost wanted to protect him, because he seemed so vulnerable. Rufus was very different, a piece of work, I guess. A strange character, quite aloof – you could never really tell whether he liked you or not. But he kind of latched on to the two of us because he didn't really have any other friends at school. He lived very much in a world of his own. He was obsessed with how mechanical and electrical things worked, and was always either taking stuff apart or making things.'

'What kinds of things?'

'Stuff that worked – I guess you'd call him a boffin. We all had our rooms at school – studies with a bed. Most pupils put pin-ups on the wall – rock stars, adolescent stuff. Not Rufus. He'd turned his room into a miniature rocket science laboratory. There was Dexion shelving everywhere, stacked with half-dismembered television sets and other electrical apparatus. And model aircraft – but not the normal kind that we kids used to make. He built remote-controlled flying bombs.'

'*What?*'

'Yep. There was a big area of wilderness behind our boarding house – we were all in the same house – and he liked to take us out and show us his latest. It would be a radio-controlled single-engine plane packed with gunpowder and a detonator, and he'd let it take off, then a short distance on would nosedive it into the ground and it would explode.'

'For fun.'

'His idea of fun. I told him it seems such a waste of effort to spend all that time building the aircraft to then go and destroy it, and he used to tell me not to be so damned dull – that life should be about excitement, about pushing your boundaries beyond your horizon. Anyhow, then he progressed into something that all of us did like. He developed a bit of software that enabled us to download the latest Hollywood movies onto our computers.'

'Pirated?'

Taylor nodded and drank some more wine. 'Oh yes. It was the early days of streaming. It would take hours – sometimes a day or more to do the download – but then we would have the latest *Batman* or *Mission: Impossible* or whatever. It was actually pretty cool.'

'And illegal.'

'Totally. But we didn't care back then, it was really exciting. And Rufus was making a small fortune selling his software to other pupils – he was minting it! He even sold it to several of the teachers!'

'Barnie never told me any of this.'

Taylor shrugged.

'So this was when you saw his *dark side*?'

'No. Not then. I thought he was pretty cool at that point and I think Barnie did too. It was what happened when were about fifteen that changed everything.' He drank some more, and was surprised to see his glass was nearly empty.

The waiter hovered with the bottle, but he politely dismissed him. Debbie's glass was still nearly full.

'Which was what?' she prompted.

'All of us more senior cadets in the RAF Corps were offered the chance to have a flight in an RAF training aircraft. The three of us jumped at it – wow! We were actually going to fly in a real RAF plane! I'll always remember the day, a Tuesday afternoon in November. It was overcast and windy. And what made it even more exciting was that it was nothing like the kind of aeroplanes we'd ever been in on holiday.'

He drank another sip. 'It was a twin-prop aircraft that was used for training the paras. The interior was basic. Totally stripped down, with canvas seating, bare metal cabin and no sound-proofing. When the engines revved it was like being inside a boom-box. And when we took off it was lumpy, bumpy and horribly uncomfortable. On top of which, exhaust fumes were leaking in. Then, almost immediately, we hit turbulence and got bounced around for the next half-hour while we tried to look out of the few windows and figure out where we were.'

'No drinks trolley, eh?' Debbie jibed. 'And no air stewards?'

'Not unless you count one grizzled RAF flight sergeant who thought, probably quite rightly, that we were a bunch of tossers.' He grinned, fleetingly, then turned serious again. 'I think we'd all had enough. All of us were feeling sick and just wanting to get back down onto terra firma. There was one guy, one of our classmates, called Will Cooper. He was very quiet, quite bookish – had a mop of hair permanently in front of his eyes, and wonky spectacles – he was blind as a bat without them. He was in particularly bad shape on the plane and had thrown up several times into a sick bag.'

Taylor shrugged. 'I was close to puking too. We finally landed, and I don't think any of us could stagger down those steps that were lowered from the fuselage fast enough. I felt woozy as hell. We all did. I think Rufus was in front of me, and Barnie. I could see Will Cooper, who was first out, swaying from right to left on the tarmac, like he was drunk. The steps were at the rear of the plane, behind the left wing. Then I saw he wasn't wearing his glasses, he was holding them in his hand. He suddenly lurched forward. Straight towards the propellor that was still spinning – the engines were still running. We all saw him. But it was like he hadn't seen it. I yelled at him. Barnie ran forward to try to grab him.' He fell silent.

Debbie was staring at him. 'What happened?'

He took a long time to answer. Over twenty years later, the image was still so raw in his mind. 'He walked straight into the propellor. Straight into. He sort of tripped as he reached it and tumbled forward. He . . .' Taylor's voice choked and he took some moments to regain his composure. 'He just – sort of – disappeared, from the waist up, into a pink cloud. For a fraction of a second. Then we were all spattered with bits of him – bone, blood, flesh, brain, everything.'

He put his glass down and sank his face into his hands. After some moments he looked up. 'I'm sorry. I've not talked about it in years.'

She gave a gentle smile. 'You don't have to apologize. That's just . . . unbelievable. Horrific. I can't imagine how . . . how you could ever unsee that.'

'I can't. I can't ever unsee it, however much I've tried. And God knows I have.'

'And the others?'

'Several of us – including Barnie and myself – had mental breakdowns afterwards. There were ten boys and five girls on the plane – and it was mostly the boys that suffered the worst. The females seemed tougher.'

She smiled. 'Maybe we are tougher.'

'I've never doubted it.' He smiled back.

'And Rufus?'

Taylor turned to look for the waiter, who magically appeared and refilled his glass. After he had walked away, he said, 'Rufus reacted in a very strange way. It was like he wasn't affected at all. He said, a few days later, that Will had been a bloody idiot. I thought at first that was just his bravado, his way of dealing with it, but later on I realized I was wrong. He genuinely thought Will had been an idiot. There was no empathy, no sense that he was sorry for Will – nor for the guy's family. He even made crude jokes about sending Will's parents the dry-cleaning bill for his clothes.'

'Seriously?'

'That was Rufus all over. Will had been an only child. His parents had lost . . . everything. Rufus had zero empathy.'

'I'm shivering,' Debbie said. 'I can't believe Barnie never told me about this. But, at the same time, I suppose I can. He had a way, if he didn't like something, of sort of pretending it had never happened. But what you're saying about Rufus's reaction – that to me fits the mould of a psychopath – or sociopath – or whatever the term is.'

Taylor sat, frowning, for some moments. It was not something he'd ever thought of. 'I remember at school Rufus always got his way. He was cunning and manipulative. I had a sense back then that he would be highly successful one day. But would he go as far as killing?' He shrugged, then gave a wan smile. 'I guess that's an opinion that, as the saying goes, is above my pay grade.'

She smiled. 'So to recap on where we are on this: shortly before he died, Barnie claimed to have something big on a rich former school friend who everyone thought was dead. The only friend you guys had who became rich was Rufus. But we were both actually at Rufus's funeral two years ago – how could it be him?' She paused. 'Oh my God, do you think he really might not be dead?'

Taylor shrugged. 'It was a *no-body* funeral. There was no coffin. It was more like a memorial service, I suppose.'

'How much do you know about how he died?'

'Rufus apparently fell off a yacht in darkness, in the middle of the night, somewhere off the coast of Barbados. I don't know all the details, but that's what his wife – widow – Fiona, told me before the funeral.'

'His body was never found, was it?' she said.

He shook his head. 'Not as far as I know. But if you go overboard in the middle of the night, in shark-infested Caribbean waters, maybe your chances of being found intact aren't great.'

'Do you have any other evidence that he might still be alive?' she pressed.

'Only that I was certain I saw him at Barnie's funeral.'

'But you could have been mistaken?'

'I tried to catch him at the end of the service, but he'd vanished. I later asked the vicar if he had CCTV of the service and he showed me the footage of the mourners arriving and leaving.'

'You saw him?'

'No. But the vicar did say if someone wanted to avoid being caught on camera, it was unlikely but possible.'

'Have you thought about going to the police, James?'

'Yes, but I'm not sure if there's a lot of point. Telling them I think I might have seen him in church but he didn't show up on CCTV is hardly going to float their boat.'

'Are you really, really sure it was him you saw in the church?'

'I'm beginning to doubt it. And yet I don't know. I really do think it could have been him. Nothing's making sense at the moment.'

She shook her head. 'Let's think this through logically. Let's say he faked his death in order to get out of some kind of trouble. Maybe his wife colluded and covered for him. She might be a good starting point.'

'Fiona? I doubt it. I heard they'd not been getting on so well in the months before he died – disappeared – whatever. And she didn't waste any time changing back to her maiden name of Davies.'

Debbie Martin gave a wry smile. 'Seems none of you Three Musketeers turned out to be so great at relationships.'

'*All for one and one for all*,' Taylor quoted. 'That was our motto, once.'

'And now carved on a headstone in the graveyard of good intentions?'

25

Paul Anthony had a lot on his mind. Three new orders had come through from Shannon for 3D printed handguns, with Bitcoin deposits received, and he thought he might go to his office this afternoon to start work on them.

But far bigger and more exciting than these was an ongoing contract he had been offered. A wealthy lady wanted her husband to meet with a fatal accident. Paul had an idea how to do this and, throwing modesty to the wind, he thought it was just brilliant.

No – more than brilliant; it was genius!

But first, Professor Llewellyn.

He opened his fridge door and admired the three cans of Diet Coke on the top shelf. Perfect, sealed, distinctive red and silver cans, indistinguishable from the ones on sale in any of a trillion shops, stalls, cafes, restaurants and bars around the globe.

No one could have told the difference, simply because there was no difference. He'd bought the empty, printed Diet Coke blanks through a counterfeiting source on the dark web, and a portable canning machine from trusty Amazon. He'd marked a number on the top of each of these three with a black felt tip: 4, 6, 8. It was the number of hours they had been in the fridge.

The process had been simpler than he'd imagined. He just poured in Diet Coke from other cans he'd purchased in a super-market, leaving a gap of a couple of inches to the top. Then he had enmeshed each wasp in a cocoon of spun sugar from the candyfloss machine, placed them at the top and sealed each can with the machine.

He removed the three cans, put them down on the kitchen work surface, and placed a clear glass tumbler beside them. Then he listened to each can in turn with a piece of kit from another of the packages that had arrived in the past few days – a stethoscope. He began with the one marked 8.

Silence.

Then he listened to the one marked 6. There was a very, very faint scratching sound. Something was alive inside it. He felt a thrum of excitement. And it was the same with number 4. Yes!

Carefully, holding a cloth in his left hand above the can marked 8, he popped the tab with his right. There was a hiss, just like normal. He peered in but could only see dark liquid, no spun sugar. He upended the can, emptied the contents into the tumbler and saw a very dead-looking wasp float to the surface.

He removed the wasp with a spoon and laid it in a saucer, then peered at it through a magnifying glass for any signs of life, however small. He could see none. He emptied the tumbler into the sink, then repeated the process, opening can number 6. And this was much more satisfying. A plump, very drowsy wasp was struggling around on the surface. All traces of the spun sugar gone, as in the previous can.

'Hello, my beauty – been gorging, have you?' he said, beaming. 'All your Christmases come at once?'

Next he opened the can marked 4. As he tipped out the contents, he could see a few strands of the pink candyfloss, but not enough for anyone to notice, and a much more active, angry wasp. It was struggling. Fighting to lift off from the Coke, fighting like a tiger.

Professor Bill Llewellyn normally got to his office around 8.30 a.m. From the reconnaissance he'd carried out, there were no security guard patrols, and no one around in the small hours. So it wouldn't make any difference whether he visited Llewellyn at 2.30 a.m. or 4.30 a.m.

He decided to repeat the experiment again, to be sure. He had plenty of time and, judging by the contents of the four jars, two containing honey and two jam, he had no shortage of volunteers.

One of them was destined to die a hero.

Well, in his eyes, anyway.

26

'Do they have snakes, Daddy?' Noah asked.

'Snakes?'

'In the zoo. Do they? Do they have big ones?' Noah, five years old, with unruly fair hair and deep blue eyes, was almost impossibly cute, Roy Grace thought, and because of that, almost impossible to punish when he was naughty – which he was quite a lot. He adored the boy with all his heart. And at times it felt that maybe Noah was a gift in place of Bruno, the son he had lost.

Grace smiled at him. He sat at the breakfast bar in their cottage, barefoot, in jeans and a sweatshirt, the main section of the *Sunday Times* spread out in front of him, his ever-present job phone underneath it somewhere, and Noah perched beside him, hyper-excited, firing questions at him repetitive fashion, about the visit to Drusillas Park zoo at Alfriston that he and Cleo had promised the kids today.

Molly, on her mat on the floor near them, was occupied with her animal farm, occasionally pressing a button that produced the bleat of a sheep, a moo, a cluck or honk or grunt. Cleo, who was happily not on call this weekend, sat at the kitchen table in jeans and a baggy sweater, with a large mug of coffee, reading *The Week*.

'They have snakes at Drusillas that could swallow a boy your size in one gulp!' Grace said.

132

Noah shrank away, raising his hands protectively. 'Nooooo!'

Grace nodded. 'They particularly like little boys who ask lots of questions.'

Noah gave him a sideways look and pursed his lips. Then he frowned. 'I bet one could swallow you too, Daddy!'

'Your father would put it in handcuffs first,' Cleo said.

Noah had an expressive face and none more so when he looked genuinely surprised. 'Put a snake in handcuffs? Wouldn't he wriggle out of them?'

Grace smiled and tenderly tapped the boy's cheek with his knuckles. 'Smart thinking – he might!' He was in a happy frame of mind. Feeling energized after an eight-mile run with Humphrey earlier this morning, and enjoying what promised to be a precious and all-too-rare Sunday with his family, having left Glenn in charge of Operation Meadow today. Kaitlynn, their nanny, was back in the States visiting family and would be gone at least a few weeks, depending how the visit went.

Half an hour earlier, he'd collected six eggs from the hen coop, and had scrambled five of them for Cleo and himself, serving them up with wholegrain sourdough toast along with some grilled tomatoes and baby spinach. For Noah and Molly, he'd made French toast – dipping both sides of the bread in egg, frying it and then dousing it in maple syrup. Noah was still scraping every tiny bit off his plate.

Grace turned to his favourite columnist, Matthew Syed, and had just started to read his piece on what he felt had gone most wrong with post-Brexit Britain when his job phone rang. Irked at the intrusion, he retrieved it from under the paper, and answered. It was Glenn Branson. 'Sorry to wake you, boss,' he said.

'Just woken yourself, have you?' Grace looked at the kitchen clock. It showed 9.50.

'Yeah, yeah! How's your morning going?'

'Noah wants to know if it's possible to handcuff a snake?'

'Of course, we've nicked plenty of reptiles in our time, haven't we?'

'That's the right answer. Anything else on your mind?'

'Actually, yes. You tasked Jack yesterday with finding the whereabouts of the yacht, *Eloise III*, and you told him you wanted to speak to the yacht's captain and to the crew member who raised the man overboard alarm on Rufus Rorke.'

'Correct.'

'Jack found out the *Eloise III* is currently in port in Cannes, having routine maintenance before repositioning to the Caribbean for the winter. We've made contact with the captain, name of Richard Le Quesne, who is currently at his residence in Antibes and is happy to speak to you in the next hour – before he leaves for Nice airport on a week's holiday. I have a number for him.'

Grace tapped it into his phone.

'The crew member who was present when Rorke went overboard is called Lance Sharpus-Jones. By happy chance, he has a flat in Sussex – in Bosham, near Chichester. He is happy to come in for an interview, the only problem being he's flying out to be caretaker of the boat on Monday morning; he's on an 11 a.m. flight from Gatwick to Nice, he'd have to come in super-early – like 7 a.m. If that's not too early for you?'

Grace suppressed a grin. 'Hope it's not too early for you, either, as I'd like you with me – as my Deputy SIO.' He enjoyed the grunt of dismay that came through the receiver.

After he ended the call he went up to his den, with his view out over the hens in the rear garden and the slope of the hill beyond, and dialled the number Glenn had given him for the yacht skipper.

It was answered after two rings by a posh English voice. 'Hello?'

'Mr Le Quesne, my name's Detective Superintendent Grace

from the Surrey and Sussex Major Crime Team. I'm sorry to disturb you on a Sunday, but we have rather an urgent situation. I understand you are a professional yacht skipper and you are currently employed by the owners of a yacht called *Eloise III*?'

His reply was polite, but tinged with suspicion. 'That is correct, Detective Superintendent, is there a problem?'

'Do you recall clients who chartered the *Eloise III* about two years ago, called Rufus and Fiona Rorke?'

After a moment's hesitation, Le Quesne said, 'Yes, indeed I do. I remember them well. Mr and Mrs Rorke. Such a tragic situation. How can I be of help?'

'They'd chartered the *Eloise III* for two weeks cruising around the Caribbean, is that correct?'

'Yes.'

'You were just over a week into the cruise, I believe.'

'Correct.'

'So you would have had time to observe the Rorkes, I imagine.'

'Meaning what, exactly?' Le Quesne asked.

'In your opinion, did everything seem all right with their relationship?'

He hesitated for a moment. 'To be honest, our clients are all extremely rich people who very much tend to keep to themselves, whether on their own or with friends. But a couple of my crew did say to me that they'd heard them arguing pretty ferociously.'

'On the night he went overboard?'

'No, a couple of times during the previous days. May I ask why you are raking this up now, Detective Superintendent?'

'Well, this may sound a little strange, but we have reason to believe that Mr Rufus Rorke may still be alive.'

'Really?' the yacht captain exclaimed. 'That certainly does sound very strange indeed. I'm afraid that's utterly impossible!'

'Why do you say that?'

'Well, for starters, on the night he went overboard, Mr Rorke and I had quite an argument. He wanted us to sail to Grenada, so they could meet some friends who were holidaying there. It's quite a long stretch and quite normal for people chartering the yacht to get passages like that done at night, so they would arrive in daylight. But the forecast was poor – force seven, gusting eight to nine. I strongly advised it would be better to spend another day in port in Barbados, as the weather would be improving the next day, but Mr Rorke was insistent – and I'm paid to, within reason, do what the client wants.'

'Understood,' Grace said.

'Mr and Mrs Rorke went to a restaurant in Barbados – the Cliff, from memory – and returned very late, both somewhat the worse for wear from booze, if I'm not giving any confidences away?'

'You are not giving any confidences away, Mr Le Quesne. This is a murder inquiry and I'm grateful for all information.'

He sounded genuinely shocked. 'Murder? Seriously?'

'If you could just tell me everything you can remember about that evening – night.'

'Yes, right, I see. Well, on Mr Rorke's insistence we sailed from Bridgetown soon after he and his wife returned to the yacht. The sea state was fairly choppy and for that reason I stayed at the helm myself rather than handing over to another crew member. It was about thirty minutes after we'd left Bridgetown harbour that the man overboard alarm was raised. This would have been around 1.45 a.m. At which time we were five nautical miles south-west of Bridgetown, from memory.'

'The alarm was raised by a crew member called Lance Sharpus-Jones?'

'Yes, a very reliable chap, who'd been a member of my crew for several years. I know he gave the Barbados Police a statement. He was due to take over from me, and had gone to the stern of the ship for a cigarette, I believe, at around 1.40 a.m. From memory, a very drunken Mr Rorke had barged into him, very apologetically, as the yacht had lurched in the swell. Mr Rorke then stood some distance from him, leaning against the deck-rail, and said something that Lance Sharpus-Jones didn't catch, then lit a cigarette. As I understand it, a few minutes later Rorke leaned over the rail and began retching. Lance turned away, then a moment later he heard a splash and a yell – a shout for help. He immediately followed the man-overboard drill – checking his watch to mark the time, throwing a lifebelt, shining a torch and raising the alarm. We spent the next five hours, until dawn, circling the area without any success.'

'Is there any possibility he could have swum to the shore, Mr Le Quesne?' Grace asked.

'In my opinion, zero. To be precise, a long way less than zero. We were, as I have said, five nautical miles from the nearest land, in rough sea, and with the additional hazard of sharks. What I can say is that, after thirty years of skippering yachts around these waters, I do know if someone does go overboard on any vessel at night, there's a very slim chance indeed of them surviving even in a calm sea. Without a buoyancy aid, even if he had been a strong swimmer, Mr Rorke would have stood no chance in that sea. The waves breaking over his head would have drowned him in a short space of time.'

'All right,' Grace said. 'Let me ask you another question – what if he didn't actually go overboard? Could he have concealed himself somewhere on the boat? Or been concealed by an accomplice?'

'I'm afraid that's being fanciful, Detective. After we abandoned the search and the Barbados coastguard took over, we returned to Bridgetown, where the police then made a thorough search of the yacht. There aren't that many places you could hide on a yacht her size, and then you'd have the additional difficulty of getting ashore without being seen.'

'That's very helpful. If I can ask you one more thing: this crew member, Lance Sharpus-Jones, would you say he was trustworthy?'

'How well do any of us know anyone, Detective Grace? All I can say is he was my Number Two. I would have trusted him to sail that yacht anywhere, in any weather, while I slept. He's a good man.'

'Not someone who might easily be coerced, perhaps by money, into helping out in a major deception?'

'Good grief, no.'

Grace thanked him and ended the call. He went back downstairs to his family. But, as was the case most of the time in his job, Operation Meadow had got to him, got under his skin. He enjoyed the pub lunch in Alfriston, where Noah messily ate most of a huge pizza, he had a beef roast and Cleo a vegetarian one, which she shared with Molly, and then an afternoon at the zoo, where he carried Molly in his arms.

But he only enjoyed it with one half of his focus. The other half had been on the job. Trying to work out how a man could have been alive, two years after vanishing overboard from a yacht.

Was the skipper, Richard Le Quesne, lying? Or his Number Two, as he called Lance Sharpus-Jones? Had Rufus Rorke given them both a massive bung to cover for him? To fake his death?

He thought about the further evidence. The torn remnants of Rufus Rorke's expensive jacket, recovered by a local fisherman called John Baker. Rorke's DNA was obtained from it, as well as the pen his wife had given him as an anniversary present, still zipped inside an internal pocket. A marine biologist and a highly regarded forensic orthodontist had both confirmed the tears on the jacket to be compatible with successional tiger shark bite marks.

All the evidence pointed, conclusively, to Rufus Rorke being dead.

Apart from that footage of him, two years later, walking along a supermarket aisle.

27

James Taylor was tapering this week in the approach to the Chicago Marathon, which meant only light, short runs. Which was just as well, he thought. It felt like a chainsaw was at work inside his skull. After leaving – or rather stumbling out of – Wild Flor at around 5 p.m. yesterday, he and Debbie had fetched up in a bar across the road, and for some reason, known only to the God of Bad Decisions, decided that ordering Negronis would be a good idea. And she was insistent on buying.

One-third Campari, one-third red vermouth and one-third gin.

And they had seemed a very good idea at the time. A second one, followed by a third, which it would have been rude to refuse. Debbie's invitation back to her apartment had seemed a good idea too, but some bit of common sense – or perhaps decency – had kicked in. If he was going to make love to this amazing woman, he didn't want the first time to be a drunken fumble.

Which was why, after a taxi ride he didn't remember at all back to his beachfront apartment in Worthing, fourteen miles west of Brighton, and a fitful night's sleep, assisted by two doses of paracetamol, he was now struggling, along his seafront route, in light rain, to complete what normally would have been an easy five-mile run for him.

And this time next week I have to run 26.2 miles! Shit!

He headed on past the pier to his left, and then the deserted pebble beach and a closed coffee stall. The sea beyond was a roiling grey. His Garmin watch told him he'd done .73 miles, just under two to go before he could turn back, and then perhaps sweat out some of the booze in the apartment block's steam room or sauna. It was 10.54 a.m. An hour ago he'd rung Rufus Rorke's widow, Fiona Davies, asking if he could speak to her, and she'd invited him to tea, telling him the boys would be at a birthday party, so they wouldn't be distracted. She still lived in the home she and Rufus had shared.

He passed the 2K marker on the pavement for the Worthing parkrun, feeling a little stronger now, a *Desert Island Discs* podcast playing in his headphones, but he wasn't listening, he was deep in his own thoughts. Thinking back to his long lunch and afternoon – and evening – with Debbie Martin yesterday. And what she had said.

Let's think this through logically. Let's say Rufus faked his death in order to get out of some kind of trouble. Maybe his wife colluded and covered for him. She might be a good starting point.

In a few hours, he would have the chance to talk to Fiona and make up his own mind.

28

Fiona Davies had texted Taylor her What3Words address. He followed the directions on his phone, suction-cup clamped to his MG's windscreen, along a labyrinth of narrow rural lanes close to the village of Bolney, some fourteen miles north of Brighton.

The final countdown started: 100 metres . . . 60 metres. Then wrought-iron gates appeared on his right. He turned in and braked to a halt in front of them, and was looking for an intercom when the gates opened. He drove along a tarmac driveway lined with laurel bushes on both sides for several hundred yards, then curving right, before seeing the spectacular, angular, black and white half-timbered facade of an L-shaped Tudor mansion. A silver Bentley Bentayga SUV was parked on the forecourt, which was paved in grey brick, and there were almost impossibly wide steps leading up to an equally impossibly grand front door, with massive gargoyles on either side.

He parked close to the Bentley, and as he climbed out the front door opened and Fiona emerged. He'd last seen her at Rufus's 'funeral', and she hadn't changed. Just like her impossibly grand home, impossibly imposing front steps and impossibly grand front door, she was almost impossibly beautiful. And impossibly posh.

Long fair hair, classic English-rose face, lace-collared blouse, wide leather belt, classy jeans and suede Cuban-heeled cowboy boots. She was accompanied by three yapping Pomeranians.

It could have all been a movie set. Except, Taylor knew, this was all real. This was Rufus Rorke country. The world he had carefully created. To impress. But who?

'Very cool wheels, James!' she said, her accent as cut-glass as it gets. 'I'm not sure I've ever seen an MGB GT in black before.'

'It's a very rare colour,' he said, a little proudly. 'They had to be specially ordered back in the 1970s. Are you into cars?'

'Well, I suppose vicariously, through Rufus. He built up quite a collection – mostly of rare Porsches.'

'Very nice. What do you have?'

She raised a hand in the air. 'I'm not that great on their names – some very early 356s, an ex Le Mans racer, an LMP1, I think it is – oh and one that sounds like a sewing-machine manufacturer – Singer.'

Taylor raised his eyebrows. 'A Singer? Awesome.'

'If you have time I'll show you.' He knelt to stroke one of the dogs, which immediately bared its teeth at him and gave a warning growl.

'Nero!' she admonished. Then turning to Taylor she said, 'Don't worry – they're just very protective.'

A few minutes later, Taylor was seated on a soft chintz sofa, in a grand drawing room filled with ornate, gilded Louis XIV side tables and cabinets. There was a fine view out across a lake, with a Grecian temple folly beyond. He noticed a very faint, ingrained smell of cigarette smoke, above the strong fragrance of her perfume, and saw a clean ashtray on the side table next to her. He sipped his Earl Grey tea, which had been served by a uniformed maid, and took a bite of his chocolate Bath Oliver biscuit. The three tiny dogs sat close to their mistress's feet. She glanced at her watch. 'I will need to shoot in an hour, to collect Robert and George.'

'That's fine, I'm grateful for your time.'

The room was immaculate, straight off the page of a photoshoot in *Country Life*. A CSI would have struggled to find any traces of two small boys ever having set foot in here, he thought.

'So, James, what was it you wanted to talk about?'

Taylor wasn't normally fazed by grand displays of wealth. His employer Tommy Towne lived in a mansion that he'd paid over £20 million for, filled with art that must have cost the same again. Just like the art in this room he was in now. But there was something about this very beautiful and self-aggrandized woman, sitting defensively, arms crossed, that was throwing him off his stride.

'I don't want to rake up any sad memories,' he said. 'But I wonder if I could ask you about the night Rufus disappeared?'

She gave him a strange look that felt almost hostile. 'What exactly is going on?'

Taylor thought hard and carefully before replying. 'I don't quite know how best to frame this, Fiona, but there are people saying that Rufus is still alive.'

Her reaction was instant and emphatic. 'What? For God's sake! I was with him – and, yes, lots of people have said our marriage was rocky, and I'm not denying that. Rufus was a serial adulterer and I nearly kicked him out several times, but in the end I didn't for one simple reason. I did love the bastard.' She shrugged. 'And, I guess, for the sake of our kids. On that night he went overboard he'd been troubled for many weeks and had started drinking heavily – which wasn't him at all. He had his vices but booze wasn't one of them. Not in the sense of being a drunk. That day, or rather night, he was in a mental state that had really worried me – I'd never seen him like it. He was – like – trying to drink himself into oblivion.'

She fell silent for some moments. Then she said, 'And the stupid bastard succeeded. End of.' She glared at Taylor.

'You don't think there is any possibility he might still be alive, Fiona?' he asked.

'Do you think Adolf Hitler is still alive, James? John F. Kennedy? Martin Luther King? Are you one of these wacko conspiracy theorists?'

He shook his head. 'No, I'm not.'

'So what makes you think Rufus is still alive?'

'Because I saw him.'

'*Saw* him?'

'Yes.'

'Tell me you're not serious?'

'I'm serious, Fiona.' Taylor looked at her levelly. Trying to read her face. 'Are you certain he's dead?'

'What kind of a question is that? How could you have seen him? He went overboard from a yacht, in the middle of the night, in the Caribbean, witnessed by a crew member. We searched for him for hours. A fisherman found remains of his jacket with bite marks from a shark on it. He's dead, James, he's been dead for over two years. We had his funeral, for God's sake!'

Taylor let it ride that it was a no-body funeral.

'Where did you imagine you saw him, exactly?' she asked.

'It was ten days ago, at a funeral. One of our mates from school – Barnie Wallace.'

She gave him an odd look. 'Barnie Wallace, did you say?'

'Yes.'

'One of your Three Musketeers at Brighton College?'

He nodded. 'Yep, that's him. Barnie, myself and Rufus. We were the Three Musketeers.'

She was silent for some moments, then she said, 'Barnie turned up here about a month before Rufus died.'

'He did? Why? For what reason?'

She shook her head. 'I've no idea. As far as I knew, Rufus hadn't seen him in years. I remember they went into Rufus's study and after a while I heard shouting. Now I think about it, that was around the time Rufus began drinking.'

'After Barnie's visit?'

'I can't remember exactly.' She frowned. 'Maybe. I'd never seen Rufus so angry after Barnie left. He told me that Barnie was desperate for money and had asked him for a loan – a very big loan.'

'Presumably he didn't give him that loan?'

She shook her head. 'Rufus told me after what a loser he thought Barnie was.'

'There had always been friction between them. Even at school Barnie was a little jealous of Rufus.'

'So Barnie's dead – very young. How did he die?'

Taylor told her.

She looked shocked. 'What a horrible thing. I've heard mushroom poisoning is agonizing. Poor guy, what a ghastly thing to happen.'

'Yes,' he said flatly.

Fiona was pensive for a moment then she said, 'OK, so you *think* you saw him – Rufus?'

'I don't *think* I saw him. I *know* I saw him.'

'How can you possibly know you saw him?'

'Look, I don't want to open up a can of worms, Fiona. Obviously I know the whole tragic story of him going overboard.'

She gave him a sad smile. 'And you gave a very beautiful eulogy at Rufus's funeral. You summed him up exactly – he'd have been proud.'

He smiled. 'Thank you. There's one thing I've never asked you – when were you made aware he'd gone overboard?'

'It was some while after – an hour or so, I think. I hadn't been sleeping well and took a prescription med. I was woken up around 2 a.m. to be told Rufus had fallen off the boat and we'd turned around and were looking for him. It was quite a heavy sea and the captain told me that it wasn't going to be easy to find him.'

'Were there any other boats around?'

She shook her head, then hesitated. 'I'm not sure but I think one of the crew said they'd seen the lights of a fishing boat and they tried to radio it to help in the search, but couldn't get a response.'

'I don't want to sound insensitive, but did you have any doubts at all that he had fallen overboard?'

'None,' she said emphatically. 'There was a member of the crew – called Lance something, a double-barrelled name – who'd been standing near him and heard the splash, and raised the alarm. And then there was that fisherman in Barbados who'd found part of . . .' She hesitated again, her voice cracking.

Taylor waited patiently.

She was crying. 'Found part of his jacket.' She sniffed and dabbed her eyes. 'I'm sorry.'

'I understand.'

'There was a pen in the jacket pocket I'd given him, a Mont Blanc. Oh Jesus.' She began crying again.

Taylor sat in silence until she had calmed down. 'Let me tell you something about Rufus when we were at school. He was a big prankster. Did you ever see any of that?'

She nodded. 'Oh yes, he loved playing pranks on people. And dressing up – we always hosted a fancy dress New Year's Eve party every year, I'm surprised he never invited you.'

'We'd all drifted apart, gone our separate ways.' He smiled sympathetically.

'Were you sober when you saw Rufus?' she asked after a moment of easy silence.

'It was around midday.'

'There's no way, James. No way you could have.'

He believed she was telling the truth. He didn't think anyone could act the distress in her face. 'Did Rufus have a brother – like a twin – even a long-lost one?'

146

'No,' she said adamantly. 'So tell me exactly what you saw and where?'

He told her what had transpired in the church. When he had finished she shook her head. 'So you really didn't get a close look at his face, did you?'

'I saw enough.'

She sipped some of her tea then put the cup down. 'I can tell you one thing, James. If Rufus is, somehow, still alive, he would have contacted me. He adored the boys, there's no way he's been around for two years and not made contact. That's my proof that he's dead, if I needed it.'

Taylor nodded. Through the window he saw a large bird – a heron, he thought. It swooped down on the lake and then rose off the water with a fish in its beak, its wings flapping slowly and gracefully. She saw it too. 'That bloody bird – steals all our beautiful fish. I'll tell you something, if Rufus were alive and here, he'd bloody well shoot it, protected species or not.'

He nodded politely. 'Fiona, do you remember the name of the fisherman in Barbados who found the remains of Rufus's jacket?'

'Yes, John I think it was – but it might have been Jim.' She thought for a moment. 'No, it was definitely John.'

'Do you know his last name?'

'Baker.' She spelled it out. 'He's a bit of a local character, I got the impression.'

'And you believed his story.'

'Why wouldn't I have? He didn't have any reason to lie – and he could have kept the pen, which was worth quite a bit of money, but he did the decent thing and took it along with the remains of the jacket to the police.'

As Taylor drove away from the house he was thinking pretty hard. Fiona Davies hadn't seen or heard from Rufus, that much he was reasonably sure of.

It was the remains of Rorke's jacket that struck him as the weak link. A fragment of cloth several miles offshore, in a vast, rough ocean. What were the chances of a fisherman netting that? One in a million? Billion? Trillion?

Had nobody asked that question?

29

Roy Grace had just asked himself exactly that question. It was 9.45 p.m., and he would have loved to have been downstairs right now, curled up on the sofa with Cleo, watching some of the latest season of *Succession* with her. But Operation Meadow had become central to his thinking and his mind was focused, as always, on how the investigation was going.

He used to go fishing off Brighton beach with his father in a small rowing boat. Then, when Jack Grace retired from the police force, he'd bought a deep-sea fishing smack that was capable of venturing much further out into the Channel. Roy had loved his days on that boat, during those few precious years his father had after retirement, before his early death from cancer. And he had loved talking to other fishermen they berthed alongside in Shoreham Harbour and seeing their catches. He was constantly amazed by the rubbish they – and he and his father – frequently pulled up: plastic waste, discarded tyres and balloons, rusted car parts, as well as bags and items of clothing. It seemed like the oceans were the world's rubbish dumps.

No one on the inquiry into Rufus Rorke's death had raised a flag over the odds on this Barbadian fisherman recovering part of his jacket. It simply appeared to be just one of those coincidences that happen from time to time. Part of the quirks – or magic – of being a fisherman.

But if Rufus Rorke was still alive then all bets were off. The *recovery* of that jacket became a game-changer.

Was it a plant? The fisherman possibly in cahoots with Rorke?

As ever the age-old detective mantra was in his mind. Check the ground under your feet. Maybe if ACC Downing would sanction it, he could send someone out to interview the fisherman – he doubted there would be any shortage of volunteers for this.

He had been through all the reports and witness statements. From the captain, Richard Le Quesne, who had a long, unblemished record. The crew member, Lance Sharpus-Jones. The Barbados police Inspector, Terry Stephens, in charge of the case. The fisherman who'd found the jacket, John Baker. The marine biologist and the bite-mark expert's opinion on the jacket remnant. The Coroner's findings.

Perhaps most significantly of all, Rufus Rorke's widow, Fiona, who stated that her husband had been stressed and drinking heavily on the night he disappeared. Norman and Glenn had interviewed her together at the time, and he remembered her clearly, having watched the interview. A beautiful but aloof lady, who clearly inhabited a world to which he would never aspire – a parallel universe whose inhabitants spent their summer days at polo at Cowdray Park, at Ascot and Wimbledon Centre Court, the Henley Regatta, Cowes Week, in between jetting off to hotspots in private jets – when her husband wasn't flying her in his multimillion-pound helicopter. A parallel and alternative universe to the one in which he lived. And he did not envy her any of it, one bit.

But, unless she was a brilliant liar, one thing he was reasonably sure of after watching her interview for almost three hours was that she was totally unaware of the criminal activity that Sussex Police suspected her husband was involved in. And it felt like she had told him the truth.

Maybe Grace would find out more when he interviewed the crew member, Sharpus-Jones, in the morning.

In the meantime, he sat in his den, viewing the compilation of recordings from the city's own CCTV, the various shopfront cameras located along either side of Western Road close to the Organica supermarket, as well as dashcam recordings from taxis and buses and, following a public appeal, footage from the GoPros of two cyclists. He had narrowed the times he was studying to twenty minutes either side of 3.25 p.m., Saturday 3 September.

For the past hour he had scanned the content of the CCTV back and forth repeatedly. Incredibly frustratingly, there was nothing captured at all of the Organica shopfront from across the street. The store itself had two cameras located above the front door, but the lenses of both had been shattered sometime prior, and not replaced. Forensics had reported that both cameras looked like they had been shot at with airgun pellets, or possibly stones fired from a catapult. Whatever, he thought – this all indicated possible prior planning.

By Rufus Rorke?

As he moved through the footage yet again, something was niggling him. Something his eyes were seeing but he had not yet connected the dots. He couldn't explain, if asked, how he knew, it was just instinct. Something was wrong. An anomaly.

He played the footage very slowly backwards, singling out one member of the crowd. A blind man, in a white jacket, wearing large dark glasses and the kind of peaked caps that only old men wear. He was holding his guide dog by its harness, some yards away from the Organica shopfront, and heading away.

He stopped the recording and played it forward again. The blind man, limping a little, one of several people ambling along. He was now heading east, approaching Organica, white stick in one hand, black Labrador leading him. Two young women walked a short distance in front, a gangly youth right behind.

But, as the footage went on, it showed the two young women and the gangly youth continuing their journey.

But no blind man.

He must have gone into Organica. Or stopped outside.

Fifteen minutes later, on the digital time clock on the screen, the blind man and his dog came back into sight. This time he held what looked like an Organica hessian sack in the same hand as his white stick. The bag didn't look heavy. Just a carton of mushrooms inside, he wondered?

Next he opened the assembly of Organica's six internal CCTV cameras, selected the one covering the inside of the front entrance, clicked to the same start time as the blind man had disappeared from view in front of the store and then hit the play symbol.

No blind man entered.

He moved the assembly on slowly. A minute, two minutes. Other people were coming in, including their suspect, the hooded man in dark glasses and scarf. No blind man.

But the hooded man was wearing dark glasses. The same as the blind man's? Had he tethered the dog outside? Reversed his white jacket so the black side was showing? Both men wore jeans and trainers.

He felt a growing beat of excitement as he looked at the other footage of the blind man on the street and went in as close as he could on his face. But the resolution was too poor to be able to see if these were the same sunglasses or not. They looked quite a bit larger than the ones the man in the store had been wearing.

But, if it was the same person, why go through the elaborate process of switching identities? There could only be one reason. Deception.

And there were two places he could think of to go, as a starting point, where he might be able to get an opinion whether the blind man and the hooded man were the same person. The first was the SuperRecognizer department at Scotland Yard. The second was the forensic gait analyst Haydn Kelly.

He yawned and looked at the time on his computer. It was 11.20. *How did it get so late?*

He heard the door open behind him and turned. Cleo stood there, in her white robe dressing gown, giving him a wan smile. 'Are you going to work all night, darling, or come to bed?'

'I'm sorry. How was *Succession*?'

'One of the best episodes ever – you missed a treat!'

'I'll try to watch it tomorrow.'

She shook her head. 'You won't, will you? Because tomorrow night you'll be up here again. I know you too well.'

'Maybe if people were considerate enough to stop killing each other, I might not need to be.'

'But then you'd find something else, wouldn't you? It's in your nature.'

He gave a defeated smile, shut down his laptop and followed her to bed.

30

Monday 3 October 2022

Paul Anthony knew that in ancient Greek mythology, Sleep was the twin brother of Death. He also knew from previous research that most hospital deaths occurred between 3 and 4 a.m. The theory, to which he subscribed, was stress caused by the body starting to prepare for the day ahead but the brain having not yet let go of all the angst from the previous day. Creating a perfect internal storm for anyone with weakened resistance.

It was a time of day he had always loved, ever since childhood. Particularly in the summer months, when as a small boy he would creep out into the garden as the dawn chorus began, armed with his catapult and a supply of ball bearings, to kill as many thrushes, sparrows, robins and any other winged creatures as he could before his parents woke.

It always amused him that his mother blamed the neighbour's cat for the dead birds she was constantly finding scattered around the garden. It amused him most of all that she never suspected him – that no one did.

And it amused him to kill.

And he could always justify it. Who was to say the life of a bird was worth more than the life of a worm it would eat, given the chance? Who made these value judgements? Stopping these vicious, savage worm-killers in their tracks gave him a real sense of community service.

Not to mention pleasure.

The kind of pleasure he was feeling now. Standing inside Professor Bill Llewellyn's fifth-floor office in the Cockcroft Building of Brighton University. He had his toolkit, not that he was expecting anyone to see him – there were only two lights on in the whole building. Well, three including this office. But there was something important in his toolkit – a slim yellow package he'd bought in a Boots pharmacy on Saturday.

The challenge facing him, and one he'd been pondering for many hours, was how to make sure which can of Diet Coke the professor drank first when he arrived in his office, in a few hours' time at 8.30 a.m., as Shannon had told him he did every single day. A creature of habit. Just like all those birds he used to shoot at dawn – those stupid things were creatures of habit too.

Being a creature of habit is always a good way to get killed. *Isn't it, Prof? A dead good way!*

He laughed out loud, but not too loud. Funny! God, sometimes he could be just so funny!

His first job was to swap the thin yellow pack in his toolbox with the one in the fridge. That done, he had the next and bigger challenge. How to ensure which can of Diet Coke Professor Bill Llewellyn drank first.

There were still eleven cans in the fridge, on the middle shelf. After a simple bit of rearrangement, there was just one can at the forefront, behind it the tub of Greek yoghurt and the pack of red grapes, and behind that the rest of the cans.

He slipped out of the office and the building, into the still-dark dawn, walked a quarter of a mile and crossed the road to the parade of shops at the foot of the Moulsecoomb estate, where he had left his inconspicuous Honda Jazz. He was smiling. Feeling good. The trap was baited.

31

'So how can I help you, gentlemen?' Lance Sharpus-Jones asked insouciantly. 'Detective Superintendent Grace and Detective Inspector Branson, if I've got your names right?'

The *Eloise III* crew member was a lot younger than Roy Grace had imagined – mid-twenties at the most. A public-school accent, a tanned *I know I'm cool* face beneath tight frizzy curls of straw-coloured hair, a puffa over a blue jumper, jeans and suede loafers, no socks. And plenty of attitude.

The relaxed way in which Sharpus-Jones sat opposite him and Glenn Branson, arms spread out across the backs of his chair and the one next to him, was a strong indicator to Grace of someone with nothing to hide. Nonetheless, he watched his eyes and body language carefully. 'What did you have for breakfast?' Grace asked.

The young man frowned, then laughed. But all Grace focused on was his eyes moving. They went left. He'd already seen, from the coffee that Sharpus-Jones was drinking, that he was right-handed. The eyes going left, in a right-handed person, meant they were going to the *memory* side of his brain, which indicated he might be telling the truth. If they'd gone right, to the *construct* side, it might indicate he was lying. Neither were foolproof but, along with other tell-tale signals of body language, in his experience they could be every bit as reliable as lie-detector tests.

'A banana and an espresso,' Sharpus-Jones said. 'All I had time for. Otherwise I'd have stopped at a workmen's cafe and had a full English.'

'What was the name of your first pet?' Grace continued.

He shook his head, bemused. 'Is this some kind of bank security question?'

'Did you have any pets, as a child?' Grace asked, ignoring him.

'Well, yes.'

'What was the name of your first one?'

He looked thoughtful for a moment, his eyes going left. 'I named him Dunce,' he said finally. 'A Jack Russell cross with something. The stupidest dog on the planet – and the best.'

Grace gave Branson a faint nod, which he picked up on.

'Lance,' Branson said. 'We appreciate you coming in. We'd like to ask you about the night that Rufus Rorke went overboard from the yacht *Eloise III*, as we understand you were the last person to see Mr Rorke alive.'

Lance Sharpus-Jones shook his head. 'Seriously? This is all being raked up again? I thought it had been put to bed a long time ago – at the inquest, which was, what, eighteen months ago?'

'Something has occurred that requires us to review the circumstances of Mr Rorke's disappearance off the yacht,' Grace said.

'Something – what exactly?'

'I'm afraid that's all I can say at this stage, Lance. Could you tell us again what happened that night?' Grace asked calmly, focused on his reply but also on his non-verbal cues.

He shrugged. 'Sure. The plan had been that after we were clear of Bridgetown harbour and on course for Grenada, I would take over on the bridge for a four-hour watch from Richard Le Quesne. But because of the rough sea state, and he's a very conscientious skipper, he stayed on at the helm. I was feeling a bit queasy – happens more than you'd think to a lot of yacht crew. I went to the stern to get some air and have a fag. As I stood there, suddenly

Mr Rorke appeared, still dressed as if for dinner in a white jacket. He lurched towards me, and as the yacht rolled, he crashed right into me. He was very apologetic – and he reeked of booze.'

He paused to sip some coffee. 'He stood leaning against the deck-rail and lit a fag himself, with some difficulty. The wind was strong and the boat was pitching and rolling crazily. I was about to go back inside, to give him privacy – we're under instruction only to talk to our guests if they instigate the conversation, when I heard him retching. I glanced at him leaning over the rail, looking like he was about to puke, then turned and walked away, out of politeness.'

He sipped more of his mug of coffee. 'I'd only gone a few steps when I heard a splash and scream for help. I turned and he just wasn't there. Vanished. Gone.'

Grace saw genuine distress in his face. Sharpus-Jones wasn't faking this.

'For a moment I couldn't believe it, I thought maybe he'd gone to the loo or something. But then I heard another cry from the sea just below me, and I realized he must have fallen overboard. I tried to see him, but it was ink black. I tried to remember the man-overboard procedure. Watch the spot, throw a lifebelt, shine a torch, then raise the alarm. I threw a lifebelt and a life raft into the water, grabbed a torch, but I couldn't spot him. I heard one more shout – cry – but it was faint. I ran up to the bridge and the captain immediately turned the yacht around, while I put out a mayday, then radioed the coastguard. I then woke all the other crew members, got them up on deck with flashlights, looking out.'

He sat for a moment, looking like a ghost, as the memory flooded back. His voice cracked. 'Oh God, I still wake up in the middle of the night, at least three times a week, wondering what I could have done differently that might have saved his life. I – I just – I—'

He was crying, Grace realized. He glanced at Branson, who gave him a nod. *Enough.*

After Sharpus-Jones had dabbed his eyes and calmed down, they thanked him, and told him they would be in touch if they needed anything more.

'You don't think I pushed him, do you, gentlemen?' he asked, looking scared suddenly.

'Did you push Rufus Rorke overboard, Lance?' Grace asked, locked on his eyes again.

The young man opened his arms expansively and grinned again.

'No, of course I didn't – why – why would I have done?'

'OK,' Grace said. 'Thank you, we're grateful to you for coming in. We don't think you pushed him, for one very simple reason. There is some evidence to indicate Rufus Rorke may not actually be dead.'

'No fucking way!'

'Anything you'd like to add to that?' Grace pressed.

'He went overboard. I'm one hundred per cent certain. As I said at the inquest, there is no way he could have still been on the yacht. And there is no way he could have survived in that sea. If he hadn't been drowned by the waves, he would have been taken by sharks – as, from what I've heard, the evidence of the remains of his jacket showed.' He was silent for a moment, then he asked, 'Out of interest, why are you bringing all this up again? What's making you think Mr Rorke is still alive? I'm telling you, man, there is no way he could have survived.'

'I'm afraid we can't tell you that, at this stage,' Grace said. 'All I can reiterate is evidence has come to light.'

Sharpus-Jones shook his head. 'If he's still alive, I'll eat my yachting cap.'

'I think we are done here,' Branson said, closing his investigator's notebook.

32

'My weekend? It was pretty shit actually, Alex, but thank you for asking,' Bill Llewellyn said as he locked up his bike. 'One of the worst weekends I've ever had, if you really want to know. But so kind of you to ask.'

The professor left an astonished Alex Petrovic, the youthful-looking head of the university's Digital Marketing team, busy padlocking his own bike, and strode angrily on towards the entrance to the Cockcroft Building, the events of the weekend preying on his mind. Out of the blue, his wife of twenty-seven years had told him she was thinking of leaving him because she suspected he was having an affair with one of his staff colleagues. It was untrue, of course, but he was now worried she might also know something about Shannon Kendall.

8.15 a.m. The first day of the autumn semester. Once, he'd have expected to see a throng of eager-beaver students pouring in through the door. But not any more, not these days. Most of the lazy bastards wouldn't be rocking up for at least another hour. There was just a handful outside the door, a few of them smoking or vaping. He pressed his card and the door slid open. He entered and made his way towards the lifts.

The shattering news from his wife made him realize he needed to sort out his shit. Particularly when he thought back to Shannon Kendall and the little trophy that he kept in his office fridge. It would not be good if that was found. He shoved it into a plastic bag and dumped it quickly into a communal bin in the corridor.

He sat down, back in his office, increasingly flustered and panicking. His mouth was dry. Parched. He needed a caffeine hit to think clearly.

He went to the fridge, opened the door, and took out the first can of Diet Coke he saw.

Then he dug the tip of his forefinger under the ring-pull.

33

Monday 3 October 2022

Glenn Branson opened the 8.30 a.m. briefing meeting, saying, 'Unusually in a murder inquiry, we are actually looking for proof of *life*.' He smiled and paused for emphasis before continuing. 'On account of the fact that our prime suspect in Operation Meadow is dead, and has been so for over two years.

'According to the findings of forensic gait analyst Professor Haydn Kelly, our suspect is a man known as – or perhaps who *used* to be known as – Rufus Rorke, whose funeral was held over two years ago. But there are two factors for us to consider here. The first being that it was a *no-body* funeral, and the second that I have found Haydn Kelly to be a reliable expert on the previous occasions when we have used his services. If Professor Kelly says this man in the supermarket is Rufus Rorke, then there's a good probability he is – certainly enough to take it very seriously. If we add to that the findings from JJ Jackson's Met Police Facial Recognition software and the school links from the association charts, then it is fairly compelling evidence.'

Will Glover spoke up. 'Sir, is it not possible this man in the Organica supermarket could be a twin – Rorke's twin?'

Branson shook his head. 'That's already been ruled out by the professor, Will. Our suspect walks with a limp, which the professor believes is likely to be the result of leg shortening following a fracture. It's highly unlikely an identical twin, even

162

if there is one, would have the same injury. But it's a good question to raise.'

The DC looked pleased with his praise.

Grace brought the team up to date on his conversations with the yacht captain, Richard Le Quesne, and with the crew member, Lance Sharpus-Jones.

'Sounds pretty convincing, boss,' Glenn Branson said. 'But do you think we should check them out further?'

Grace nodded. Branson then turned to the financial investigator, Emily Denyer. 'Emily, I'd like you to take a good look at the finances of Richard Le Quesne and Lance Sharpus-Jones. We need to see if either – or both – of them had any regular payments into their bank accounts. And if they could be traced back to Rorke – as bribes. An issue we will have is Bitcoins, which we know Rorke was very familiar with – and perhaps other cybercurrencies.'

'I discovered something last night, sir,' she said. 'Which may be significant. In the month before Rorke went overboard, he liquidated shares to the value of approximately £9 million, through the wealth management company Baker Stewart, of which he was a high-net-worth client. He then appears to have bought a number of speculative cybercurrencies that roughly equate to this amount.'

'For what reason, do you think, Emily?' Glenn Branson asked.

'There are different reasons people buy blockchain currency – cryptocurrency – sir. The legitimate one is investors speculating with it. Criminals use it because it's almost impossible to trace the transactions. Instead of the cash being held in a conventional bank account, where you have an account number and a sort code, you get a crypto-wallet – say a Bitcoin one, which can be between twenty-five and thirty-five alphanumeric digits long. That is where your money is, and that code is your only way of retrieving it. Lose the code and you've lost your money – for ever – there's no other way to retrieve it and no friendly bank manager you can speak to.'

Branson frowned. 'But that's crazy.'

Denyer shook her head. 'You and I might think so, sir. But if we wanted to hide transactions from the police then it's a brilliant way to do it. The only way I could see what Rufus Rorke has done with his nine million pounds of cryptocurrency is if I had the code. There is no bank manager I could speak to. No one. The codes are the only thing.'

'And where do you find those?' Branson asked.

'On his computer – or smart phone. That's the only way.'

'Presumably you haven't?'

'If he did go overboard from the yacht, the chances are his phone would have gone with him. If his crypto-wallet was on it, it could well be lost for good.'

'Nine million smackers?' Potting said.

'Yes, the lot.'

'A nice little haul for Davey Jones's locker,' Potting said.

'Meaning what, Norman?' Velvet Wilde challenged.

'Puts a whole new meaning on *money down the drain*, doesn't it?' he replied. 'I may not be as rich as Rufus Rorke but at least when I log on to check my bank balance, I don't get told all my money is at the bottom of the Caribbean Sea.'

'OK,' Grace said. 'Let's see if Le Quesne or Sharpus-Jones's bank accounts take us any further forward.'

Will Glover put his hand up. 'What about if either of them has a crypto-wallet? Which Emily cannot access?'

Potting butted in. 'In which cases, young William, we are Donald Ducked.'

This time everyone, including Grace, grinned.

'OK, I want you all to look at the screen,' Grace said, pressing a button on the remote control and turning to look himself.

It showed the blind man walking along crowded Western Road, heading east towards the Organica store, with the time log in the top right-hand corner. Then walking back from the store just over twenty minutes later.

'If I was blind,' commented Norman Potting, 'I wouldn't go out shopping in the middle of the day when it's all crowded. I'd go in the night, in darkness. Wouldn't make any difference, would it?'

'That's cruel, Norman,' Velvet Wilde said.

Grace ignored the handful of titters and glared at him. 'Not very helpful, but thank you for the tip, Norman.'

'Always, chief,' he replied cheekily.

Addressing the team, Grace said, 'I sent this footage to Professor Kelly for analysis very early this morning, because I have a feeling this blind man is in disguise, and is in fact, as Norman calls him, our Phantom Mushroom Switcher.'

He went on to explain the blind man's disappearance from the screen, after he approached the entrance to Organica, and his reappearance twenty minutes later, after Barnie Wallace had emerged. Just as he paused the playback, his job phone buzzed with an incoming text. He glanced down at the screen. It was from JJ Jackson. It said, simply:

In haste, more later. It looks like the same person, but we're not 100%

Branson turned to Potting. 'Norman, I need you to drop everything else and go to the city CCTV in the Control Room – with Will. Get all the controllers in there looking for this blind man, tell them about the disguises and the way he walks. We need to track him, see if we can find where he starts and finishes in Brighton – or Hove. We've got over five hundred cameras covering the city, there can't be that many blind men with black Labradors.'

'Got to feel a bit sorry for the poor bastard, haven't you?' Norman Potting said.

'Sorry?' Jack Alexander asked.

Potting nodded. 'Bad enough being dead, but to be blind as well? That's a real bummer.'

34

Paul Anthony's right foot was tapping. A steady tap-tap-tap-tap-tap.

It did that when he was nervous. Anxious. And he was so anxious this morning that instead of his normal Armagnac and cigar with his double espresso, following his breakfast almond croissant he'd had a second Armagnac and was now contemplating a third.

Waiting. Staring out at the grey sky, across the grey sea, at the wind farm. Today, those white spindles looked like skeletal arms rising from watery graves. He shuddered.

That was always the worst part of what he did. He baited the traps, then all he could do was wait. He was trying to remember a line in a Shakespeare play he'd seen once with his wife – *ex*-wife – *was* wife – *still is wife? Othello*, it was called. A big tall black guy was talking about a web, about snaring as great a fly as someone called Cassio with so small a web.

He smiled. Fly – wasp. A sign?

On his laptop he checked the *Argus* newspaper online. Stupid, he knew. It was only 8.45 a.m. Professor Bill Llewellyn would barely be in his office, barely opening his fridge, barely taking out his first can of Diet Coke of the day.

And perhaps his last.

But he needed to move on. He was working on a challenge that had come in. And unlike despatching Bill Llewellyn, this was a proper client. Paying full whack.

But, all the same, along with this tap-tap-tapping foot, he wondered, *Hey, Bill Llewellyn, how you doing this morning? Or should I call you Lechy Lew?* He smiled. He liked that.

35

Monday 3 October 2022

Bill Llewellyn wasn't actually doing that great. The professor was shivering and perspiring heavily. The weekend's events had really shaken him up.

He could barely hold the Diet Coke can, his hand was shaking so much. Trying desperately to think clearly, with his brain frozen like the way a computer screen freezes and needs rebooting. What if his wife did know about Shannon Kendall? What if she was thinking of reporting him to the university?

What did he have here he should destroy? Wipe from his computer? Oh Jesus.

His chest was pounding, crazily. It felt like a heavyweight boxing fight was happening inside it. Sapping his energy. He sat down in his chair, behind his desk. *Think, think, think.*

How would he explain about Shannon to Bethan? Thank God he'd now got rid of the trophy underwear. That had been smart.

Maybe if he just put on the charm and convinced her that what they had was worth fighting for, she might change her mind and not leave him. He must ring her immediately to try to save his marriage.

He reached over to his desk phone, tapped her number out on the keypad, giving himself a moment before picking up the handset and propping it between his shoulder and the side of his face. He needed caffeine – a shot of caffeine to jump-start his brain. He popped the ring-pull of the drink can, heard the hiss of escaping gas, and gulped down mouthfuls of the sweet-tasting nectar.

As the ringing tone started, he felt a sharp, burning pain in his mouth and then in his throat. Instantly the handset fell from his shoulder and he dropped the can, splashing him and everything around with cola. What? What had just happened? What on earth was in that can? A bee? A wasp? How? His panic levels rose.

Rivulets of perspiration were flooding down his forehead, stinging his eyes, half-blinding him. He managed to remove his glasses, dabbed his eyes with his handkerchief and looked around.

It took a few seconds for Llewellyn's near paralysed brain to process just what had happened. He stared ahead, his eyes wide. A new fear now began to grip him.

He could already feel his throat tightening, or was that his imagination? His pulse was racing. He made his way over to the fridge, side-stepping the puddle on the carpet and, feeling increasingly unsteady, almost fell over. He reached the fridge, grabbed the door handle, and for a moment stood, steadying himself. The tightening in his throat was increasing and he was having to work harder to breathe. He was wheezing. And feeling a little giddy.

He pulled open the door, reached for the top shelf of the fridge and pulled out the slim yellow package, six inches long, labelled EpiPen. With increasingly shaking hands and fumbling fingers, he managed to tear the package open, then with difficulty, his fingers reluctant to obey the instructions his brain sent them, he prised open the lid and took out the pen inside, letting all the packaging fall to the floor.

It was getting harder to breathe, his throat felt as though a steel ring was clamping it tighter and tighter. He tugged off the top of the pen, stabbed the needle end into his right thigh and pressed the plunger.

Nothing happened.

He frowned and pressed harder. Harder still.

'What?' he gasped. 'What – the—?'

The EpiPen was empty. They'd sold him a dud pen?

He staggered back towards his desk. Had to get to this desk, to his phone, to dial 999.

He was sort of – sort of swaying.

Spinning brain.

Spinning, a giddily spinning body.

Fighting for breath now.

Trying to focus.

That damned desk was ahead. Just a few feet in front of him. He just had to reach it.

He stumbled to the right, then to the left. Almost at the desk now. He reached out both hands to grab the edge, to steady himself.

But he was too far from the edge. His hand flailed on empty air. Then he hit the carpet, face down, barely aware of the sticky wetness, and the partially flattened can of Diet Coke wedged uncomfortably under his right thigh.

As he lay there, he heard a disembodied voice. A female voice. Bethan's voice. 'Hello?' she was saying. 'Hello, who is this? Who is this please?'

She had a nice voice. He liked her voice.

He died listening to it.

36

Malling House, the Sussex Police HQ, was situated on the northern edge of Lewes, the county town of East Sussex. The sprawling campus, which also housed the HQ of the East Sussex Fire and Rescue Service, got its name from its crown jewel, the handsome and imposing eighteenth-century Queen Anne mansion that dominated the entrance and housed the top brass of both services.

Most of the rest of the buildings were bland and functional, except for the Control Room, an incongruously futuristic-looking, two-storey brick structure. The 999 call centre for the Police and Fire services for the county was located inside, as well as stations, of ten monitors each, showing CCTV footage from the 1,320 cameras located around the city of Brighton and Hove, and other key hotspots across the county, manned on a 24/7 shift rota.

Now, at midday on the first Monday in October, two of the three operators, along with Norman Potting and Will Glover, were focused on footage from the cameras in and around Western Road, Brighton, from just over three weeks ago, mid-afternoon, Saturday, 3 September. They were looking, among the teeming Saturday shopping crowds, old and young, smart and shabby, weird and even weirder, for a blind man in a white jacket, wearing large dark glasses and a peaked cap, with a black Labrador guide dog.

'Gottim!' Will Glover shouted suddenly. 'Camera 6!'

The CCTV operator, a diligent woman in her forties, now a wheelchair user after being knocked off her bike by a van driver ten years ago, instantly freeze-framed the image. It showed the blind man, with his dog, turning left a few blocks west of the Organica supermarket onto Preston Street, a road lined with restaurants that led down to the seafront.

'Click it forward!' Will urged.

She did so, but all that happened was the man and his dog disappeared from view.

'OK, he's heading for the seafront, what cameras do you have along there, Elaine, that might pick him up?' he asked.

'There's one either side of the bottom of Preston Street,' she said. 'Another, a quarter of a mile further along to the east, and one a similar distance to the west. Unless he vanishes into thin air, we'll pick him up.'

Allowing their target only a couple of minutes to reach the seafront, in case he had started to run, she then selected the recordings from both these cameras, found the correct time and date, then let them play on adjoining monitors. Monitor 1 showed east and Monitor 2 west.

Will watched both of them intently. He saw an androgenous man, his hair a kaleidoscope of primary colours, shoot past on an e-scooter. A drunk-looking female in a bride's rig, followed by a posse of similarly inebriated-looking hens wearing sashes. Two smart-suited Asian men arguing fiercely. A mother dragging a reluctant child along beside her.

No blind man and his dog.

After fifteen minutes, there was still no sighting of him.

Will went over to Norman Potting, who was studying all the CCTV footage from the same time but to the north of Organica, in case. He told him the findings.

'Disappeared into thin air, did he?' Potting retorted.

'It seems that way, sir,' Glover said.

Potting shook his head. 'Listen, sunshine, this isn't my first rodeo. If I've learned anything in over thirty years as a copper it's that nobody disappears into thin air, unless they're an illusionist called Derren Brown, right?'

Glover nodded, dubiously.

'A blind man and his dog turn left and head down Preston Street towards the seafront, then don't appear on any more CCTV cameras. Correct?' Potting said.

The DC nodded again.

'Right, so, in the absence of any UFO sightings around this time, it's safe to assume they've not been captured by aliens and spirited away to Planet Zog, wouldn't you say?'

'I would, yes, Norman.'

'So I'm all ears. Where are they?'

'I – I've no idea.'

'Oh yes you have. You want to be a detective, then you've got to have an idea. A hypothesis. So do you have one?'

'I do. The blind man turns into Preston Street and does not appear the other end. So perhaps he gets into a parked car somewhere along there, or in a road off – there is just one – and drives away.'

'A blind man gets into a parked car and drives off?'

'If he's faking being blind, then yes, and it seems probable from what Detective Superintendent Grace said that he is faking it. Instead of driving, he could have got into a taxi. Another hypothesis is that he lives somewhere down Preston Street or off it. It's a busy street of mostly restaurants. Some of them surely will have outward-facing CCTV cameras, and might give us something. I also have a further hypothesis.'

'Which is?' Potting encouraged him.

'That he went into a restaurant with his guide dog and had a meal. In which case we should be looking at the footage on the cameras at the bottom of the street over a much longer period after he entered it.'

'All good points,' Potting agreed. 'But you are overlooking one more thing.'

Glover gave him a puzzled look.

'Criminals can be crafty bastards. Often when they are being pursued they will turn and double back in the direction they came from. We need to check the footage along Western Road, either side of Preston Street, for at least two hours after he went in.'

'As well as any private cameras in Preston Street around then?'

'You're cottoning on. And we need to check the taxi companies. A driver would remember picking him and his dog up. We can do that while we're watching more footage. And then it's time for some shoe leather.'

'Shoe leather?' Will Glover asked.

'Good old-fashioned detective work,' Potting replied. 'It's not all about sitting on your jacksie watching television. We'll go door-knocking down Preston Street. See if we can find the black hole into a parallel universe our blind man went through.'

The DC frowned, then realized Potting was joking. It wasn't always easy to tell with him.

37

The row of ten run-down-looking lock-up garages Paul Anthony owned, where he had his office, were pretty much tucked away. They were situated a short distance north of the Shoreham Harbour main road, along a weed-strewn track between a modern furniture warehouse on one side and the rear of an equally modern industrial estate on the other. It was a tiny pocket of land that time, and the world, appeared to have forgotten.

He'd bought them from a man who restored classic race cars, who had moved his business to more prosperous premises near Goodwood, twenty-five miles to the west, but left behind his name. *Chris Snowdon Garages, Portslade* was the address.

Inside his office, accessed through a door to the left of the up-and-over – which was firmly sealed shut and airtight – was a plush, windowless world that belied the shabby exterior. Well insulated, air-conditioned and sound-proofed, with wall-to-wall carpeting and a Bang & Olufsen sound system.

A bank of six computer screens, each with its own dedicated server, sat above a wide desk, on which were a keyboard, mouse and a framed photograph of his twins, Robert and George. He sat for a moment, with a pang, staring at their mischievous faces beneath their messy blond fringes. Dressed in T-shirts, jeans and trainers, they were perched on one wing of his precious ice-blue Singer Porsche 911 Turbo. He missed the boys and he missed his cars too. One day he'd figure a way to get the cars back. The boys would be a bigger challenge. He might just have to accept their permanent loss and compensate by becoming their secret, mysterious benefactor.

The rest of the space was taken up by a sofa, a recliner armchair, a kitchenette with a quality coffee machine, a fridge-freezer, a well-stocked bar and a cigar humidor. There was also enough tinned, frozen and long-life food to enable him to stay here for six months, if not longer, in the event he needed to go to ground. Behind the sealed up-and-over door of the adjoining garage was an en-suite bedroom and bathroom. All in all, he thought, it wasn't a totally shit place for a dead man to have to hang out in.

He never used one computer and server for more than one job, destroying and replacing them straight after, to make it even harder for the police to track him down, if they were trying. Not that they had much of a chance as every email he sent, and every web search or instruction, was routed through twenty-two servers around the world, each with its own firewall to keep out prying electronic eyes. And many of those servers were located in countries that weren't exactly known for helping police – whether local or international – with their enquiries.

But despite all the high tech in here, at this moment Paul Anthony was peering at his phone, at the top stories of the online version of the *Argus* newspaper. Anxiously waiting for news of Professor Bill Llewellyn.

Right now, no news was bad news.

And there was no news. Plenty of news of other stuff: of Green MP Caroline Lucas and environmental issues; of a bunch of lowlife scum who had set fire to a homeless person in a churchyard; of a potential big-money purchase of a footballer by Brighton & Hove Albion.

No Professor Llewellyn.

It was 1 p.m. and he was getting impatient. Had it all gone

wrong? He took his lunch out of the fridge, a pastrami and Swiss on rye he'd bought earlier from a deli in Kemp Town and, because it amused him, a can of Diet Coke. As he popped the tab he raised the can. 'Cheers, Bill! Down the hatch, eh?'

He was planning to tell Shannon about the professor's demise and how he had done it. They would be bound together in conspiracy to murder – whether she liked it or not. It would be an end to that tiny bit of love, commitment, affection – whatever – that she always seemed to hold back. He would now have her loyalty and affection and adoration, one hundred per cent. They were now bound together, with the future all mapped out.

She had proven herself to be a fine wingman, great front of house for him. She was brilliant at taking care of the 3D printing of handguns – and orders were coming in at a decent rate. As well as screening their customers. Villains were fine, terrorists were not. If people didn't like his moral code they could fuck off. Terrorists could fuck off, anyway.

But at this moment he had a very much bigger fish to fry. Dermot Quince Bryson. Who the hell named their child *Quince*, for God's sake? Whatever, that wasn't his problem. Dermot Quince Bryson's ex-wife, Kimberley, was willing to pay one million pounds for him to be killed. And she was serious. And she had the means, as she had already demonstrated.

Five hundred thousand pounds' worth of Bitcoins had been deposited into his crypto-wallet three weeks ago.

And she was one sassy piece of work.

One of his requirements was to see each client's face before he agreed to take them on, but of course they could never see his. He always conducted this via an encrypted FaceTime meeting, in which he sat in semi-darkness, his face pixelated, and spoke through a voice modifier.

In this potentially very lucrative meeting, Kimberley Bryson had told Mr Oswald, as she knew him, everything about her husband she thought might be helpful. First and foremost of which was that Dermot Quince Bryson appeared to be a total shit. That, at any rate, was her press release. Did he believe her? Actually, yes. And even more so after meeting him. There were few things Paul Anthony liked less than unpleasant people who had made a fortune and then wanted to show the world how rich they were. It would all add to his pleasure in despatching him. And there was something else that would add to it even more, something that went back in his past . . . He broke off his thoughts mid-bite of his sandwich as the headline flashed up on his phone: BREAKING NEWS. BRIGHTON PROFESSOR FOUND DEAD IN OFFICE.

Paul Anthony froze for an instant. Then, his heart racing, he put the rest of the sandwich down on his desk and read on.

> University of Brighton Professor of Artificial Intelligence Bill Llewellyn, 53, was found dead in his fifth-floor office at Brighton University earlier this morning. The cause of his death is at present unknown, but Sussex Police have said they do not believe it to be suspicious and are not looking for anyone in connection with it.

He was halfway through reading the article when he was interrupted by a sharp knock on the door.

He frowned, momentarily on edge. No one ever came here, apart from one person. All his small amount of post, which was mostly utility bills, was delivered to a poste restante address. Instantly, he tapped the keyboard, to pull up the image from the concealed CCTV camera above the door. Moments later, he smiled with relief. But not joy.

38

Roy Grace sat at his desk, his lunch, a tuna and cucumber sandwich, lying in front of him in its unopened packaging. Glenn Branson sat opposite, crumbs from his massive blueberry muffin littering much of his side of the desk. Even more fell, like a snow flurry, as he took another bite and talked at the same time, but he didn't seem to notice. He glanced at his watch – it was just gone 2 p.m.

'You're looking a lot better, less bruised, but dare I say . . . a bit glum, matey?' Branson said.

Grace shook his head, then gave a wry smile. 'Got Cleo's uncle and auntie arriving for a few days – their annual visit to their nephew and niece.'

'Nice,' Branson said. Then sensing Grace's mood added, 'Nice – not?'

'He's eighty-seven, deaf as a post and refuses to wear a hearing aid because he says it makes him look old.'

'Aren't you entitled to look old when you're eighty-seven?'

'He's a stubborn bugger, and he knows everything – everything about everything.'

'Handy.'

'Not when you have to listen to how he would reform the police before, during and after every meal. He's a right pedant – used to be a building inspector and tells me everything that's wrong in our house.'

'And the auntie?'

'Five minutes with her ailments and doom-mongering and you're done.'

'Sounds like you're in for a party! Want to come and kip at our place? I owe you!'

'I wish.'

Focusing back on work, Branson said, 'So Norman and Will haven't found our blind man yet?'

Grace shook his head. 'They've got a ton of CCTV footage from premises along Preston Street, but no sign of our blind man and his dog. A few taxis, and a couple of illegally parked cars. They've put out an appeal to all local taxi firms, for drivers who might either have picked him and his dog up, or alternatively were in the vicinity of Preston Street around that time and might have picked him up on their dashcams. The *Argus* are going to show one of the CCTV images of our blind man and his dog walking along Western Road in tomorrow's print version, and it's going to go up online before then.'

Branson took another bite, delivering another flurry of crumbs onto the desk, oblivious to Grace's frown.

'You know you're eating pure sugar, don't you?' the detective superintendent said.

'Got blueberries in it – one of my five-a-day.'

'Dream on,' Grace said. 'Heart attack on a plate – or in your case, on my desk.'

'So you think your tuna sandwich is the healthier option? Know how much mercury and plastic is in that tuna? Did it say *sustainably caught* on the package? Because that's bollocks too.'

'Is there anything we can actually eat?' Grace asked with a smile. 'Eggs are bad, even free-range ones because they force hens to keep ovulating. Plants are sentient, according to the latest thinking, so it's cruel to eat them.'

'Muffins!' Branson said, with a triumphant grin and a final spray of crumbs.

'Of course. Shall we focus? I've got a meeting at half past with the ACC, who's anxious to know progress on Operation Meadow.'

Branson grinned and opened his arms expansively. 'All hail, Assistant Chief Constable Nigel Downing. Who's never done a day's honest coppering in his life! He was a Highways Planner, for God's sake, Roy! He's a seagull manager.'

'A what?'

'You've not heard the expression? *Seagull managers* are the ones who fly in, cause mayhem, crap all over everything, then fly away again.'

The ACC had been a so-called *Direct Entry* police officer. People brought in from outside the force, usually at middle-management level, to help bring a broader outlook into the police, and better management skills. Their introduction had long been a source of controversy within the force, but Grace's view was that, so long as they understood the limits of their actual operational policing expertise, there was a lot of value to the scheme. 'Yadda . . . yadda . . . yadda . . .' he said. 'We agree to disagree, Glenn, now focus!'

'I'm all ears.'

Grace, who always tried to keep his desk tidy, frowned again as his colleague leaned back in his chair and folded his arms behind his head, clearly having no intention of clearing up the mess on his desk. Ignoring his sandwich, although he was hungry, he said, 'Disappearing.'

'Disappearing? Natural selection?' Branson frowned.

He shook his head. 'I'm thinking about Rufus Rorke. Haydn Kelly is convinced he's both the man in the supermarket and that he's the blind man. So let's go with that for the moment. When you're in a court of law, smart barristers, for both the prosecution and defence, constantly bring up previous cases as setting legal precedents. I can think of a number of cases where villains have faked their own disappearance to avoid justice. One of the most famous was the MP John Stonehouse. He ended up with long sentences, right?'

'He did. So Rufus Rorke was declared dead after seemingly vanishing overboard from a yacht off the coast of Barbados, while on holiday with his wife. Yet he has now been positively identified by Haydn Kelly on two occasions. Kelly is an expert witness with a highly dependable track record. Could we have another John Stonehouse situation here? He faked his death on a beach in Miami and was found living in Australia with his mistress. Perhaps his Achilles heel was his love life?'

'So how do we find him?'

'I have an idea. Fancy a trip to Barbados?'

'Are you kidding?'

'Let's see if our Highways Planner buys it.'

39

Paul Anthony studied the image on the central one of the five monitors above his desk carefully. It showed the figure who had just rapped on the door standing huddled beneath an umbrella in the pelting rain. He continued to study it closely for a few seconds more, before feeling confident enough to walk over to the door.

He slid open the top and bottom bolts, and as he pulled the heavily reinforced door open he could smell the Jo Malone 'Peony and Blush Suede' she had worn for as long as he had known her, before he saw her. As always, to her credit, she had done such a good job on her disguise.

'Hi,' he said flatly, stepping aside to let her in.

'You all right?' she asked equally flatly, folding her umbrella and striding in like she owned the place – which in a sense she did. Well, part of it anyway.

She peeled off her hooded black sou'wester, then her peaked cap, handing them to Paul like he was a flunkey in a grand hotel.

'All good,' he answered, hanging up the sopping-wet garments. 'How are the boys?'

'Missing their dad.'

The same questions, the same answers. All that was different was the day of the week and the time that they met. Two people who hated each other, bonded by a common deceit and the love of everything money could buy. 'What are you doing here?' he asked.

'You'll find out in a minute.'

'Coffee?'

'And something stronger with it,' she said, flopping down theatrically on the wide sofa and placing her Chanel bag beside her, its gold chain lying like a small snake on the floor. 'Can you believe this weather?'

He poured them each a generous measure of Haig Club Blue and carried one glass over to her. As he strode back over to the coffee machine to make her usual – a double macchiato – he heard the pop of her handbag clasp, then the click of her Dupont lighter and, moments later, the first tantalizing, rich and sweet aroma of her Lambert and Butler reached him. So good he had to strongly resist the urge to ask her for one. Behind him the Gaggia spat and gurgled.

'So I think we have an interesting development,' she said.

He turned and saw her tap the end of her cigarette in the ashtray on the table beside her. 'Development?'

Fiona looked elegant and chic, as she always did, whether going to a charity ball or putting the bins out, when there were no domestic staff around to do it. Today she was in a white rollneck, with a horsey scarf around her neck, skinny ripped jeans and knee-high crocodile-skin boots that looked a million dollars – and had probably cost more, he thought with a wry smile. And, he had to admit, whatever it was she'd had when they'd first met and started dating, she still had, in spades.

Unless you knew her, he rued. Behind the visual facade was a seriously cold, unsexy personality. Obsessed with ageing – she was only thirty-six for God's sake – her preparations for bed took over half an hour, with unguent after unguent, climaxing with a face mask that made her look like she was auditioning for a role in a remake of *Scream*. Most of her days were taken up with gym, Pilates and mixing disgusting-looking vegan gunk for her supper. And yet she still ingested, daily, the best part of a pack of fags, as well as what doctors recommended as the weekly quota of alcohol units.

It was so different in those early hedonistic days when he'd fallen in love with this wild, rebellious, posh bird from a titled – if impoverished – family, who drank, ate and snorted everything that came her way. On their very first date, she'd looked him in the eye and said, '*Rufus, if it's illegal, immoral or fattening, I want it!*' And, over the ensuing ten years, he'd done a great job of supplying everything that met those criteria. Although she'd always, somehow, kept her figure trim.

He walked across the floor, holding a perfectly made macchiato, handing it to the woman he had contemplated killing three years ago, before realizing she was more useful alive. He was stuck with her – probably for life. Just as she was stuck with him. Each bound by a secret they could never, ever tell.

He returned to his desk, sat down in his chair and spun it around to face her. 'So?' he asked. 'An interesting development?'

'Very. One you won't be pleased about.'

40

Jamming his sopping wet umbrella in the rack in the entrance hall of the main building, the original Malling House itself, Grace climbed the handsome staircase – which always smelled freshly polished – to the top floor, where the chief constable, deputy CC and the ACCs had their offices. It all felt very different to him, in a good way, ever since the arrest and departure of his nemesis, Assistant Chief Constable Cassian Pewe.

Being summoned to a meeting by Pewe had always felt like a scary summons to the headmaster's office, taking him right back to his early trembling schooldays. But no longer. Coming here was now as it should be – he was going to report to his senior officer and have a constructive discussion with him.

He rapped on the panelled door facing the top of the stairs, and heard the faintly gruff voice of ACC Downing call for him to come in. Stocky and muscular with a boxer's physique and short hair, he had a no-nonsense, straightforward air about him.

He stood and shook Grace's hand warmly, with a powerful grip. Then he frowned. 'Blimey, Roy, you've been in the wars.'

'It's a long story, sir, for another time,' Grace replied. Downing offered him tea or coffee, which he declined, then the ACC indicated for him to take a seat in one of the elegant chairs in front of his desk, and sat back down.

Grace reflected for an instant on the many past occasions he'd sat in this chair, getting a grilling from Cassian Pewe, sharp

186

but fair ACC Peter Rigg, and before him an antagonistic ACC, Alison Vosper.

Downing really was different, a breath of fresh air, in Grace's opinion. He had the sense that, having only been very recently promoted, replacing a temporary ACC who had gone on to an ACC role in another county, he was still feeling his way, as well as preferring to be a team player rather than superior boss.

The room was as grand as ever, with its fine view out over the front lawn and the gently sloping silhouette of the South Downs beyond, but it somehow felt lighter, airier, more welcoming.

Downing, jacket off, in his white shirt, with epaulettes bearing crossed tipstaves inside a laurel wreath, and black tie, smiled. 'So, Roy, the Chief is anxious for an update on Operation Meadow.' He spoke with a broad Scottish accent. 'People in the area are shunning mushrooms in shops and stores and market stalls, not helped by what the *Argus* and the *Sussex Express* and other people are saying – and there was an alarmist piece on the Danny Pike show on the radio this morning. Do you have any suspects – a prime suspect perhaps? Are you anywhere close to an arrest?'

These were the first questions Grace knew he would be asked; he'd been prepping for them on the short walk over, through the rain. 'At the moment, sir, our prime suspect is a dead man.'

Downing looked predictably puzzled. 'Would you like to elaborate?'

Grace told him all he knew so far.

'So a blind man is captured on CCTV walking with his guide dog towards the front entrance of the Organica supermarket and is not seen again for twenty minutes. During that same twenty minutes, a person in a hoodie and dark glasses is picked up on the supermarket's internal security cameras. This person leaves the store and vanishes into thin air, and then, hey presto! Our blind man and dog reappear. Is that about the size of it?'

'It is, sir, yes.'

'And you have opinions from the Met Facial Recognition Team, corroborated by the forensic gait analyst, that this person in the checkout queue and this blind man could be Rufus Rorke, who might not be so dead after all?'

'Yes, that's correct, sir.'

'Despite the convincing evidence that Rufus Rorke drowned at sea two years ago.'

'No body was ever recovered,' Grace replied.

'Remains of a jacket containing his DNA, as well as a distinctive pen his wife had given him, I understand? Bite marks on the fabric consistent with a shark attack? You've interviewed the yacht captain yourself as well as the crew member who was near him when he went overboard. Correct?'

'Correct, sir.'

'Is there any part of their stories you have doubts about?'

'Not their stories, no.'

'I've read the Barbados coroner's report – it's pretty conclusive,' the ACC said.

'It is a thorough report, sir. If indeed Rorke had been attacked by a shark in the water – and the remains of his jacket found by the fisherman is evidence of this – then his body would be unlikely to ever be recovered. But if we follow the science – and we have two separate areas of forensic science, Facial Recognition and Gait Analysis – both indicate that Rorke may indeed still be alive.'

Downing looked at him, puzzled. 'Are you saying the Barbados coroner is wrong, Roy?'

'Someone is wrong or someone is lying, sir. We know from past experience working with Professor Kelly that the way everyone walks is as unique as their DNA.'

'You're saying no two people have an identical way of walking, Roy?'

'That's right.'

Downing looked sceptical. 'I would say that's a bit of an exaggeration.'

'Not in my experience so far, sir, no. But even so, we have two other factors to add in – the Facial Recognition, and that shortly before Rorke disappeared, he was the prime suspect in Operation Stenographer, the investigation into the murder of lottery winner Pauline Ormonde.'

'I recall that case.'

Grace nodded. 'At the time, Rorke was on the National Crime Agency's radar as well as Europol's. It was suspected he was supplying 3D printed weapons, among a range of other services, via the dark web, and then he was linked to Mrs Ormonde's murder.' He paused to let this sink in before continuing. 'It was a very convenient time to disappear.'

Downing scratched the back of his neck. 'You've not convinced me yet, Roy, but I hear what you're saying.'

That was a lot more than he'd ever have got from Pewe, Grace thought.

'So, Roy, where do you take the investigation from here?'

'I intend to contact DC Carruthers, who is working undercover on the dark web, to follow up all this information and see where it takes us. I also would like your support to my decision to put twenty-four-hour surveillance on Rorke's "widow", Fiona.' He indicated quote marks with his fingers as he said the word *widow.*

Downing reacted with a predictable frown. 'That kind of surveillance is a big ask.'

'I know, sir. But I think we might have a John Stonehouse situation – that Rorke's disappearance might not be what it seems. Remember John Darwin? The man who faked his death by drowning after his canoe capsized – and later turned up in a photograph with his wife, Anne, in Panama? He was another one. It's worth exploring – to see if Fiona Rorke might just lead us to her husband. And if she doesn't perhaps their children might.'

To be effective, surveillance required three teams of eight people around the clock. Sussex Police only had capacity for a maximum of three such operations at the same time, and they were always in demand. As well as there being a major budget issue to contend with.

'And your rationale is?'

'From our intel, Rorke and his very posh wife had a pretty toxic relationship in the months before his apparent death.'

'So they went on an expensive, idyllic private cruise in an attempt to patch things up, perhaps?' Downing suggested.

'I have a different hypothesis, sir. Rufus Rorke and his wife shared a love of two things: money and their twin boys, but not in equal proportions. She loved money and he loved the boys. From what I've learned about Fiona Rorke, money was the number-one priority, the children came second. If her husband had been arrested – and subsequently convicted – she would have potentially faced losing all the wealth she enjoyed, under the Proceeds of Crime Act. So my hypothesis is that they hatched a plan to fake his disappearance.'

'And all this is based on the findings of your forensic gait analyst and the Met Facial Recognition Team?'

'So far, but I need more, sir. Which is why I want you to sanction flying one of my team to Barbados to interview the fisherman, John Baker, who found the remains of Rorke's jacket.'

'What do you think one of your officers will get from this Mr Baker that the Barbados Police and coroner failed to get?'

'The truth,' Grace said, levelly.

'What reason would the fisherman have to lie?'

'My dad was a deep-sea fisherman for a few years after retiring from Brighton Police. I used to go out with him and know from experience the ocean is a very big place. The word is that Rorke allegedly went overboard in the early hours of the morning, in a force seven gale, five miles off the coast of Barbados. He's attacked by a shark, which rips an arm and part of the shoulder off his white dinner jacket. Two days later, the rest of the jacket winds itself around one of the ropes of a fishing net, a few nautical miles from the yacht's known position at the time Rorke went overboard. The probability of that jacket wrapping around that rope is infinitesimally small, even if John Baker happened to be fishing in the vicinity of where Rorke went overboard. But there's something that bothers me even more – something I've been thinking about a lot that I don't think anyone has properly considered.'

'Which is?' Downing asked.

'I don't know about you, sir, but, if I fell off the back of a yacht into the oggin and I was wearing a jacket, that jacket would severely restrict me from swimming. I'd want to get it off, along with my shoes, as quickly as possible.'

'What about if the shark attacked him almost immediately, before he'd had the chance to remove it?' the ACC posited.

'That gives me another problem. So the shark bites off his arm and part of his shoulder – even if it didn't touch him again, those injuries would be fatal, he'd bleed out very quickly and lose consciousness almost instantly.'

'I agree.'

'Is he really going to take his jacket off before he does lose consciousness? Bearing in mind he's now in agony, being tossed around in a raging sea? I don't think so.'

Downing was staring at him and Grace could see the penny had dropped. 'You're saying how can the jacket have come off his body?'

'Exactly, sir. He would either have suffered more bites from the shark, or passed out and died from loss of blood, or drowned first. So how did the jacket come away from his body? Surely it would have gone down with him.'

Downing nodded. 'How do you explain the blood on the jacket?'

Grace smiled. 'I can't – maybe John Baker can.'

'If he's not told the Barbados Police, why would he tell one of your team?'

Grace smiled again. 'Maybe they didn't ask him the right questions. I know someone on my team who will – and has the best chance of getting honest answers.'

The ACC nodded slowly. 'I see where you're coming from, Roy. But it's still a big ask.'

'I'm going to need you to trust me on this, sir.'

Nigel Downing stared at him for some moments. 'Do I have an option?'

'You can say no, sir.'

'And why would I want to do that?'

'So that you don't look an idiot if I'm wrong.'

Downing smiled back. 'So don't be wrong.'

41

'I said you wouldn't be pleased about it,' Fiona Rorke said, and pulled her cigarettes out of her handbag. The stub of the one she had just crushed out was still smouldering in the ashtray. She was nervous, he could tell. Her hands, with their exquisite nails, were shaking. She only chain-smoked when she was nervous.

'You always were good at understatement,' Paul Anthony retorted, standing up and walking over to his cocktail cabinet. He poured himself two fat fingers of Haig Club Blue then sat back down opposite her again, frowning. 'What the fuck?'

'What the fuck indeed, Rufus. What the fuck were you doing at Barnie Wallace's funeral? Are you mad?'

'Paying my respects.' He shrugged.

She lit her cigarette, inhaled deeply then blew an angry jet of smoke towards the ceiling. 'Showing your face there was completely crazy. Pure arrogance. There's two of us in this, right? We're partners here.' She glared at him and drew on the cigarette again.

She was right. They were partners. Reluctant partners who hated each other, held together by the bond of mutual greed.

When the police were closing in on him, because of his stupid error over the CCTV cameras on the Ormondes' house, Fiona was only too well aware that if he went down, she stood to lose a very large part of her lifestyle under a confiscation order. So despite the fact they had been in the early stages of divorcing, they'd struck their own kind of Faustian bargain.

She got to carry on living the moneyed life of luxury that she'd always considered her birthright. But the price was that she would forever have to conceal the truth – or face prison for being an accessory to murder, along with the loss of most of what she had. He reinvented himself in a new life, and the price for him was never seeing his sons again. Nor anyone else he had ever known or loved, although the latter wasn't important. The boys were. But not as important as evading prison.

'Seriously,' she said. 'Just what the hell were you thinking? When you jeopardize yourself you jeopardize both of us. I still don't think you've told me the truth about how Barnie sussed you. What did you do, turn up to an old boys' reunion dinner or something?'

He grinned and downed his whisky. 'Hey, come on, credit me with a bit more than that.' The smell of her cigarette was tantalizing him more and more. 'How's your wine, by the way?' he asked.

Fiona looked at him almost incredulously. 'You want to know about the wine at a time like this?'

'I always want to know about the wine.'

During their years together they had amassed a formidable collection of rare high-end Bordeaux and Burgundies, across many of the finest vintages of the last century. They were stored in the extensive cellars beneath the house where Fiona now lived, which had once been their shared home. She had always drunk heavily and when she was getting drunk she became reckless.

There had been too many occasions, each of them resulting in a row, when she had staggered down to the cellar to get a second bottle of wine, and without considering the value of the bottle, grabbed something rare and popped the cork. One memorable night he'd been out and when he arrived home around 11 p.m. he was greeted by her, sitting on the sofa in front of the television, totally sloshed, an almost empty bottle of red wine on the coffee table, telling him in a slurred voice that the wine was crap and she'd almost choked on a mouthful of sediment.

The bottle was one of their most prized, a 1947 Cheval Blanc, considered one the world's finest wines and possibly the finest vintage year ever. It was worth £14,000.

'The wine is very happy,' she said. 'I take it for walks with the dogs, and it enjoys that.' She drained her glass of whisky.

'Very funny.'

'It's a very funny question you asked, Rufus, when we have such a big fucking problem.' She shook her head, tossing her blonde hair disdainfully. 'You and I loved watching true crime on television. Don't you remember – and we didn't just hear it once but many times – detectives talking about how they would turn up to the funerals of murder victims, in order to study the mourners, because the killers sometimes went along to watch.'

'I remember that well, Fi.' Then he hesitated. That had always been his pet-name for her. Was the hit of whisky making him affectionate? There was no hint of affection in the way she was glaring at him. 'Barnie's funeral wasn't the funeral of a murder victim, it was a poor bastard who'd been a victim of mushroom poisoning.'

'All part of the nice, low-key service you offer your clients, eh?' she said with unveiled sarcasm, stubbing out the cigarette already down to the butt and delving in her bag for the pack again. 'The Sussex media has been all over it for the past week. Headlines screaming "The Phantom Mushroom Switcher".' She shook her head. 'Nice discreet job – not. I never realized I'd married a total fuckwit.'

'Hey! That's not fair. It would have been fine if that idiot woman golfer hadn't gone and picked those damned death caps. It would have been a perfect murder. She's the fuckwit here.'

'What are you going to do about Taylor?'

'I'm on it.'

She lit her cigarette. 'You are? Do you call turning up to Barnie's funeral being *on it*?'

She blew more smoke at the ceiling.

God, he wanted to cadge one from her. But that would have been a show of weakness. 'You forget, I look very different now, unrecognizable.'

She stared at him with a look almost of pity, as if she was watching a pleading puppy in an animal rehoming centre. 'You and James Taylor go back to what age? Eleven?'

'About that.'

'At Brighton College until eighteen?'

He nodded.

'I'd recognize my best friends regardless of what they did to their faces or hair. After we've known someone even a short while, we don't look at their features or notice their hair. It's their mannerisms – how they move, all the little subtle nuances. That's what we clock.' She took another drag. 'You were presumably in disguise at the funeral?'

'Of course.'

'So James Taylor *might* have thought it was you but there was no way he could have been completely sure, without actually going up to you and talking to you.'

The rich, sweet smell of her cigarette was driving him nuts. 'Can I cadge one of those off you?' he asked, finally.

'Buy your own, you tight bastard,' she said.

He gave her a bemused grin. 'Hey, come on, Fi!'

'It's *Fiona*, to you.' She clipped her handbag shut, as if to show him she meant it. 'You know what you are? You're a twat.'

That really stung. Paul Anthony felt his cheeks redden. *Twat.* No one had ever called him a twat before in his entire life. Until now. Anger flared inside him. Anger fuelled by guilt, because she was right, it had been incredibly stupid to go to the funeral.

'You've put us both in danger. Now there's only one thing you can do. Understand what I'm saying?'

He hesitated. 'I think so.'

She shook her head. 'Do you? Really? You and your Three Musketeers bullshit. *All for one and one for all.* Barnie had cottoned on to you and was threatening to blackmail you, and you got rid of him. What's your plan with James Taylor? Are you going to let him keep sniffing around?'

'No, of course not.'

'So what are you going to do?'

'I told you, I'm on it. I'm thinking about it.'

'You don't need to think about it, Rufus. You know exactly what you have to do.'

42

Gloom descended on Roy Grace the moment he rounded the final bend in the cart-track driveway to their cottage, and saw the ectoplasm-green Prius, with the disabled sticker on the wind-screen, parked behind Cleo's Audi.

He had once been given a tour of the Old Bailey. He was taken along a passageway below the courts that led to the cell where, in former times, a convict who had received the death penalty would be held for his or her final days. The passageway grew narrower and narrower as the condemned person approached the cell – a symbol that there was no going back.

That was how he felt now as he approached the front door of his home, much earlier than usual, at Cleo's request, so they could have a meal together with her uncle and aunt on the first night of their stay.

Maurice and Eileen Morey were very particular about eating at precisely 6 p.m. every evening, because they had read it was healthy. Roy Grace, who rarely even got home before 7 p.m. on a good night, reckoned, uncharitably, it was so that the pair of them, who were verging on morbidly obese, could fit in a second snack – biscuits and cheese or cake – before retiring to bed.

Normally he loved coming home and into their cosy – if higgledy-piggledy – cottage in the middle of farmland, eight miles north of Brighton. But the sight of Maurice and Eileen lounging back on the sofa, and the sound of her moaning Brummie voice, made him wish for his job phone to ring, summoning him out on a new murder investigation. But at least there was the smell of something good cooking.

'I mean, when did you last buy cod, Cleo? And as for haddock, well, the price is crazy now.'

'Have you tried pollock, Auntie?' Cleo said.

'I wouldn't give pollock to me cat.'

Grace, who'd always had a professional interest in regional accents, knew that the Birmingham accent had evolved during the Industrial Revolution, when that city had become a major centre for metalworking. There was even a theory that factory employees were forced to speak in a whine so that they could be heard above the howl and grinding of machinery. Now it served for Eileen to make herself heard above the almost deafening volume of the television.

Maurice, dressed in what looked like hand-me-downs, was lounging back, looking like a badly stuffed scarecrow, holding the remote in one hand and a glass of beer in the other. While the television was on at near maximum volume, one glance at him told Grace he wasn't understanding much of it.

'Hi, Maurice!' Grace greeted him. There was no reaction until he shouted even louder.

He received a warm beam of recognition for his efforts. 'Roy! Eee-up lad!' He raised his glass. 'Helped myself to a beer, hope you don't mind?'

Maurice and Cleo's father, Charles, were chalk and cheese. Charles, who was in his late sixties, was a successful businessman, urbane and great company. Likewise, her mother was an elegant, smart lady, interested in all and everything.

'I'm good, lovely to have you both here,' he lied.

Maurice looked at him with a puzzled expression. 'What you say?'

'LOVELY TO HAVE YOU HERE!'

The old man patted his chest, then shook his head. 'Not good, the old ticker. Still, I'm here, eh?'

'You look pretty robust to me.'

Maurice stared ahead at the television, not hearing him, then turned back. 'Tell you something, Roy. When I was deputy chief planning officer in Leeds I'd never have passed a staircase like yours here.' He shook his head. 'Too steep, and that handrail – that just wouldn't do.'

'That's too bad,' Grace replied.

'What did you say?'

Grace shook his head then turned to Cleo's aunt, encased in voluminous folds of what appeared to be repurposed curtains, with steel-grey hair that looked like she'd ironed it herself. 'Hi, Eileen, how was your journey?' He bent down to give her the approximation of a kiss and noticed the fusty smell of mothballs.

'Dreadful,' she said. 'We had to stop to charge the car and there was only one charger working – and someone was on it. Two hours we had to wait. You know how much the electricity costs on the motorways? It's robbery. And I was just telling Cleo about the price of fish – can you believe how expensive it is now?'

'Somebody at work was telling me they do great value prawns at Lidl,' he replied.

Eileen didn't react.

Cleo had once referred to her uncle and aunt as *mood hoovers* and she was right, Grace thought. He just wanted to be anywhere but in this room with them. Giving them all a cheery smile he said, 'Just going to nip upstairs and say goodnight to the kids, and get out of this suit.'

Sensing his awkwardness, Cleo said, 'I'll get you a drink, darling – what would you like?'

He shook his head. 'Just something soft, I'm on call this week.'

As he climbed the stairs, he heard Eileen's moan about something else over the sound of the news.

He ducked into their bedroom, closed the door and called Jamie Carruthers. The DC answered almost immediately. 'Good evening, sir.'

'Jamie, could you take another close look to see if anything pops up on the trade in 3D guns in the Brighton area – particularly linked to the name Rufus Rorke or any alias he may be using. And, also, could you run a check for anyone on the dark web using the terms *accidental death* or *no police investigation.*'

'Absolutely, sir.'

'I take it you've not made any significant progress re contract killers?'

'Not yet, but we are following up one possible lead of someone trying to recruit a killer on the dark web. But,' he cautioned, 'we do come across these regularly and mostly they don't lead to anything.'

Grace thanked him and asked him to keep him posted. Ending the call, he changed into casual clothes then went to say goodnight to his children, staying with them for a good long time, much preferring the sound of Molly sleeping to the drone of Maurice and Eileen's voices.

43

Monday 3 October 2022

Three painful hours later, as they stood in the bathroom, Grace squeezing toothpaste onto his electric brush, Cleo said, 'I'm sorry to inflict them on you. You're very patient with them.'

'I am?'

'You are.'

He shrugged. 'Family is important. You're lucky to have so many relatives still alive. Make sure you ask them everything you could ever think of that you might want to know one day – because when they're gone, all their knowledge is gone too.'

'Sound advice as always, my fearless detective!' She kissed him on the cheek. 'So how was your day – before you arrived home and it all went south?'

Grinning, he replied, 'It was fine. Yours?'

'A bit sad, actually. We had a professor from Brighton Uni who died of anaphylactic shock – possibly from a wasp sting. You know, it's strange how things go in cycles.'

'Cycles?'

She nodded. 'We have weeks – months – when all the victims brought into the mortuary are sudden deaths from heart attacks, strokes, falls, road traffic accidents. Then in the space of less than a month we have two fatal mushroom poisonings and now a wasp sting – which is a kind of poisoning too. At least two of them accidental.'

'There's nothing accidental about Barnie Wallace's death,' he said.

'Have you made any progress?'

He yawned. 'I think we might have done.'

When he'd brushed his teeth, he padded out in his dressing gown to check on Noah and Molly, then stood for some moments, reflecting on what Cleo had just said.

At least two of them accidental.

He went back into the bedroom and closed the door. Cleo was already curled up beneath the sheets, her bedside light off – unusual, because she normally filled in her five-year diary then read for a while. Probably she was exhausted by their house guests, he thought, as he climbed into bed, kissed her, then lay back against the pillow, suddenly feeling very wide awake.

At least two of them accidental.

Lottery winner Pauline Ormonde's death, in a fall down her stairs, had been seemingly accidental. Until CCTV footage of Rufus Rorke approaching her house had emerged. There were two prior cases of apparent accidental deaths possibly linked to Rorke that Operation Stenographer had uncovered. One was a wealthy man who'd been having an affair, who'd fallen to his death from the balcony of his Kemp Town apartment while his wife was sunning herself in Majorca.

The other was a retired postman, whose refusal to sell his central Brighton cottage was blocking a development of over two hundred townhouses from taking place. He'd been knocked down and killed cycling home from his local pub, in a hit-and-run that was never solved.

After Rorke's death, with their resources stretched, the police had not pursued either as there had seemed no chance of a conviction. Grace made a mental note to look at the files again in the morning.

44

James Taylor had been thinking about Debbie constantly since their lunch on Saturday. She was under his skin in a way no one had been since those early days when he'd first met Marianne and had been smitten with her.

He felt the same about Debbie now. But he was also unable to stop thinking about Rufus, and what Debbie had said. Could Rufus have killed Barnie?

His apartment was on the seventh floor of a modern complex in the Bayside in Worthing. He had views to the east of the coastline of Brighton and Hove, and straight ahead across the English Channel to the geometric layout of the Rampion wind farm.

Right now he was focused on a layout of his own on the bed in the spare room. His *flat lay* – his running kit for the Chicago Marathon next Sunday. He had only been in this apartment for two months, and the sea views, especially on this glorious day, continually distracted him. To the east he could see the whole of the Brighton coastline and the cliffs of the Seven Sisters beyond. And as he stared once again out at the wind farm, to the south, he had no idea he shared this same view with Paul Anthony, just eleven miles east of him along the coast.

The weather forecast for Chicago was, unhelpfully, anything from eight degrees to the mid to high twenties. It might be sunny, it might be raining. It would probably be windy. One of the forecasts he'd looked at online had even predicted sleet. He looked

204

down at his orange running cap, his top – a sleeveless vest – and his lightweight shorts, his socks, his state-of-the-art trainers that had received a rave review in the latest edition of *Runner's World*, and his supply of nutrition gels. And finally, reluctantly, at his body-worn water supply, which he had just read was banned in US marathons as a terrorist risk ever since the Boston bombings. He was going to have to leave it behind.

He smiled wryly. During his days as an easyJet pilot, airport security had been one of the banes of his life. He remembered one occasion, a decade or so ago, when a particularly jobsworth security officer at Gatwick had removed a metal fork from his carry-on bag and confiscated it. He'd had a stand-up row with the man, shouting did he really think if he was going to attack someone in his own plane he would use this small fork rather than the heavy-duty axe that was part of the equipment in his cockpit?

He glanced at his Garmin sports watch. He would need to leave here in two hours to arrive at Heathrow in good time for his 15.35 flight. Four days there would give him just about enough time to adjust to the time zone. Chicago was six hours behind UK time. Rule of thumb was it took a day for each hour to get over jetlag. But, from his years of experience flying long-haul for easyJet, he reckoned it took four days, max. For sure, if you were in the better-quality air at the front end of the aeroplane, which was why he was flying Business Class today, as always.

And after Chicago, he was off to a few days of luxury at Barbados's best hotel, Sandy Lane – courtesy of his boss. Not that he would be spending all his days there sunning his tum – he was a man on a mission. A very specific mission.

45

Tuesday 4 October 2022

So, OK, it wasn't the screaming front-page splash Paul Anthony had been hoping for, it was buried away on page 9 of the *Argus*, but at least there were several column inches and a photograph.

SUSSEX AI PROFESSOR KILLED BY WASP STING.

Accompanying the article was a head-and-shoulders photograph of Professor Bill Llewellyn in a mortar board and black gown.

He settled down to read the short piece. According to the post-mortem, Llewellyn had died from anaphylactic shock after being stung by a wasp. The highly respected professor knew he was dangerously allergic to wasp stings and always kept an EpiPen in his office, but despite having used it, he was pronounced dead on arrival at the Royal Sussex County Hospital yesterday morning.

The article ticked all the boxes. And what mattered most of all was that the professor was dead and there was, seemingly, no hint of suspicion about his death.

Shannon should be more than pleased! He would invite her to dinner tonight to celebrate. And to suggest that they were now bound together by a deadly secret.

He messaged her, suggesting dinner at Tosca in Shoreham, again. He liked the food there and especially the long narrow layout. It was a restaurant where it would not be easy to recognize someone, particularly at his regular table in the rear, and in

Shoreham, a few miles west of Brighton, it was less likely he would be spotted by anyone who might have once known him.

She messaged back almost instantly. 'Sounds good.'

Clearly, she hadn't yet read or heard the news, unless she was just being discreet. He would tell her later, and then they would celebrate with a glass of Champagne. Or two. Maybe more.

Meanwhile, he had business to attend to.

Three handguns to print, and James Taylor and Dermot Quince Bryson's deaths to arrange. Bryson had made the mistake – not dissimilar to himself, Paul Anthony reflected – of marrying an utterly ruthless woman and then dumping her in favour of a younger model.

In one of those bizarre – happy – coincidences that no one could have made up, Shannon had reported that Dermot Bryson reached out quite independently, wanting to buy an untraceable 3D printed handgun. Paul Anthony prided himself on his research, he liked to know everything he possibly could about his victims. Dermot Bryson could not have made it easier for him. Loud, misogynist, racist, homophobic, arrogant and massively boastful, he'd made a point, on the first occasion they'd met online, of showing him the £300,000 Richard Mille wristwatch he wore. And only a few minutes into that first meeting Bryson had tried to buy into his business.

It was going to be a real pleasure arranging his accidental death. But one thing Paul Anthony had learned, and something that had become a strict rule, was never to rush a job. When an approach was made to him over the dark web to kill someone in a hurry, he advised them to try elsewhere.

Masterpieces were seldom painted in twenty-four hours. And he prided himself that the tragic accidental deaths of his clients were all masterpieces.

Dermot Bryson's death would truly be one.

Paul Anthony was going to deploy a method of killing he had

first read of in a comic when he had been eight years old – something that had captured his imagination, as well as setting him
with a challenge he could not resist.

It was Dermot Bryson's passion for fast cars that made him
the ideal subject – or should that be *muse*?

Muse.

He liked that word. All his victims were his muses. Oh yes!
Barnie had been one. And now James Taylor was on the cards to
be another. What was that Agatha Christie novel? *And Then There
Were None.*

Boo hoo.

Fiona's words yesterday afternoon had been echoing in his mind.

'*You don't need to think about it, Rufus. You know exactly what
you have to do.*'

Of the three of them at school, James Taylor had always been
the straight bat. Barnie was the wild card – he'd always considered
him a harmless loser, until the day he'd turned up at his front
door, desperate and threatening blackmail.

He tried to focus, but the spectre of James Taylor descended
again, clouding his mood and fogging his thoughts. He tore
abstractedly at the skin of his right thumb with his teeth. Fiona
had been right yesterday, of course she had been, just as she
always was, and that hurt.

He shouldn't have gone to the funeral. But it had been such
fun!

And, thinking it through, he wondered how much danger,
actually, could Taylor be? He was a very different character to
Barnie. Barnie had been a desperate man. Somehow – and he
never thought he would have had the brains – Barnie had
tracked him down, just a couple of months ago, through a dealer
in classic Porsche cars. A company called Paragon, through
which Paul Anthony had bought several of his prized collection
in his former life. He had been unable to resist visiting them a

year ago, partly to test out his change of appearance – and it had worked. No one, not even the boss, Mark Sumpter, had recognized him.

But, somehow, Barnie had found him through that slender connection. He'd turned up again recently at his Kemp Town apartment one morning, desperate for money and threatening to blackmail him. It turned out that Barnie had been following him for some months and taken a ton of pictures of him, all smugly uploaded to the Cloud.

Barnie would settle, he told Paul Anthony, for £50k, promising that would be the end of it.

But he knew Barnie too well. The man was a weasel and that would never have been the end of it. The only end of it would be the day Barnie was inside a coffin. And, if he was honest with himself, that was part of the reason he had taken the risk of going to his funeral. To see for himself that the little shit was in that box, and wasn't coming back out.

He'd not expected so many other mourners to be there. Who the fuck was going to mourn that loser, Barnie Wallace? Were most of them, other than Taylor and a handful of close relatives, there for the same reason as him? To celebrate? He was reminded suddenly of the story he'd heard about the funeral of Hollywood legend and tyrant Harry Kohn, the founder of Columbia Pictures: that the reason so many people had turned up was to make sure he was really dead.

Taylor was a different animal.

With Barnie, he knew right away what he wanted – paying off. Barnie was always coming up with money-making schemes at school, none of which worked. But Taylor had never been motiv-ated by money, right back in their early schooldays. He was the *decent* one of the Three Musketeers, the *honourable* one, almost the *goody-two-shoes*. So what on earth was he doing going and interrogating Fiona?

The last time he'd met him, some years ago, he was an easyJet pilot, respectable, married with a young son, seemingly set up for life. They hadn't seen each other for several years. Jamesy gave him a great eulogy at his funeral. So what was his interest now in digging around into something that was no concern of his?

Because he had recognized him in church?

How?

Maybe Fiona was right.

One thing was certain. There was no way he was going to risk Taylor exposing him. If his old school friend continued to bugger about, asking questions, telling people, like he'd told Fiona, that he'd seen Rufus Rorke at a funeral, he would kill him. James might think they'd once been good friends but the truth was he'd never actually cared that much for him. He'd actually always liked loser Barnie more than Taylor. He'd been almost sorry to have despatched Barnie. He really wouldn't feel any emotion at all if he had to kill goody-two-shoes Taylor.

One of the tasks he would give to Shannon would be to find out everything she could about him. Strengths and weaknesses. And the best way to kill him – making it appear an accident, of course. In fact, the way James was acting at the moment, making him look stupid to Fiona, killing him would be a pleasure.

He was a private pilot these days. Small planes crashed frequently. Pilot error, mechanical error, whatever. If he got any nosier, it would be *goodnight, Jamesy*. Wouldn't be too hard to arrange.

But, in the meantime, Taylor was a sideshow. He needed to focus on the current main event. And suddenly, he felt hungry. The thought of killing Taylor, he realized, had given him an appetite for breakfast.

That had to be a sign.

46

Roy Grace woke as usual, shortly after 5 a.m., and the first thing he did was check the recently instigated Chief Officer's Briefing Sheet, which gave a summary of the day ahead – including who the duty SIO, gold and tactical commanders were, all serious incidents that had happened overnight, as well as sudden deaths of apparently healthy people during the past twenty-four hours. The professor at Brighton University who had died from an apparent wasp sting was listed.

Then he took Humphrey for a run across the Downs at 5.30 a.m., during which he reflected on what Cleo had told him the previous night. About the professor who had died from a wasp sting. On top of the recent death of the golf captain who had died from eating death cap mushrooms. Like Barnie Wallace.

Accidental deaths happened all the time. He had long been aware that next to being in a car or on a motorbike, the second most dangerous place in the world – the place where you were most likely to die – was in your kitchen. The seemingly harmless domestic kitchen quietly hosted a litany of things that could kill you – fires, treacherously slippery floors, wonky stepladders, dodgy electrics, gas leaks, choking, toxic chemicals including bleach, and potentially fatal bacteria like salmonella were among its deadly arsenal. Cleo had even had one tragic kitchen death when a young mother had leaned over to empty the dishwasher and was stabbed through the eye by a protruding boning knife.

So two fatal mushroom poisonings and a fatal wasp sting occurring within a couple of weeks of each other wouldn't ordinarily have struck anyone as suspicious, but it was the way Cleo had said it. She had good instincts for when something was wrong, and he could feel from the tone of her voice last night that she was uneasy.

And it echoed his own concerns.

Barnie Wallace and Rufus Rorke had both been at Brighton College school together. Rorke had 'died' over two years ago but was now possibly still alive. He'd been under suspicion of operating a service of creating fatalities and framing them as accidental, through the dark web. Now Barnie Wallace had died from a death that might have seemed 'accidental' had it not been for the CCTV in the Organica supermarket.

Was there history between the two of them?

He had been planning on a quick breakfast after showering when he got back, and being at his desk by 7 a.m., where he would then dig a little deeper into all three of these deaths. But, he rued, as John Lennon said: *Life is the stuff that happens to you when you're busy making other plans.*

And in this case *life* was Cleo's aunt, already berthed at the breakfast bar at this early hour, dressed in what looked like a circus marquee suspended from her shoulders by straps.

'Good morning, Eileen!' he said breezily, standing at the bottom of the stairs. 'How did you sleep?'

'Morning, Roy. To be honest, I'd forgotten how noisy the countryside is. Sheep bleating in the night, then the cockerel, crowing. If it was mine I'd wring its neck and cook that bird.'

He had debated making a dash for his car but hesitated out of politeness.

It cost him an hour of his life he would never get back.

47

As a result, Roy Grace only just made it to the office in time for a slightly awkward meeting with Glenn Branson. He'd had to explain to his friend that due to the complexity of the investigation, he was taking over the SIO role. It was not a reflection on Glenn, but Roy's experience told him it was time to take charge. They went straight from this meeting to the morning briefing on Operation Meadow. Norman Potting and Will Glover informed the team they had made little progress in discovering how the blind man and his dog had seemingly disappeared down Preston Street.

But Glover had done something on his own initiative, which further reinforced Grace's view that the young DC had the potential to be a good detective. He had checked for any parking tickets that had been issued in Preston Street around the relevant time period. There were five, and he would be following up on these today, to see if any could take them further forward. There had been little progress from the other current lines of enquiry.

Grace thanked him and then said, 'We need to learn a great deal more about Barnie Wallace. As we know, that information may come from his electronic footprint.' He turned to Branson. 'What have we had back from Digital Forensics so far?'

'Nothing yet, boss. I spoke to Aiden – he said they're struggling with Barnie Wallace's laptop password, and the same with the phone. EJ went to see his girlfriend to see if she knew or not and doesn't reckon she does. Unless she's fibbing.'

Grace cursed, silently. Most people were lazy about their passwords, creating simple to remember ones, such as their date of birth. Digital Forensics had a raft of algorithms they used and could get into most computers and phones fairly easily. But if someone had a mind and know-how – not hard – to create something really difficult then sometimes, as he knew from bitter experience, it could take days, or weeks, or even much longer.

He had once seized a phone from a murder suspect that the Digital Forensics team had been running an encryption-busting program on for three years, so far, going through combinations to try to break the password, still without success. He shook his head angrily, still in a grumpy mood, he realized, from having any possible joy he might have woken up with sucked out of him by Cleo's aunt. 'Glenn, hello, this is a murder inquiry.' He felt restless.

'What do you want me to do, boss?'

He shook his head in frustration.

Finally, shortly after 9.30 a.m., Grace was able to settle at his desk. As was his routine, he scanned the reported or investigated overnight incidents in the county, then the pages of the *Argus*. He stopped when he reached the piece on Professor Bill Llewellyn and read it carefully. As soon as he had finished he called the number of the duty CID Inspector at Brighton police station – known by the moniker of Golf-99 – who would be out of the Daily Management Meeting by now.

The phone was picked up by DI Mick Warburton. 'Sir!' he said. It came out as a gasp, as if Grace was the sole mountaineer holding the rope from which the caller was dangling over a precipice.

'Mick, can you tell me anything about the death of Professor Bill Llewellyn at Brighton University, who died yesterday from anaphylactic shock? Is there anything that hasn't appeared in the media about this?'

'Apologies about my voice, sir – bit of pasty just went down the wrong way. Anything suspicious, is that what you're driving at?'

'Yes.'

Could Llewellyn have made enemies? Did this have any of the hallmarks of a Rufus Rorke accidental death?

From the information the Major Crime Team had accumulated on Rorke, immediately prior to his apparent death, he operated in the rarefied world of the seriously wealthy, charging a substantial fee. Professor Llewellyn's world was one of academia, he wasn't in that financial league.

'Your officers who attended found him dead, on the floor, with an EpiPen beside him. And they presumed anaphylactic shock?' Grace asked.

'It was confirmed by the post-mortem,' DI Warburton replied.

'I need you to recover that EpiPen, I want it forensically examined.'

'Well – yes, of course, sir, but it might be difficult. It might have been binned.'

Grace silently cursed the different worlds that normal police officers and Major Crime detectives inhabited. To him, everything was suspicious. Not so much to the average overworked, exhausted response coppers who were daily run ragged. 'It would be really helpful to find it if you can, Mick. OK?'

Ending the call, he immediately rang Emily Denyer, the financial investigator. He asked her to find out everything she could about Professor Llewellyn's finances.

Next, he entered a search on his computer for the two previous cases of seemingly accidental deaths that Rorke had possibly been linked to, nearly three years ago, which had emerged in Operation Stenographer. Grace noted down the key details and case references. Then he called Glenn Branson.

'No promises, mate, until I've got it sanctioned – how do you fancy a trip to Barbados?'

'You're kidding! My auntie came from there! You mean, like, all expenses paid for me and Siobhan? Two weeks in a fancy hotel?'

'Not exactly. I need someone to fly out and have a chat with a fisherman called John Baker.'

'I'm your man.'

'Of course you are.'

48

It was dark outside the restaurant window. Tonight was an ebb tide, the shimmering lights on the bitumen-black water of the Adur were steadily disappearing as the emptying river turned into a mudflat.

Flat.

That was how Paul Anthony felt at this moment. Flat as the Champagne now tasted. What the hell was wrong with the young woman sitting opposite him? He stared at her. Across the silence, across the table that now seemed as wide and dark as the river outside. Across their untouched starters, hers getting warm, his going cold.

He'd thought she would be so happy, be all over him. Instead she sat in silence, back to the window, looking as dark as the night outside behind her. She just sat, endlessly pushing a piece of mozzarella around the bowl with her fork, without raising a morsel to her mouth. She seemed at the moment like a total stranger.

Wasn't this what she had wanted? Had she forgotten their recent conversation? Because he sure as hell hadn't.

'*Could you shoot that bastard, Llewellyn? I'm not sure I could, however much I would like to,*' she had said.

'*What if I could produce someone who could?*'

'*You mean a hitman?*'

'*Exactly.*'

'*I don't think so, no. I guess that's not in my DNA. I don't think*

I could live with having paid someone to murder him, however much I hate him, however much I want him dead – or however much I'd like to cut his dick and balls off and shove them down his throat.'

'I don't know,' she said suddenly, quietly, so quietly it was almost a murmur. 'I – don't know.'

'He was a total bastard,' Paul Anthony prompted, the three grilled sardines on the plate in front of him untouched.

She continued staring at the piece of mozzarella on her fork, without answering. Seemingly deep in thought.

'Shannon?' he prompted.

She gave him a rather sad smile. She looked stunning tonight, he thought. She was wearing a simple black dress, a gold chain-link necklace, and the way she was wearing her blonde hair, long, falling either side of her face in twists, suited her so well. She reminded him more than a little of the actress Margot Robbie. So smart, so beautiful.

And yet tonight, so remote.

Suddenly, as if making a decision, she popped the piece of mozzarella in her mouth, followed by a slice of tomato and chewed that too. Then, decisively, she raised her Champagne glass and held it up. Paul Anthony raised his. They clinked.

He said, 'Louis, I think this is the beginning of a beautiful friendship.'

She smiled. A smile that melted him. '*Casablanca*?'

'Right.'

'My favourite movie. The only thing is, my name isn't Louis.'

'And mine isn't Lee Oswald.'

'Yeah, and maybe it isn't Paul Anthony, either,' she said sarcastically, unaware she was actually right about that one. 'Maybe this whole relationship isn't real. Maybe I'm not actually involved with someone who creates fatal *accidents*.' She stared hard at him. 'Do you know what I wish right now?'

'What do you wish?'

'I wish we could go back and change what has happened.' She tilted her head back, tossing some of her hair away from her face, revealing her long, slender neck. And at that moment, he was suddenly crazy with desire for her. He wanted to kiss that neck, wanted to hold her slender wrists in his arms, wanted to take her with him to the ends of the earth and back – as long as she stayed onside.

'Shannon, babes. That professor was a piece of scum, a pervert who deserved to die. You said so yourself.'

'Yes, but . . .' She was searching for the right words. 'I just wish you'd been clearer when you suggested what you were going to do.'

'I thought I was pretty damned clear. I thought you were onboard with it. Jesus, Shannon, the man *raped* you. And I'm sure others too. Did I tell you what I found hidden in his office – in his fridge of all places? The underwear?'

She nodded. 'You did.'

'That night you told me you'd been raped by Llewellyn, I asked you how you'd feel if he were to die an accidental death? Do you remember?'

She nodded slowly.

'Do you remember what you said?'

She was silent for a long time, before she nodded again. 'I do. I said I'd feel the world had been rid of one piece of vermin.'

'And now it has. So what's your problem?' He smiled gently.

'I don't know – I—' She fell silent again. 'I guess I didn't know how I would feel if he actually died.'

'And how do you feel?'

She frowned. 'I thought maybe I'd feel great.'

He smiled at her. 'So feel great!'

She looked at him for a long time. 'I guess – I guess – we can't change what's happened, we can only change how we react to it, right?'

'Right.'

'So, yes, he was a rapist and a pervert and a liar. So, maybe, good riddance.' She gave an uneasy smile. 'Maybe. Perhaps I'm just overreacting. Maybe I should treat it as an act of chivalry!'

'That's more like it! He was a piece of shit.'

'Be careful, Paul, I could pick up on a few of your faults too, you know,' she said teasingly.

Feeling the ice thawing, if not actually melting, he said, 'Well, nobody's perfect!'

'You're good on your movie quotes, aren't you? *Some Like It Hot*, right?'

'Very hot,' he said.

Her face broke into a smile and she winked at him, seductively. Then, as if it was the punchline of an inside joke only the two of them shared, she said, 'And maybe a little waspish.'

49

Roy Grace was trying to remember who it was who said, 'Guests are like fish. After three days they begin to smell.'

Sitting in his office at 6.45 a.m., after leaving home extra early to avoid being trapped by Eileen for a second morning, he googled the quote and saw it was attributed to Benjamin Franklin. Well, that Founding Father was wrong, Maurice and Eileen had begun to stink after just two days – but then, he reasoned mischievously, they hadn't arrived in the freshest of condition.

But hey, as his mum used to say: *There's nowt so queer as folk.*

Relieved that the unwelcome invasion was coming to an end today and that he and Cleo would have their home back, he applied himself to the follow-ups on the lines of enquiry he'd set for Op Meadow.

He was impressed that, overnight, an attachment had come in from Charlotte Mckee in Digital Forensics, accompanied by a note:

Sir, I'm working back from 'most recent' to oldest. Knowing the urgency of your investigation, I thought I should send you the first downloads from Barnie Wallace's phone that might be of interest. Attached are files containing photographs for the two weeks prior to his death.

Good news is he left his geotagging settings switched on. I think the latter might be worth focusing on, as Barnie

Wallace has only taken photographs of one subject during all this time. The subject seems a pretty busy person and the photographs seem to me to be clandestine, taken without the subject being aware, using the zoom lens. Let me know if you want further analysis of any of the photos.

Grace opened the file. Charlotte's note about the geotagging was good news. If Barnie Wallace had switched it off, they could not have got the precise geographic location to within a few feet. It was a truism that criminals were rarely as smart as they thought. And it was another – not one to boast about – that many crimes were solved not by the brilliance of the detectives but because of the stupidity – or carelessness – of the criminals.

As he looked at the photographs, he immediately recognized the subject, from his shape and clothing, as the man he'd seen behind Barnie Wallace in the Organica supermarket. There were dozens of photographs of him, all seemingly taken by a zoom lens, which had the effect of blurring the background, making it difficult to identify precisely the locations. But they all appeared to have been taken in and around the city of Brighton and Hove, and all dated within the last few weeks.

And in all of them the subject was wearing a baseball cap and dark glasses, and either a Covid mask or a scarf obscuring their chin. One was a close-up of the driver's window of a car, appearing to be emerging from an underground car park, with the subject's face visible through the glass, heavily masked. Grace sent the images to JJ Jackson at the Met's Central Image Investigation Unit.

Next he turned his attention to the photograph showing the car window. It was too tight on the window to reveal much of the car itself and the background was out of focus. But he could see the door handle. Someone who really knew their cars should have enough clues to figure it out, he thought. He forwarded it to Luke Stanstead, suggesting someone either in Roads Policing or in the Forensic Collision Investigation Unit would be able to help.

Next, he copied into a file all the ones of the subject walking, and sent them to Haydn Kelly for analysis. It had been some while since he'd had a series of photographs as a line of enquiry, and he knew with the speed technology moved, that he was probably out of date with what could currently be obtained by forensic interrogation of cameras or photographs. He searched the Sussex Police database for the number of CSI photographer James Gartrell and dialled it. Moments later, it was answered by the man's familiar, very precise voice.

'This is James Gartrell.'

Grace had always liked the dependable, tall silver-bearded Crime Scene Investigator. He explained what he needed.

After some moments of silence, Gartrell replied, 'Can you ping me the photos over, sir?'

'Right away. I'll send them by WeTransfer.'

'I'm under pressure at the moment, sir, how quickly do you need my analysis back?'

'Yesterday.'

'I'll be honest with you, sir, I won't be able to start looking at them until the weekend, I'm backed up with urgent work – and I'm actually on my way to a crime scene as we speak. If you need this done sooner, you'll have to speak to ACC Downing, and get him to pull rank.'

'The weekend will be fine,' Grace assured him.

Ending the call, Grace then scanned through all the photographs again. The one common denominator was that the subject was making sure, every time he ventured out, that he would be hard to recognize.

Barnie Wallace's obsessive interest in photographing him was obviously for a good reason. None of the photographs appeared

to show anything particularly interesting, nor remotely comprom-
ising. They were just of a man walking around Brighton – and
once, driving. They were boringly innocent, dull.

But Barnie, the secret photographer, had died after taking
them. Poisoned, possibly, by a switch of mushrooms by the man
he had been photographing, who had turned the tables on him?
Why?

There was one glaringly obvious reason.

And it was the only one he could come up with at this moment.

He was acutely aware it was four weeks since Wallace's death,
and it was normal when an investigation was progressing slowly
for another Major Crime Detective to carry out a review. While
part of him knew that another pair of eyes on a case could be
helpful, there was always, too, the issue of one-upmanship and
professional jealousy. Over the next couple of days, one of his
colleagues, Detective Superintendent Andy Wolstenholme, was
due to carry out such a review. Grace wanted to ensure he had
covered every possible base before that happened, having
recently taken over the role of SIO.

He turned to his policy book and looked at the lines of enquiry
and actions he had noted. It was a long list, beginning with the
surveillance on Rorke's widow, Fiona Davies, which had started
last night. She'd stayed home, no visitors. Hopefully the analysis
of the photos Barnie Wallace had taken would give them at least
the location where Rorke was now based. And would the team
be able to find Professor Llewellyn's EpiPen to see if it had been
tampered with?

And where the hell had Rorke – if he was the *blind man with
dog* – disappeared to?

Financial investigator Emily Denyer had come back, showing
there were no unusual deposits in the bank accounts of either
the yacht captain, Richard Le Quesne, or the young crew member,
Lance Sharpus-Jones.

Then Grace frowned. There was something in Rufus Rorke's disappearance overboard from *Eloise III*, other than Rorke, that was missing. Something no one had mentioned. His phone had been in his stateroom with his wife – and had revealed nothing of interest. But how come no one had mentioned his computer? Surely he would have had a laptop with him on board? Particularly as he clearly did his financial transactions in Bitcoins – and perhaps other cybercurrencies.

He felt a beat of excitement. Had no one thought of this?

And, significantly, where was it?

50

Saturday 8 October 2022

The Victory Vintage, it was called. That's what Fiona had told her husband, a few years ago, when she'd arrived home lugging a light-coloured pine box, with a triumphant smile, then put it down, very carefully, on the hall floor. She could still remember their conversation.

'This is special, my gorgeous!' she'd said. 'So bloody special! I think we should have one bottle to celebrate, it's not every day you're going to see this.'

'What is it?' Rufus had asked.

She vanished into the scullery then returned with a hammer and chisel and began to lever open the top of the case. 'I just got it, at an auction at Christie's – this is something else.'

'OK.'

'Seriously, this is something else.'

'I believe you, Fiona.'

The top of the case broke and a strip of wood with a nail attached came away. She lifted an arched piece of wood from inside, discarded it, then reached inside again, lifted out a bottle and held it up triumphantly. It had a red top, with dark contents, but most of the glass below the neck was obscured by the yellowing, faded label. At the top of the label was a large, ornate 'V'. Further down he saw the date, '1945'.

She was feeling ridiculously pleased with herself.

'1945?' he'd said.

'Uh-huh.'

'Is that the sell-by date?' he asked, teasing.

'You're a bloody philistine,' she'd replied. 'This is not only one of the finest wines on the planet, this is a piece of history. That "V" you see?'

He nodded.

She explained that Chateau Mouton Rothschild commissioned the artist Philippe Jullian to design it, to commemorate the end of the Second World War. It was one of the most sought after and collectible wines in the world. He hadn't asked her how much she'd paid at the Christie's auction; he knew she would think nothing of paying upwards of £100k for a case of fine wine.

There were eleven bottles left after they'd drunk that one on the night she'd brought the case home. It was pretty nice, he'd had to admit, although he hadn't thought it was *that* special. But then, as Fiona had always told him, he didn't have much of a palate – he cared much more about how booze made him feel than what it tasted like.

Right now Fiona was feeling special. And especially bold and playful after a nice little glass of Dutch courage – a few fingers of neat Scotch. She needed it, because tonight she had a date – and he would be here in half an hour!

The boys were away on a sleepover. She was ready, dressed to kill – or preferably seduce – in the short, black, slinky Chanel that showed off her fine legs and her equally fine cleavage, minimal bling, her seriously classy Audemars Piguet watch, and her sensational Louboutins.

She'd laid the table for two and was properly pushing the boat out, with a few touches of Domestic Goddess thrown in, such as the candles, the flowers on the table, the elegant lobster salad starter, the tournedos Rossini with chilli broccoli and fondant potatoes all prepped, and the cheese soufflé to finish. But what was going to impress Robert Drummond most of all was her choice of wines tonight.

On their previous – and first – date in the London restaurant Scott's, he'd chosen extravagantly off the wine list and had delighted in telling her that wine was one of his passions. He'd been utterly fascinated to learn about her collection, although Fiona liked to think it hadn't just been the lure of that that had made him accept her invitation to dinner tonight.

Two hours ago she'd put a bottle of Roederer Cristal 2014 into the wine cooler in the kitchen. An hour ago she'd added a Corton-Charlemagne 2000. But now she was about to fetch the ultimate *wow* from the cellar. Her three Pomeranians followed her to the door to the cellar, but that was where they always stopped. Although they were named after three of the most brutal Roman emperors, Nero, Caligula and Tiberius, they were wusses when it came to the cellar stairs. They would stand at the top, refusing to descend and each barking in turn at some unseen enemy down in the darkness below.

With the dim lights on, Fiona made her way in the chilly air along the brick floor. As she walked through the interconnecting cellars lined floor-to-low-ceiling with racks of single bottles, magnums, jeroboams and even larger bottles still, she wrinkled her nose at the damp, musty smell, vinous in parts where a cork or seal had failed and the wine was leaking.

Reaching the end of the far cellar, which housed many of the jewels of the collection, she saw the two empty slots in the Victory Vintage section of the racks. Until three days ago, there had been just one empty slot – the bottle they'd drunk on the night she had bought them – but now there was another space, vacated by the bottle Fiona was planning for them to drink tonight. It was standing upright on the floor, keeping cool and out of the light. She knew all about sediment. It was important to let an old bottle stand for at least a couple of days and preferably longer, to allow it to settle before decanting it.

She knelt, closed her fingers tightly around the neck of the precious bottle and held it up. It was a little dusty after several years down here, but she was pleased to see the level was still high up the neck – something she always checked. If it was high, the chances were the wine was still fine.

She smiled. If this beauty didn't blow her wine buff date's socks off – and hopefully his underpants too – nothing would.

Then, looking at the two empty slots, she smiled again, but now for a different reason. One of the first things Rufus had done after buying this property, ten years ago now, was to put a substantial safe down at the far end of the wine cellar, where she thought it extremely unlikely a burglar would find it, or even the police in the event of a raid. It was concealed directly behind the Victory Vintage bottles.

Rufus used to keep large quantities of cash in the safe, converting them into Bitcoins then back to cash, laundering them through a London casino that was a haunt of high rollers. He wouldn't be pleased if he knew what she kept in this safe currently.

It was his Apple laptop. The one that, on the night of Rufus's *disappearance*, it was agreed she would throw overboard.

Except of course she hadn't done that. Instead she'd concealed it among her belongings in her suitcase, and when the Barbados Police had searched the yacht, they had been too polite to start rummaging through the clothes of Rufus Rorke's grieving widow.

Rufus would not be at all happy to know she still had it, and so far she had never told him. She was well aware it contained enough information to have Rufus put away for much of the rest of his life.

She didn't intend telling him any day soon, because she knew how ruthless he was, and what he was capable of doing. And how he dealt with people he considered to be obstacles or threats.

She had told no one about the laptop or where it was hidden, but she had left a sealed letter, to be opened in the event of her death, with her solicitor.

Fiona looked at those two empty slots again and smiled, knowing what was concealed behind them. She liked to think of it as her insurance policy. Then, carrying the bottle upstairs, she turned her attention to one of the things in life she liked doing best.

51

Paul Anthony was doing one of the things he liked best. Thinking about his girlfriend – and hopefully partner for life – Shannon.

He liked her name. He liked that she was everything Fiona was not. Warm, tender, caring, so caring. Too caring?

OK, so she'd had a bit of a wobble over his despatching of Professor Llewellyn, and to be honest that was becoming his one concern about Shannon. Was she too soft? Killing was power, the ultimate power, the ultimate thrill. There was nothing to match the utter euphoria of a successful kill. She'd learn that in time, he would be a good teacher. Ridding the world of vermin. There was no sensation on earth like it.

Which was why he was standing here in the pitch darkness with his night-vision goggles, a few miles north of Brighton. Only the faintest sliver of a new moon up there in that big, wide, dark sky, above this narrow, dark country road, Sparrowhawk Lane. He knew the local police were after him, but he was entirely confident he could still go ahead and kill his target right under their noses. He found the thrill intoxicating.

He reminded himself not to look at that new moon through glass, that was unlucky.

The lane cut through the forest, just half a mile from the entrance to the house – or rather *fuck-off mansion* – of the man he was here to despatch, whose name was Dermot Bryson, along with his new girlfriend, but that couldn't be helped. Collateral damage.

Shit happened. Anyhow, she was guilty by association, just like most of his collateral damage victims always were. Hang out with the Devil and you take your chances, he figured.

Actually, strike that, he thought. *I'm* the Devil. But, hey, let's not get bogged down in semantics.

If everything went to plan – and it always did when Paul Anthony organized it – Dermot and Tracey would be dead in seventeen minutes. The app on his phone was doing the count-down as it sucked in and processed data from the magnetic tracker he'd placed under Dermot Bryson's bright red, million-pound Ferrari, three nights ago.

On confirmation of Bryson's death, which Shannon Kendall would send to his client by video via the dark web, another half a million pounds would be added to the first half a million that Bryson's ex-wife had deposited into his Bitcoin account a month ago. And of that he had no doubt. This was a well-paid job. But not all of them were charged this amount of money. The price he charged related to the complexity of the killing and the wealth of his client. He called it his *affordability calculator*!

Dermot Bryson's extremely bitter ex-wife Kimberley would not be defaulting on her payment. Not when he had the recording of her giving him explicit instructions to murder her former husband, and agreeing on the way it would be done, as well as agreeing the payment schedule – half on acceptance of the contract, half on delivery.

Dermot Bryson, a recovering alcoholic, revelled in fast cars. And because he no longer drank he always drove himself when going out on a date.

Earlier tonight, Bryson had whisked Tracey Dawson off to dinner at very fancy Gravetye Manor, fifteen miles away from his house. Paul Anthony, concealed in the woods, reckoned that Bryson had been doing well over 70mph down the fast tree-lined straight in his Ferrari, as he'd passed by him. And from the footage taken by the two surveillance cameras he'd placed up trees along this lane over the preceding two weeks – and had now removed – this was the speed at which Dermot drove regularly along this stretch of road. He only braked slightly for the long curve that led up to, and past, the entrance to his property. A suitably grand entrance, with electric wrought-iron gates between pillars topped by round stone balls and the customary CCTV apparatus that went with it.

It was Paul Anthony's hope, and plan, that – no doubt charged up by a fine dinner and the high of a great date – Dermot Bryson would be going just as fast on the way back home tonight.

He'd learned everything he needed to know to kill Bryson in the best – and most profitable – way, as the tycoon was already a customer of theirs whom Shannon had supplied with a 3D printed Glock-style handgun.

It amused him that over the past couple of weeks Dermot Bryson had come to consider them as friends and – dare he say it – almost trusted confidants, although they'd never met. One of the important things Bryson had told him was all about his neighbours.

There were just five other houses accessed along Sparrowhawk Lane. The occupants of one were currently abroad on a cruise, which left just four near neighbours for Paul Anthony to be concerned about. All of them were elderly, or at least knocking on a bit, which meant they probably weren't night owls. That was confirmed by the clips over the past fortnight that had been automatically downloaded to his phone every morning. If any of them did go out, they were home again by 11 p.m.

Most importantly for his plan, none of the others had gone out tonight, so the only vehicle likely to be coming down the lane at this hour would be Dermot's Ferrari. Of course there was always the possibility of a random police car on patrol but, in a month, none had been along here. To make absolutely sure, he had used a stolen *POLICE ROAD CLOSED* sign, which he placed strategically at the other end of the lane.

Sixteen minutes to go. The night air was calm and Paul was pleased about that. Yesterday's torrential rain would not have been good, because Dermot might not have driven so fast. On the other hand, rain would have made the road slippery. Slippery would be good, but Paul didn't need it to be slippery. Just fast.

Fifteen minutes. His nerves began tingling, but he knew exactly what to do about them. A deep breath for eight through his nose. Then eight back out through his mouth. Repeat three times.

It worked. He was calm again.

Fourteen minutes.

His own transport, tonight a Land Rover Defender, registered under one of his false and untraceable identities, was parked down a woodland track a quarter of a mile walk away. An awkward walk, because he was wearing gum boots two sizes too big, to fool any footprint or forensics analyst – once bitten, twice shy – although they were stuffed with foam to minimize their flopping about on his feet.

Thirteen minutes.

He looked at the tiny red dot on the map app on his phone, and was pleased to see that Dermot Bryson was driving very fast. It showed that the Ferrari was on the A27, the dual carriageway, out of Brighton and just passing the Sussex University campus. His speed was currently 95mph.

Keep it up, big guy! Love it!

Twelve minutes.

Eleven.

Ten.

In the still air he could hear – or perhaps imagined he could hear, very faintly at first – the scream of the Ferrari's engine.

Nine minutes.

The red dot was moving closer.

The scream was getting louder.

Eight minutes.

Louder and closer still.

Seven minutes.

Now!

Paul Anthony strode quickly over to the ancient, solid chestnut tree that stood to one side of the lane, part-way around the curve, far enough around that you could not see it from the direction from which Dermot was approaching.

Earlier, under the cover of darkness, he had secured an object, four foot tall and six inches in circumference, to the trunk of the tree. He now set to work with it. When he had finished, the countdown was at five minutes.

Please God don't let anyone else come along now!

It seemed like God was in a good mood – or busy elsewhere. Or whatever.

Four minutes.

Three minutes.

The scream of that engine was getting tantalizingly close.

Then he heard a different scream. A howling wail. Tyres on tarmac. The Ferrari's speed on his app plunged. 70mph. 50mph. 30mph. 20mph. Zero.

What?

Then he heard the blast of a horn.

52

'You're scaring me, Dermot,' Tracey said.

He was steering with his right hand. His left hand was on her knee. 'It's OK, babe, I'm always careful.' He winked at her.

'Slow down, please slow down. Please, Dermot, can we go just a little slower?' She sat, held tight by the arms of the racing seat, in the sumptuous velour of the interior, looking on high alert at the lights of the dials on the dashboard. The headlights lit up the trees ahead.

He wasn't going any slower.

Then she screamed.

Dermot saw it too. 'Shit!' he shouted, stamping on the brakes as hard as he could.

The car juddered, slewing right then left then right, then left again. Somehow holding a more or less straight line.

And came to a halt.

Inches away.

Tracey stared in shock at the two yellow eyes. They were staring back. In equal shock. The creature frozen in terror. Standing in the middle of the lane.

'Dumb fucking animal!' Dermot Bryson had both hands back on the wheel. He gave a full blast of the Enzo's massively loud airhorns. 'Get out of the road!' he yelled.

Either the horns or his voice did the trick. The deer got out of the road and into the forest.

236

He floored the accelerator, rapidly changing the gears up as the car launched itself at the dark horizon, and the speedometer swung back around, passing 70mph. Then his hand went wandering again, settling back on Tracey's knee.

He squeezed it, then put both his hands back on the rectangular leather-covered wheel. The curve was coming up fast. If he gave a slight dab on the brakes to pull the nose down, then kept a balanced throttle – something he'd learned from his coach, John Powis – he could take the curve without reducing speed.

He gently applied the brakes, then put only the lightest pressure on the accelerator, hurtling into the curve at 75mph on the clock, confident there would be nothing coming in the other direction.

'SHIT!' he screamed.

At the oncoming headlights.

Tracey screamed too. In utter terror.

Headlights that were racing towards them. Straight at them.

He swerved hard left with no time to brake.

Tracey screamed again.

The headlights were still coming at him.

He tried to swerve right but the car wasn't responding to the steering wheel, which was suddenly jerking wildly in his hands.

The lights were dazzling him. Blinding him.

'Oh God, oh God!' He felt the tyres scrubbing sideways as the car, still travelling at the speed of a missile, started to swap ends. He turned the wheel the opposite way but too late. Momentum had taken over.

He was no longer the driver but a passenger. Just like Tracey.

Then he saw the tall, dark silhouette hurtling towards them.

Or were they hurtling towards it?

53

Through his night-vision goggles, Paul Anthony watched the pirouetting Ferrari rip through the four-foot-high barrier of reflective aluminium foil he had stretched across the lane, fastened to a tree on each side. It was still travelling at around 60mph, he estimated, as it hit the tall oak tree broadside, just at the rear of the driver's door.

And disintegrated. Accompanied by a massive boom, like a corrugated-iron warehouse dropped from a great height onto another corrugated-iron warehouse.

Parts flew in all directions, immediately followed by an aftermath of sounds of metal clattering across tarmac, heavy objects crashing into the surrounding undergrowth, then, after several seconds, a metallic ping . . . ping . . . ping . . . ping . . .

And finally a long hissing sound.

Then silence.

Oh dear, Paul thought. It sounded like the radiator was spewing out hot water. That would be an expensive repair. He really did not want to think what a Ferrari radiator would cost to replace.

Not that this was something that would be preying on Dermot Bryson's mind just at this moment. The thought made him smile, as he walked towards what was left of the cockpit of the car. Through his goggles he could see the front end had been torn away, the engine section and front wheels were lying upside down a good hundred yards along the road, partially in a ditch.

But he focused his attention for now on Dermot Bryson. The man he had been hired to kill was still buckled into his contoured racing seat in the remains of the cockpit, deployed airbag lying white and limp on his lap. His arms were straight out in front of him on the steering wheel with the round yellow boss and prancing horse motif, looking for all the world as if he was ready to continue with his journey, bar one small detail. There was just a bloody, jagged stump above his shirt collar, where his head should have been.

Paul listened carefully, but all he could hear was the silence of the night. And still the faint hissing. Good. He switched off the app that had plotted Bryson's journey here and activated the phone's camera. He photographed Bryson's headless torso in the car. Then, striding into the woods, found the man's head in a gorse bush but conveniently looking out with a bemused expression. No mistaking who this was!

He took a sequence of photographs with his night-vision camera. Then he carried on with his examination of the scene. Tracey was on the far side of the lane, lying close to a tree, entangled in her seat belt and part of her seat, with her skull split open and the contents leaking out. *Good girl, at least you were wearing your seat belt*, he thought, as he took another photograph.

Next he photographed a large amount of twisted black metal around the base of the oak tree the Ferrari had struck. Then, a bit of artistry he was very pleased with, he found the metal gearbox gate, a hallmark Ferrari detail, lying all on its own on a fern. There were seven notches – gates, he knew they were called – and the gear-lever had a shiny round knob. He was tempted to take it, use it as a paperweight, it would make a nice souvenir. But maybe not, he decided.

He spotted a framed, damaged section of glass with a rubber surround, that looked like one of the windows that had been blown out. And finally, a deployed airbag lying in the middle of the road inside some red and black twisted metal wreckage.

He photographed that too. Happy days!

Then, aware he might not have much time if one of the neighbours came to investigate or called the emergency services, he turned to the task of removing the evidence. Beginning with unfastening the ties from around the trees, he went on to pick up the pieces of foil with his hands. *Shit* – he'd imagined the foil would have just ripped in half, but it hadn't; it had exploded like a fucking bomb and there were fragments everywhere, some small pieces so tightly embedded in the tree trunk that he couldn't get them out.

Nevertheless, with the aid of the portable vacuum cleaner he had brought in his rucksack, a bin liner and a powerful torch, he scoured the road for every other fragment he could find. And, last of all, he removed the tracker.

As he worked, he constantly looked around and listened. He had his excuses all prepared, that he was driving along, the Ferrari went tearing past him at a crazy speed and the driver appeared to lose control on this bend. But no one came. His excuse lay in his head, unused. He hadn't been able to find the Ferrari's dashcam, which had clearly sheared off its stem, but he was not overly concerned as it wouldn't show anything out of the ordinary.

It was over an hour before he was satisfied, and felt confident enough to head back to his Land Rover. When he got home, he would have a celebratory whisky and cigar, and then send the photographs to his client, along with the invoice for the fifty-per-cent balance.

Job done!

54

Monday 10 October 2022

Paul Anthony, breakfasting out on the terrace of his apartment, was in such a fabulous mood! It wasn't just the glorious, unexpected, Indian summer weather that was making him feel so sunny, nor the fact that beautiful Shannon was naked in the master bedroom en-suite shower. It was most of all the front-page splash of the local newspaper, the *Argus*, which had been delivered alongside the other newspapers he also read daily. And the dramatic images of the wrecked Ferrari beneath the big, shouty headline: SUSSEX MILLIONAIRE AND GIRLFRIEND DEAD IN HIGH-SPEED SMASH.

Paul Anthony smiled, took a sip of his Armagnac then blew a smoke ring. Job done. Too bad about the girlfriend but, he pondered, the ex-wife, Kimberley, probably wouldn't be too upset about that addition when she found out. He stroked Montmorency, lying on the floor beside him. 'Not bad, eh boy, value for money?'

Even the dog looked impressed, staring at him with those big brown eyes. That was the thing about dogs, Paul Anthony thought. You could go out, kill someone, kill a dozen people, and when you came home, your dog would jump up and down and lick you. They were non-judgemental, unlike cats. A cat would just look at you and know what you'd done.

He slipped Montmorency a piece of leftover toast. The dog wolfed it down and immediately looked at him, imploringly, for another. 'Basta ya!' he said. 'We'll go for a walk in a bit, you can have your breakfast after that. Where would you like to go? Up to the Dyke? Telscombe? A nice long walk, eh?'

Most days the dog walker, Joe, took him. But Joe was away with his wife, Liz, in their new motorhome. Paul Anthony didn't mind, he liked walking him and it was good bonding, getting him to practise walking like a guide dog should. He kept a white panel van down in one of the lock-up garages behind this building, for the main purpose of taking Montmorency out.

The van was signwritten Kingsway Electrical. Its licence plate was a clone of the one owned by the real Kingsway Electrical, whose services Paul Anthony had used when he'd first rented this apartment. The boss was a man called Mike Shaw. He'd bought the van off him when he was replacing it with a new one and had never removed the company markings.

One time when Shaw had been working in the apartment, Paul Anthony had slipped the electrician's driving licence out of his wallet and photographed it and he now had an exact copy. Just in case he should ever get stopped by the police.

But why would he be? He always drove carefully, courteously, and scrupulously within the speed limits. Unlike that tosser, Bryson.

He'd checked his Bitcoin account yesterday, after sending the photographic evidence of Bryson minus head to his client, and the second half of the payment had already been made. Speedy Gonzales! Prompt payers. He liked prompt payers. Not that he got a lot of repeat business – he was more in the one-off game, with clients like Bryson's wife, Kimberley.

Callously dumped after twenty years – at least that was her account to him – Kimberley Bryson was a satisfied customer, and so she should be. The divorce hadn't yet been finalized, so legally she was still Dermot Bryson's wife. And as such, she stood to inherit her late hubby's entire estate.

Happy days for her, if Bryson's listing in the top 350 of the *Sunday Times* Rich List was anything to go by. He raised his glass. 'Fill your boots, Kimberley!' Then he gently stroked the back of Montmorency's head before glancing at his watch: 9.20.

Behind him, through the open patio doors, he heard the sound of the shower still running. Shannon. He smiled. Sex after a killing was always the best, seriously, *the best.* They'd spent most of yesterday in bed, fuelled by Champagne and a delivery of pizzas at lunchtime and Thai in the evening. She was something else. Perfect for work, and perfect for pleasure.

He drank a little more Armagnac and took another long puff of his cigar. Montmorency sighed. Getting restless.

'Soon, boy!' he said and tickled the back of the Labrador's head again. Then, staring out across the sea, flat as a millpond, at the wind farm on the horizon, he reflected what a great career move death had been.

The only issue, he had learned, was around the laws of perpetuity, which forbade you from leaving money to yourself when you died. But of course, as with all laws, there had been ways to circumvent that, even if it did mean a pact with Fiona. And judicious use of Bitcoins.

Rufus Rorke, missing at sea, had been declared legally dead by a Sussex coroner. So tragic, so sad. Boo hoo.

On the third day he rose again on the dark web – no disrespect intended – as Lee Oswald.

Such a clever name, he prided himself.

Oh, and Paul Anthony. Such a nice and very useful name.

Most of the proper money he had made in his first incarnation was safely buried in the blockchain that was Bitcoin. It didn't require all the ID crap that banks requested, under the money-laundering regulations. All it required was the code, safely backed-up. Perfect for a dead man!

He'd created *Paul Anthony* very carefully, bit by bit, with the aid of a few contacts in the right places. Paul Anthony was thirty-eight years old, divorced, who ran a successful international property development company and had an annual income, post-tax, in excess of £250,000 – more than enough to have satisfied the landlords of his current smart abode.

With his usual thoroughness, he'd covered every detail of Paul Anthony's life, down to his Jersey, Channel Island, passports and driving licence, his Aviva health insurance policy, and his annual generous donations to the range of charities he supported.

And all would have been fine if he hadn't had contact with that total loser Barnie, who had recognized him.

It hadn't been clever of Barnie to try to blackmail him.

But then, Barnie had never exactly been the brightest bauble on the Christmas tree.

Although maybe, as Fiona had suggested, he hadn't been too bright himself attending Barnie's funeral, either. But he honestly hadn't expected James Taylor to be there – he didn't even know James was still in contact with Barnie.

And he'd only wanted to attend for just one reason. To gloat. Were there many pleasures in life greater than that?

Barnie was plain dumb, but James had always been smart. Although of course, Paul Anthony knew, he himself was far smarter than both of them. Always had been.

If you really thought you saw me, James, my boy, I strongly advise you to forget about it – if you know what I'm saying. I know more ways to kill someone and make it look like an accident than you've had hot breakfasts.

His thoughts were interrupted by the very pleasant smell of a freshly showered Shannon, wrapped in a towelling robe, a kiss on the back of his neck, and a pair of elegant hands massaging his shoulders, then sliding down inside the collar of his dressing gown and nuzzling his ear. 'Come back to bed.'

He tilted his head up and kissed her on the lips. Then he said, 'Explain that to Montmorency. He needs his walk.'

She gave him a sultry look. 'And I need to feel you again. Inside me.'

He grinned. 'Why don't I make you some breakfast, take Montmorency for a walk, then come back and we spend the rest of the day in bed?'

'Don't we have work to do? Our new clients who would like their shiny new guns?'

He grinned again. 'We do have work to do, but it could be done in bed. Isn't that what laptops are for?'

'Hmm.' She was leaning over him and looking at the front page of the newspaper on the table. Abruptly, she pulled away and her mood changed. 'What the hell?' She sounded genuinely angry.

'I'm sorry?' he queried. 'What do you mean?'

'The girlfriend died?'

'Collateral damage.'

The sudden change in her tone of voice startled him. 'What the fuck does that mean? Was she involved in his slimeball activities?'

'By association.'

She pulled up a chair opposite him and sat down. 'By association? What association?'

'She must have known he was a slimeball, but she liked the idea of a fancy lifestyle, fast cars, flashy houses, high-end restaurants.'

Shannon was frowning in a way he did not like. 'Paul, when we first met, I really admired your attitude - philosophy - whatever. You eventually told me you create accidental deaths for people who deserve to die?'

He nodded. 'Yeah.'

'Really?' She leaned close on her elbows. 'So explain to me - convince me - why, exactly, Tracey Dawson deserved to die?'

55

Roy Grace's phone had rung again, moments after he'd ended the call, this time from Roads Policing Inspector James Biggs. And now a copy of the *Argus* lay on his desk, with a dramatic photograph of the rear half of a wrecked Ferrari taking up much of the front page. Inset below was a smaller picture, showing the front end of the car, clearly some distance away.

The headline: SUSSEX MILLIONAIRE AND GIRLFRIEND DEAD IN HIGH-SPEED SMASH.

He had already had the details from James Biggs. It appeared the driver, Dermot Bryson, a wealthy businessman, had lost control of the car on the approach to the entrance to his country home, a few miles away from the police HQ in Lewes. Grace had also been, unenthusiastically, privy to a number of photographs taken by the Forensic Collision Investigation Unit, which fortunately for the general public had not made the pages of the *Argus*, but through which he was now scrolling on his screen. They did not make pretty viewing – particularly the photographs of the two victims.

Ordinarily, as Head of Major Crime, he wasn't concerned with fatal road traffic collisions, but both Biggs and he had a gut feeling there was more to this accident than was initially apparent. And, as he stared at the photograph of a lacerated, severed head lying in undergrowth – which very definitely was not going to be appearing in any newspaper – he was thinking hard.

In his long years as a homicide detective, he had learned never to take anything at face value. Dermot Bryson was an extremely rich man. Grace had googled him and discovered that he had a passion for fast cars, and held a motor racing licence. Bryson regularly raced a number of exotic classic cars he owned in fixtures around Europe. Earlier this year he had raced a Lola at the Goodwood Members' Meeting. And only two weeks earlier he had raced a short-wheelbase Ferrari at the Goodwood Revival, narrowly missing a podium place.

He clearly knew how to handle a potent car.

So what had gone wrong here?

Three questions went around in his head. He couldn't help it. Twenty years of being a detective, of being endlessly lied to by suspects, of looking at things that all too often were not as they seemed, had made him suspicious of just about everything. The same three questions he always posed:

Why him/her?

Why here?

Why now?

James Biggs said that data the FCIU had obtained from interrogating the Ferrari's onboard computers indicated the car had been travelling at excessive speed at the time it left the road.

Showing off to his girlfriend? But this was a man who knew how to drive fast cars fast. He was unlikely to have been drunk as apparently he was not a big drinker any more, according to his social footprint.

And, Biggs informed him, there were other things that had made the first attending Forensic Collision Investigator, DC Rideout, who was nobody's fool, think this wasn't a straightforward accident. He was concerned the pattern of tyre marks on the road were indicative of someone taking evasive action rather than losing control from going too fast. Swerving to avoid a deer had been one possibility considered at first.

The post-mortems of both Dermot Bryson and his girlfriend, Tracey Dawson, would show whether alcohol or drugs had played any part in this crash. But at this moment, Grace was staring intently at the photograph James Biggs had just sent through, of an item that had been found in the glove box of the wrecked Ferrari.

Not something that would have come as an optional extra in any motor car, however exotic, in most countries of the world.

It looked like a heavy-duty Glock .44mm handgun. It fired the kind of rounds that wouldn't just stop someone in their tracks: depending on where it was aimed, it would either blow a football-size hole through the target's midriff, or take most of their head off.

It was a weapon of choice for a killer. But most concerning of all to Roy Grace was that, according to the Sussex Police firearms expert to whom Biggs had given the weapon for examination, and to make it safe, it wasn't an original Glock weapon, but an illegally manufactured version made using 3D printed components. Equally deadly and a lot harder to trace, because there would be no serial number and no record of it ever having been made.

A ghost gun.

So just what nefarious business had Dermot Bryson been involved in that required him to carry a handgun in the glove box of his car? And did it have any bearing on the accident that killed him? Ordinarily, people did not carry firearms in their cars, unless they were either crackpot sociopaths or paranoid about their security.

He googled the man's name, and after going through several Dermot Brysons, found the Wikipedia page, with the photograph that corresponded to the one James Biggs had sent on Bryson's driving licence and the rather more distorted face on the FCIU photograph of Bryson's severed head.

Just as he began to read about Bryson's business activities, which ranged from construction, engineering and venture capital to a global container business with offices in several countries including China – all seemingly legit – he was interrupted by the sound of the door opening, and Glenn Branson's voice.

'You're looking pale, Roy, you need a few days in the sun – you should try the Caribbean!'

Grace gave him a sideways look. 'I've actually been working while you've been sunning your tum.'

'I wish.'

'So it rained – the whole time?'

Branson shrugged and, as he regularly did, turned one of the chairs facing Grace's desk around the wrong way and straddled it. 'It rained. It rained for all two days I was there.'

Grace stared at him. 'You want me to start crying?'

'A bit of sympathy would be nice.'

'You didn't go there to sodding sunbathe!'

'Yeah, well, I thought I might at least get a few hours on the beach. At least it was warm rain.'

'I'm sorry to bring up the name John Baker – I hope he didn't interrupt your holiday too much?'

Ignoring Grace's sarcasm, Branson said, 'Found him – got lucky, he was just back from a three-week fishing trip. But, as I said on the phone, I didn't really get anything extra of value from him. He told me he'd already said everything he had to say in the statement he gave Barbados Police two years ago. I emailed that to you.'

Grace nodded. 'I read it.'

'I asked him how he even connected the remains of the jacket he'd fished up – wrapped around one of his net ropes – with Rufus Rorke. He said he saw a photograph of Rorke in the newspaper; he was at a restaurant called the Cliff with his wife, and was wearing a distinctive white jacket, and Baker put two and two together.'

'Did you get *anything* that wasn't already in his statement?' Grace was thinking about what he was going to say to ACC Downing when he asked him about Glenn's trip.

Branson grinned and wiggled his fingers in the air. 'You need to cover your butt, right?'

'I need to solve this case.'

'Well, the one thing I got was that John Baker was lying.'

'You did?'

Branson smiled, looking very pleased with himself. 'He was very definitely lying.'

'What was he lying about?'

'How he found the jacket. And why he contacted the police.'

'You're certain?'

'Everything about his demeanour tells me I'm certain. He's not exactly a man of many words. I think what he said was well rehearsed. But he couldn't remember the precise details of what he'd already told the police and there were several contradictions. He was no doubt comfortable with the local police, but as I questioned him he became uncertain, clearly agitated, and was definitely hiding something. My contacts in Barbados are continuing their interest in Baker and will come back to me if they find anything new.'

'Great. So anything else that you found out while you were on the island?'

'I spoke to a number of Baker's associates and the impression they had was that his story was all very convenient and they were not sure if they believed him. Two of them told me they were convinced he was lying.'

'OK, well done. So it seems less and less likely that Rufus Rorke did go overboard and get eaten by a shark and more and more likely he is still with us.'

'AKA the Phantom Mushroom Switcher?'

'Indeed. There's another thing that's been bothering me about this jacket – remains of – which is *why*?'

'Why the jacket?'

'We have an eyewitness – a member of the yacht crew, who says he saw him go overboard. Wouldn't that be enough to satisfy people that you had died – to go overboard off a boat several miles off the coast, at night, in a rough, and shark-infested, sea? It almost feels that the addition of the fisherman finding the jacket remains is gilding the lily a bit too much.'

Branson nodded. 'Maybe it was done for extra precaution?'

'Maybe. OK, so meanwhile we've got something else come in.' Grace nodded at the paper.

Branson, scanning the front page of the *Argus* upside down, said, 'Shite, that's no way to treat a Ferrari! Or does it come in kit form like that, with instructions and you have to assemble it?'

Grace smiled wryly.

'Guess if I was going to snuff it in a crash, doing it in a Ferrari would be a lot classier than in my clapped-out car,' Branson said.

Grace grimaced, well aware just how reckless Branson's driving was. 'Do me a big favour, mate?'

'Yeah?'

'Just don't snuff it in a crash.'

Branson stared at him, wide-eyed. 'Hey, I'm qualified – I've got my advanced permit and my pursuit TPAC ticket!'

Just as he was about to reply, Grace's phone rang. It was Inspector Biggs, and instantly he had Grace's full focus.

'Guv,' he said. 'My team at the scene have recovered a dashcam from the wrecked Ferrari. It was buried deep in a hedge some distance from the main crash site itself, and appears to have sheared off in the impact. The broken stem is an exact match with the base still attached to the top of the dashboard in the Ferrari's cockpit.'

'Have you recovered any footage from it, Biggsy?' Grace asked.

'We have, boss. I think you need to take a look at it. Something's seriously not right here, and that's confirmed by what's been found at the scene.'

'Which is?'

'Take a look at the footage first, guv. Start at twenty-two minutes in. Then bell me.'

Intrigued, Grace said, 'Ping it over.'

'On its way.'

Sixty seconds later, the file began to download on Grace's screen.

56

Paul Anthony was looking across the table at her. His cold expression was unnerving her. 'You want me to explain why exactly Tracey Dawson deserved to die?'

'I do, Paul. This is not what I signed up to. I thought most of your business was in 3D guns and that you only helped arrange *accidents* for people who really did deserve to die. I'm not convinced about Tracey Dawson. And I'm not convinced it's just a few of these *accidents* you have been involved in.'

He looked back at her evasively. That same weaselly expression she'd seen before, when she'd forced him to explain something she was really not happy about.

'Listen, babes, that girl, Tracey, is just collateral damage. Unfortunate, but sometimes shit happens in my line of work.'

His words horrified her. '*Shit happens?* Is that all murdering an innocent person means to you?'

'You need to understand, Shannon,' he said.

'Understand what, exactly?'

He stared back at her in silence for some moments. 'Do you have a view on guilt by association?' he asked, finally.

'I don't. And what's that supposed to mean?'

'Take Fred West, for example. He murdered at least twelve young women and girls, burying them in his garden, as well as horrifically abusing his own daughter. His wife, Rosemary, maintained her innocence for thirty years. Don't you think she was guilty by association, at the very least? Dennis Rader operated in Wichita, Kansas, binding, torturing and killing ten people over a fifteen-year period. He was married with two daughters. Was it possible his wife, who was an intelligent woman, didn't know – or at least turned a blind eye?'

'Tracey Dawson is a different situation entirely,' she said. 'This was only their third date.'

He looked hard at her. 'How do you know that?'

'You are paying me to know everything.'

He smiled and was relieved to see a slight thaw in her expression. But it was only fleeting before the coldness returned. 'I'm concerned,' she said. 'I'm concerned about who you really are. Do *you* even know who you are any more?'

57

As James Biggs had instructed, Grace, with Branson standing beside him, selected a point in the recording around twenty-two minutes in, then clicked to make it full screen. Both of them watched.

It was footage from a forward-facing dash camera. From a vehicle travelling at very high speed at night – Dermot Bryson's Ferrari, Grace presumed. A digital clock in the top right-hand corner of the display showed 23.19. Headlights lit up a section of road he immediately recognized as the dual-carriageway stretch of the A27, where the Sussex University campus would be to the left and the Amex football stadium over to the right. The Ferrari was travelling recklessly fast, switching lanes, undertaking and overtaking at near insane closing speeds. He watched the digital readout in the bottom left corner of the screen: 110mph; 115mph.

'This is not going to end well,' murmured Branson.

'It doesn't,' Grace replied.

The speed reduced dramatically as they approached the roundabout for the Cuilfail tunnel, then shot past 120mph as the car accelerated down the hill towards the Beddingham roundabout. It slowed sharply at the bottom, then, taking the roundabout at a rate that would have been impossible in his own Alfa Romeo, Grace thought.

The car began accelerating again, but only for a short distance

255

before turning off the main road onto what was little more than a heavily wooded lane, barely two car widths.

Then something loomed ahead.

An obstacle in the road.

Two tiny bright lights.

The Ferrari decelerated fiercely, swerving left, right, left, right. He could almost feel the driver fighting to keep it pointing forward. The digital readout plunged. 70-60-50-40-30-20-0.

Barely a few feet in front of them, a deer, with massive antlers, stood in the beam, frozen, staring straight at the camera with big yellow eyes. Then, after several seconds, it bolted into the night.

'Shit!' Glenn Branson said. 'Remember Tony Warren – became a chief super over in Worthing?'

'Yeah, he was my boss at Gatwick for a brief time.'

'He totalled his car in a deer strike on Christmas Eve two years ago – and put himself in hospital for a month with a busted hip and ruptured spleen. You seriously do not want to hit one.'

'And how was the deer? Did it carry on helping Santa with his deliveries?'

'And I thought I was the sick one here!'

The car began accelerating again and in moments the speed readout was above 80mph. The road ahead was dead straight, and the speed rose again.

A bend was coming up.

As they approached, the speed dropped: 75; 70.

Whoever was driving must know this road well, Grace thought. If not, they were a total idiot. But if this was indeed the Ferrari's dashcam, and it was Dermot Bryson driving, then yes, he would know this stretch of road like the back of his hand.

Then, as the headlights showed they were entering a long, sweeping curve, Grace almost missed a heartbeat, as a pair of dazzling headlights came from the opposite direction, straight towards them.

Straight towards a head-on collision.

'Jesus,' he murmured under his breath.

The car's lights veered to the right. So did the oncoming lights, getting brighter with each fraction of a second.

Then to the left.

So did the oncoming lights.

Yards away now from a massive collision.

Suddenly, the lights in front of the dashcam swerved sharply right. For an instant, all they illuminated were trees and shrubbery.

An instant later there was an intensely bright flash, and the camera appeared to be cartwheeling into a darkness, showing streaks of light, like sparks, either side.

'Jesus,' Branson said. 'I'm perspiring!'

'Quite a ride,' Grace said grimly. 'Want a replay?'

Without waiting for an answer, he played the footage again from the same place, slowing it right down after the deer incident, watching mystified. A car, going like a bat out of hell had come the other way, head-on at them – how on earth had the two vehicles avoided colliding?

By Dermot Bryson driving off the road? Swerving to avoid it?

He was struggling to make sense of what he had seen. And the speed at which the oncoming vehicle appeared to be travelling.

The team in the FCIU were highly skilled in their forensic examinations of both crashed vehicles and the crash scene. Whoever had been driving in the opposite direction would have left massive tyre tracks on the road, as would Bryson's Ferrari. He had a whole bunch of question marks in his head.

'What do you know about who was driving and what the car was?' Branson asked.

'We're about to find out.' He dialled James Biggs' number.

The RPU Inspector answered on the first ring. 'Quite a show, right, boss?'

'A shit-show and a half, Biggsy. But I'm sure Glenn will have seen a car chase in a movie to top it,' Grace replied and glanced up. His colleague nodded with a grim smile. 'He's been watching it with me, I'll put him on speaker.'

'*Bullit?*' Branson suggested. '*Fast and Furious?*'

'And the rest . . .' Biggs replied grimly.

'So what do we know about the other vehicle, the oncoming one?' Grace asked him.

'That's the interesting bit, boss. There's no trace of any other car.'

'No trace? What do you mean *no trace?*'

'Just that, boss. There's no trace of an oncoming car. There's nothing to indicate it was there.'

'But it's on the recording – the headlights. Coming straight at Bryson's Ferrari at immense speed.'

'Yes, it is.'

'It must have braked.'

'You'd expect a car coming the other way at speed, on a narrow road with barely enough room for two cars to pass, to have stamped on its brakes, right?' the RPU Inspector said.

'Stamped on them and then some,' Grace retorted.

'Exactly. You'd have expected both drivers, no matter how inebriated or intoxicated from drink or drugs, to have braked like crazy. But the only skid marks we've found on the road are from Bryson's Ferrari. Nothing from the opposite direction and no sign of debris from any other car either.'

'Nothing at all?'

'Nothing.'

Great, Roy Grace thought. We've got a ghost gun and now a ghost car. 'This isn't making a lot of sense, Biggsy.'

'You're right, boss. I don't think this is an ordinary double fatal RTC. I feel that you and the Major Crime Team should run this investigation. The RPU and the FCIU will retain the scene, of course. We've still got the road closed, and we need it closed for quite a bit longer, but we've a posse of angry locals.'

'Have you moved the bodies yet?' Grace asked.

'Yes, they were recovered to the mortuary. We had the coroner's officer, Michele Websdale, attending the scene yesterday, and at that point we didn't have any reason to suspect this was something other than a straightforward driver-run-out-of-talent accident. Since then, with what we've found, I've requested a Home Office post-mortem and the coroner has agreed.'

'Do you know who the pathologist will be?'

'Nadiuska De Sancha.'

Grace was relieved. Nadiuska De Sancha was good news, efficient and pleasant to work with. 'The PM is planned for 8 a.m. tomorrow?'

'It is. At the moment I have one of my officers attending but I think it should be yours, boss.'

Grace made a mental note to send one of his team over to the mortuary, to attend, as soon as he ended this call.

'Where's the gun?'

'I've had a Tactical Firearms Unit make it safe and remove it as an exhibit.'

'And the residents are angry about the road closure?'

'Fuming about it. About all the vehicles everywhere – the RPU, the Forensic Collision Investigations Unit, the coroner's officer – who left with the bodies – and all the rest. As the Yanks might say, this is a right howdy-doody.'

'So what have you got that's making you so suspicious?'

'Something I'd like you to see.'

'Tell me?'

'I'd like you to tell me, when you've figured it out. You're the sharp detective, I'm just a humble traffic cop.'

58

Monday 10 October 2022

Memories of yesterday – the good and the bad – were flooding back to James Taylor, as he sat back in his cosseting seat up at the sharp end of the early morning American Airlines flight from Chicago to Miami, fighting periodic, savage bouts of cramp in his right hamstring and left calf. Boarding was complete and they would be taxiing shortly.

The good had been the series of WhatsApp messages from Debbie, wishing him luck, followed by her genuinely joyous reply after he sent her his result. And a row of kisses.

The bad had been his alarm ringing in his hotel room at 4.45 a.m. and, forty minutes later, still a little jet-lagged, walking through the cold, dark streets of Chicago in his running gear, with an old jumper for warmth over the top, and hoping the queue for the line of portaloos wouldn't be too long.

There were nearly fifty thousand entrants and most of them were already on the streets, heading in the same direction as he made his way towards Wave 1, Gate 9, Corrall C. Organizers always wanted you there long before the start time, and at least, he had hoped, he would have the opportunity for a good long warm-up before the start.

The queues through security had been hellish, and although he'd allowed himself the two hours advised by the organizers, by the time he'd finally reached the start for his wave, he'd barely had enough time, given the long queue for the toilets, to have a final, much needed pee and dump his bag in the bag drop. He only managed a five-minute warm-up before discarding his old pullover in a charity bin.

But once the race had started all of his annoyance was forgotten. He'd loved the buzz of the crowds lining the city's streets, who were cheering, honking horns or ringing bells, loud, motivational music blaring out of speakers. And he remembered growing more and more tired, getting confused where he was, whether in New York or Chicago – the buildings looked so similar – as he hit the same mental and physical wall most marathon runners hit around the 20-mile mark. That's when the real race begins, he knew.

Those last few miles had been a real struggle and he'd had to push harder and harder to maintain his pace, despite the regular energy boosts from the gels in his nutrition plan, repeating his mantra over and over. *Remember why you're doing this . . . Remember why you're doing this . . .* His mantra for each of the eighteen marathons he had run so far. Reminding himself why he had started running in the first place.

For Marcus.

His older brother and role model, Marcus. Marcus had always dreamed of becoming a pilot and that dream had been infectious. That day, almost twenty years ago, he would never forget. As teenagers, inseparable and always competitive with each other, they'd been racing each other on their pedal bikes down the steep hill on the far side of the Devil's Dyke. Marcus, always the more daring, whooping with delight, had overtaken him on a blind brow. And hit a van coming up the hill, head-on.

Even more tragically, he hadn't died, but instead had been condemned to a living death. A brain-damaged tetraplegic, Marcus lived for a further twelve years in a specially adapted bedroom at their parents' house.

It had plunged Taylor into a deep depression. Every time he went into that room, he was thinking that it should have been him in that bed. Then, just a few days before he had died, Marcus had summoned Taylor to his bedside and, in his wonky, croaky voice that always made him sound like he was drunk, had whispered, 'Just go for it. Promise me. Live your life for both of us. Almost every time I sleep, I dream I'm suddenly able to run again. I dream I'm running a marathon and running it so fast my legs leave the ground and I'm flying. Make that dream come true. Do that for me, bro. Make me even more proud of you than I already am.'

Taylor promised him he would.

Chicago had been a tough one and he'd finished almost a full minute slower than his personal best. All the same, he'd been elated going through that finish line yesterday in the time of 3.29.15. Elated and totally drained.

But he'd recovered fast enough to meet an old friend and former easyJet colleague Robert Boyd, now a private pilot also, based out of Chicago. They'd had a drink at the Green Mill jazz club – one of Al Capone's haunts where the mobster had had a permanently reserved booth – and then a hefty steak at Mastro's and probably a bit too much red wine. In fact, definitely too much red wine, or was it was the bourbons before? More likely a combination of both, on top of being dehydrated from the run.

Whatever, he was sure feeling it now. In addition to the cramp, he was low on energy, but boosted considerably by the satisfaction that he now had another marathon medal, carefully packed in his bag, which no one could ever take away from him. His nineteenth. And boosted even more by the two dozen kudos 'likes', emojis of clapping hands from fellow runners and messages, on his Strava app. He scrolled through them, replying briefly to each.

One was from a running buddy from Worthing, Haydn Christmas. **Awesome run! Well done.**

A second from another Worthing runner, Oliver Dunn. **Smashed it, mate!**

And another, from Stuart Baulk. **You only went and blew the bloody doors off!**

The messages were putting a big smile on his face. Then he yawned, regretting his decision to book such an early flight. But he wanted to make the most of his brief break in Barbados, and to arrive in daylight so he could at least have a couple of hours on the beach, and get his leg muscles working with a gentle swim.

He winced as his calf muscle cramped again, and he leaned forward, rubbing it vigorously. Three and a half hours to Miami, then a four-hour flight to Barbados. And tonight, courtesy of Tommy Towne, who was as generous as he was at times crazy, he would be sleeping in luxury.

When he'd told his boss he was going to Barbados, Tommy had picked up the phone and called the manager of the Sandy Lane hotel, requested the best suite they had available and insisted the entire bill, extras and all, be charged to him. Towne had demonstrated similar generosity to him a while back, when Taylor had split up with his wife, putting him up in a suite in Jersey's Royal Yacht hotel, one of the finest on the island, for several months.

He hoped to have a good long sleep tonight, and a day chilling on the beach tomorrow, then on Wednesday begin the task he had set himself. To see if he could find the fisherman, John Baker, who had recovered the remnants of the white jacket.

To see if it would take him any closer to the truth about Rufus Rorke.

59

Roy Grace drove his Alfa, with Glenn in the passenger seat, past Lewes and down towards the Beddingham roundabout. They were approaching the scene of the accident.

A short distance past Firle he braked and turned off the A27 onto a minor road, densely wooded either side, and drove along it for a quarter of a mile. He was intrigued by what James Biggs had said – or rather had not said: a Ferrari, a multimillionaire and his girlfriend, a 3D printed gun in the glove box. 'You wanted a more challenging murder case to work on, matey; I think we've just got one.'

'Yep, sounds it.'

Ahead, just before a bend warning sign, he saw the familiar cluster of police and forensic vehicles that signalled a major RTC.

He pulled the Alfa up behind the last vehicle in the line, a marked Roads Policing Unit car, angled across the road, protecting the scene, and they climbed out, Grace taking his time.

'You're still not recovered, are you, mate?' Branson said, genuinely concerned. 'You need some X-rays, I think, you might have internal damage.'

'I'm fine.' Grace closed the door. 'Do you hear that, Glenn?'

'What? I can't hear a thing.'

'Exactly. The previous vicar of St Peter's told me he'd been to Auschwitz and said it was the strangest feeling, because there was utter silence, you couldn't even hear birds singing. I've noticed the same thing sometimes at murder scenes out in the countryside or woodlands. And at fatal RTCs too. It's as if there really is some vibe in the air that spooks all the wildlife into staying away.'

Branson reflected for some moments, then said, 'Maybe it's the reaction to being so struck by the horrors that our brains blank out the sound of birdsong?'

'There's the detective in you, looking for the rational explanation.'

He shrugged. 'I've heard that too, but I'm a realist. There must have been countless generations of birds born in those areas since the end of the war and the liberation of those camps. I'm not saying it's impossible there isn't some bad vibe in the air around them, but I think there's maybe another reason people don't hear it.' Branson looked at Grace. 'Sometimes I think you're too sensitive a soul to be a cop. Maybe you'd have been a good parish priest, or a counsellor.'

Grace glanced at him. 'You don't have to be a hard, cynical bastard to be a detective, Glenn.'

'No, but maybe it helps.'

Roy grinned.

'Do we need our onesies?' Branson asked.

The detective superintendent shook his head. 'From what Biggsy's told me, it sounds like every man and his dog's trampled all over the scene before they realized there might be something more to it. And, besides, you never look that great in one – they kind of cramp your style.'

'And they make you look like a sperm.'

'Thanks for the compliment.'

'Any time.'

They strode towards a marked police car, a line of blue and white tape stretched across the road behind it. An irate woman of around sixty, with a foghorn of a voice, was haranguing the scene guard. She was dressed in a puffa, with baggy jeans and wellies, a tangle of grey hair and holding a restless lurcher the size of a small donkey by the lead.

'Do you realize, officer, yesterday the High Sheriff of East Sussex and his wife had to *walk* to our house to lunch because of all this idiocy?'

'Madam,' the officer replied calmly, 'two people died on Saturday night. We need to understand what happened and the victims' loved ones need to understand too.'

'It's perfectly simple: that idiot Dermot Bryson always drove like he was a flipping – what's his name, that racing fellow? – Lewis Hamilton. All of us knew he was an accident waiting to happen – it's a mercy he didn't kill any of us in the village too.'

'It may be helpful if you gave a statement, madam,' he said, doing his best to placate her. 'If you let me have your name and phone number, someone will be in touch.'

She huffed. Ignoring her, Grace and Branson signed the outer cordon scene guard log, and walked a short distance up the road towards the inner cordon.

'See, it's not my imagination,' Grace said. 'I can't hear any birdsong. Can you?'

They both stopped for a moment. Branson cocked his head. There was a very distant sound of a combine harvester, but nothing else. Silence. He frowned. 'Have you got me at it too, now?'

'Imagining the silence?' Grace quizzed.

'When I was a young kid, my mum taught me how to make clouds disappear. She told me I had magic powers and that I could dissolve clouds. If I just stared at a small cloud hard, really hard, and kept staring at it, it would break up and disappear.'

'Did it work?'

Branson nodded. 'Often it did. For a while I thought I was really special and that I did have magic powers - you know, that I had a gift – like that kid Danny Torrance in *The Shining*.

Then I told a science teacher at school and he explained that clouds didn't last long anyway – a few hours at the most, and many change shape and dissipate in minutes, whether anyone was watching them or not. I experimented and realized he was right. And yet, you know, I do still look at clouds today and make them dissolve.'

Grace smiled. As they walked on, he caught the scent of wet grass and the sharper, ranker smell of hogweed. In front of them, a single autumnal leaf zigzagged to the ground. Continuing around the bend, the large, square-sided Forensic Collision Investigation Unit truck, parked in front of the inner cordon, came into view.

Startled by a whirring sound, they looked up, to see a drone pass a short distance above them and then hover in the air. On the far side of the cordon one of the FCIU Team, in overalls, was holding the controls and being directed by a similarly attired DC Simon Rideout, the Forensic Collision Investigation Unit officer currently in charge.

Grace had met the young detective on a couple of previous occasions and had always warmed to him. He did one of the grisliest jobs imaginable, and yet seemed always to manage to balance charm, humour and respect perfectly. Someone who looked less like a Forensic Collision Investigator would be hard to imagine.

Rideout was tall with the warm, smiling face of a natural entertainer, this effect enhanced by his head of thick, long, fair hair and a magnificent moustache twirled at each end. He could have been the compère on a cruise ship, or a famous stage magician. Instead he worked his magic on computers, lasers, mathematical calculations on the angles of bends and the speed of vehicles. He could tell if an indicator was on or off at the time of the collision. From minute clothing fibres on seat belts and on seats he could prove who was sitting where, as well as a whole host of other vital information. Over recent

years he had carved a reputation as a brilliantly incisive investigator – the nearest Sussex Police had to a Sherlock Holmes
of fatal traffic collisions.

Grace could see the sweeping curving clockwise lines of
coloured cat's eye markers and numbering cones, and then an
abrupt change in direction to the left. Matching the path of the
swerving Ferrari in the recording he had just seen.

He signed the second log, ducked under the red and white
tape, and was immediately greeted by the amiable Inspector, a
stocky figure with a buzz-cut, who always exuded an air of both
authority and efficiency – not something mutually compatible in
every police officer, in Roy Grace's experience. Biggs was an
innately kind man, and Grace often wondered, after twenty years
as a traffic cop, how much horror and tragedy he had seen, and
would forever have to live with.

A hive of activity was going on behind him.

'Morning, boss.' Then the RPU Inspector frowned and peered
more closely at Grace. 'I hope the other fellow came off worse.'

'He did,' he replied with such feeling that Biggs looked startled.

'Don't tell me you were in a bundle, boss? A proper roll-around?'

'Quite a grave one, actually.'

Biggs frowned. 'You've been checked over?'

'I wish everyone would stop bloody asking me that! It was over
two weeks ago. I'm on the mend. It's good to see you, Biggsy.
How's your lovely Nadine?'

'She's a lot better, boss, thanks for asking.'

'Glad to hear it, please give her my love. So – what do we have?'

'Apart from confirmation of a stat I heard recently?'

'And that is?' Grace asked.

Biggs beamed as he enlightened him. 'Fifty-two per cent of
all road traffic collisions happen within five miles of the drivers'
homes?'

'I didn't know that, but it makes sense. I also heard that in eighty per cent of collisions that happen between 11 a.m. and 1 p.m., the driver hadn't had breakfast.'

'Could make a great ad,' Biggs said, with typical gallows humour cynicism. 'Eat your Shreddies or get in your car and become one.'

Grace shook his head good-humouredly. 'You've been doing this job too long, mate.'

'Tell me about it. One hundred and thirty-two more shifts and then I'm done. Got the chart on the wall.'

It was something Roy Grace heard all too often these days and it made him sad that so many really good officers, like Biggs, were literally counting down the days to their retirement. But, equally, he could understand it. Once, in his father's time, and during his own early days on the force, the police had the public with them. In recent times, a handful of corrupt officers, and an even smaller number of officers who were sexual predators, had hit and dominated the nation's headlines. Added to that had been some tragic deaths during blue-light pursuits, and right now it felt as if the police were Public Enemy No. 1.

'So what do we have?'

'I'm hoping you'll tell me that, boss. I'm going to hand you over to Simon Rideout. But essentially, we have a Ferrari, travelling at high speed but, from the pathologist's report, driven by someone completely sober and not on any drugs, on a road familiar to him. He swerves left to avoid an unseen obstacle, swerves right, left again, then rotates, fatally, off the road into the woods. We will need to check that there were no mechanical defects with the Ferrari once we've recovered the vehicle.'

Grace glanced at Rideout, who was kneeling a short distance away and picking up something with gloved hands, which he then bagged. Dotted around the tarmac, and in the weeds at the edges, were numbered cones, used at crime scenes to mark items considered to be possible evidence by the FCIs. Sunlight seemed to be glinting off something marked by a few of them.

Over to his right, he saw the final yards the Ferrari had travelled, into the woods. Shrubbery torn away, a small sapling mown down by the car, which had then hit and scarred a large oak, before striking more trees, breaking up in the process. There were small cones on and around the path. He stared at the car's mangled cockpit and rear end in one place, the front wheel assembly in another, and the engine, still in its bay, on its side in a partially demolished bush.

'Not as pretty as when it came out of the factory, is it?' Biggs said.

'Looks to me like a masterclass in how to deconstruct a Ferrari.' Grace gave him a grim smile.

'Just needs a couple of bolts, a bit of panel beating, a lick of T-Cut and it'll be back on the road in no time,' James Biggs said.

'And it probably will be,' Grace said, thinking about the unscrupulous motor trade. Some rogue would doubtless one day turn this mess back into a handsome Ferrari on a lot, and the purchaser would be none the wiser. He looked around, taking in the scene. 'So you said there are no skid marks from the oncoming car, and there's something you want me to see?'

Biggs nodded. 'Simon Rideout feels something doesn't make sense about this and I agree with him – actually not just one thing, several things, boss.'

'Like a guy with everything to live for trashing himself and his girl on a road he's driven a thousand times?'

'That's a good place to start. Next up is that car coming from the opposite direction – you've seen the dashcam footage – it's impossible that the other car didn't brake. But we can walk further up the road and you won't see any sign of the kind of tyre marks you get before a collision or a near-collision, like we have from Bryson's Ferrari. We'll get some house-to-house done for doorbell or other private cameras to see if that comes up with anything.'

They walked on around the curve. As they passed more yellow cones, Grace saw several more glints of reflected sunlight. He stopped by one cone, numbered in marker pen, 27. It was beside a jagged piece of foil no more than two inches square. Frowning at Biggs he asked, 'Chocolate wrapper?'

'If it is, boss, and it came from the Ferrari, Dermot Bryson would have to be a major chocoholic – seems there's enough foil to wrap a hundred bars.'

As he spoke, Biggs pointed out several other cones with glinting fragments beside them, but Grace was already there. He'd been wondering about the foil – the more he looked around, the more bits of it, marked by cones, he noticed. 'So, if it's not been wrapping chocolate, why do you think there's so much of it around, James?'

The Inspector shrugged.

'DC Rideout's team are saying the car the Ferrari hit, head-on, was made of foil and disintegrated. They've found foil embedded in the front of the Ferrari and in the tree trunk.'

'And the driver disintegrated too? Into thin air?'

'It's the best I can come up with, boss. Unless you believe in ghosts. Ghosts that drop aluminium foil in their wake.'

Roy Grace nodded at Rideout who was walking towards them. 'Been in an accident, sir?' the FCI detective asked.

Grace nodded. 'I'm fine, thanks, Simon. So what have you found so far?'

'We're baffled at the moment by the bits of foil we've found around the scene, sir. We've been looking at a few heavy foot-wear marks we've found in the ground around the trees. We'd normally associate boot prints with the fire service, but some of the prints seem further afield than the fire service team would have needed to go when they attended, so I've requested the CSIs to take a look at them. James Gartrell's photographing them with a scale ruler and we're using a Crownstone plaster cast to collect impressions of them. I'm also looking for dirt, examining the cleanliness of each bit of foil to understand if it's fresh or been there a while. We're also using CSIs to look for any discarded items from people in the area, especially those around trees – cigarette ends, drinks containers, or fibres caught on branches.'

Grace nodded.

Rideout continued. 'My team are also looking for alien objects on or around the wreckage of the vehicle. We're checking for body tissue in case it struck someone, although that doesn't appear to be the case here, or paint transfer – or in this case embedded foil.'

Grace looked around. He noticed two sturdy trees on either side of the road and walked over to one, studied the base of the trunk, then crossed over and studied the other in the same place. Then he turned back to the FCIU detective. 'Do you have any hypothesis about how this accident occurred, Simon?'

'Initially I would have said he'd come around the corner and swerved to avoid an animal. But now I've looked at the dashcam, that doesn't work. But the oncoming car has vanished and left no trace. It's like it was never there and yet I can see headlights in the recording. Do you have any thoughts, sir?'

Grace looked down at the ground again, at several of the cones marking foil fragments. 'Something's not right, for sure, that's what I'm thinking, Simon.'

'And me, sir.'

60

Paul Anthony opened the What3Words app on his phone screen, and tapped the area he had selected on the map, along the coast a few miles east of Brighton. Within his target area, up came: **fear.insulated.organist.**

He smiled. *Fear.* That was a good omen for sure. *Insulated*? He'd need to figure that one out. Or maybe not. Perhaps the meaning was crystal clear. Insulated meant protected. Yes! Another good omen!

Omens were everything. Portents. Or whatever they were called. When things were meant to be!

Although the boss inside his head wagged a finger at him, like someone chanting in a pantomime. *Oh no they're not!*

He always came close to convincing himself that he did not obey the boss inside his head. But never quite close enough. The boss had been there all his life, like a mocking, domineering shadow he could not shake off. Sometimes it told him to be brave, to remember he was the best, the smartest, the toughest, King of the Hill. Other times it told him to rein it in, take his foot off the gas, lie low.

Organist.

This was a very good omen indeed.

His next victim, Toby Carlisle, had expressed a wish to be lowered into his grave to the sound of an organ – a live one, not recorded – playing sea shanties. Apparently Toby Carlisle had a love of the sea and wanted to be buried at sea. Paul was very happy to expedite his wish. A bit sooner than Carlisle had antici-pated – a good forty years sooner, perhaps, but that was what his client had ordered. So unfortunately Toby Carlisle wasn't going to have any say in the timing of his demise.

But, hey, he thought breezily, do any of us?

His client, a charming guy called Steve Lampard, was Toby Carlisle's husband, a tall, fit, muscular hunk who had made a fortune out of nightclubs, bars and gyms.

Assuming Steve Lampard was telling the truth, and he did believe he was, Toby Carlisle was an ungrateful little shit. Under the cover of his hobby of deep-sea fishing, Carlisle had for some years, before meeting Lampard, operated a very lucrative drug-smuggling business, regularly collecting consignments of heroin and crack cocaine in floating containers fitted with transponders in the middle of the English Channel, dropped by a French fisherman counterpart, and then passing them to a third party in a dinghy, in the dead of night, a few hundred yards off the Sussex coast.

All had been fine for a while, until one night, approaching the agreed rendezvous location with the dinghy, he'd been dazzled by searchlights from almost every direction. His boat was boarded by the Coastguard and impounded, along with his cargo of drugs, with a street value of over £800,000.

With all his assets frozen under the Proceeds of Crime Act, Carlisle was flat broke and unable to afford private legal representation. He had no option but to throw his lot in with a harassed, overworked and underpaid legal aid solicitor, who cheerfully advised Carlisle he was looking at the wrong end of a ten- to fifteen-year sentence for drug trafficking.

Out on bail, Toby Carlisle met Steve Lampard in a Brighton bar and it was lust at first sight. Followed by love, at least on Lampard's part. And his first act of love was to hire a top solicitor and top brief. The brief found a small but vital error in the chain of evidence and an elated Toby Carlisle walked free.

He and Steve married a month later at the Brighton register office.

Steve bought him another boat so he could continue with his passion for fishing – but hopefully not any more drug trafficking. He'd never been on the boat himself. He told Paul he got seasick just looking at ads for cruises.

Two months later, Lampard arrived home at his Tongdean Road mansion unexpectedly, in the middle of the afternoon, to be greeted by the sight of his husband's naked white bum pumping up and down on a lounger by the indoor pool. The recipient beneath him was a younger man Lampard had never seen before.

Paul Anthony would have preferred a bigger gap of time between arranging Dermot Bryson's demise and then Toby Carlisle's. The boss inside his head felt the same and told him so. The boss warned him to put the brakes on, slow it down, let the dust settle first. Give it a month at least. But Steve Lampard was one angry man. He wanted it NOW.

And, hey, Paul had given a lot of workload to his very able assistant. Between them, surely they could cope with fitting this one in?

It was all going so well again, apart from that little hiccup a couple of years back – now almost forgotten. Even the cynical boss inside his head had been forced to admit he was impressed with how well he had recovered from that little blip.

It had gone brilliantly to plan with Barnie Wallace. Until a random, dumb, middle-aged lady golfer who didn't know a mushroom from a banana, had gone and stuck a spoke – or more appropriately a five-iron – into all his careful plans.

But Dermot Bryson – that had been text-book perfection!

Although now he had the *James Taylor* shaped blip. That would just be a blip. One more wrong move by him and Taylor would be history. Nothing was going to stand in the way of Paul's new incarnation in his slightly stepped-back role, and blossoming love.

So lucrative and such fun, to boot!

The boss was saying, *Slow down, man. Wait. Give it a month or so.*

The smart thing, he knew, would be to go to ground, lie low, let the dust settle. It wasn't smart to execute another contract (he liked that term, just so apt . . .) so soon after this situation, when the police would for sure be all over Barnie – and perhaps Professor Llewellyn too. But he had already agreed the delivery date with his new client, and Mr Oswald's reputation for always delivering on time was impeccable.

And, besides, with this one there really was very little that could go wrong.

He stared at the word *organist* again.

According to Steve Lampard, he and his husband, Toby, had shared with each other the kind of funeral they wanted, in case one of them died suddenly. Sweet that they loved each other so much, Paul thought. Never mind a burial at sea with an organ playing as his body went overboard; with Steve Lampard's money, Toby Carlisle could have the entire London Symphony Orchestra playing. But Paul guessed it would be difficult to get them all assembled on a boat, and not great if the sea state wasn't calm – and the English Channel wasn't calm most of the time. Not so great to have all your mourners vomiting over the side.

He looked again at the What3Words.

fear.insulated.organist.

Definitely an omen.

The boss inside his head warned him that not all omens were good ones.

Paul Anthony told the boss to get lost.

61

The flight from Miami to Barbados was delayed, the pilot giving one of the myriad excuses that Taylor himself had used during his days as an easyJet pilot. Late arrival of cabin crew/late departure from the previous location were two of the favourites. This time it was a bag in the hold whose owner had not boarded. Probably a drunken idiot, Taylor thought, but nevertheless he was reassured by the security process. And he was very happy to see a text from Debbie when he switched his phone back on after landing.

Looking forward to seeing u when u get back 😊 XX

When the doors opened and he stepped out into the balmy, 30-degree afternoon heat, at 4 p.m. local time, Taylor had a big smile on his face. And an even bigger smile when he saw the placard held by a smartly suited man on the far side of the immigration control: *Sandy Lane Hotel – Mr James Taylor*

Ten minutes later, he was in the back of a blood-orange-coloured Mercedes taxi, heading north. It was now 4.20 local time and the driver told him it would take around forty-five minutes to reach the hotel. His name was Tony Skeete. An amiable man with a thick greying beard and a solitary gold tooth among an immaculate set of shiny white molars. He spoke with a strong voice, Bajan accent inflected with what sounded to Taylor like the occasional tinge of Irish.

277

'First time in Barbados?' Skeete asked.

'No, I came a few years back,' he replied.

'You here on vacation?'

'Partly.' The aircon was icy and Taylor cracked the window a little. Instantly he felt the warmth of the afternoon air and the sun on his face. He calculated that with luck he'd have a good hour on the beach before dusk, get his legs working again in the water. 'Can I ask you something – you're a local, right?'

'I'm local as they make them. Straight out the box.'

Taylor smiled. 'So you know a lot of the locals on this island, right?'

'Sure I do, pretty much most of 'em. Most of the ones that matter, anyhow. There's only 280,000 of us that we know about. Sure I know a lot of them.'

'Ever heard of a fisherman called John Baker?'

'John Baker? You mean the shark man?'

'The *shark* man?' Taylor felt a rush of excitement.

'Anything you want to know about sharks, John Baker's your man.'

'So he's a shark fisherman? Like that guy Quint in *Jaws*?'

'The one Robert Shaw played, right?'

'Yep.'

'John Baker knows all about sharks, but he don't fish 'em.'

'Could you take me to see him – are you available tomorrow?'

'You want to see John Baker?'

'Yes.'

'I can take you up to where he keeps boats but there's no guarantee he's going to be around. He got a big boat that he goes far out into the Atlantic – four hundred miles – for maybe twenty days at sea. He got a day boat too, for lobster and inshore fishing – you may be lucky.'

'Is it possible to call him?'

Tony Skeete shook his head. 'Don't have his number, I just know where to find him, up in Moontown.'

'How far's that from the hotel?'

'About a twenty-minute drive.'

'So we'd just have to take pot luck?'

'Pot luck,' Skeete replied.

Thirty minutes later, they swung into a smart, barriered entrance with a bored-looking security guard in a booth in the centre. He grinned at Skeete and raised the barrier.

'Tony, could you take me up to Moontown tomorrow, see if we can find him?'

'What time?'

'When do you think might be the best time?'

'Mid-morning be as good as any.'

Taylor figured on having a lie-in and an early swim. 'How about 11.30?'

'11.30 tomorrow. Got you covered.'

62

If you ever think you're having a bad day, or that life is treating you like shit, pop along to your local mortuary, Roy Grace thought sometimes. Check out the refrigerator doors. Look at the name tags. Mostly such ordinary names. Because on the other side of those doors were such ordinary people. Well, technically no longer people, just the shells of what were once people. Fathers, mothers, husbands, wives, brothers, sisters, loved ones. Human beings.

They were no longer having good or bad days. But you could guarantee one thing, and that was that all the people who had loved them were having days that ranged from pretty shitty to God-awful. For many, their worst days ever. And he never forgot that.

But also, in a bizarre way, Grace found his regular visits to the mortuary to be almost life-affirming. There were some cultures he knew where, if people saw a dead body, they would laugh – because they were celebrating. Someone had to die that day and it wasn't them. He could understand that, not that he had ever laughed at a body. Far from it. But every time he came here, it made him feel grateful for what he had. For simply being alive, and for all he had in this world that he loved – such as his wife, his children, their dog, their hens, his friends, his job and his colleagues.

There were two separate post-mortem rooms in the Brighton and Hove City Mortuary. This was so that when a potentially suspicious death was handled by a specialist Home Office pathologist there was no risk of cross-contamination with the more routine post-mortems that were carried out daily.

Ordinarily, anyone killed in a road traffic accident would be given a thorough but brief post-mortem by one of the local pathologists, unless foul play was suspected. Its purposes would be to establish whether the cause of death was from their injuries sustained in the accident or whether the cause of the accident was due to a medical condition, such as a heart attack, stroke or diabetic hypo. But, because of the suspicions raised by Inspector James Biggs at the scene, which Roy Grace had agreed with, the two victims were now going to be subjected to far more elaborate, time-consuming and expensive Home Office pathologist post-mortems.

The process was just starting now, at a few minutes to 8 a.m. It was Roy Grace's duty as the SIO to attend, or for continuity, to delegate another detective from his team should he need to leave. He was currently attending with Branson so that they could discuss Operation Meadow during what promised to be a long and slow day, and assess any findings from the pathologist.

In the cold, gloomy room, all gowned up in green, wearing cloth caps and gauze masks, were: the Spanish-born pathologist, Nadiuska De Sancha; the coroner's officer, Michelle Websdale; CSI photographer James Gartrell; Grace's wife, Cleo; and her deputy, Darren Wallace. The latter two had carried out a forensic recovery of the bodies from the scene. This involved placing bags over the head, hands and feet of the deceased – and, in Dermot's case, the head separate to the body. Then they were packaged into individual white body sheets, rolled up and sellotaped at each end – 'cracker wrapped', as Norman Potting had once described it, with his grim gallows humour – then placed inside body bags, which were zipped up.

Grace looked at the body bags, each lying on a steel table, each tagged with a brown exhibit label. Last week Dermot Bryson was a very rich man with a Ferrari worth over a million quid. Now he was a crime scene exhibit. He looked at Tracey Dawson's label, wondering what her story was. Someone hard as nails, or a soft, kind young woman with her whole future ahead of her, perhaps swept off her feet by Bryson? Or an accomplice in whatever nefarious activities he was involved in that required him to keep a gun in his glove box?

Then he thought back to the crash scene.

Glenn Branson said something he did not hear, he was so wrapped up in his thoughts.

'Hello!' Branson said again. 'Anyone home?'

That got through. Grace looked at him with a startled grimace. 'Sorry, I was miles away.'

Branson looked at the body bags and shivered. 'Wish we both were. It was a lot warmer in Barbados.'

'That footage we viewed from the Ferrari's dashcam. I've just realized what it is that's been bugging me.'

'Which is?'

'So a car's coming the other way around that bend, towards the Ferrari, right?'

'Yes.'

'But we didn't see any headlights on that footage of an oncoming car before the bend. We only saw the lights of the oncoming car when they were actually head-on.'

Branson frowned. 'What are you saying?'

'Bear with me. There are no turn-offs along Sparrowhawk Lane, until you get to the main road at the far end. There's only one property along the lane that had outward facing CCTV, Cobhouse Lodge, and Biggsy said they'd checked it and it didn't pick up any vehicle coming from the other direction fifteen minutes either side of the time of the crash.'

'There was a lot of foil on the ground. What was all that about?'

'A ghost car that turned to fragments of foil on impact, perhaps.'

'Ghost car?'

Grace nodded. And in response to his colleague's frown said, 'I'm just going to step out and make a call.'

He walked out into the corridor and went into the privacy of Cleo's little office, where he sat down at her desk, smiling at the tiny frame containing a photograph of himself, Noah and Molly. He called Jack Alexander. When he answered, Grace said, 'Jack, I need a roll of mirror foil, four foot wide and thirty long, as soon as possible. Find a local supplier for this and call me back as soon as you have. I also need to know all the local firms who could supply this, and any who have sold rolls of this size in the past month.'

The DS said he would be right on it.

Grace could hear the unasked question, *why*, in his voice.

Instantly he ended the call his phone rang again. It was Jonathan Jackson from the Met's Central Image Investigation Unit.

'Sir, we've got a result for you on the CCTV you sent through of the blind man with his dog.'

'Tell me?' Grace said, feeling a surge of adrenaline.

'The footage wasn't great, but we have run it through our new Facial Recognition System. The algorithms are much better these days and it looks at loads of measurements between the eyes, the nose, the mouth, the chin et cetera. It kicks out a handful of possible matches, but it still takes a human to compare and make a decision. I had one of my best officers, Andy Eyles, look at it.'

Grace could hear the excitement in his voice. 'And, JJ?'

'We're now sure it is your dead man walking. Rufus Rorke.'

63

Taylor felt much more refreshed after a long early swim across the clear warm water of the bay, out to the raft anchored in the middle and back, followed by a sensational breakfast. Then he wrote a postcard to his ten-year-old son Harrison, which he did whenever he was anywhere abroad. Although he had no idea whether Harrison ever saw them, or if Marianne destroyed them – he wouldn't put it past her, he rued. He had given it to the front desk to post.

Now in shorts, a short-sleeved linen shirt and beach shoes, he sat in the back of Tony Skeete's Mercedes taxi, watching the passing scenery and thinking about the questions he would ask fisherman John Baker if – he hoped to hell – he was around.

The road was bumpy, badly in need of a lot of repair work. To their left they passed a plethora of large signs. *BEAUTY AND THE BEACH. LAS VEGAS SLOTS – 777! CHESTERTONS LUXURY SALES AND RENTALS.* Out of his right-hand window he could see what looked like a smart department store, then a Rubis filling station. A short distance on they passed, on their left, a series of gated, ocean-fronting mansions, and on the right a long row of wooden chattel houses. Tiny, rectangular wooden dwellings, with a front door and a solitary front window, some clearly loved and some very dilapidated.

After twenty minutes, Skeete slowed sharply. 'Moontown!' he said.

On his right, Taylor saw a beat-up-looking, dark red single-storey building almost groaning under the weight of a satellite TV dish and an industrial aircon vent. On the wall, in white paint, one sign read, *BANKS – THE BEER OF BARBADOS*, and another, *SENSIBLE SHOPPERS SHOP WITH US!*

To his left was an open-sided building, a pitched corrugated-iron roof supported on stone columns painted turquoise and white with the sea visible and alluring beyond. There were several people in the open space, none of them appearing to be doing anything.

'The fish market,' Skeete said. Then he added, 'You're in luck. I see John Baker, let's hope he hasn't been on the rum yet.'

Taylor's watch told him it was 11.55 a.m. 'Sun's not over the yardarm.'

'Yardarm? What's that?'

'Just a saying.'

'I'll introduce you, then I'll leave you to do whatever business you have with him.'

They got out of the car. Taylor noticed immediately the rank stench of fish in the air, as he glanced at a large official-looking sign hanging high up. *NOTICE – FISHERIES DIVISION*, and a blackboard fixed to one column with the catches of the day marked and chalked up. There was a large free-standing refrigerator in one corner, and a long slab, on which sat weigh scales at one end, and a small, headless conger eel at the other, beneath a cloud of flies. The whole of the wall facing the sea was one long, tiled washbasin, like a raised trench.

He wrinkled his nose at the smell, looking around, wondering which of the dozen or so men in here was John Baker. Several were looking at him, eyeing him curiously, and one, a youth in a baseball cap, with a row of beads around his neck, with definite suspicion. There was a listless atmosphere, as if the business of the day was now over. Several open bottles of beer and rum sat on a table, and he noticed at least three of the men holding glasses containing the dark liquid.

Tony Skeete began talking earnestly to a man of around sixty, who was wearing old Crocs, faded green shorts that finished well below his knees and a grey T-shirt. He was solid and muscular, his shaven head looking like it had been hewn from a block of ebony.

'Mr Taylor, this is your man, this is Mr John Baker. He's happy to talk to you.'

Taylor strode over and held out his hand. 'James Taylor, nice to meet you.'

Baker looked at him for a moment, with large brown eyes that seemed tinged with some deep sadness, as if appraising him. He shook Taylor's hand back, a solid, almost crushing handshake, and said nothing for some moments. He seemed like a man who had no need to hurry anything, as if he had all the time in the world.

Taylor broke the awkward silence by adding, 'I appreciate your talking to me.'

'You're English?' Baker asked. His voice was deep, quiet and thoughtful.

'I am. Ever been there?'

'My wife was from Newcastle. I lived there once. But she died.' He unconsciously fingered a ring hanging low down on a silver chain around his neck.

'I'm sorry.'

'It was a while back.' He looked at Taylor inquisitively and with a faint, wistful smile. 'How can I help you, Mr Taylor?'

'An old friend of mine – a very old and good friend – was lost at sea off a yacht off the coast of Barbados, a couple of years ago. I understand you found his jacket when you were out fishing?'

Baker seemed to stiffen. His face gave little away but there was wariness in his eyes now and he looked at Taylor more intensely. 'I found part of a jacket. Wrapped around one of my net ropes.'

'I heard he might have been the victim of a shark attack – is that what you think? I understand you're an expert on sharks.'

Baker shrugged – just the tiniest hint of unease. If Taylor had blinked he would have missed it. 'I killed a few.'

'You think a shark got Rufus Rorke?'

He was silent for a moment, as if reflecting. 'Maybe, or maybe the shark just saw the jacket floating free and took a bite at it, then spat it out when it realized it wasn't a fish. Sharks don't have colour vision, only black and white. For sure the teeth marks on the jacket were from a tiger shark.'

'I understand there were bloodstains on the jacket – that matched my friend's DNA. Wouldn't that indicate the shark had got him?'

'I never saw any blood on the cloth. But the police are clever with their forensic stuff. You know?'

Taylor nodded.

'What exactly is your interest?' Baker asked.

'His widow asked me to find out more about his death,' he lied. 'She's distraught and doesn't think the police have been telling her the whole truth. Can I ask you, how did you know it was his jacket? The ocean's a big place.'

Instantly, he clocked the flash of unease across the fisherman's face, before Baker glanced down at his chunky digital mariner's watch. 'I got to go over to my boat in a minute, the engineer's got the gearbox out.'

'I won't keep you. I am just curious how you knew it was his jacket.'

Taylor noticed him curl and uncurl his hands. 'I didn't. After I untangled it from the rope I slung it on the deck – it's always good to have rags on the boat, although I could tell it had once been some kind of a fancy jacket, I saw the Savile Row name in the label. Like I said, I lived in Newcastle with my wife for some years, and I know what Savile Row is. I wondered how come that got into the sea – didn't sit quite right. Then I got back and I saw in the papers about this man lost overboard.'

'Rufus Rorke?'

'Yeah – yeah, that was his name. There was a photograph of him and his wife taken at a fancy restaurant earlier on the night he disappeared, in the paper. I saw he was wearing a white jacket that looked pretty much like the one I'd fished out the water. First, I thought about not going to the police, because of the hassle – seems like I was right.' He smiled.

'You've had a lot of hassle?'

Ignoring the comment, John Baker said, 'Anyhow, I contacted a police lady I know – she's the sister-in-law of another Moontown fisherman. Next thing I know I've got police all over me like a rash, asking questions and stuff, and where exactly had I found it. They sent a dive boat out to the location, but they didn't find nothing, of course.'

'Of course?'

He hesitated and looked uncomfortable. 'You go overboard five miles out to sea and the body could be anywhere, if it ain't inside the belly of a tiger, could be damned well anywhere. But I'm betting a tiger got him.' He shrugged again. 'I wish I had more for you. I'm sorry 'bout your friend.' He did look genuinely sorry.

Taylor thanked him, realizing this was all he was going to get. As he climbed back into the Mercedes, Tony Skeete asked, 'Get what you wanted?'

Taylor didn't reply for some moments. He was thinking about John Baker's body language. About those flashes of unease. And he reflected on one of the last things John Baker had said. *But they didn't find nothing, of course.*

What had he actually meant by that? The impossibility of finding anything in the vastness of the ocean? Or had it been a slip of the tongue?

64

'Are you going to tell me exactly what we are doing?' Glenn Branson asked.

'It's a scientific experiment,' Grace replied glibly.

'You dragged me out of a nice cosy post-mortem to stand in the middle of a cart track in pissing rain and falling darkness, in the cause of science?'

'Welcome to the real world of being a detective, matey.'

They were standing part way around a bend in the cart track that led to Roy Grace's cottage, a quarter of a mile on. It was 7 p.m. and almost fully dark. Rain that had begun as a light drizzle was now falling steadily. Jack Alexander had been delegated to stand in for them at the post-mortem, for the rest of the procedure.

It quietly amused Grace that his friend, colleague and protégé was so totally baffled, as between them, ignoring the rain, they unspooled the roll of four-foot-wide mirror foil across the cart track. Using two lengths of baler twine, Grace secured one side to a tall sapling on the left. There was no convenient tree, but to their right was the open-sided barn with the rusted tractor that had not moved in all the time Grace and Cleo had lived here, and looked like it never would. But finally it served a purpose, as he and Branson, struggling with some difficulty against the wind, finally got this end of the foil, again using baler twine, attached to the sub-frame at the bottom, and higher up around the steering wheel, and pulled it tight, being careful not to tear it.

'Oh, I get it,' Branson said. 'We're going to play moonlit reflective tennis, right?'

Grace grinned. Branson was right, it did look rather like a shiny tennis net strung across the track. He walked back across and checked again that it was secure against the sapling.

'When are you going to tell me what the hell you are doing?'

'You're a detective, you figure it out.'

'I didn't join the police to stand getting sodding soaked in the middle of farmland with my lunatic senior officer farting around with Bacofoil.'

Grace started striding back towards his Alfa, parked a hundred yards or so back. Branson trudged after him, conscious of his polished shoes getting increasingly sodden as he splashed through mud and then stubbed his foot on a rut. When they reached the car both of them climbed in. Grace started the engine. 'Put your phone on record and hold it on the dash – imagine it's a dashcam, pointing forward.'

Branson frowned, and then clicked. 'I think I just got what you're doing!'

'No shit, Sherlock.'

As Branson complied, Grace put the car in gear, the headlights on full beam, and accelerated hard. He continued accelerating as they began rounding the bend. Then his colleague suddenly cried out, 'Jesus!'

The lights of an oncoming vehicle were coming straight at them, head-on.

'Wow!' Branson yelled, excited.

Grace continued accelerating as the lights came closer, larger, closer, larger. He swerved just a little, to the left then to the right, and each time the lights came at them.

'This is crazy, Roy!'

There was a blaze of white and a burst of flashes like fireworks exploding, then, as Grace braked hard, there was no longer anything in front of them except darkness, and a startled rabbit hopping across the track some yards ahead. He brought the car to a halt.

Branson looked at him, shaking his head. 'Shit. I could easily have thought it was some vehicle coming right at us.'

'Exactly, you'd never know it was our own reflection.'

'That's a smart experiment. All those bits of foil on the road around the Ferrari. I hadn't sussed.'

Grace raised a finger. 'Remember one of the first rules at a crime scene?'

'Clear the ground under your feet?'

Grace nodded. 'What are little bits of foil doing on a country lane? Are they there by coincidence, or could they just be connected to the crash?'

'So Biggsy's instincts are right.'

'This is just a hypothesis, but it fits with what we saw on the Ferrari's dashcam. You and I just saw oncoming headlights, but no advance flare of light before we rounded the bend, right? Which we would have seen, even if an oncoming vehicle had its lights on low beam.'

Branson nodded.

'Dermot Bryson had a handgun in his glove box. You only carry a handgun if you are planning to kill someone, or if you have an enemy you are afraid of. Someone who wants to kill you.'

Branson nodded again.

'Looks to me like someone wanted to kill Dermot Bryson but make it appear an accident. Whose MO might that be?'

'Rufus Rorke, possibly?'

'Rufus Rorke indeed. His funeral was held two years ago. But he's been identified by the Met Police Facial Imaging team walking along Western Road in Brighton with a white stick and a guide dog, a few weeks ago. Blind, but with good enough vision to tell a death cap mushroom from a field mushroom.' He shrugged. 'Of course, this is all hypothesis.'

'Nothing so far from surveillance on his supposed widow?'

Grace shook his head. 'No. But what I don't get is, if it is Rorke, what the hell is he doing back on this turf? At the time he supposedly went overboard from the boat, he knew he was about to be nicked on a raft of serious charges, murder, conspiracy to murder and the rest. He was facing twenty-plus years in jail. It doesn't make sense that he would come back to Brighton. That's what makes me unsure it really is him. He'd have to be nuts to think he could start operating here, under our noses, and not get spotted by someone – and potted.'

'Hubris,' Branson said. 'How many criminals have you potted over the years who would have got away with it if it hadn't been for their hubris? Their smug confidence that all cops are thick as shit, and they're the smart ones?'

Grace nodded. 'You're right. A lot.'

'So let's go find this guy. See if it really is Rufus Rorke, and let him see who's really the smart one.'

Grace grinned. 'I like your style.'

'There's something I've been thinking about. The association chart.'

'Tell me?' Grace frowned, looking distractedly at his phone screen.

'OK, so we know Barnie Wallace and Rufus Rorke were at school together. If Rorke has come back from the dead and murdered Wallace, in addition to Dermot Bryson and his girlfriend, what was the motive? Are they all connected?'

'I think we may have some answers.' Grace held up his phone so Branson could read the message on it. A text from Aiden Gilbert.

Call me when you can, Roy, in the morning. We have good news re Barnie Wallace!

'Sounds promising,' Branson replied. 'Sounds like they're in the rest of his devices.'

'Meanwhile, we've got some foil to clear up. We don't want to be litter louts in the countryside.'

65

The wind rattled the patio doors that opened onto Paul Anthony's terrace. Tonight they were firmly closed and the rain, flung at the glass by an increasingly strong sou'wester, sounded like buckshot.

Inside the warmth of his living room, Paul sat at his leather-topped desk, laptop open in front of him, Van Morrison playing through the speakers, a Cohiba burning in the ashtray and a tumbler of Haig Club Blue on the rocks on a coaster next to it.

And a beautiful woman, in ripped jeans and a loose, sexy blouse, leaning affectionately on his shoulder, crystal coupe of Billecart-Salmon Champagne in her hand.

All was good with the world. He used to tell Fiona that the secret of life was to know when it was good. And right now it didn't get much better than this.

Two pinpricks of light appeared in the distance in the darkness. They disappeared, then reappeared. A ship, way out in the Channel. Not a good night to be at sea, much better to be in here in the snug warmth, on terra firma. With a beautiful lady.

Shannon was looking at the English Channel too, but not at the bitumen black one through the windows. She was focused on a bottle-green version on Google Earth on Paul Anthony's laptop screen. On a section of sea some miles off the coast to the east of Newhaven Harbour. 'That's where Toby Carlisle goes fishing,' she said, and with her forefinger on the trackpad moved the cursor to a point some miles further offshore. 'That's the shelf where the sea deepens. I've interrogated the boat's satnav and that's the area he fishes around. And because of its depth – 120 metres – it's a good place to scuttle his boat after . . .'

She let the unspoken word hang in the air.

He looked up at her with a smile. 'How did I cope before I met you?'

'You know exactly how you coped. You coped fine. The question you should ask, is how you are going to keep me onside with your skewed moral compass.' She strode across the room and, holding her glass, lay back on a leather sofa, kicking her barefooted legs over one of its arms.

'You're judging me? Seriously?'

'When I met you, I thought you operated under some kind of moral code and I liked that, I respected you for that. You gave me the impression you were providing justice in a world where justice is too often the victim instead of the result. Sure, I was shocked that you did really sort out Professor Llewellyn. Shocked, but at the same time, I kind of liked you for doing it. He was a piece of shit and the world is a better place without him. But is the world a better place without Barnie Wallace? Dermot Bryson sounds like another slimeball, but did Tracey Dawson deserve to die just for dating him? Do you actually have any moral compass at all, or are you doing this purely for the money, using altruism as a flag of convenience?'

'Hey, Shannon! That's a big one you're laying on me. We should be having fun tonight!'

Before she could respond, one of the three mobile phones on his desk rang. All of them were pay-as-you-go – burners. Only Shannon knew two of their numbers. And only one person knew the third, which was the one ringing. Anthony stepped out of the room with it, wondering what problem or demand she was going to throw at him tonight. Was one of their sons unwell?

'Hello,' he answered, curtly as always.

'Mr Rorke?'

He was startled to realize it wasn't Fiona. It was a man, his voice deep and slow. A voice he recognized but was taking a moment to remember. How had he got this number? For an instant, in sheer panic, he wondered whether to hang up. But the caller knew his name, and he was sure he did know the caller. 'Who is speaking?' he asked, guardedly.

'John Baker.'

'Hey, John!' he said, startled. 'Long time no speak. How – how are you?'

'I been better, Mr Rorke. Maybe you can 'splain to me what's going on?'

'What do you mean, John? Explain what, exactly?'

'Last week I had a British police officer – a detective – asking me questions about your disappearance. Seems like he wasn't too convinced you were dead. Then today, I had someone else asking 'bout you, said he was a friend of yours, said your wife – widow – had asked him to find out more about your death.'

'What?' Paul Anthony exclaimed, and saw Shannon looking at him through the glass door. 'Fiona?' he said softly and turning away. 'He said she'd wanted to know more?'

'That's what he said, Mr Rorke,' John Baker said flatly. 'And I'm wondering what is going on. You paid me to give a story about finding your torn jacket, with shark bite marks on it, to the police and you said that would be the end of it. I did what we agreed, and used the jaws of a tiger I killed a few years back. Did a pretty good job, I thought. Now I'm starting to feel real uncomfortable. I didn't get paid enough to deal with all this stuff. So I called your Fiona and she said to phone you.'

'I can send you more money. This man who came to see you today. What was his name?'

'Taylor,' Baker said. 'James Taylor. Said he was a real good friend of yours. He wanted to understand more about how you died, so he could explain to your – *widow.*' He said that word with a sarcastic tone. 'You know him, this Mr James Taylor?'

'Oh yes,' he replied darkly. 'I know him.'

66

Shortly before 7 a.m., Grace, holding a mug of coffee in his hand, stood in the conference room of the Major Crime suite. He'd not had much sleep after calling ACC Downing last night to inform him that the deaths of Dermot Bryson and Tracey Dawson were being treated as murder and of his suspicions about Rufus Rorke, giving him reason to put this investigation under the same Operation Meadow umbrella as the Barnie Wallace inquiry.

He'd lain awake in bed, his brain racing, thinking about everything he needed to do today on the dual investigation. And on the way in this morning, he'd called Aiden Gilbert and left a message.

He was now studying the association chart for Dermot Bryson, which was pinned on a whiteboard next to the one for Barnie Wallace. Two men murdered in ways that made their deaths look like accidents. The MO of the perhaps not-so-deceased murder suspect, Rufus Rorke?

The death of Brighton University professor Bill Llewellyn was also on the radar for this same inquiry, having been brought to his attention by both a Sussex coroner and Cleo as another unusual death. But Grace didn't feel, at this stage, that he had enough to connect it to these two, and that for the moment it might be a distraction.

Barnie Wallace had a clear link to Rufus Rorke, through their schooldays. But there was nothing at all, so far, to link Wallace to Bryson – nor to Bryson's girlfriend, Tracey Dawson. He sat down and began making a number of updates to the agenda for the 8.30 a.m. briefing he had called for Operation Meadow. But, just as he started, Glenn Branson came into the room, wearing the kind of shouty suit, shirt and tie combination that, Grace thought, was more appropriate for a 1950s seaside spiv. 'Morning, early bird,' the DI said chirpily.

Grace looked up at him then covered his eyes in mock horror.

'Dazzled by my brilliance?' Branson asked.

'Glad to see your tailor hasn't lost his sense of humour, matey.'

Branson looked mock-offended. 'My tailor is a man of the ultimate taste and discernment. And now I wouldn't be seen in any other suit than a Gresham Blake one.'

Grace shook his head. 'Do you need me to remind you again why detectives wear suits, with shirt and tie and clean shoes?'

'So we give a respectable image when we turn up to people's homes or business premises.'

'Precisely. In order to give them confidence. Not make them feel that you're about to produce a string of dodgy watches from your inside pocket.'

'So you don't like my threads?'

'It's a very nice whistle, suit, threads, whatever you want to call it. But you're a detective. You need to be just a tad more discreet – in my humble opinion.'

Branson, stroking the front of his jacket, looked hurt. 'I actually thought this *was* discreet – respectful, like, it's mostly black, yeah?'

'Maybe if you put a flashing purple lightbulb on your head, you might look a little more discreet.'

Just as Branson frowned, Grace's job phone rang. It was Aiden Gilbert. Grace put him on loudspeaker.

'Roy, good news, we've broken the encryption on Barnie Wallace's computer and accessed more photographs from his phone.'

'Nice work, Aiden.'

'Most of the credit goes to Charlotte Mckee – she broke the phone first, and then she found the password to the computer hidden on the phone – winner winner, chicken dinner!'

Grace laughed.

'I think we've got quite a lot of stuff, but I don't know what's going to be helpful to you and what isn't.'

Grace looked at his electronic diary. As was normal in the early stages of a murder inquiry, his PA – shared with several other Major Crime Team detectives – had cancelled all his non-urgent meetings. 'I can be with you in half an hour, Aiden.'

'I'll put the kettle on.'

67

Roy Grace always thought that Haywards Heath police station looked far too big a building for the requirements of this quiet, affluent small town, fourteen miles north of Brighton, in the heart of the West Sussex countryside. Populated by just forty thousand people, a substantial number of whom were commuters to London, a little over half an hour away by train, the town had a relatively low crime rate, despite being named, so one rumour had it, after a highway robber called Jack Hayward. It was a rumour Grace liked to believe.

Since being built, the creatively designed, three-storey 1960s building had housed not only all the wide variety of police officers and support staff required for the town, but it had also been the HQ of both the West Sussex Roads Policing Team, COMMS, where all 999 calls came in, as well as forensic imaging. Today, while still a live police station, that was only a small part of the work that went on inside.

From a distance, with its smart, modern exterior, the police station could have been mistaken for the corporate headquarters of any number of multinational finance or insurance companies, until you drove closer, and saw the police vehicles filling much of the car park. It was when you approached the back entrance that you began to realize that, no matter what the exterior of a police station told the world, the staff entrance was almost invariably a reinforced steel door, with a handful of people smoking outside, accessed by a keycard that instead of opening onto a grand foyer, puts you at the bottom of narrow steep stairs as lavishly appointed as a fire escape.

Which was where Grace and Branson found themselves now, shortly after 8 a.m. They climbed up the two flights, passing the Crime Management Unit floor, and reached the second storey, where the Sussex Digital Forensics and Cybercrime units were housed.

Grace held his passcard to the keypad, but all he got was a beep and a flashing red light. He cursed, but at the same time respected the security of this unit being so tight it would not even allow access to the Head of Major Crime for the two counties.

'Not as important as you thought you were, eh, boss?' Branson quipped.

Grace narrowed his eyes at him. 'All right, smartypants, try yours.'

Branson did. As he pressed the card to the pad there were two sharp beeps and a green light. He pushed the door open and held it for Grace, who stood there, shaking his head at him. 'What?'

Branson grinned.

'What?' Grace said again.

Still grinning he tweaked his jacket lapels. 'You just need influence, boss. Like what I have.'

Shaking his head from side to side, Grace walked beside his colleague along a short corridor lined with warning posters about passwords and into the large, open-plan office that was the nerve-centre of the Digital Forensics team. There was an atmosphere of quiet, studious energy in here. Casually dressed people, mostly in their late twenties and thirties, worked at the rows of two-abreast workstations lined down each side of the room, each with a single keyboard and twin screens. Many were cluttered with personal stuff – water flasks, mugs with slogans – and the walls were lined with whiteboards, all with writing and diagrams. On one partition, he saw a yellow hazard warning sign that read: *WARNING. HANGRY. DO NOT APPROACH (UNLESS WITH FOOD)*

He grinned, then saw the figures of Aiden Gilbert and Jason Quigley, two of the most long-serving people in this department. Wearing their ID lanyards around their necks, both were dressed in what was pretty much the male uniform here of polo shirts over jeans and trainers. They greeted the two detectives with warm smiles. Gilbert, energetic, with his silver hair brushed forward and his blue polo shirt long and baggy, could have been a famous Shakespearian actor who had just stepped out of rehearsals for a brief moment. Quigley, tall and shaven-headed with a neatly trimmed beard, exuded debonair, almost avuncular charm. This small corner of the large room was now the only section dedicated to computers, Grace knew.

When he'd first visited this department, many years back, then known as the High Tech Crime Unit, it was tucked away in the basement of the old CID headquarters, Sussex House, and computers were the main focus. Today, it was increasingly all about the phones.

'So your reprogrammed card worked, Glenn?' Gilbert said.

'Worked a treat!'

Grace looked at Gilbert then Branson, and saw he'd been pranked. 'Bastards!'

Grinning, Gilbert said, 'Sorry, Glenn, I'm afraid I'll have to deauthorize your card now. Can we get you anything to drink?'

'I'm good, thanks,' Grace said.

Branson nodded, the same.

'Have a seat, gents,' he said, indicating two spare swivel chairs at the empty workstation next to him. As they perched on them, he said, 'I think we've found something of interest from interrogating Barnie Wallace's computer – in particular from the folders of photographs, in addition to the ones we've already sent you from his phone. I'll take you down to Charlotte Mckee afterwards, she's in the process of doing a full extraction from his phone and laptop.'

Quigley brought up an image of what looked a pure work of art. A length of chargrilled fish, topped with prawns and stalks of dill and surrounded by a tiny lake of green sauce. A row of edamame beans was elegantly laid out around the rim of the plate, like a string of beads.

'From the photographs on his computer there seem to be only two subjects Wallace took photographs of – the first is food,' Quigley said. He showed several art images of dishes in succession, some still photographs, some frenetic videos of Barnie Wallace in his kitchen cooking in speeded-up time. 'Raw ingredients,' Quigley continued. 'Cooking utensils, ingredients in prep and in stages of being cooked, and finished dishes and plates of food.'

The image on the screen changed to a photograph of a tall man in a long coat, hoodie, face covering and dark glasses, against a Brighton residential street background. He was immediately familiar to the two detectives who had been working on the initial images that had been sent to them. 'This is his other subject,' Jason Quigley said. 'A tall man whose identity we don't know. There are literally hundreds of photographs of him, all taken through a long lens – a Tamron 400mm on a Nikon D5300 camera.'

'You can tell the camera and lens make, from the photographs?' Grace asked, impressed.

'The lens, camera make, model and location to within approximately twenty feet, and time, Roy,' Aiden Gilbert butted in.

'I always knew you were a smart guy, Aiden, I didn't know you were a genius!'

'I'm not! It's all built into the camera's memory, unless the person using it disables it. Maybe Mr Wallace didn't know about that.'

Grace thought hard for a moment. 'Can you get the images of this man's face enhanced, Aiden?'

'The best people to do that are the Met Facial Imaging Team, up in Lambeth. But they'll only be able to help if there is a crime connection in their area.'

'There is,' Grace replied. 'Our suspect – the man we might be looking at – we now believe committed a murder in Bond Street about a year ago where he shoved a man into the road, under a bus. It was caught on a shop's outward-facing CCTV.'

'Good,' Gilbert said. 'This fellow always seems to have been careful not to show too much of his face – in the photos he wears a baseball cap and a face mask a lot of the time, or a hoodie and mask or scarf high up his face.'

'Not surprising, since he's dead,' Grace said.

The two forensic investigators both looked bemused. 'He's been photographing a ghost?' Quigley said.

Grace smiled. 'OK. What can you tell me about the location of these photographs? Is there any pattern?'

'There is,' Gilbert said, sounding very pleased with himself. 'I'll show you on a map. But Charlotte Mckee will have a lot more on this for you, from his phone.'

'This camera – the Nikon D5300 – how easy would it be to identify where it was bought?' Branson asked.

'Not easy at all, it's one of their most popular models – there are literally thousands of them out there. But in terms of the pattern of photographs, Jason and I have done a matrix and the majority are around an address in Kemp Town. When we narrow it down further, it points to Arundel Terrace. Again, Charlotte will be able to give you more on this, I'm pretty sure.'

Grace knew the road. One of the city's finest addresses – a row of grand, elegant, terraced Regency buildings facing directly onto the English Channel. They had once been individual houses, but most of them now, if not all, were divided into apartments. His late, former wife, Sandy, had said more than once that if they ever won the lottery, Arundel Terrace was one of the places she would love to live.

'Can you pinpoint any further than that?' he asked.

'Yes. But not the exact number – I can narrow it down to three – approximately mid-terrace.'

'Three is good.'

Moments later, they saw a sequence of numbered photographs on the screen. He got as far as number seven when Branson exclaimed, 'Bloody hell.'

'You took the words out of my mouth!' Grace said.

A tall figure in a hoodie, bulky black jacket, jeans and trainers, and with a very confident, erect posture, was striding up a street towards the camera, but clearly unaware of it. The background was blurry, but looked like the sea in the distance.

Grace looked at the date and time on the photograph: 2.12 p.m., Thursday, 1 September. The coordinates were next to it. He turned to Branson. 'Looks very much like our mushroom switcher again. Two days before he strikes.'

'Could be his identical twin,' the DI retorted with a grin.

'The coordinates, Aiden. Where do those put him?'

Quigley tapped his keyboard. After a few moments a map of part of Kemp Town seafront appeared. 'Chichester Terrace,' he announced.

Grace, born and raised in the city, had a good knowledge of its streets. 'If I was going to walk from an apartment in Arundel Terrace to Organica supermarket, that is one of the streets I would choose as part of my route. This is two days before the mushroom switch? Is he on a recce?'

Quigley brought the image of the man back up and zoomed in tight on his face. He was wearing a scarf that covered his nose and lower part of his face, and his hood came down low over his forehead. His eyes were concealed by large sunglasses. 'Looks like someone not too keen to be recognized.'

Branson nodded slowly. 'And just like the Switcher. Same good posture.'

'What we need now is the CCTV footage from Organica for that afternoon, Thursday, September the first. On the assumption they still have it,' Grace said. 'See if we can spot him doing a recce.'

'We're getting there, aren't we? Slowly but steadily,' Branson said.

Grace smiled. 'You know what they say about science? It advances one funeral at a time.'

'And we're one funeral in. Two to go.'

'Let's hope we can keep it to that.'

They were interrupted by a sudden roar of laughter.

Gilbert and Quigley stood up. Grace and Branson joined them and they saw a tall, bearded man giving a speech, with the attention of everyone in the room.

'Good news!' whispered Gilbert. 'It's a leaving assassination speech. It means there will be cake!'

'You mean we can have it and eat it?' Branson said.

68

Ten minutes later, Grace and Branson, each awkwardly holding a paper napkin balancing a crumbling slice of coffee cake, sat on chairs at the far end of the room with Digital Forensic Examiner Charlotte Mckee and Team Leader Lisa Roberts. Both women, exuding enthusiasm, were in their early thirties. Mckee had long light brown hair, a striped jumper, black leggings and trainers; Roberts was sporting cropped blonde hair, a green track-suit top, jeans and trainers. Also present was DC Ruth Venus from the Major Crime Team.

Another member of the team, Digital Forensic Examiner Gabriella Weston, similarly dressed to Mckee – apart from a white bobble hat – and affectionally dubbed by Mckee as the Tea Lady, appeared with two steaming mugs for Grace and Branson, who were by now both desperate for a drink.

On Mckee's desk, amid the clutter of a notepad, Thermos, Scotch-tape dispenser and electronic apparatus, was an evidence bag and, next to it, Barnie Wallace's phone, plugged into her computer. On her right screen was an exquisite photo-graph of a chain of dachshunds, and on the left it was all black with white lettering; at the top it read: EXTRACTION COMPLETED SUCCESSFULLY.

Grace and Branson scanned the headings:

Contacts. 372
MMS
Pictures. 9,750
Videos. 375
Documents. 8,500
Email. 26,232
Call logs. 956
Advertising ID
User Dictionary
SMS 883
Calendar
Audio/Music. 335
Ringtones
Archives
IM
Locations
Browsing data
Files. 871

It reminded Grace of something his former colleague Ray Packham had said to him, years back. *Give me an hour with someone's computer and I'll know more about them than their partner does.* And something that Aiden Gilbert had said to him only a year or so ago. *Looking into someone's computer – or phone, now – is like looking into their soul.*

So this was the deceased Barnie Wallace's soul. Would it provide the reason, from beyond his grave, why he had been murdered?

'So, gentlemen,' Mckee said in her very friendly and rather posh voice that reminded Grace quite a lot of Cleo's equally upper-crust voice – far posher than his own. 'Are you looking for anything specific?'

'We are, Charlotte,' Branson jumped in. 'We are interested in Wallace's movements in the four weeks before his death, in particular. And any calls he made during that period.'

'OK, that should be easy.' She took a swig of water from her Thermos, then tapped her keyboard. 'I'm sure you both know how paranoid so many people are about the idea that their every movement is being tracked?'

Grace nodded.

'And being injected with microchips to make us all love the Bay City Rollers,' Branson added.

Charlotte Mckee frowned.

'She's too young,' Grace said. 'You're dating yourself.'

'Me?' he exclaimed. 'You're a fine one to—' But before he could say anything else, Mckee continued.

'The government doesn't need to inject tracking devices into anyone. We all carry them around with us all day long, anyway – in the form of our mobile phones.' She smiled. 'If you have your phone's Wi-Fi switched on, then it says hello to every Wi-Fi router it passes. Which means, these days, every house, shop, restaurant and institution. Ruth and I can tell you from this extraction not only Barnie Wallace's movements during the time period you need, but how long he spent in each location.'

'Can you tell us what he was thinking when he was there, Ruth?' Branson asked.

'Not yet.' She smiled. 'But just give it a few years.'

69

Wednesday 12 October 2022

'Kill him?'

It was the way Paul said the words that shocked her the most. There was no emotion, just pure matter of fact. He could have been talking about cancelling a magazine subscription.

'What exactly do you mean *kill him*, Paul?'

'Is there some part of those two words you don't understand, my gorgeous?' he replied with an inane, almost simian grin. His voice sounded a little woozy from too much whisky. In a short while, he would be even more woozy after pouring that bottle of Corton-Charlemagne 2008 – which was currently on ice – to go with their evening meal of lobster salad.

She looked at him, feeling almost as if she was seeing him properly for the first time. As if up until now, beneath his carapace, she'd felt there was actually a decent person, just with very skewed morals. But she wasn't thinking that any more.

'Kill. Him,' Shannon said, with perfect enunciation. 'I understand both words perfectly, Paul. Explain something to me, you're a linguist, aren't you?'

'A linguist? Me?'

'You speak French, Spanish and German.'

'*Ein bisschen,*' he replied with a knowing grin.

'What does that French expression *le petit mort* actually mean? I know that literally it means *the little death*. It refers to making love. Is it that the male falls asleep after coitus? Or is it that some men die *on the job*, as it were?'

'I'm not quite sure of your point,' he said.

'Good,' she said. 'Now we're on the same page.'

'On the same page? But different dictionaries?'

Shannon cocked her head and sipped some Champagne from her round glass. 'Five minutes ago, we were talking about arranging the accidental death at sea of Toby Carlisle, who clearly is a shit. He fits your profile, or your moral code, he's legit – in your warped view of what is legit.'

'Warped view?' he challenged, feigning a pained look.

She ignored him. 'Now, having killed one of your Three Musketeers, you want to kill the other? Is this how you reward friendship?'

'This is not a good time to go moral on me, Shannon. We have a major issue we have to deal with.'

'Clearly.' She drained her glass, walked over to the fridge, removed the bottle of Billecart-Salmon and emptied what was left into her glass.

'What exactly is your problem?' he asked.

She rounded on him, trying to hold down her pent-up fury. Fury at herself for allowing herself to have been so much taken in by him. And fury at his sheer callousness as the body count continued to rise. At the same time, she felt afraid of him. Afraid of this man who was her lover but was also a monster she felt she no longer knew – or perhaps never had known.

'You know what my problem is, Paul. I signed up to this life because I thought you had principles. What I believed was your moral code. I never loved it but I tried my best to understand it, and because I love you, I went with it. But the more time I spend with you I've begun to realize that was all bullshit, you don't actually have a moral code. You'll sell guns to anyone who'll pay your price. You will kill for anyone who will pay your price or kill anyone who might be a threat to you. What happens to me if I ever become a threat to you? Will I have a fatal accident too?'

He stared at her with what looked like genuine astonishment. 'That's what you *really* think? You know, Shannon, you ask a lot of questions.'

'Because the more I know you, the more questions I have.'

'I thought you were enjoying – you know – us,' he said.

'I was. Before I knew what you were really like. I should have guessed then, when Professor Llewellyn died.'

'I thought it was what you wanted.'

'I wanted him to suffer for what he did, but it wouldn't have crossed my mind to kill him. Someone – I don't know who – once said there are only two tragedies in life. The first is not getting what you want. The second is getting it, and that's the real tragedy.'

'I'll tell you who said that,' he replied with a triumphant smile. 'Oscar Wilde!'

'You surprise me.'

He smiled. 'I'm full of surprises. So what surprises you about my knowing Oscar Wilde?'

She had to think for a moment. About the way to express it. The surprise was that he could be so brutal, callous, a cold-hearted killer one moment, then show himself to be cultured in another. 'How well do you know his work?'

'I did a thesis on him at school. I've always liked the bad boys.'

'So you'll know Wilde also said that each man kills the thing he loves?' She looked at him pointedly. 'Are you going to kill me one day too? Professor Llewellyn, Dermot Bryson, Tracey Dawson. Toby Carlisle. Then Shannon Kendall?'

He raised his hands. 'Hang on, you're now objecting to Toby Carlisle?'

'Toby Carlisle is fine. But I'm telling you, I don't want you killing James Taylor.'

'It's too dangerous not to, babe. Just as it's too dangerous to stay still. We have to protect our backs, always. That asshole Barnie Wallace was taking photos of me. The police will be interrogating his camera, phone, computer. At some point, they're going to figure it's me and they're going to be able to work out roughly where I am. And it's not going to take them long to know that you are shoulder deep in this operation too. We're not in the business of being nice to people, we're in the business of not getting caught, whatever that takes.'

'I'm telling you I don't want you to kill him.'

'So what are you going to do about it?' He gave her a look so full of arrogance she felt like throwing something at him. He stood and walked, a little unsteadily, over towards the bottle in the ice bucket. And suddenly looked so damned attractive. And hurt. Or was *hurt* her imagination?

God, she felt conflicted. Intoxicated on a combination of the Champagne and being in his presence.

'Look, Paul, I am getting near breaking point here. I'm beginning to think I don't want to be in this *business* any more.'

'Well, as I've said before, don't you think it's a bit late for that?' He lifted the bottle from the ice bucket and wiped it with a cloth.

She stayed silent.

'Shannon? Come on, Shannon, talk to me.'

After some moments, to hell with it, she dropped the bombshell she'd been waiting to land. 'I know about Fiona, and I know about your secret past.'

He spun around to face her. 'How – how the hell? I mean, what do you know about Fiona?' He was clearly flustered and frowning deeply. 'You bugged me?'

She gave him a knowing smile, saying nothing for some moments, and could see that infuriated him.

'You bugged me, right?' He raised his voice to almost a shout.

'I worked for three years programming espionage software. I was just being diligent. I know you are bound together by this pretty big secret, am I wrong?' she said, glaring at him questioningly.

To her surprise, he backed off and seemed even to relax a little. Almost as if glad it was out in the open.

'If you know about that, then, yes, we do have a big secret, but that is all, Shannon. I swear Fiona and I are not an item, and neither of us would want to be back together in any other way than for business.'

'So you're not fucking her then. That's good to know. But there's a small matter here that's a bit awkward. From what I've discovered you're supposed to be dead.'

He looked shocked. 'That can never get out. Never. You, me and Fiona are the only ones who know this. We are all in it together and could destroy each other.' He paused. 'But we won't, will we? Because then we'd all be fucked.'

Shannon sat there a while, smiling. Grinning. 'Funny, isn't it?'

'What? What the hell's so funny?'

'How we're the three now!' she replied.

'What do you mean? What three?'

'The three of us now bound together. All for one and one for all, united we stand, divided we fall.'

70

James Taylor had been looking forward to a week of relaxation in pure luxury and making the most of Tommy Towne's generosity. Sun, glorious sea swimming, massages, great food. Catching up on his reading, and watching some movies in his large suite. But it just seemed a shame not to be sharing it with someone.

Someone called Debbie Martin.

His thoughts, ever since his meeting with John Baker, had been a jumble. He spent a sleepless night, his brain whirring, presenting him with conundrum after conundrum. Maybe it had been irrational, he thought, to have expected the shark man to have laid his suspicion that Rufus was still alive, to rest. But that's what he had genuinely hoped for. Confirmation that Rufus had died at sea. Confirmation that he'd been mistaken about him in the church at Barnie's funeral.

Instead he was now more certain than ever that his old school pal was still alive.

So what should he do next?

He thought about it during a long swim, then over a sushi lunch with a couple of beers, followed by a large glass of rosé wine. He needed to talk it through with someone, someone he could trust.

Debbie Martin.

He was thinking about her constantly. She was under his skin, he knew. Taking him back to schoolboy crushes. He wished she was here, with him. Then, waking on his sunbed sometime after lunch, with a wild thought, he texted her.

What u doing the next five days? Fancy joining me in Barbados?

He looked at his watch: 3.21 p.m. England was five hours ahead. It was 8.31 p.m. for her. What the hell? He sent it.

Then he planted the flag beside his sunbed into the sand. It was a signal for one of the beach staff to come over. And when the smiling young man did, Taylor ordered a Martini. What the hell? He was on holiday. Might as well get smashed.

But before his drink had even arrived, his phone pinged with a text.

It was from Debbie.

When he read her message, totally surprised, he beamed with joy. And, later, he barely slept a wink that night.

71

Thursday 13 October 2022

On the split screen behind Grace were two photographs of their prime suspect. Both showed a tall figure in a hoodie, bulky black jacket, jeans and trainers and very confident, erect posture. The first was the familiar photograph of the man in the Organica supermarket checkout queue. The second was him walking, with the sea a blur behind him. Written across this one was: *POI – Chichester Terrace, 2.12 p.m., Thursday, 1 September.*

Because he had so many actions to delegate, Grace had drafted in two additional full-time members, the former detective Polly Sweeney, who had already been working in conjunction with Jamie Carruthers, and DS Jon Exton, who had also been a member of his team previously, before being seconded to a stint in Professional Standards, the division that policed the police.

When everyone was assembled in the room for the 8.30 a.m. briefing, he began by bringing them up to speed on the information received from the Digital Forensics team, showing the photographs extracted from Barnie Wallace's computer and adding that he had sent some of them to Jonathan Jackson at the Met's Central Image Investigation Unit to see if they could get a match to the man standing behind Barnie Wallace at the Organica supermarket checkout.

Next he gave his reasons for treating the deaths of Dermot Bryson and Tracey Dawson as murder, and for bringing them under the umbrella of Operation Meadow.

Velvet Wilde raised a hand, and when Grace nodded, she asked, 'Sir, with three murders, does that make the suspect a *serial killer?*'

'That's not a term I would want us to use, Velvet – and it would be particularly unhelpful if the press began using it.' He shot Glenn Branson a warning glance that carried a message: *Do not say a word to Siobhan.*

'The technical definition of a serial killer is someone who kills three or more persons, usually with a considerable gap between the killings, which is not the case here. My hypothesis is that we are potentially looking at a contract killer.' He turned to Stanstead.

'Luke, the report from Digital Forensics is that our man is living somewhere in the middle of Arundel Terrace. I imagine all the apartments there are either owned or rented, but some will be sublet. I'd like you to start by contacting the Electoral Register department for Kemp Town and get all the names of the occupants, except for the two end properties, which we can discount for now. Having done that you'll need to start phoning the letting departments of the local estate agents to see if any of them have rented out a flat there in the past three years. Check online on places like Rightmove too.'

'Yes, sir,' the researcher said.

Next he turned to DC Glover. 'Will, I want you to go to Organica and view their CCTV for the afternoon of September the first, to see if you can find this character then, doing a recce perhaps.'

Glover looked proud to have been given a solo action. 'Yes, sir,' he said.

'Chief,' Norman Potting said, 'young William here and I extended our search for outward-facing CCTV cameras in the Preston Street area yesterday, and I think we found something interesting yesterday evening. If I may put it up on the screen? It's footage from a Ring doorbell camera.'

'Go ahead,' Grace said.

Potting tapped his keyboard. A grocery list appeared. Followed by an upside-down naked woman in a Halloween mask.

'Treating us to your family album are you, Norman?' Velvet Wilde asked.

A photograph of Donald Trump dressed as a Barbie doll appeared. Then the screen went blank. Potting muttered an apology. Then a series of images came up, showing a street of elegant Regency terraced houses, each with a columned porch. Parked in front of one was a white Ford Transit van, sign-written in large letters, Kingsway Electrical. The time and date showed top right: 15.36, 03/09/22

Eleven minutes after the Phantom Mushroom Switcher had done his stuff, Grace calculated. 'I know that firm!' he said. 'Owned by a guy called Mike Shaw – he did some work on my house with Sandy years back.'

'That might come in handy, chief,' Potting said. 'If you see what happens next. This is the road that connects Preston Street with Regency Square.'

Seconds later, the blind man with his dog came into view.

''ello, 'ello, 'ello, what do we have here?' EJ Boutwood said.

He walked along the far side of the pavement, and out of sight behind the van. Temporarily, everyone presumed.

'Now watch!' Potting said, excitedly.

Everyone was watching. For several seconds nothing happened. A Post Office van went by, followed shortly after by a helmeted cyclist.

But the blind man did not reappear on the far side of the van.

'Has the dog stopped for a pee or a dump?' Jack Alexander suggested.

Potting wagged a finger in the air. 'Keep watching,' he said, enjoying his moment in the sun.

Twenty-eight seconds later, the van drove off. The blind man and his dog had vanished.

'Great conjuring trick,' Nick Nicholl said.

'Derren Brown or Penn and Teller?' asked Polly Sweeney.

'Can you show us the driver, Norman?' Grace asked.

Potting froze the recording then zoomed in on the passenger window. The driver, on the far side, was indistinct, fuzzy. It was just possible to see he was wearing a baseball cap, dark glasses, and face mask.

Jon Exton read out the licence plate letters and numbers. Grace noted them down.

'I think I still have the boss of that firm in my contacts,' Grace said and pulled out his personal phone. It took him only seconds to find the mobile number of the proprietor. As it rang, he put it onto speaker, so everyone could hear.

It was answered by a friendly-sounding, 'Hello?'

'Mike Shaw?'

'It is!'

'It's Roy Grace.'

'Well, hello, sir. This is a blast from the past. I keep reading about you in the *Argus*, over the years. Expecting to see you as chief constable any day now!'

'You'll have to wait a while yet, Mike. Listen, I'm calling you on police business. One of your vans was parked between Preston Street and Regency Square on Saturday, September the third. Can you give me any information about what it was doing there and who was driving it?'

'Saturday, September the third? We don't work weekends, except for emergencies, Roy. Are you sure it was one of my vans?'

Grace read him the licence plate details.

'That's an old vehicle, Roy,' he said. 'I moved it on at least a year or so ago – if not longer.'

'With your company name still on it?'

'The chap who bought it said he'd take care of removing it – all part of the deal. It was sign-painted, but he said he would livery it up in his own colours.'

'Do you remember the name of this person? And his address?'

'To be honest, we've a number of vans and I always chop them in after a couple of years – I'm out on a job at the moment, I'll look at my records when I get back to the office.'

Grace thanked him and turned to Stanstead. 'Luke, run a PNC check on the registration right away, please.' He moved on. 'Dermot Bryson, who died on Saturday night, had a 3D printed Glock-style handgun in the glove box of his Ferrari. We need to know why he felt he needed to carry a gun.' He turned to DS Exton and to Polly Sweeney. 'You two have always been good at digging deep into characters. See what you can find out about Bryson's personal and business dealings. Emily Denyer might be able to help you on this by looking into his financial dealings.'

'Boss,' Exton asked, 'I'm not a firearms expert. Could any Tom, Dick and Harry buy a 3D printer and knock out a working gun?'

Polly jumped in. 'The answer's no, Jon. I've done some reading up on it and it's a highly complex process. For starters they'd need to find the blueprint or digital files for the firearm. They'd need a highly expensive 3D printer capable of printing materials that could withstand the stresses involved in firing a gun – it would need to be an industrial grade printer that can work with metal alloys. There's highly complex calibration required, and also all the components like springs and the firing pin. In addition, they would need ammunition.'

'So if I wanted a gun, why not just buy the real thing?' Exton asked. 'It wouldn't be hard if I had the right contacts, would it?'

'Any normal handgun – or any firearm – you buy would be traceable, Jon,' Polly said. 'The attraction to a villain of a 3D printed one would be that it would have no serial number.'

'And where would someone buy a 3D printed gun, Polly?' Exton asked. 'The dark web?'

'That's where I'd go shopping,' Polly replied.

'Sir,' Luke Stanstead said. 'Got the response back on the Ford Transit – it is still registered to Kingsway Electrical.'

'It is?' Grace replied, puzzled. 'Is it possible that Mike Shaw could have sold it a couple of years ago and it's still registered to his firm?'

Nick Nicholl answered. 'If the new owner says he'll deal with the paperwork and notify the DVLA of change of ownership, it is possible, boss.'

'And the reason you'd do that, Nick, is so it can't be traced back to you?'

'So long as the new owner pays the insurance and keeps their nose clean, no one will be any the wiser, boss.'

Grace thought for a moment and made a note. Then he looked back at DS Potting. 'Norman, you and Will seem to be our CCTV wizards right now. While Will goes to Organica, you go back to the Control Room and see what ANPR and local CCTV hits we can get on this van. Index, Golf Sierra, One Seven, Charlie Papa November.'

'On it, chief,' Potting said.

Grace's phone rang and he saw it was Mike Shaw. He answered it, raising an apologetic hand to the team.

'Roy, I'm not going to get back to the office tonight – been called out on an emergency. I'll be able to confirm the name of the guy I sold the van to first thing in the morning. It's on the tip of my tongue.'

Grace thanked him, and felt they were finally moving forward. He was on fire!

72

James Taylor was on fire! He had the butterflies in his stomach of a schoolboy waiting to meet his first date.

Debbie Martin would be entering the arrivals hall any moment now. And he had the hotel driver, Tony Skeete, waiting outside in his Mercedes. It was coming up to 5 p.m., an hour and a half or so of daylight left. Enough for her to see something of the island as they headed to the hotel. Although he could scarcely believe she really was on that plane and that she was about to appear.

And then she did.

An apparition in large sunglasses, denim shirt, skinny jeans and white trainers that looked fresh out of their box, pushing along a large, smart, black suitcase. Her fair hair, cropped to near the shoulder, looked like she'd just stepped out of a hairdressing salon, not off an eight-hour flight. She was looking around, and when she saw him, she pushed her glasses up onto her forehead and her face exploded with joy.

They hugged hard, really hard, as if this moment, bizarre in some ways that it was, meant everything in the world to both of them. They kissed, almost innocently, on each cheek. Then, hesitating for an instant as they looked into each other's eyes, their lips touched, just once, just fleetingly.

And Taylor felt a bolt of electricity spark through him. There were a million things he wanted to say, but for a moment he was almost struck dumb, by her radiance, her presence, her faint rich cologne, by the fact she was really here. 'How was the flight?' he said, and immediately felt it sounded lame.

'Oh, you know, it was tough having to slum it in Business Class.' She gave him a mischievous sideways look. 'That was very naughty of you. I'd have been happy to have actually slummed it!'

He shrugged, then with a slightly embarrassed smile said, 'You deserve it.' He took her bag and they walked out to the taxi.

Ten minutes later, sunglasses still on her forehead, leaning back in her seat, her window cracked to let in the balmy air, Debbie suddenly gave a big smile. 'I can't believe I'm here,' she said.

'Nor me.'

'Sandy Lane! Not that I want to talk about him, but it was Barnie's dream of taking me to Barbados one day to stay in Sandy Lane. He said we would fly Business Class, that was another of his dreams. I guess sometimes dreams come true – just not in the way we imagine.'

He smiled. 'I've booked you a separate room – I don't want you to feel under any—'

She gave him a mock frown. 'Really? I haven't got *that* much luggage!' She reached out a hand and gripped Taylor's. Squeezed it hard. So hard he could feel her nails digging in.

Then she leaned over and gave him a long, soft kiss on the cheek.

Tony Skeete drove in discreet silence.

Taylor felt smitten. He squeezed her hand back. God, how much he wanted her. And she was here. And not playing any games with him. And suddenly he felt a little guilty. Sure, he had invited her because he really fancied her, but he had another agenda too, that he was going to have to broach. But maybe not now, not tonight.

'So tell me,' she said. 'Chicago, were you happy with how you did overall?'

'I didn't get a PB, but got fourteenth in my age group.'

'Out of fourteen?' she teased.

He feigned a look of hurt. 'There were fifty thousand runners – over sixteen hundred in my age band!'

She squeezed his hand again, tightly, then kissed him on the cheek and whispered into his ear, 'I hope you haven't used up all your strength?'

He felt a crazy tingling of desire deep in the pit of his stomach. He whispered back into her ear, 'I saved some for you.'

'Hey, lovebirds, none of that in the back of my taxi!' Tony Skeete said. 'This a nooky-free cab!'

They all laughed.

'Got you covered, guys!'

Taylor looked at Debbie and the look she gave him back totally melted him. *I could fall in love with you,* he thought. *I really could.*

73

Friday 14 October 2022

'Lee Oswald,' Grace said, in his office, just as everyone was coming in for the morning briefing. Holding his phone to his ear and writing the name down. 'Thanks, Mike. Anything you can remember about him – his appearance, any distinguishing features?'

There was silence for a moment. Then the electrical contractor, Mike Shaw, said, 'He was tall, Roy, but to be honest I didn't get a good view of his face – he had a baseball cap, dark glasses and most of his face was covered. He was very polite, well-spoken, paid me in folding.'

'If you think of anything else about him, let me know.'

'Of course. Has he been using it for something illegal?'

'I'm afraid I can't tell you, Mike. Let's just say I don't think he's using it to provide electrical services.'

'A bit stupid of me really, to have trusted him. I should have notified the DVLA myself.'

'Yes, you left yourself open to any fines he racks up. I'm not an expert on this area but I'd advise you to notify the DVLA right away.'

'I will.'

Grace ended the call.

'Lee *Harvey* Oswald?' Jon Exton questioned. 'The man who assassinated President Kennedy?'

Potting wagged a finger in the air. '*Might* have assassinated Kennedy, Jon.'

PETER JAMES

'Should have known you'd be a conspiracy theorist, Norman,' Velvet Wilde said.

Ignoring them, Grace turned to Sweeney. 'Polly, ask Jamie Carruthers to do a full check on the dark web on the name Lee Oswald, to see if it gets any hits. Luke, then you need to go through all the letting agents in the city to see if a Mr Oswald has rented in Arundel Terrace.'

Just as the researcher was about to reply, his phone rang. Glancing at the display, Stanstead said to Grace, 'Sir, it's one of the estate agents.'

'Take it, Luke.' He turned to DC Glover. 'Will, how did you get on at Organica?'

The detective spoke up. 'Sir, I have a section of recording from the Organica CCTV that fits with the timeline that our suspect was seen in, on September the first, two days before he made the switch. If I may play it?'

'Go ahead.'

Will pressed the remote and overhead footage began to play. It showed a checkout counter – the same one, Grace recognized, where the mushroom switch had been made. Their suspect came into frame, dressed exactly as he had been half an hour earlier, on the CCTV footage of him walking along Chichester Terrace. He had a small hand-held Organica woven basket in which were just a few items. Two clear containers of what looked like field mushrooms. They both looked identical, to Grace, to the one where the suspect had made the switch on Barnie. A packet of nuts and what looked like a box of protein powder. He paid cash, then produced his own carrier bag from inside his coat pocket, and placed the items inside. It was green and emblazoned with the name Waitrose.

Grace made a note about checking the CCTV on local Waitrose stores as a possible line of enquiry. But he was aware there were several and it would be a big drain on resources to go back through weeks of footage in them all to see if they could spot their suspect. It was one for the back burner if all else drew blanks.

'So,' Branson said, 'looks like he was doing a dummy run.'

'They call it *test purchases* in retail,' Polly Sweeney said.

'Test purchase indeed,' Grace said.

'Maybe he just likes mushrooms,' Potting said. 'He's a real—'

Jack Alexander's groan stopped him in his tracks. 'You've already given us all the mushroom jokes, Norman,' he said.

'Oh no, I haven't – I've plenty more!'

'Save them for your Christmas crackers,' Velvet Wilde said.

Grace clocked the sudden look of sadness on Potting's face. Velvet had unintentionally touched a raw nerve. Grace knew that after his fiancée had died, tragically, the seasoned old veteran, estranged from his four former wives and his children, had told him he'd had Christmas dinner last year on his own in a Brighton steak house. Fortunately, this year looked like it should be a far happier day for him as he and his new love, Heather, were spending Christmas together. They had booked a break in Lanzarote to meet up with her two children, who lived on either side of the globe, and Potting seemed elated to be getting more involved with her family. So far, her cancer treatment was showing only positive signs. He was pleased Potting had found a new partner and just hoped for him that it worked out.

'So two boxes of field mushrooms,' Potting said thoughtfully. 'One to empty and replace with the death caps. The other to match how they are presented in the box, before he seals the death caps up?'

'Clearly our man's no fool,' EJ Boutwood said.

'Someone who charges a million pounds for a hit and gets it – if this is our man – isn't going to be a fool,' Grace said gravely.

'Sir,' Stanstead said, ending his call. 'That was the rentals division of the estate agents Stiles Harold Williams. They handled the rental of the penthouse flat of number 118 Arundel Terrace eighteen months ago to a man called Paul Anthony.'

'Paul Anthony?' Grace repeated back, then wrote it down. 'Do a Google search as well as the police national database and try to find a Paul Anthony that fits the bill. Did you get a physical description?'

'No, sir, the agent who dealt with him has left the firm.'

'OK, we may need to track that person down. Did you ask them about Lee Oswald?'

'I did, sir. They don't have anyone of that name on their books.'

Grace turned to the financial investigator. 'Emily, see what you can come up with from the estate agents' records. These flats in Arundel Terrace are all high-end properties. They must have taken references, a chunky deposit, and presumably a standing order for the rental payments.'

Stanstead was already tapping the name into Google. Keeping his eyes on the screen he said, 'There are a lot of Paul Anthonys.'

'Of course there are – *if* this is our man. He wouldn't make it easy. No other rentals from anyone else, yet?'

'Not so far, sir. I'll ping Aiden Gilbert – in case he can help. We should get a quick answer on the dark web.'

Grace turned to Potting. 'Any dice from the Control Room CCTV or ANPR, Norman?'

'A double-six, I would say, chief!'

'Really?' He raised an intrigued eyebrow.

'I've been analysing the photos of our suspects you sent from Barnie Wallace's laptop. They were mostly clustered in the vicinity of Arundel Terrace, which coincides exactly with the timeline of his mobile phone from Charlotte Mckee. The CCTV and ANPR hits are again clustered in that area. The van has been clocked around the city, and further afield, but the majority of sightings are within half a mile of Arundel Terrace, which indicates that's where our Mr Oswald is based.'

'Nice work, Norman,' he said, and looked down at his notes then looked in turn at Polly Sweeney, then Jon Exton. 'Anything on Dermot Bryson yet? To give us any reason he might have needed a gun? For self-protection or because he was planning to shoot someone?'

'We worked late into the night with Emily,' Polly Sweeney said. 'She can explain it best.'

Emily Denyer looked down at her tablet. Grace had noticed this highly efficient investigator, who wore bright red lipstick, always seemed nervous at first, blushing when she was the sudden centre of attention, but once she got into her stride, her confidence grew rapidly.

'Until eight years ago, Dermot Bryson was just a trader on the London Metal Exchange, earning good money – around £250k annually with a bonus of up to £100k. Good money but nowhere near enough to finance his current lifestyle. He set up an offshore fund investing in a cryptocurrency start-up, which appeared to make a very substantial and rapid profit, but there was more going on that I haven't yet got to the bottom of, but I strongly suspect an involvement in scam websites – phishing for people's bank details then cleaning them out – but all the time washing the money through his crypto-currency dealings.'

'Like Bitcoin, you mean?' Nick Nicholl asked, looking a little puzzled.

'Exactly, that kind of thing,' she said.

'So he could have made any number of enemies,' Glenn Branson said.

'Including his wife,' Denyer said.

'His wife?'

'Kimberley Bryson. I ran a search on her, and she's a piece of work,' Denyer replied. 'Five years before she married Dermot Bryson, Kimberley was charged with GBH after she attacked her then lover. It appears a smart brief got her off on a technicality.'

'Did Bryson know this when he married her, Emily?' Exton asked.

'I've no idea.'

'Would you have married her, knowing that?' Nick Nicholl asked the DS.

Branson, looking pained, said, 'Not sure I would have done.'

Polly Sweeney's phone rang. She answered it discreetly, but, for some reason, everyone in the room sensed it was something important. Almost all eyes were on her as she politely thanked the caller and put her phone down. Then she looked at Roy Grace.

'That was Jamie, sir. I asked him to run the searches on the dark web for the names Paul Anthony and Lee Oswald. And he's got a result.'

'Which is?' Grace asked.

'They're the same person!'

74

Friday 14 October 2022

'It's hard not to feel in the pink here, isn't it?' Debbie said with a teasing grin.

Taylor grinned back. They were seated in the warm air on pink cushions; all the waiting staff in pink and white, and the large umbrella above them, shading them from the sun on their table out on the dining terrace, was also pink.

Taylor, in shorts, linen shirt, flip-flops and a Panama hat was feeling just insanely happy. Debbie wore a loose white top over her bikini, her fair hair tucked up inside a white baseball cap, and large dark glasses with a discreet Ray-Ban logo at the edge of the frame. She was leaning across the table on her elbows, hands steepled, with the lunchtime wind rippling the surface of the sea behind her. She looked even more gorgeous than ever, he thought, and he was feeling crazy for her.

Spontaneously, he reached across the table, took her right arm, drew her hand towards him and kissed it. 'Am I dreaming?'

She raised her glasses with her free hand, and looked at him with her clear blue eyes. 'Yep. Right now you're having a night-mare. When you wake up it's going to be even worse!'

'Then I'll stay asleep.'

'Good plan.'

Debbie turned and looked at the beach behind her. A small bay of white sand, and a long line of sunbeds with pink mattresses, beneath pink parasols. 'I read something once about this place.

I think it was that late film director and food critic, Michael Winner, walking along this beach on New Year's Day with John Cleese. Cleese apparently turned to him suddenly and said: *You know, there must be more to life than this.'*

Taylor laughed. 'And is there?'

She cocked her head provocatively. 'You tell me?'

'Since you arrived yesterday, no, there isn't. There isn't anywhere in the world or anyone I would rather be with than you.'

'I feel that too, I really do.' She gently pulled his arm towards her and kissed his hand, one finger at a time. Then she looked up at him, quizzically. 'Is it just coincidence you're in Barbados, or is there something you've not yet told me?'

'You've not really given me much of a chance to tell you anything since you arrived!'

She leaned further over and punched him playfully. 'Too busy flirting?!'

Both realized a shadow had fallen. A middle-aged, rather prim-looking waitress stood discreetly by the table, with a bottle of rosé in an ice bucket, on a silver tray. They grinned. The waitress did her best and failed to hide a grin too. 'I heard nothing!' she said, breaking into a warm laugh.

She set the bottle down, opened it with a corkscrew then asked, 'Will the gentleman or the lady try the wine?'

Taylor indicated to Debbie.

As the waitress departed, saying she would return to take their food order, Taylor raised his glass and they clinked. 'Cheers,' he said.

'To more to life than this?' Debbie replied.

'I think to want any more would be greedy.'

She nodded. 'I agree. I don't want any more than this right now, but I do want to know why you are here – why Barbados?'

He sipped the cold wine and it tasted so good. He immediately took a longer sip. He didn't have to pilot a plane again until next

Tuesday, when he had to pick up Tommy Towne from Jersey and fly him to a meeting in Brussels. Out of long habit when he worked for easyJet he'd always maintained a twelve-hour bottle-to-throttle rule. So for now he could throw the rule book to the wind and enjoy the next few days of pure hedonism. 'Why Barbados?' he replied.

'Uh-huh. You could have gone anywhere in the Caribbean or anywhere else. Rufus Rorke supposedly disappeared off the coast of Barbados. Is it pure coincidence you're here?'

He shook his head, then glanced up as their waitress brought them menus and thanked her. Turning back to Debbie he said, 'Let's order and then I'll tell you what I've found out.'

'Has it been worth the trip?'

'Bugger Rufus. You've been worth the trip!'

She narrowed her eyes at him. 'You're out of practice dating, aren't you, Taylor?'

'Why do you say that?'

She grinned again. 'Because you're so bloody cheesy!'

'I'll take that as a compliment,' he retorted.

75

Saturday 15 October 2022

At 5.30 a.m., in the misty drizzle and near-total darkness, the convoy of three vehicles rolled out of the parking lot of Brighton police station, turned left and proceeded downhill towards the brightly illuminated London Road.

The lead vehicle was a black Audi containing Armed Response officers from the Tactical Firearms Unit. Behind them was a plain white Transit van, inside which were eight members of the elite Public Order Team. Bringing up the rear were Roy Grace and Glenn Branson, in an unmarked Ford. This was the order in which they would arrive at their destination, and it was the order in which everyone would enter the building, with Grace and Branson last, after the apartment had been made secure.

Branson drove, with Grace in the passenger seat beside him. Both detectives, who had shed their suit jackets in favour of stab vests beneath heavily padded fleeces clearly marked POLICE, were tense. The only sound in the car was the monotone clonk-clonk of the wipers.

Each passing street light strobed across Branson's face. He looked stiff, anxious, tired, Grace thought, not his usual perky, jokey self. Grace had felt tired too earlier but not any more. As always on the way to a raid, he felt the buzz of excitement as adrenaline coursed through him – but tinged with apprehension. Everyone was highly trained and well briefed and knew exactly what they had to do, but he was only too aware from

336

past experience that things could easily go wrong on raids, and sometimes very badly, very quickly.

All three vehicles maintained radio silence. Surprise was the key element in any raid, and if Paul Anthony/Lee Oswald was indeed Rufus Rorke, then, with all his guile, it was possible he had equipment tuned into the police radio network. It was also highly probable that he would be armed.

From the maps of Arundel Terrace they'd studied, as well as Google Earth, there were just two ways of gaining access to the property – the main entrance at the front, and from a fire escape door at the rear. They also had a floor plan and good video of the interior of the penthouse, which Stanstead had found from an old listing on Rightmove.

All three vehicles, as prearranged, pulled up a block short of the building, double-parking, blocking in a few cars, but hopefully not for long, Grace figured. The firearms officers, menacing shadowy figures in their dark clothing in the misty rain, climbed out of the Audi, brandishing their semi-automatics. Then the Public Order Team clambered down from the van, each in blue combat kit, wearing body armour and helmets with visors. Their leader for this operation was a tough sergeant, Monica Dawes, who had once been a police diver before that unit had been disbanded. They stood in a circle as Grace and Branson approached.

'All good?' Grace asked.

'Ready, sir,' Dawes said.

Then he looked ahead at the handsome front facade, weakly lit by a street light. Black railings lined the steps up the porches of each front door. He stepped out into the road and looked up, at roughly where he thought Rorke's apartment was. There were no lights on anywhere in the building. Good. Dawes delegated two officers from the Public Order Team to cover the front entrance.

The rest of them headed into the mews that ran behind the building and lined up, the firearms officers ready to enter first after the door was opened. One public order officer, a man-mountain, stood holding the bosher – the big red battering ram. Grace checked everyone's position, then gave the order to start.

They all shuffled to a halt at the top of the steps, silent, apart from several of them panting. Ahead of them was a drab door. Grace knew from the Rightmove plans this was the fire door at the rear of the penthouse.

The sergeant turned to Grace for his instruction to proceed. Grace nodded. The firearms officers positioned themselves to the right of the door and one signalled, with his free arm, for everyone to stand well back. Then the man-mountain stepped up to it and swung the bosher with seemingly all his force. It just bounced back, showering a few wood splinters and flaking paint. Looking very determined he took a second swing, and this time the door visibly shook and seemed to give a fraction. He paused for breath for an instant, then swung it again.

The door burst open and hung at a drunken angle. Immediately he stood aside and the two firearms officers squeezed past him and rushed in, screaming at the top of their voices, 'ARMED POLICE! ARMED POLICE!'

Grace heard their voices, repeating the same words for some moments. It was followed a couple of minutes later by, 'ALL CLEAR! ALL CLEAR!'

Grace and Branson held back, until Sergeant Dawes, who had entered the flat after the firearms team, came to the front door and said, looking slightly crestfallen, 'The place is definitely empty, sir.'

'Empty?'

'There's no one here. Doesn't look like there's anyone living here, sir.'

'What? What do you mean? The letting agents confirmed they have a tenant living here!' Grace retorted.

'Maybe he hasn't moved in yet?' the officer suggested.

Grace shook his head. 'We know from the agents their tenant is living here, and in residence.'

The officer gave him a look that implied otherwise.

Shit, Grace thought. He and Branson each slipped on a pair of protective gloves and turned on all the lights. They walked around the sumptuous apartment. In the living room he noticed immediately the stale reek of cigar smoke, as if it were ingrained in the place, but there was nothing to indicate Rufus Rorke or indeed anyone else was currently actually living here. The whole place was as sterile, pristine and lacking in any personal touch as a vacant hotel suite.

He and Branson continued walking around, going from room to room. There were no photographs, no mail, no half-drunk or empty bottles. Nothing in the massive fridge or freezer compartments. Nothing in the dishwasher. The kitchen bin was empty and spotless. Nothing in the two bathrooms or their cabinets. The bedding in each of the rooms, with stacked cushions and pillows, looked professionally made and untouched.

Walking over to the conservatory-style windows he opened one door and shone his torch out across a deserted, equally spotless terrace, Grace turned to Branson. 'Are we sure we're in the right place?'

'We are. This is the apartment rented to our friend, Paul Anthony. No question.'

'Does he smoke cigars? Do we know if Rufus Rorke did? We need to find out. Because someone here has been smoking them. Recently.'

'Done a runner, do you think, sir?' Sergeant Dawes said.

Grace shrugged. 'We know from the estate agents that our suspect has been paying his rent – apparently from a bank in the Seychelles, which makes it hard to trace who exactly.'

'It doesn't look like anyone's living here,' she said. 'You couldn't keep a place this neat and tidy. It doesn't even look like either sofa has been sat on in a while. Would he have a vehicle in the car park – if there is one?'

'There isn't,' Branson replied. 'The residents all use lock-ups.'

Grace sniffed hard. 'But someone has been in here, smoking a cigar – can't be that long ago – a few days?'

'So where is he?' Branson asked.

Grace rubbed his eyes, looking around carefully. He opened a drawer in a table that he realized, with a beat of excitement, they'd missed. It too was empty. 'What we do know about Rufus Rorke is that he's very good at disappearing. But, if you're going to do a runner, why go to so much effort to clean up behind you?'

'Unless he was never here in the first place, boss,' Branson suggested. 'Perhaps he just rented this place as a possible bolt-hole?'

'That doesn't fit with what we know from Aiden Gilbert and Charlotte Mckee – Barnie Wallace's movements, the subject he photographed, the location. I'm pretty sure Rorke was here. And he's now trying to give the impression he was never here.'

'What's that old boast of the SOCOs? That if someone has ever been in a room, no matter how long ago, give them enough time and they'll find the evidence to prove it,' Branson said.

'There may be a quicker way,' Grace said.

'What's your thinking?'

'The clue is in the cleaning.' He smiled.

'Are you going to leave me in the dark?'

Grace patted him on the arm. 'Nah, it'll be dawn soon.'

76

Saturday 15 October 2022

'He's dangerous,' Debbie said, suddenly, keeping her voice low although there was no one either side of them. 'Really dangerous. As I said to you at lunch.'

'About having something of the night about him?' Taylor replied.

'Exactly. And now after seeing your fisherman – John Baker – you're even less certain that Rufus is dead, right?'

They were lying on their sun loungers, beneath a large pink umbrella. She was drinking sparkling water and had a Linwood Barclay paperback on the table beside her. Taylor was sipping an espresso and flicking through *Flight International* magazine. He glanced at his watch. It was 11 a.m. here in Barbados, 4 p.m. in England. The whole glorious day stretched out ahead, and they had some of tomorrow, too, before flying back in the evening.

'Right. The more I think back to our schooldays, the more I realize just what a dark side he had. Maybe I didn't see it as *dangerous* then. But he did nasty pranks, ones in which people got hurt.'

'Such as what?'

'I guess the one I remember clearest is when we were only about twelve or thirteen, there was a bully a lot older than us called Terry Hawkins. He used to steal sweets and food from smaller boys – and girls – literally just snatch them out of their hands and then eat them in front of them, gloating. So one day

341

Rufus decided to get even by pulling a chair out from under him as he was sitting down. Hawkins almost had to go to hospital with the injuries.' He shrugged. 'Another time he put a small ants' nest in Hawkins' bed. That kind of thing.'

'You could argue Hawkins deserved it.'

'You could. But Rufus did stuff when people didn't deserve it too.'

'He must have got found out – didn't he get expelled?'

'He was always adamant it wasn't him doing it. He was a very convincing liar and good at passing the blame onto someone else.'

A jet-ski rasped across the bay, just beyond the swimming marker buoys. Over to their left, Taylor saw a couple sitting on the anchored raft a couple of hundred yards out from the shore.

'I'm worried about you,' she said. 'We've just found each other – I don't want anything to happen to you.'

He looked at her and raised his sunglasses for a moment. 'Thank you.' He smiled tenderly. 'But I'm a big boy.'

'Rufus is even bigger. You are kind, he's nasty.'

'You really do think Rufus might have killed Barnie, don't you?' he said.

'What do you think, James?'

'If – and it's getting a smaller *if* by the day – Rufus is really still alive, then I can see his motive.'

'Someone murdered Barnie – someone who had a reason to. He was trying to blackmail an old schoolfriend who he said had faked his disappearance. That has to be Rufus. You reckon you saw him at Barnie's funeral, and now you've met the fisherman who allegedly pulled his half-eaten jacket out of the sea – and you didn't believe his story. So it kind of fits rather too well, don't you think?'

'It looks that way.' He finished his coffee and put the small cup down.

'What is your interest, James – why do you want to know about Rorke? Is it just curiosity – or something more I should know?'

He smiled. 'Wouldn't you be curious in my position? I deliver the eulogy at an old school friend's funeral and two years later I see him.'

'Or think you see him?'

'No, now I'm convinced I saw him. Then you tell me about Barnie trying to blackmail an old friend who faked his disappearance and suddenly I get a lot more intrigued.'

'And this fisherman here, John Baker, has added to the mystery.'

'He has.'

She sipped some water. 'Have you told anyone your suspicions? Anyone, James, anyone at all?'

'You sound really worried.'

'I am. I'm very worried – for you.'

He shook his head. 'I guess the only person other than you that I've told is Rufus's widow – or supposed widow, Fiona.'

'She told you she was on the yacht when he went overboard, right?'

'But she never saw him go overboard, she said it was a member of the crew who did.'

'That person could have been lying.'

He nodded.

She was silent for a moment. A water-ski boat's engines roared as it powered forward, pulling a skier up and onto the surface of the water. 'OK, if you can get enough evidence to be as certain as you can that Rufus Rorke is still alive, what are you going to do with it?'

'Maybe try to meet with him, ask him what the hell he's doing.'

'Why?'

'Because, if Rufus did kill Barnie, I want to help the police track him down and get justice for him.'

'There's something I haven't yet told you about Rufus,' she said. 'Barnie was friends with a guy who worked for – well, not exactly *for* Sussex Police, but the Crown Prosecution Service, who make all the decisions about prosecutions. Barnie told me – this was probably the last time I saw him – that his friend had said that just before he disappeared, Rufus Rorke was on the verge of being arrested for murder.'

'Seriously?'

'Seriously. And they believed it wasn't just one murder he was responsible for – the police thought there were others.'

Some of the heat seemed to have gone out of the morning sun. He looked at her hard. 'You mean like a serial killer?'

'I don't know exactly, but yes, something like that. That's why I'm worried about you digging too deep. If you do locate Rorke, don't go and see him, don't let him know. I suspect he didn't just kill Barnie because he was blackmailing him, but it was more because he had recognized him. That's what makes it so dangerous for you. Why do you think he didn't just pay Barnie off?'

'Because he couldn't be sure Barnie wouldn't either come back for more money at some point, or worse, blab to someone?'

'Exactly, James. Blab to someone. He couldn't risk Barnie telling someone. So what makes you think he would take a risk on you?'

77

Saturday 15 October 2022

The damned dog was barking. Paul Anthony looked at his watch for the hundredth time. Unusually for him, he'd lain awake for much of the night before finally drifting off well after 4 a.m. Now something had woken him and it wasn't just Montmorency. It was a beep, an electronic alert, but not a text or WhatsApp or email alert. Shannon stirred too. 'Gurrurr?' she murmured.

The police could not be here, he thought. There was nothing at all in Arundel Terrace to link to this address here. And they'd travelled here in a Nissan Leaf that had not been out of the garage in over a year.

All the same, he was concerned. He slipped out of bed, calling to Montmorency to be quiet, and hurried, naked and anxious, through onto the carpeted floor of the room that served now as his and Shannon's office as well as living room, and looked at the bank of CCTV monitors above his desk. They covered all 360 degrees around the entire complex of garages. He saw, to his relief, the reason the dog was barking. Monitor 3 showed an urban fox rummaging inside a bin it had managed to knock over. It was only Montmorency's second night here and the dog hadn't got used to all the different sounds and activities around this row of lock-up garages.

He turned on the lights then hurried over in the cold air, stroked him and calmed him. 'Good boy, good boy! We'll go walkies soon, OK?' But he was still well aware it wasn't just the

345

barking that had woken him. It was something else. He looked at his phone and saw an app pulsing. And realized.

Montmorency whined at him.

'OK, boy!' He pulled a treat out of a drawer in the kitchen area and gave it to him. The dog took it in his soft mouth, then padded over to his beanbag and settled down to crunch it.

Paul Anthony tapped the app. Seconds later, he was looking at a video of the interior of the Arundel Terrace flat. One of the concealed motion-activated cameras, which covered each of the rooms, showed two men, one black and shaven-headed, one white with short fair hair, both wearing padded jackets with POLICE emblazoned across their chests. He stopped and played it from the start.

The time clock read 05.34. Three-quarters of an hour ago. There were a number of police officers breaking into his flat.

He smiled, he'd been expecting this. They wouldn't find anything in the apartment. And they wouldn't find the Kingsway Electrical van that was parked in a lock-up garage two streets away, rented in a completely different name. They wouldn't find it for a good five years, when the lease ran out. And he would be long gone from England.

'That's our apartment!' Shannon said. He'd been so absorbed he hadn't noticed her coming over and now standing beside him, hair tousled, pink dressing gown pulled tightly around her. Shivering, he put an arm around her and felt the warmth of her body through the dressing gown. 'Shit, is that today?'

'You get it now? What I said about the need to keep on the move?'

She looked up at him. Her eyes looking wider than ever in her still sleepy face. 'Shit. If—?'

'If?'

'If we'd been there, we'd be busted.'

'Which is why when I say *leave*, we leave.'

She walked over to the coffee machine and switched it on. 'Is it always going to be like this?'

He shook his head. 'It's only like this because of that twat Barnie Wallace. Which is why we can't take a risk with Taylor. Capiche?'

She pulled two ristretto capsules from the dispenser then eyed him warily, without saying anything.

'Capiche?' he said again. 'Unless you want to take the risk of spending a very long time in prison, which I do not.'

'I've not actually committed any provable offence, Paul,' she said.

'Other than accessory to murder and conspiracy to murder?' he said and cocked his head with a smile.

She placed a small cup beneath the spout, pushed a capsule into the machine and hit one of the two illuminated buttons. It began rumbling. Seconds later, the tantalizing aroma of coffee spread through the room. 'Don't play games with me,' she said icily. 'And don't threaten me.'

'No one's playing games and no one's threatening you. You just need to get real.'

'I have a very long spoon,' she said darkly, pushing in the second capsule.

'Long spoon? Meaning?'

'You must have heard that expression, being who you are?'

He frowned, shaking his head with a bemused smile.

'He who sups with the Devil should have a long spoon.'

'The Devil? I'm taking that as a compliment.'

'Coffee?'

He nodded.

'So where do we go from here?' she asked.

'Marbella's very nice this time of year. Spanish winter sunshine. I've a gorgeous villa with a heated pool, in a gated complex, and a whole new identity there, where no one's got a cat-in-hell's chance of finding us.'

'Except we just have to get there.'

'That's all taken care of. But first you need to earn your keep. Taylor flies for a gazillionaire, Sir Tommy Towne, who lives in Jersey, and he keeps one of Towne's planes, a Pilatus, at Brighton City airport in Shoreham. The larger plane, a Citation jet, is parked at Southampton airport. I need you to find out which plane he's flying next and when.'

She handed him his espresso. 'Sure, shall I phone him and say, "Hey, Mr Taylor, my boss wants to know when you are next flying so he can put a bomb in your plane?"'

'Haha.' He put the cup down and wiggled his hands in the air. 'I think we need a little more subtlety. I know where he lives, because two years ago my dearly beloved non-wife, Fiona, mailed him a ton of stuff about me so he could write my eulogy and he recently sent her a change of address card. Sweet. It's an apartment block in Worthing, just ten miles from here. I can give you the apartment number. I'm sure with all your grasp of espionage technology you can suck all the information out of his phone. We just need his calendar. Or does that offend your morals?'

'Are you going to kill him?'

'I'm just going to have a cosy chat with him.'

'You expect me to believe you?'

He pointed at the door. 'I'm not forcing you to stay, you're free. If you don't like this – us – you can just walk out the door.'

She walked up to him and kissed him on the lips, hard. 'Consider it done.'

'He was in Barbados two days ago, so we may need to be patient.'

'Didn't Tolstoy say the two most powerful warriors are *patience* and *time*?'

He put his arms around her and pulled her towards him. 'I never give you enough credit for your intellect.'

She looked up at him again with those big wide eyes. 'Mediocrity recognizes nothing higher than itself. It takes talent to appreciate genius. You clearly have talent.'

He laughed and hugged her tighter than ever.

But then, as he looked into her eyes again, he saw something. Something he could not put his finger on, something that unsettled him.

Deeply.

Can I trust you or should I kill you too?

78

'Just the job I signed up to when I joined the police!' Glenn Branson said. 'Did I ever tell you I was a binman once, for six months?'

'No, I must have missed that part when I read your CV,' Grace said. 'Good prep for being a copper though, most of the time we're just collecting garbage – human garbage.'

There were four wheelie bins in the open-sided brick store behind No. 118 Arundel Terrace. One was for glass, one for re-cycling, the other two were for rubbish from the five apartments in this building. Grace had radioed for two CSI search officers to attend as soon as possible, but in the meantime he had opened the lid of the first rubbish bin and hauled out a knotted black bag. He and Glenn, now in torchlight in the pre-dawn darkness, wearing their latex gloves, were rummaging through the contents.

Branson pulled up an envelope, with a stain on it, addressed to 'Anthony & Sara Macaulay, Flat 3, 118 Arundel Terrace.' He showed it to Grace. 'Wrong bin bag, boss.'

Grace nodded. He should leave this job to the trained search officers, he knew, this was what they did better than anyone else, but it could be some while before they got here. In the interim, fuelled by disappointment and anger at being outsmarted by Rorke, he pulled out another bag, all the time thinking about him. He was pretty confident a mistake hadn't been made and they had raided the right apartment, and that Rorke had sensed it coming and fled. After cleaning it to the point of sterilization.

But, Grace knew from long experience, criminals made mistakes. A few years back he'd secured the conviction of a killer who had shot dead a postmaster in a raid, thinking the skin-tight downhill racer suit, balaclava and surgical gloves he had worn would ensure he left no DNA at the scene, either from his skin or hair, and he'd been correct. Then, after fleeing with the cash, the idiot had dumped his gloves in a bin a quarter of a mile from the scene, and James Stather's forensic team had had a field day with all the DNA inside those gloves.

Which was why, acting on his hunch and past experience, he wanted to go through all the bins now. A call to the Control Room, twenty minutes ago, had established there'd been no pinging on any ANPR camera of the Kingsway Electrical van in the past four days. It could be that Rorke had some other means of transport as well, but he figured it was the van he would most likely have used if he was going to dispose of the bags of rubbish off-site. Which meant they might well be here, in one of these bags, in one of these bins.

'Ye gods!' Branson exclaimed, wrinkling his nose as he peered into an opened white bin bag and pulled out the putrid entrails of a chicken, with bits of paper stuck to it.

Grace looked at him quizzically.

The DI held up one strip of paper with printing down it. 'A Waitrose receipt, boss,'

'Any name? Credit card details?'

'Too damp to read.'

'Bag it,' Grace said. Then his phone rang. It was Chris Gee, the Crime Scene Manager, telling him that two search officers would be with them in half an hour.

Ending the call, Grace turned to Branson. 'Let's try to put

ourselves into Rufus Rorke's mindset. He's faked his disappearance and thinks he's got away with it. He changes his name and starts back in business again, bold as brass, advertising his services on the dark web. Something alerts him and he does a runner from his flat, forensically cleaning it first. Who or what has alerted him?'

'The fisherman in Barbados – John Baker?' Branson ventured. 'After I talked to him? Maybe I spooked him?'

'Maybe. I'm hypothesizing here. Let's say Rorke kills his old school buddy, by all accounts a total loser, Barnie Wallace. The motive looks like it could be that Wallace was blackmailing him. It would have been the perfect murder. Someone dying from mushroom poisoning – especially a former professional chef – wouldn't have raised a flag if that Dyke Golf Club captain hadn't died two weeks later. Then we have Dermot Bryson and his girlfriend, Tracey Dawson, dead in a high-speed smash that clearly is more than it seems. Accidental death, Rorke's MO. Not to forget the professor, Bill Llewellyn, which might or might not have any relevance.'

He looked hard at the DI. 'So imagine for a moment you are Rufus Rorke. You've come back from the dead and set yourself up in a cushy pad in the city you know. You've gone back to your old lucrative business of flogging 3D printed guns, and being a hired assassin who makes his victims' deaths look like accidents. Something spooks you. Could be a call from the fisherman you gave a big bung to, to give a cock-and-bull story about finding the remains of your jacket, to reinforce the story of your disappearance off the back of a yacht.' He raised his eyebrows. Branson nodded.

Continuing, Grace said, 'You figure the police may be moving in on you. Barnie Wallace has told you – and I'm speculating here – that he'd taken a ton of photographs of you. You'll figure that the police now have Barnie's camera, laptop and phone, and from your knowledge of technology, you know that the police will be able to pinpoint where you live from the data embedded in these photos. You clean out your rented, fully furnished, apartment to the extent that it looks like no one was ever there. So where do you go?'

'Abroad somewhere?' Branson ventured.

Grace nodded slowly. 'Maybe. And if he has gone abroad he could be anywhere in the world by now. But let's look at why he disappeared in the first place – it was because he knew he was on the verge of being arrested. He pulled off a pretty fancy disappearance, all belt and braces. Until you showed up and talked to John Baker. So, yes, possibly Rorke has panicked and fled to a bolt-hole abroad. But I'm guessing he's a raving egotist and narcissist. Who knows how long he's been doing this? And how many victims there were before the slip-up involving Pauline Ormonde that led to him faking his death as a last desperate throw of the dice? Until now, he's seemingly not put a foot wrong. My bet is that he's still around. Just a copper's hunch, I can't add any weight to it.'

'If you're right, how do we find him? We have to wait for him to make another mistake?'

Grace smiled. 'There's a good chance he's already made one.' He nodded at the wheelie bins. 'We just need to find it.'

79

'Twenty minutes late, but they're taxiing now,' Shannon said, turning up her nose at the smell of cigar smoke. It was particularly strong at the moment. Dense and cloying, and it was annoying her as she sat, perched at Rorke's desk, barefoot, in a black roll-neck sweater and jeans, two computer screens open in front of her.

Paul Anthony, reclining on the sofa with a cigar, large whisky and his laptop, was concentrating on the image on his screen of the interior of a Pilatus PC-12 aircraft, the type James Taylor flew. He looked up with a frown. 'Sorry, who's taxiing?'

She shook her head in mock astonishment. 'Hello? Duh! Julius Caesar? The Queen of Sheba?'

He raised a hand in the air as a signal of recognition. 'Ah, yes, brilliant!'

'I know. I am actually more than brilliant. I'm a genius!'

She was rewarded with a pained smile. 'And so modest with it,' he mocked.

'*When virtue and modesty enlighten her charms, the lustre of a beautiful woman is brighter than the stars of heaven, and the influence of her power it is in vain to resist.*'

She grinned at his reaction. He was frowning. 'Oscar Wilde also?'

'A little bit before his time. Akhenaten.'

'Who's he?'

'Tutankhamun's uncle.'

'You had an affair with him, did you?'

She beamed. 'Yep, I'm pretty sure I did, in a former life.' She was on a roll today. She'd hacked the Barbados airport information and found the flight home to London that James Taylor was booked on. Interestingly, with a travelling companion, she'd told Paul. None other than Barnie Wallace's widow. Which made everything just that little bit more dangerous still. Another dense cloud of smoke engulfed her.

'That really stinks!' Shannon said, waving smoke away.

'My cigar?'

'Yes, it's foul.'

'You've never complained before.'

'Well I'm complaining now.'

He looked at her and she glared back. 'Seriously, it stinks. It makes everything stink.'

'I thought you liked it.'

'There's a lot of things you *thought*, that you got wrong, Rufus.'

'Don't call me that, it's a dangerous habit to get into.'

'Couldn't you just send a warning to Taylor? I'm really worried about this.'

'We've been through it a dozen times.'

'Killing the professor, killing the innocent girlfriend in the car and now you're about to kill James Taylor. And you *thought* I would be happy. I've told you before I didn't sign up to that. And I didn't sign up to being killed by passive smoke.'

He put the glass on the table, and the cigar in the ashtray, then jumped up and walked across to her, putting his arms around her. 'I like that you don't wear perfume,' he murmured, seductively, in her ear. 'Fiona always smelled like she had been dunked in the stuff.'

Shannon shook him away. 'I'm concentrating.'

He peered at the screens. The right-hand one showed the interior of the cabin of a Boeing 777. Two seats were highlighted in red.

'Is that them, all cosied up in Business?'

The left screen showed a flight path across the Atlantic from Barbados to London.

'They're due to land at 0641 tomorrow,' she said. 'But that's subject to congestion at Heathrow – early morning's the busiest time for inbound flights. Once we know the plane has landed I can calculate the time he'll arrive back at his Worthing flat and get across there. He's got a distinctive car, an old black MGB. I can cycle over there and hang around in the car park. I'll follow him out, get in the lift with him, and' – she held up a small piece of black electronic kit – 'have sucked everything out of his phone by the time we get to his floor.'

'I like your planning,' he said.

'I don't like yours. And if you want to smoke any more of that stogie, do it outside.'

'I'm meant to be invisible.'

She looked up at him and, suddenly, she saw something pathetic in him. He was for a moment like a whining schoolboy. 'So take the dog for a walk and smoke all you like out there. It's dark, no one's going to see you.'

'This isn't the time for an argument, Shannon.'

'You're dead right. So we're not going to argue. You're taking the dog out. End of.'

Looking at her, as if unsure what to make of her mood, he drank a slug of the whisky, jammed the cigar in his mouth, grabbed his coat and Montmorency's lead and stepped warily out into the darkness.

80

'Missing you already,' he said, hugging Debbie outside the entrance to her flat, in one of the old Victorian villas just above Brighton Station.

She grinned. 'That's so cheesy, Taylor. What was it I said about you being so cheesy?'

He looked at her for a moment; tired and pale, her brief tan was already largely faded after their long flight, and her hair was scrunched into a ponytail that popped out of the rear of her baseball cap. But in her fleece-lined denim jacket, ripped jeans and tall trainers, she was, to him, so beautiful and very self-assured. He shrugged. 'Yeah, well, it may be cheesy but it's true. I want to see you again, soon. Like very soon.'

She put her hands on her hips and grinned. 'You're flying tomorrow with your boss? To Brussels?'

'Tomorrow morning. I'll be back on Friday night.'

She nodded thoughtfully. 'Well, what's wrong with tonight – or do you need your beauty sleep before flying?' She nodded at his MG. 'You could either come here in your little black rocket, or I can come and find you.'

'Both plans are good.'

She smiled. 'They are.'

As he drove off, and glanced in his rear-view mirrors, and could see her standing on her doorstep waving goodbye at him, his heart was heaving. After his split-up with his wife, he felt he finally had his life back. And he was in love, he realized. Truly, hook, line and sinker in love.

81

Roy Grace was about to enter the conference room for the 8.30 a.m. briefing on Operation Meadow, when his phone rang. It was the Crime Scene Manager.

'Chris, good morning,' he said, and stepped to one side as a couple of his team walked past.

'Sir, I thought you should know right away, we've found something of interest in one of the bin bags,' Chris Gee said.

'Tell me?'

'It's a receipt from a company called PPB in Dartford. It's for a roll of industrial-size mirror foil, purchased on October the fourth. Sounds like the same kind of foil that we found fragments of at the Ferrari crash scene.'

Grace thought for a moment of the implications. The chances of two different people buying this product, who both lived in Arundel Terrace, were infinitesimally small. It was further evidence that Rorke had been living there.

'Brilliant work, Chris,' he said.

Ending the call and thinking hard, he was interrupted by Norman Potting's voice. 'Morning, boss.'

The DS was walking past him and about to enter the conference room. 'Norman!' he called out.

Potting turned.

Grace brought him quickly up to speed with the information he'd just received from Gee. 'I'd like you to go straight up to

Dartford, take Velvet, and see what you can find out about who the purchaser was and how they paid, and if you can, from the store's CCTV, what vehicle he arrived in. I'm assuming a van for a roll that size.'

'Dartford in the Monday morning rush hour on the M25, boss?' Potting said with a wry smile. 'Glenn gets Barbados and I get Dartford, lucky me.'

'Count your blessings, Norman.'

'Ran out of fingers to count them on a long time ago, boss.'

As Potting headed into the room in search of DC Wilde, Grace punched his right fist in the palm of his left hand, repeatedly, excitedly. This, he thought, could be the first, possible, vindication of the raid. Then he heard Glenn Branson's voice behind him.

'You're looking full of beans!'

He turned and grinned at the DI. 'I am.'

'Oh?'

As Grace updated him, Branson nodded. Then said, 'As you say, he would have needed a van to collect a roll that big. We can get an ANPR check of that area done.'

'That warehouse is just off the M25,' Grace said. 'How many vans do you think will have been on that road?'

'Maybe he's been careless enough to use his Kingsway Electrical van?'

'Maybe, and we need to do that urgently,' Grace said. 'But we might get an even better result from a description of whoever purchased the foil – see if it matches Rorke. And maybe we could get really lucky if the foil company have internal CCTV. I'm sending Norman and Velvet there.'

'I've been thinking, boss,' Branson said.

'OK?'

'If Rorke had faked his disappearance, why would he return to the city where he's known? Even if he's changed his appearance. You and I know from the Facial Recognition Team that recognition is done mathematically, not strictly by physical appearance – so he would likely be recognized regardless of how much he altered his looks. Wouldn't Rorke know this? Why would he stay around?'

'He's got away from us once by faking his disappearance, and that's bolstered his confidence. Made him think he's invincible. And he is – until, as I told you, he makes a mistake through hubris.'

'And now he has made one, right? With the receipt for the foil?'

'Remember what we were talking about at the crash scene, investigating a murder?'

Branson frowned.

'About clearing the ground?'

'Yeah, of course. *Clear the ground beneath your feet,* right?'

'Exactly. Rufus Rorke has failed to clear the ground beneath his. He should have taken all the rubbish from his apartment to a tip – or at least somewhere a long way from his place.'

'Ironic, isn't it, that sometimes the same rules apply to both us and the villains.'

'It is. Now all we have to do is go catch him.'

'And we've no idea where he is.'

'At least we know where he was.'

'And that's going to help us?'

'It's one less place to worry about where he might be.' Grace smiled grimly. 'We can eliminate Arundel Terrace.'

'Which only leaves us with the entire rest of the world to search.'

He nodded. 'That's about the size of it. Until we get a break.'

'Until – or *if?*'

'We've found one mistake. Jamie Carruthers is watching the dark web like a hawk for any activity that could be him. He will make another mistake – people like Rorke always do, especially when they're spooked. And from the fact he's vacated his apartment, it looks like we've at least succeeded in doing that.'

He was interrupted by his phone ringing. Looking at the display he saw it was the ACC, Nigel Downing.

Waving an apology to Glenn he answered it. 'Good morning, sir.'

Downing was not a happy bunny. 'Roy, good morning, this whole Operation Meadow seems to be getting quite expensive, budget-wise. You had a surveillance team on Fiona Davies, and they came up with nothing positive. Earlier this morning you organized a raid on what turned out, apparently, to be an empty apartment. I'd like to see you to review what you're doing and get an update? I've got a free slot at midday.'

Ending the call, for the first time since working with the ACC, Grace was feeling uncomfortable echoes of when Cassian Pewe was in that role. And the truth was: the ACC had a point, and he suddenly had a big moment of doubt. He stood still, not ready to enter the conference room just yet, trying to take stock.

They were looking for a suspect who had died over two years ago. They'd put surveillance on his 'widow', which had yielded absolutely nothing. They'd just raided an address linked to their suspect to find absolutely no trace of him at all or any sign that he had been living there, other than the stale smell of cigar smoke and a single receipt. For mirror foil. And, at this moment, he had no way of establishing whether the fragments of foil found at the crash scene were from the roll supplied by the company PPB in Dartford. Maybe in time the forensic labs could prove it – or not. But, even so, unless Emily Denyer could link the credit card payment to an account the suspect held, they would still be no further forward.

They desperately needed a break. He walked through into the conference room, hoping to hell one of his team had some good news.

82

Paul Anthony was having an anxious morning. According to Shannon, James Taylor's flight from Barbados had touched down at London Heathrow at 7.11 a.m., forty-five minutes late, despite having made up some time thanks to a tailwind, due to being stacked for over half an hour.

He'd allowed half an hour for the couple's checked baggage to come through, and calculated they should be on the road by around 8 a.m., give or take. Into the heart of rush hour on the M25 – or the world's biggest car park, as it was less affectionately known.

Assuming Taylor was being a gentleman, and dropping Debbie home somewhere in Brighton, the earliest he would reach his apartment in Worthing would have been around 10 a.m. But, just to be safe, he'd despatched Shannon on the electric bike at 6.30 a.m. for the half-hour ride to Worthing, giving her time to arrive with still some cover of darkness. She would be in place in the Bayside apartment block's underground visitors' parking area by now, carefully avoiding any CCTV cameras.

When she returned, all being well, she would have captured the entire contents of the pilot's phone. Although all he actually needed to see was Taylor's diary. To establish which airport he would be flying from tomorrow to pick up his boss from Jersey and fly him to Brussels. And on which aircraft. For a short-haul job like that, almost certainly the Pilatus. Too bad for Taylor's boss the plane would never arrive in Jersey.

Too bad for Taylor too.

Too bad for Shannon, perhaps. He needed his wingman. But she was nobody's fool and must be sensing the tension in their relationship, too; he could see it in the way she looked at him sometimes. He just needed to keep treating her well and make sure she knew how trapped she was. Then be ready to strike.

Disposal of a body at sea was always a good plan, and he had the advantage that he did not exist. A no-body murder committed by someone who was long dead was getting as close to the perfect murder as it got. A few miles out to sea, and properly weighted, her body would never be found. And he had a very nice power-boat in the marina at Puerto Banús just along from Marbella.

For now, though, he would continue to play the charmer and – OK – not smoke a cigar indoors for the rest of today. He could live with that. Maybe it would do his health good. He grinned at the thought that not smoking would do his health a lot more good than it might do Shannon's.

But, just to rebel, he lit a Cohiba now. And smoked it, accompanied by a small drop of cognac – well, not that small. As he blew a large smoke ring and watched it slowly rise to the ceiling, he imagined Shannon lounging in a fancy bikini, topless, on the padded foredeck of *Naughtyboy*. After sharing a bottle of Champagne with him. And making love for the last time. Followed by her surprised expression as she opened her eyes from a drugged sleep to feel the weight of the anchor chain he was winding around her ankle. Then *bye-bye, Shannon.*

Plop!

He hoped it wouldn't come to that. But he wasn't betting on it.

83

There was something about the white shirts with epaulettes that the top brass of Sussex Police wore – males with black ties, females with black and white chequered cravats – that gave off a clinical air of authority. The shirts always looked immaculate, with something of the military about them.

Until this morning, Grace had always enjoyed a cordial relationship with Nigel Downing, but today the ACC appeared to have swallowed a Cassian Pewe pill. By way of a greeting, as Grace settled into the chair in front of the large desk, Downing asked in a crisp tone, 'Were you ever a fan of that TV series, *Blackadder*?'

Pewe had been a past master at asking questions that were carefully disguised trapdoors, and one lesson Grace had learned from him was to avoid giving a direct answer, although he doubted Downing was trying to trick him. 'With Rowan Atkinson and Hugh Laurie, sir?'

'That scene when Blackadder says, *It's like a blind man in a dark room looking for a black cat that isn't there.* Did you see that?'

Playing along, Grace replied, 'I've never seen it, but Norman often quotes it.'

Downing nodded hard, several times, his face softening to a smile. 'You know what I'm about to say, don't you? Because that's what seems to be happening on Op Meadow since the start. You've been looking for a dead man, in an apartment, where he doesn't live.'

'I actually think that's a bit harsh, sir, but I take your point.'

'OK, enough said on the matter, but we need to make sure we are not falling in love with a hunch. I've seen countless prisons in countries around the world where innocent people are rotting in jail thanks to detectives biased by their hunches rather than the facts. I just don't want that to happen to you.'

'I understand, sir.'

'Roy, I appreciate you've had many years' experience as a detective on the front line of Major Crime, and I'm just a relative newbie. But what I hope I bring to the force is an occasional fresh perspective on the way things are done. We have a lot of anxiety in the city of Brighton and Hove over two fatal mushroom poisonings, with the perpetrator still at large. Admittedly one might have been accidental, but the other, Barnie Wallace, was clearly intentional. Whether or not he was targeted or just unfortunate is something we still do not know, do we?'

'I'm pretty sure I do know,' Grace said. 'He was specifically targeted.'

'Based on the facts or just a hunch?'

'Based on twenty years of experience as a detective on Major Crime, as you've just said, sir, and the evidence we have already found.'

'And your twenty years of experience tells you that the death of two people, in a high-speed crash in a Ferrari, is the work of the same person who switched Mr Wallace's mushrooms in the Organica supermarket?'

'It does.'

'Both acts perpetrated by a man who has been dead for over two years?'

'Correct.'

'A *blind* man – but not in a dark room this time?'

Grace saw the creases of a smile in the ACC's face. 'He didn't have a black cat with him either, sir.'

'Roy, you're a dog lover, right?'

Frowning at the apparent non sequitur, he replied, 'I am, yes – my wife and I love dogs.'

'I love them, too,' the ACC said. 'You recently solved a major case involving the illegal trade in dogs, and full credit to you for that.'

Grace wondered for a moment if his boss was losing the plot. Then Downing said, 'You know the Chief has dogs too.'

Grace frowned again. He knew that the chief constable of Sussex, Lesley Manning, was a big dog lover. Where was this going?

Downing smiled suddenly. A big, warm beam of a smile. 'Roy, she's breathing down my neck. We've got three bizarre deaths in Sussex in the past few weeks. A mushroom poisoning, a university professor, and now a prominent businessman – and his girlfriend – in a car accident that might not be so accidental.' He opened his arms, expansively, shooting his cuffs in the process. 'You're the Head of Major Crime, so I have to turn to you for the answers the Chief wants. I'm on your side, Roy, I believe in you, but I need something for her. So, dog lovers the three of us, just throw me a damned bone!'

84

Paul Anthony, wearing his leather jacket, lined gloves, jeans and helmet, wheeled his Ducati out of the fourth garage along in his row of lock-ups and into the pre-dawn darkness. He stood for a brief moment and reflected, wryly, that it was fortunate he wasn't the sentimental type.

Three Musketeers. Then two. And now it was about to be just one. One dead man not quite as dead as most people thought. But which one of us is actually going to die, Jamesy? Let me tell you something, it ain't going to be me, old mate. Sorry.

The sky was clear and he could see the lights of a gazillion stars above him. It was going to be a beautiful day for flying. He smiled. A beautiful day for dying. For plummeting out of the sky.

A pannier hung either side of the motorbike, one containing all the few possessions he was taking with him, together with a yellow hi-vis jacket and an orange hard hat. The other containing the weapon that would kill James Taylor. Both weighed a similar amount. Symmetry. He liked symmetry.

Closing and locking the door for the last time – not that there was a lot of point in doing that: smartyboy Detective Grace or one of his colleagues would get here, eventually. By which time he would be safely ensconced in his beautiful hillside property on the outskirts of Marbella, and smartyboy's team would be looking, once again, for someone who no longer existed.

He mounted the machine, then switched on the ignition and

lights and fired up the Panigale V4's engine, letting it warm up for some moments, enjoying the burbling rumble as sweet, to his ears, as any of the finest orchestral symphonies. Then he gave the throttle a couple of sharp twists, just for the hell of it, the exhaust crackling like a firework in the silent, still air. He glanced at his watch: 6.03 a.m.

Shannon had left fifteen minutes ago, towing a large suitcase on wheels, to rendezvous with a taxi on the main Shoreham Road a few hundred yards away. It would take her to Gatwick airport, where she would board the 10.05 easyJet flight he had booked her on to Malaga. And from there the Blacklane limousine he had also booked would whisk her the few miles to his villa. He would arrange for his loyal hound, Montmorency, who he had put temporarily into kennels, to be collected and join them later.

He clicked the bike into gear, twisted the throttle, released the clutch and accelerated away, feeling the sense of exhilaration he always got on this machine, but keeping to the speed limit, despite the temptation to blast up through the gears on the quickshifter. By tonight, all would be good again. No more Fiona to pester him. No more James Taylor to worry about. And Shannon. Well, he would decide about that soon.

Downloaded onto his phone, zipped securely in his breast pocket, he not only had Taylor's calendar, but also his flight plan for this morning, from Shoreham to Jersey. It was all prepared, ready to be filed when Taylor got home. Shannon had done a brilliant job of sucking out the entire contents of his phone in the brief journey from the parking lot of his apartment to his floor in the communal lift. Taylor, totally unwitting, had even chatted pleasantly to her while she was doing it.

Minutes later, he heeled hard left at the roundabout in front of the Ropetackle arts centre, crossed the Adur, and shortly after, at the next roundabout, moved over to the right and slowed down as his headlights picked up the first speed bump on the narrow Brighton City airport approach road. He accelerated again, past several private houses, then slowed right down as he passed warning signs, one of which said: *WEAK BRIDGE*. And another: *CAUTION BRIDGE SURFACE SLIPPERY WHEN WET*.

On the far side of the bridge, the road dipped down beneath a short tunnel and he gave the bike another playful burst of speed, loving the echo of the exhaust against the walls and roof. Then he immediately slowed as he saw rows of industrial buildings ahead and the poor state of the road. He passed mostly modern warehouses, the BlueSky Shoreham Business Centre, then a row of buildings that were little more than dilapidated sheds, before the shadowy shape of the white Art Deco terminal building came up on his left. No lights were on in any of the windows. Good. He knew the airport went live at 8 a.m. but had been hoping there wouldn't be too many people around at this hour. Just a couple of security guards, with a big area to patrol, Shannon had found out for him.

He cruised slowly on past the terminal, the engine barely on tickover now, looking left and right for somewhere to park the bike where it wouldn't be noticed – for long enough, anyhow. A little further on was the heliport area, where he'd once kept his own Agusta. But before that he saw a messy-looking open space to his right, between two old and shabby warehouses. He pulled up, switched off the engine, kicked down the stand, dismounted, removed his helmet and placed it on the saddle, then removed the contents of the panniers – the black leather bag containing his laptop and several other items, and a black velvet bag. It looked innocent enough, the kind of outer bag an expensive handbag might come in. But its contents were a lot more deadly than a handbag.

Carrying the bags and knowing exactly where to go from the map Shannon had made, he strode back, guided by the beam of the small Maglite torch he'd brought with him, and checking his watch as he crossed the deserted car park in front of the building – 6.21 a.m. He passed the green-framed windows of the Hummingbird cafe and glanced at the opening hours, thinking he could murder another coffee. But like the airport itself, it didn't open until 8 a.m.

He carried on, heading towards a mesh gate between two corrugated-iron buildings. It was about seven-foot high – the kind of entrance gate you might see on any public tennis court, he thought. It was hardly going to keep anyone determined out. There was a large yellow sign on it that read: *PILOTS' GATE – THIS GATE TO BE KEPT CLOSED AT ALL TIMES*. It was held shut with a large padlock. To the right was a plethora of warning signs. *NO HI-VIS NO ENTRY . . . CAUTION, NOISE LEVEL OF 85 dB(A) OR ABOVE. CAUTION, AIRCRAFT MANOEUVRING AREA AHEAD.*

He debated for some moments whether to pick the lock, then decided it would be just as easy to climb over. He first slung his laptop bag over the top, guiding it down the far side carefully, in stages, with his fingers through the mesh, then repeated the process with the black velvet bag.

Then he caught a sweet whiff of cigarette smoke.

He froze.

Another whiff of smoke. Laughter.

Shit.

It was coming from the end of the passage between the two buildings. The building on the left, he knew from the map, was part of the main airfield hangar. The one on the right housed the firefighting vehicles and equipment.

He pressed himself against the wall on his right and held his breath, listening. *Don't come this way. DO. NOT. COME. THIS. WAY.*

He was close to hyperventilating. If they came down here they would find the two bags. He cursed his stupidity. His laptop, for

PETER JAMES

God's sake! His laptop lying the other side of the gate, out of
reach. With everything on it. And the velvet bag. Jesus.

Was he losing his touch. Had he lost the fucking plot?

Then he saw a tiny flare of red, like a laser dot, followed by a
shower of tiny sparks. The cigarette butt hitting the ground. More
laughter. Two males, maybe twenty yards away, both with deep
voices, their conversation crystal clear in the silent early morning
air. They were talking about football, about Brighton and Hove
Albion's chances in the game this coming Saturday.

To his relief, the voices became quieter. They were walking
away.

He continued waiting. Until he could no longer hear them at
all. Then he hauled himself up and over the gate, jumped down
on the far side and stood and listened again, shivering a little
from the cold, despite his fleece-lined leather jacket.

Silence.

He picked up both bags and hurried along the passageway
between the two buildings and came out into the open space in
front of them. The vast structure of the hangar was to his left,
and to his right was a much smaller building. The pre-dawn sky
was beginning to lighten. Within half an hour he would no longer
have darkness to hide in.

He checked again and still could not hear any voices. He risked
briefly switching on the torch and shining it on the hangar doors.
They were shut. Shut and no doubt locked. He went over and
tried them, just in case, and they would not budge. As he had
expected. But they would be opened soon, well ahead of the
airport going live at 8 a.m., he was sure, in order to start towing
out the aircraft that would be flying this morning. He needed
somewhere close by where he could lurk.

Then he saw it, the perfect place! A hundred yards or so
across the apron he saw, in the steadily increasing light, the
silhouette of the parked refuelling truck appearing out of the

darkness like a developing Polaroid photograph. He hurried over to it.

Standing on the far side, he removed the yellow hi-vis tabard from his bag and donned it. Then he put on his orange hard hat. Wording printed along the front of it read: CAA INSPECTORATE.

Across the chest of the tabard were the words CIVIL AVIATION AUTHORITY INSPECTORATE.

Craving a coffee even more now, a strong one, a double espresso or an Americano, he perched on the vehicle's front bumper and settled down to wait. As he did so he thought about a US serial killer he'd read about, long ago in his former life, who had been sentenced to death by a US judge. The venerable judge had asked the man if he had anything to say, and he'd replied, 'Yeah, have a good time on earth, sugar.'

He'd always thought that was a cool response. And he was thinking now, and it brought a big smile to his face, about James Taylor.

Have a good time on earth, Jamesy. All two hours of it, or so, that you have left.

85

Roy Grace went and sat down in the conference room shortly after 7.15 a.m. The morning briefing wasn't due to start until 8.30 but he had a lot of prep to do. He wanted first to review the footage of the blind man and the photographs taken from Barnie Wallace's camera on the big screen in the room. He had a growing feeling of despondency.

Yesterday morning the ACC had asked him to throw him a bone. Grace had hoped that an ANPR camera in the vicinity of Dartford, where the roll of foil had been purchased, might have shown up the Kingsway Electrical van, but it hadn't. Nor had any of the city's CCTV cameras picked it up either side of the time when the roll was collected.

The search of the bins at 118 Arundel Terrace had revealed nothing else, either. The only positive he had, so far, came via Jonathan Jackson at the Met's Central Image Investigation Unit. The additional photographs they had sent of the man in the Organica supermarket, and who was the subject of the photographs taken by Barnie Wallace, had been analysed further, and Jackson said they were pretty near one hundred per cent certain it was Rufus Rorke – despite superficial alterations to his face.

As he began to play the footage of the blind man, he was running through, in his mind, all his lines of enquiry. They had not yet come up with any conclusive reason Dermot Bryson had carried a gun in his car. Just speculation that he'd been involved in dodgy dealings in drugs and cybercurrency. His team had not found any copycat killings anywhere else in the UK. Emily Denyer, the financial investigator, had found evidence that Bryson was moving major amounts of cash around through Bitcoins and other cybercurrencies, but was, so far, unable to establish any criminal activity – and in the past few days after his death all activity had ceased.

Almost out of desperation, he'd had the team look at the Brighton University professor, Bill Llewellyn, just to see if there was any link to Rufus Rorke there, but they'd been unable to establish anything.

Anaphylactic shock from a wasp sting looked certain to be the coroner's verdict. As evidence of this, a wasp had been found in the professor's oesophagus during the post-mortem. It was late autumn, the time when wasps were at their most aggressive and carrying the most venom. Even so, he was still not satisfied that this was a tragic accident and that was why he was keeping it as part of the overall investigation. Llewellyn's EpiPen had never been recovered – presumably thrown away by someone who was unaware of the importance of preserving everything around a sudden death. Llewellyn was a chauvinistic drunk that no female at Brighton University would be shedding any tears over, but with the total lack of evidence to the contrary, not a murder victim.

He was feeling tired this morning, after a restless night in which he could not stop his brain from churning, churning, churning. Something must have spooked Rufus Rorke. Or maybe it was his MO to keep disappearing. Playing some kind of Dead Man's Hide and Seek. He could be anywhere in the world now. But he could have lived and operated anywhere in the world after going off the back of that yacht – so why did he return to Sussex? Sheer hubris? A belief that he was invincible? To cock a snook at him – *So, Roy, you nearly caught me last time but I fooled you by dying . . . now I'm back, operating under your nose and you still can't catch me!*

Grace knew there were criminals with out-of-control egos who did actually think like that. He knew also they were the ones most likely to make a mistake. Rufus Rorke had made one, two years ago. He was bound to have made another – they just had to find it.

'Morning, boss,' Jack Alexander said, walking in looking perky, holding a large mug of coffee.

'Any progress on the source of the guns, Jack?'

'The Ballistics team at the Firearms Unit have said the gun in the Ferrari's glove box was a viable weapon, but probably only good for one or two shots – which I understand is the case with most of these printed weapons. But there are a wide range of 3D printers capable of printing the components in that gun. I've got a list of all the manufacturers of the ones capable of producing a working firearm, and it's a big one, boss – and they are all over the world. Colombia, the US, China, India, Argentina, the Czech Republic. To give you a sense of what we're up against, there are currently 168,000 3D printers in use in the UK.'

'That's why villains like these 3D guns,' Norman Potting said.

Grace looked up – he hadn't noticed the DS enter the room.

'No serial number on them,' Potting continued. 'They're untraceable, as we know.'

Grace nodded, only too aware he was facing yet another blind alley in this investigation. The internal phone began warbling. Nick Nicholl, who had also just come in and was standing close to it, picked up the receiver. 'DC Nicholl, Major Crime,' he said.

Grace turned back to Alexander. 'Jack, did the Ballistics guys say if that gun had ever been fired?'

'Boss!' Nicholl interrupted with an urgency in his tone. 'You need to listen to this!' He tapped a button on the phone and seconds later they all heard the voice of DC Jamie Carruthers.

'Sir, I've been contacted from a woman on the dark web. She wants to speak to you and no one else. She says she knows where Paul Anthony is.'

86

At 7.25 a.m., a red and yellow chequered SUV with blue rooflights, marked Fire Crew on the door, drove around from behind the terminal building, and pulled up opposite the hangar in front of the corrugated-iron building with large windows that had a yellow sign sticking out. *BRIEFING ROOM C.*

Paul Anthony, shivering a little more now, watched from behind the fuel truck as two men in thick blue sweatshirts, baggy blue trousers and trainers climbed out of the vehicle, unlocked the Briefing Room door, entered and switched on the lights. Moments later, he saw them come back out, walk over to the massive hangar doors and start to slide them open, with a loud screeching and clattering sound. The superstructure of the hangar looked far larger in the growing daylight than it had in shadowy darkness.

After a minute or so the doors were fully open and he could see a few of the light aircraft parked in there, a couple partially cloaked with silver protective covers, and a small Cessna jet. Hopefully the Pilatus that Taylor would be flying was in here too.

Somehow, he had to get in, without being seen. He had the tabard and hard hat, and the spiel to go with it if he did get challenged, but better if no one saw him. He looked at the windows of Briefing Room C and saw the two men moving around. Then they came out again, got into the SUV and drove off.

He couldn't believe his luck!

The moment the vehicle was out of sight, he made a dash for the hangar and entered it, passing a yellow tug that looked like a lawnmower without a blade. *AIRCRAFTCADDY* was stencilled down the side. He breathed in smells of engine oil, rubber, paint and varnish in the cold air, and looked around. There were at least a dozen small aircraft in here, but it didn't take him long to locate the one he was after. The Pilatus PC-12 was a pressurized single-engined turbo-prop aircraft. From the front it resembled a Second World War Spitfire. It was gleaming, sleek, like a bird of prey, sitting on small wheels with fat tyres.

He looked around carefully for any sign of anyone else in here. The place was deserted. He smiled. It had been worth the wait. Well worth it.

Then just as he reached the Pilatus he was startled by a howling banshee wail, like an air-raid siren. *Shit*, he thought. *Shit, shit, shit.* He looked desperately around. Had he triggered this? How?

Then it stopped, slowly, taking several seconds to wind down. He breathed out. A routine test, he figured, either a fire alarm or a crash alarm.

He looked around carefully, but could see no one. Then he reached for the aircraft's rear-door handle and pulled it. As he had expected, it was unlocked.

87

Roy Grace went to his office with Glenn Branson ready to take the call from the anonymous female. Moments later, his phone rang.

'This is Detective Superintendent Grace,' he answered calmly. 'Who am I speaking to?'

'I can't give you my name,' the woman said. She sounded young, he thought, in her twenties, nervous but punchy, her accent classless, Home Counties. 'I know you are looking for Paul Anthony, and I know where he is.'

Grace frowned. On his strict instructions, his team had not made Paul Anthony's name public, not at either of the two press conferences on Operation Meadow, nor in any other way. 'Can you tell me why you think we might be looking for Mr Anthony?' he asked, keeping his tone calm and polite, not wanting to risk spooking her.

'Because I'm not an idiot,' she retorted.

'OK,' he said, continuing to think hard. 'Do you know Paul Anthony yourself?'

'Maybe.'

'OK, you *maybe* know him and you are not an idiot. What is your reason for wanting to tell us his whereabouts?'

'Because someone needs to stop him.'

'Stop him from doing what?'

'From what he's doing.'

'And what are you aware of that he is doing?'

'He's a killer – a murderer – he's totally psycho. He's about to commit another murder; you might be able to stop him. But you may not have much time.'

Grace considered his reply very carefully, thoughts swirling through his head. She didn't sound like a crackpot, so who was she? How did she know they were looking for Paul Anthony? How did she know what he was about to do?

Unless there had been a leak from within his team, which he strongly doubted, how did she know? 'Do you want to save this person's life? The person you say he is about to murder?'

'I do, he's a decent, innocent man.'

'Can you tell me who he is and where he is?'

'I can, yes, but before I do, I want immunity from prosecution. Can you give me that? In writing?'

'What exactly are your concerns about being prosecuted?' he asked, still keeping his tone gentle, caring.

'I've been working for him, doing stuff for him. He lied to me about what he was really doing.'

'What kind of stuff?'

'On the dark web. Supplying criminals with stuff. I could just disappear right now and you'd have a hard time finding me, you might *never* find me. But I don't want to, I want to stop this bastard. That's why I called. Please.'

Grace waited a beat, then said, 'Look, it's not in my gift to grant anyone immunity from prosecution, that's not how the system works. But—'

'That's not good enough,' she said. 'I'll give you an hour to think about it, and then I'll call you back.'

She terminated the call before Grace had a chance to reply.

88

Tuesday 18 October 2022

Taylor was in a hurry. He had intended to arrive at the airport by 7.30 a.m. for the 08.15 take-off slot filed on his flight plan. Out of habit he liked to leave plenty of time to check the aircraft, and if possible grab a coffee from the cafe.

But thanks to a minor accident as well as roadworks clogging up the rush-hour traffic, it was 8.10 a.m. when he finally pulled into the parking area in front of the Brighton City airport terminal. The flight plan he had filed yesterday with Air Traffic Control, as normal, only allowed a thirty-minute window for take-off. His was 08.15–08.45. He was going to have to rush his pre-flight checks, which he never liked doing – and he had to hope that the duty ops team had towed the Pilatus out of the hangar and onto the apron, ready to go.

He parked the MG, grabbed his battered overnight bag and his flight logbook, and hurried in the cold through the pilots' gate and along the narrow corridor between the two buildings. To his relief he saw the Pilatus was out of the hangar, parked just over the yellow line indicating the start of the apron. An airfield operative he knew, Des, was detaching the yellow towing tug from the front.

As he strode over he glanced at the orange windsock, which was indicating a light sou'westerly – the normal prevailing wind. Then reaching the Pilatus he did a quick walk around, thanking Des for getting the plane out.

Reaching the aircraft, he lowered the front door and climbed up the steps into the immaculate cream and tan interior, which reeked of fresh polish, and had the same thought he always did boarding this aircraft. It looked so tiny on the outside, yet it was like a Tardis inside.

Behind the cockpit, which could be closed off for privacy, was a spacious boardroom configuration of four large first-class-style leather seats, with tables, and another two seats further back, with the curtained-off baggage stowage area beyond, in the rear. He glanced briefly around, checking out of habit that all looked in order, and that the private company employed to stock up the stores of drinks and nibbles, and sandwich selection in the fridge, had done their job. Then he glanced at his watch again: 08.14. Shit.

He dumped his bag on a passenger seat and secured it with the belt, planning to move it to the rear stowage area later, after he landed in Jersey, then grabbed the canvas bag hanging in the cockpit and hurried back down the steps. He made another fast inspection walk around, checking that nothing looked damaged and there were no leaks, then removed the pitot covers from the tubes under the wings, followed by the nose wheel chock and put them in the bag.

Then he climbed back on board, pulled the door shut and entered the cockpit. Hanging the bag back up on its hook, he sat in the left seat, loaded up the nav computer with the route, then opened the tech log to confirm the aircraft's current technical status was serviceable, as expected.

It was still fairly quiet at this hour out on the airfield, but he could hear the faint clatter of a helicopter. He zoned the sound out, and everything else, to focus.

Finally, when he was satisfied, he clipped on his harness, unhooked the headset from above him, pulled it on, and pressed the transmit button on the radio. It was 08.19. Although now known as Brighton City airport, historically it was Shoreham airport, due to its location, and all Air Traffic Control communications continued as from Shoreham tower. 'Shoreham tower, Golf Alpha Victor Uniform Zulu PC12 on the main apron with information, request start clearance for Jersey.'

The air traffic controller's voice was calm and crisp as he approved the request.

Taylor fired up the Pratt and Whitney turboprop engine and let it warm up on idle power, while he spent the next few minutes carefully ticking through the checklist. The fuel tanks were full, which gave him a range of 1,500 miles, more than ample to collect Towne, fly him from Jersey to Brussels and return – a round-trip of approximately 1,000 miles.

'Tower, Golf Uniform Zulu request taxi,' Taylor replied.

'Golf Uniform Zulu taxi Kilo One for runway Two Zero.'

Taylor's adrenaline began to surge as it did every time Air Traffic Control gave him the signal to proceed to the runway. This was in some ways the biggest buzz of flying, the rising excitement during the minutes immediately before take-off.

He replied and opened up the throttle, enjoying the rise in pitch of the engine and the increased thrashing of the large propellor in front of him, then the plane began to move forward, jolting on the uneven surface, as he headed at a gentle taxiing speed out across the airfield.

Five minutes later, he was in place, and the runway, a narrow strip of black tarmac with white markings, stretched out ahead of him. There was no sign of any other plane on the move. And he still had twenty minutes in hand. The controller's voice came through his headset.

'Golf Uniform Zulu are you ready to copy clearance?'

He responded that he was ready to copy. He was feeling like an excited kid, he couldn't help it, and there were other pilots he'd spoken to over the years, mature adults like himself, who still got the same thrill in these final moments. The day you didn't, he thought, would be the day you should hand in your ticket.

'After departure you are cleared right turn on track Goodwood, remain outside controlled airspace.' The controller continued with the instructions before eventually giving Taylor clearance for take-off.

Now his adrenaline was really surging.

Taylor pressed firmly on the brake pedals then opened up the throttle. The aircraft juddered as the engine howled. This was the moment he loved best of all. For the next thirty seconds or so, until he was airborne and away, he owned this runway and all the airspace around him. For the next thirty seconds, the whole train set was his!

He released the brakes and the plane rolled forward, accelerating rapidly, bumping faster and faster, the ribbon of tarmac unspooling in front of him. He watched the speed. 50mph . . . 60 . . . 70 . . . 80. He gently pulled back the control column. The nose of the plane came up and the bumping stopped. He was airborne.

Then he heard another sound, like a bump, somewhere behind him.

He turned his head, puzzled. But could not see anything amiss.

89

She was on the phone again exactly one hour after she had hung up. She hadn't exactly endeared herself to Roy Grace. He had a place in his heart where he kept a special loathing for people who had the arrogance to think they could hold the police to ransom.

But he was well aware she was one of the few live lines of enquiry he had at this moment. 'This is Detective Superintendent Grace,' he said, doing his best to sound calm and patient.

There was just silence. It went on so long, Grace, still puzzling how this young woman knew they were looking for Paul Anthony, worried she had hung up again.

Then, after a good ten seconds, she said, 'So immunity from prosecution. What can you offer me?'

'Can you give me your name?' he asked.

She was silent.

Grace continued. 'Once I know who I'm talking to, there are a number of avenues I can follow with the Crown Prosecution Service and the judge in any future trial. The more help you give me now to apprehend Paul Anthony, the greater credit you will get for your assistance and this, I promise, will help you very much. If you can show that your actions now save someone's life, that will also be a massive benefit for you. But, tell me first, what are you concerned about? What do you think you are going to be prosecuted for – if anything?'

'Possibly accessory to murder, but I was being coerced,' she replied.

Roy Grace had been thinking hard during this past hour, about how she could know what she claimed to know about Paul Anthony. The only possible way, he had concluded, was that she had been in some kind of relationship with him. And had been involved in the evacuation and clearing out of his Arundel Terrace apartment. Had she been living there with him? And now they'd had a falling-out? And her loyalty had changed?

'OK, I'll put my trust in you. I hope I'm making the right decision. My name's Shannon.' She took a deep breath. 'Paul is a control-freak, and he has been threatening me with his coercive behaviour and making me do things I would never have done before I met him. I am petrified of him, and I need to do something to stop him. He is at Brighton City airport. He's gone there to kill a pilot called James Taylor.'

'How is he planning to kill him, Shannon?' Grace asked, still keeping his voice calm.

'I don't know – I don't know. I think a bomb. A bomb on his plane. Or something.'

90

Taylor decided the noise he had heard behind him, somewhere in the back of the aircraft, must have been a crate of drinks or snacks that had not been properly stowed. He put it out of his mind and concentrated on flying the aircraft and the Air Traffic Control instructions. They were climbing steadily, approaching the first ceiling he had been given.

He clicked the mic button. 'London Control, good morning,' he said and gave the full call sign. 'Golf Alpha Victor Uniform Zulu passing three thousand five hundred feet climbing four thousand feet to remain clear of controlled airspace on track Goodwood.'

Then, as he released the push-to-talk mic button, he heard a voice right behind him, muted slightly by the headset clamped over his ears.

He froze.

A voice he had not heard for many years. That same, confident, disdainful *I'm the BIG I AM and you are nobody.*

'Nice eulogy you gave me, Taylor. You hit all the right notes. I was impressed. Too bad I never got the chance to thank you before now.'

He turned his head, as much as he could, to see Rufus Rorke, standing right behind him, holding a small, black cloth bag in his right hand, and with a smile on his face that was pure, utter venom.

91

Glenn Branson and Roy Grace raced from the Sussex Police HQ on blue lights, siren wailing. It was a sixteen-mile drive to the airport, and even at speed it was going to be twenty minutes before they got there. Branson drove, while Grace was on his radio, patched through to Shoreham Air Traffic Control.

A Roads Policing Unit patrol car as well as an officer on a motorbike were already at the scene, at Brighton City airport.

The controller was polite and calm and spoke with a clear voice. 'Golf Alpha Victor Uniform Zulu, piloted by James Taylor, left Shoreham air space four minutes ago,' he said.

'He needs to land at the nearest airport, immediately,' Grace said. 'We believe there may be a bomb on board. Can you contact him?'

'I'm looking at his flight plan, sir. He should currently be in radio comms with London Control. I'll ask them immediately.'

'Thank you. What is his destination?'

'The flight plan we have filed is for Jersey, Channel Islands.'

Grace glanced up, through the windscreen, and wished he hadn't. They were on the wrong side of the road, hurtling towards the Cuilfail tunnel, and a cement lorry was heading uphill straight at them. Abdicating responsibility for his imminent death or survival to Branson, he looked back down at his radio. As he did so he felt the car swerve violently, the constant wail of the siren making it hard to hear what the man was saying.

'Jersey, Channel Islands?' Grace repeated.

'Yes.'

'Can you find out from London Control which is the nearest airfield he can put down at?'

'Looking at his flight plan, it would be the Isle of Wight.'

'OK, tell London Control to ask him to put down urgently at Bembridge in the Isle of Wight.'

'Wilco.'

Grace's brain was racing. From memory, the hovercraft, HoverTravel, was the fastest route from the mainland to the island. But that wasn't fast enough right now. He radioed to see if the helicopter, shared between Sussex, Surrey and Kent, was available. He was told it would be in fifteen minutes, after dropping off an injured motorcyclist at Guildford Hospital. He put in a request for it to head for the Isle of Wight immediately after.

Then he radioed Shoreham tower again to update the controller.

The controller replied, 'Golf Alpha Victor Uniform Zulu is not currently responding to London Control, sir, although he did check in a short time ago on the frequency.'

92

Rufus Rorke unhooked the headset above the co-pilot's seat and donned it. 'Always nice to know what's going on, isn't it, Taylor?' He held the velvet bag to his side. It contained a heavy brass knuckle duster. Sometimes, Rufus thought, you could be just a bit too modern, a bit too hi-tech, a bit too digital where analogue might do the job better. Firing a gun in the pressurized cabin of an aircraft was just plain dumb. In some situations Uncle Johnny could be a far more effective weapon.

And he liked the double-entendre of the name.

When he had been a child, his mother's brother, Uncle Johnny, had been his favourite relative. A tall, flash guy who had a dealership selling used high-end cars, Uncle Johnny had in his youth been a county middleweight champion. He'd taught him how to box when he was just seven years old. Taught him painfully. Uncle Johnny had given him a cool pair of red, white and black gloves for his seventh birthday, and then had begun to coach him into becoming a boxer himself. Once a week he'd come over in a tracksuit. When it was fine they'd go out in the back garden, and when it was wet, into the garage, and Uncle Johnny would bash him to hell and back.

He taught him to duck, weave, parry, the jab, the cross, the hooks and the uppercut. He learned pretty fast that if he didn't do it adroitly, his uncle would have no compunction about slamming a massive sucker punch into his face that would floor him.

During the school holidays, from the age of eleven until he was fifteen, Uncle Johnny would knock him flat on his back several times in each session. It angered him, not because it hurt – and it did hurt – but much more because it humiliated him. He never complained, he took it, he knew he was learning, and there was something else he was gaining from this, too, something that would serve him well in his career now. And that was how to bide his time.

It all changed a couple of weeks after his sixteenth birthday. He'd put on a sudden spurt of growth over the previous months and was now, at six foot tall, only a couple of inches shorter than his uncle – who still called him *little guy*, though. He'd decided it was finally time for action.

With surgical precision, using a razor blade, he cut out all the interior padding of his right-hand boxing glove, just leaving the thin outer skin. Then he carefully inserted a knuckle duster against the knuckle area of the glove.

He'd had the foresight to buy an identical pair of gloves, from money he'd saved, and kept them hidden beneath a bunch of clothes in a drawer in his bedroom.

The next Saturday, when his uncle turned up, it was pelting with rain, so they went into the double garage, and his uncle reversed out both of his parents' cars. Then, as their ritual always went, his uncle would start his stopwatch, they would tap gloves, then step back two paces and, holding their hands up, protectively, would begin their cagey moves, darting forward, back, sideways, stabbing tentatively, feinting, looking for that opportunity to land a punch that counted.

Uncle Johnny wasn't going to put him on the floor today, no way, José.

He dodged a massive punch that came out of nowhere, narrowly skimming his right ear, then walked into a stinging left uppercut. He saw the demon in his uncle's eyes; the sparkle and glee of that old killer instinct; the smile on his face, the smile of a guy who knew he had the upper hand and was toying with his nephew.

And he saw the gap. Seized the moment, and slammed that heavily loaded right fist with all the force he could deliver, straight at his uncle's face. For some reason, Uncle Johnny tilted his head down, and he struck between the bridge of his nose and the front of his temple. There was a loud crack and blood sprayed from his nose.

It was followed by a weird, giddy look in his uncle's eyes, then he dropped to the ground like a sack of potatoes and lay still.

Uncle Johnny spent three days in hospital suffering from concussion, during which he was diagnosed with a fractured skull. No one could figure out how this had happened from a blow from padded sparring gloves. The surgeon concluded there must have been an existing weakness that Uncle Johnny had sustained from a car crash a few years before. He was never quite himself again, after that blow, for the rest of his life.

Rufus Rorke went to a pub that night and got drunk for the first time in his life. But he wasn't drowning his sorrows, he was celebrating.

It had just felt so good!

93

'Golf Alpha Victor Uniform Zulu, do you read me?'

Through their headsets both men heard the crackly voice of the air traffic controller, calm but urgent.

His eyes not leaving Taylor's, Rufus Rorke raised the velvet bag, just a few inches, but enough. Threatening. His expression said, loud and clear to Taylor, *Do not respond.*

'This is London Control. You are instructed to land immediately at your nearest available airfield. Repeat, land immediately.'

There was a silence as both men looked at each other.

'Your aircraft is in immediate danger. You may have a bomb on board. Do you read me, Golf Alpha Victor Uniform Zulu?'

Rufus Rorke shook his head and checked the mic was off before he spoke. 'You don't have a bomb, Jamesy, my friend, you have me. And I'm much more devastating.'

'So you really are still alive,' Taylor said, calmly.

Rorke pursed his lips into a smile that was not reflected in his eyes. 'You knew that, didn't you? The moment you saw me in church you knew that. So why all the buggering about, going to Fiona, then going to John Baker in Barbados? What have you been hoping to achieve? What do you want?'

'What are you hoping to achieve by being a stowaway, Rufus?' Taylor retorted. 'If being dead has made you rich enough to afford to come back to life, surely you can afford the air fare to Jersey? On a good day you could fly there on easyJet for twenty-seven pounds.'

'Answer my question, James. What is it you want? The same as that asshole, Barnie? You planning to blackmail me too?'

'Since I gave your eulogy, Rufus, I think I'm entitled to ask a few questions when I see you very much alive two years later.'

'You always were the goody-two-shoes, weren't you?' Rorke sneered. 'Barnie, the eternal loser – a total tosser. You, the eternal swot. What did we all have in common? The Three Musketeers. How come we were even friends back then?'

'Golf Alpha Victor Uniform Zulu? Golf Alpha Victor Uniform Zulu, do you read me?' The London air traffic controller's voice came through their headsets again.

'Remember our English master, who was so big on Oscar Wilde?'

Rorke gave him a sideways look. Shannon and he had been quoting Wilde. Coincidence? 'English wasn't really my subject.'

'You should have listened, Rufus. Wilde said about someone: *he hasn't an enemy in the world, and none of his friends like him.*'

'Are you trying to fuck with my head, Taylor?'

The pilot shook his head. 'It's been fucked up a long time ago, Rufus. Shall I respond to the controller?' He watched the instruments. They were climbing steadily: 15,000 feet; 15,500; 16,000. The English Channel was below them.

'Yes.' He raised Uncle Johnny higher, even more threatening. 'Tell ATC you are diverting for operational reasons. And not a word more.'

For operational reasons was code to Air Traffic Control that there was a problem of some unspecified nature, which enabled you to divert from your flight plan without giving necessarily any further reason.

'Do you seriously want me to disobey an ATC instruction to divert immediately?'

'You're listening to me now, not ATC.'

'Going to kill me if I do say any more, are you?'

In reply, Rufus Rorke swung the velvet bag hard at the large square glass screen in front of the co-pilot's control column, that housed key duplicated instruments – the compass, airspeed indicator, attitude indicator, altimeter, turn coordinator, heading indicator and vertical speed indicator.

It shattered, imploding from the weight of the knuckle duster into a spider's web pattern, with some of the glass falling out.

'Jesus! You're crazy! What the hell are you doing?' Taylor shouted. 'Do you want to kill us both?'

'Have you forgotten that I have both a full, multi-engine, instrument-rated pilot's licence and a helicopter licence? I know exactly what I'm doing. We're going to Brest, initially, then we'll head on to Ouessant.'

Ouessant immediately rang an alarm bell to James Taylor. It was a small island off the coast of Brittany, where a couple of years ago he'd flown Tommy and his family for lunch at a seafood restaurant with a great reputation. At the tiny airfield, Air Traffic Control was shut between 1030GMT and 1300GMT and there was no Customs and Immigration – they required contact in advance. The closest main airport was Brest. If you were up to something nefarious in a light aircraft, such as this Pilatus, Ouessant wasn't a bad choice.

'I can recommend a good restaurant there, Rufus, if you like oysters and lobster,' he said, trying to bring this crazy guy back to reality.

'Funny. Answer my original question, Taylor. Why did you go to Fiona? Why did you go to John Baker in Barbados? What do you want? Money, is it?'

The ATC controller's voice came through again. 'Do you read me?'

Rufus Rorke raised Uncle Johnny even higher still. Taylor got the message.

'London Control, this is Golf Uniform Zulu. Diverting to Brest for operational reasons.'

'Golf Uniform Zulu diverting to Brest,' the response came back immediately. 'What is the nature of your emergency?'

Rorke gave him a cut-throat sign.

Obeying him, Taylor did not respond.

'Repeat, what is the nature of your emergency, Golf Uniform Zulu?'

Rorke ripped Taylor's headset off him, then tore out its wire.

'What the hell do you want, Rufus?'

'No, you tell me what *you* want, Taylor.'

They were flying along the coast. Taylor looked up at his old school friend. 'Funny, isn't it? There we were as kids, and here we are twenty years on. Barnie's dead. You're dead – well – not quite as dead as everyone thought. You must have made a lot of friends for so many people to turn up to your funeral. And yet Fiona rang me to ask me to give the eulogy because she couldn't find anyone to do it. Had all the rest of the people in that rammed church turned up just to make sure you were dead?'

'That's not remotely amusing, Jamesy.'

'You're the only person who calls me *Jamesy.*'

'You still haven't answered my question.'

'Let me guess, Rufus. You killed Barnie, didn't you? Because he was blackmailing you. And now you've come to kill me, because I've rumbled you too.'

'You always were too smart for your own good, Taylor.'

Taylor saw the black bag rising to swing at him. He ducked sideways and as he did so, he pushed the control column fully forwards, retarding the throttle as he did so, to limit the stresses on the airframe.

The aircraft bunted over, descending steeply. The velvet bag swung past his face. Rufus Rorke was hurtled by the negative G-force up onto the roof of the cabin. Then, as Taylor pulled the control column fully back, as far as it would go, Rorke, still clinging to the bag, smacked down on his stomach onto the boardroom table.

Then Taylor put the plane back into an abrupt steep descent again, before reverting violently into another steep climb.

Rorke had anticipated it. And was ready. He clung to the table that was securely fixed to the cabin floor. But it was all he could do to just hold on as the plane continued to climb, steeper and steeper, until they were almost vertical, as he hung desperately to the table top, Uncle Johnny sliding to the rear of the cabin, somewhere behind him. Powerless to stop him, he saw Taylor reach up, grab the co-pilot headset, and pull it on.

Rufus Rorke knew they could not keep climbing, they would soon reach the Pilatus's operating ceiling of 30,000 feet. Then Taylor would have to level out.

And he would be ready.

94

So far, none of the ten police officers who were now searching the vast area of the airport complex had reported any sign of Rufus Rorke. He could be anywhere, Grace knew. He could be long gone too. The detective superintendent stood with Glenn Branson in the Air Traffic Control tower of Brighton City airport.

It was rectangular, with tall, wide windows sloping outwards, giving a 360-degree view. A narrow, curved worktop ran around much of the circumference, on which sat a large number of computer screens, of varying sizes – some displaying maps, the rest rows of digits or lines of text – binoculars and several telephone sets, and Grace noticed the usual office clutter of water bottles, mugs, a Thermos flask, and cables everywhere. Some of the equipment looked almost brand new, while some looked like it dated back to the Second World War – when this airport had been a significant base for the RAF.

There were one controller and two trainees on duty, all casually dressed, seated on basic but supportive-looking chairs. Alan Moss, a jovial, lightly bearded man in his late forties, with a mop of silver hair; Darren Fry, a studious-looking man in his mid-thirties, with dark hair and dark-rimmed glasses; and Danny Robinson, tall, burly, hair shorn to stubble, wearing a cable-knit sweater and with the physique of a rugby player.

Moss had been pointing out the flight path, designated by a white line, that the Pilatus was currently on, almost due west towards Southampton and the London Air Traffic Control centre at Swanwick, and then south out across the English Channel, passing close to the Isle of Wight.

'Oh shit!' Robinson exclaimed and pointed at the air traffic monitor.

'What the hell?' Alan Moss said.

'What?' Grace asked.

Moss pointed at the large radar screen in front of him. It looked like a Cubist painting in bottle green, light green, light brown and black. The map was populated with letters and numbers in white and orange. On it, Grace could see the south coast of England, the Channel Islands and the north and north-west coast of France, the land masses showing in light brown.

'That's the Pilatus,' he said with an urgency in his voice, pointing. He clicked his mouse and zoomed in. The call sign appeared in white. *Golf Alpha Victor Uniform Zulu*. Next to it in orange were the numbers 180. 'That's the designated altitude, 18,000 feet. We allow a tolerance of 200 feet deviation either way. Look!'

Grace could see the altitude rise to 190, 200, 201, 220. Then it started going back down. Within moments it was 170 . . . 160 . . .

'What's going on?' he asked.

Moss didn't respond to him for some moments. 'Golf Alpha Victor Uniform Zulu, this is Shoreham tower, are you still on frequency?' With his headset on one ear Moss put the ageing and rather well-worn desktop telephone to the other to speak directly with his counterpart at London control centre at Swanwick by conventional landline. At the same time London repeated their increasingly anxious attempts to regain comms with the erratic Pilatus; 'Golf Alpha Victor Uniform Zulu London control radio check.' Silence. They tried again.

Still silence.

The huddled group in the Shoreham ATC room then all saw the aircraft start climbing steeply again. 220 . . . 230 . . . 240.

Moss turned to his colleagues. 'We have a rogue aircraft, we need to get all planes well clear out of the way.'

'What the hell is going on?' Grace quizzed him.

Moss shook his head. 'The pilot's not responding in any normal way. His current rate of climb is very steep – as if he's performing aerobatics. That's causing me concern.'

'Concern?' Branson repeated.

'This aircraft – the Pilatus – has a pressurized cabin,' Moss said. 'If there was some catastrophic failure of the pressurization, it could lead to oxygen starvation, hypoxia, and that could be one explanation for the pilot's erratic behaviour – or, he could be drunk or high on drugs. But I know the pilot, James Taylor, he's a very reliable man.'

All three of them could now see the plane was levelling out, at close to 30,000 feet. Then it began to dive. Vertically. Before seconds later pulling up steeply again, then rolling to starboard.

'Jesus,' Moss said. 'Those are far higher G-forces than a commercial pilot would be used to. He's in danger of blacking out.'

'Is there anything else that could explain his behaviour?' Branson asked. 'Like a malfunction with the plane's systems? Something gone wrong with the autopilot?'

'Or a bomb detonating?' Grace asked.

'Unlikely,' intervened Robinson. 'Any bomb, however small, would almost certainly either destroy the aircraft or bring it straight down.'

The other two air traffic controllers nodded in agreement.

'If it didn't detonate fully, might it destroy the aircraft's pressurization, but not the cabin itself?' Grace asked.

Darren Fry, looking deeply studious, as if he was an expert on these matters said, 'Possibly, if it was a small explosive – like a hand grenade, perhaps. But . . .' He shook his head. 'Very unlikely.'

'What about some kind of sabotage?' Grace asked. 'Or someone tampering with the controls – a hijacker?'

'We could request assistance from the military,' Moss said. 'They have Quick Reaction Alert jets – Typhoons – based at RAF Coningsby in Lincolnshire that can fly supersonic over land in emergencies. One could be alongside the Pilatus in under fifteen minutes and tell us what's going on in the cockpit.'

Grace nodded. 'What CCTV do you have around the airport?' he asked.

'We don't have much,' Moss said. 'There is some in the main hangar, but that's about it.'

'The main hangar? Is that where the Pilatus would be parked?'

'It is.'

'The hangar's kept locked overnight?'

He nodded. 'The Ops team open it in the morning and tow out any aircraft with an early flight plan filed.'

'How do we view the footage from the time the hangar was opened this morning until the Pilatus was towed out?' Grace asked.

'There's a monitor in the management office,' Moss replied. 'I'll call down and see who's in there who could do the playback for you.' He reached for the radio on the work surface in front of him.

95

Taylor rammed the control column forward, holding the plane in a near vertical descent, with every ounce of strength in his body. The sudden change of direction had the desired effect of catching Rorke out, and hurtling him head first, hard, into the windscreen in front of the co-pilot's seat, dazing him, the force of the descent then keeping him there.

The altimeter was spinning: 25,000, 24,000, 23,000, 22,000.

And Taylor's brain was spinning. Thinking. Trying to figure out how he could not only outwit but disable Rorke. The one advantage he had was that Rorke was not buckled in. He just had to keep flying manoeuvres that threw him around the plane, and hope to somehow disable him or knock him out.

In the First World War dogfights, something that had always interested Taylor, German pilots learned a tactical turn, named after its pioneer, fighter ace Max Immelmann. You climbed vertically, almost hanging the plane from its nose, then went over backwards, rolling simultaneously to the right or left.

He was well aware that if you tried such a manoeuvre in a commercial airliner there was a serious risk that the stresses would be too great and the plane could break up. But in this seemingly bulletproof Pilatus, he was confident of it working. He pulled the control column back hard, screaming out of the near vertical descent into a steep climb. And saw Rorke literally fly past him into the rear of the aircraft.

He turned and saw Rorke had collided with the seats and there was blood on his face. He looked dazed.

Quickly getting his bearings, checking the satellite navigation, he began levelling out. As he did so, he turned the radio frequency selector, pressed the transmit button on the mic and said, 'This is Golf Alpha Victor Uniform Zulu. Mayday! Mayday! Mayday!'

96

In the Shoreham Air Traffic Control tower, Grace, Branson and the three controllers listened for London's response to the Mayday call.

'Golf Alpha Victor Uniform Zulu, advise the nature of your emergency?'

There was a long silence.

London tried again. 'Can you tell us the nature of your emergency?'

There was another long silence.

All of them looked at the tiny upright arrow on the screen, with the numbers beside it. Golf Uniform Zulu was climbing steeply again and heading out away from the shore, over the sea.

'I'll suggest to London it's time to alert the military,' Moss said. 'We need someone to take a look at what's going on up there.'

Then the pilot suddenly blurted out, crackly, muzzed by interference, 'Oh shit – no!'

97

Tuesday 18 October 2022

Uncle Johnny struck Taylor squarely, with maximum force, on the side of his forehead, with a loud crack. Taylor, strapped in his seat, slumped over, instantly unconscious.

Or maybe dead, Rorke speculated. Hoped.

The plane seemed to be holding level flight. They were at just over 27,000 feet. He glanced out of a window and down at the clouds a long way below. Quickly unclipping Taylor's seat harness, he removed his headset and, struggling, pulled his old friend's limp body off the seat and onto the floor immediately behind the cockpit. Then he sat in the pilot's seat, blinking his eyes against the bright sunlight, briefly studied the controls, checked the fuel, clipped himself in and pulled on the headset. And instantly heard a calm, but anxious-sounding voice.

'Golf Uniform Zulu, are you reading me? Golf Alpha Victor Uniform Zulu – London radio check.'

Reading you loud and clear, now fuck off, he thought and smiled. Rorke responded, perfectly calmly, disguising his voice as best he could to sound like James Taylor's clear diction. 'Reading you strength five, how you me? We had an emergency, lost our instruments, and the autopilot went rogue, but I've now managed to disengage it and we are good to continue with our original flight planned route.'

'Golf Alpha Victor Uniform Zulu, thank you for this update. Are you confident you do not need an emergency landing?'

'Affirm I do not require an emergency landing. Will proceed to destination as per flight plan.'

'Descend immediately to your assigned flight level one eight zero and report when level.'

'Wilco. Golf Uniform Zulu descending to flight level one eight zero on heading 240 degrees.' Rorke immediately began the descent, maintaining his bearing.

There was a brief sigh of relief among the gathered occupants in Shoreham tower, overhearing what appeared to be a return to normal operation.

After further calm exchanges, the Pilatus pilot said, 'Thank you for your assistance, London.'

Rorke smiled. He had bought himself a few minutes without interference.

His first task was to familiarize himself with the controls. All cockpits had the same basics and similar layouts but from the YouTube videos of the Pilatus PC-12 he'd studied, it seemed this particular aircraft's autopilot was a little trickier to figure out at first. He was going to need the autopilot in a short while, so he focused on that first. He got the hang of it quickly and turned his attention back to flying the aircraft. He checked the altitude, noticing the plane was starting to climb very slightly up from 18,000 feet, and adjusted the trim. Then he checked his position. He was well south of Bembridge airport on the Isle of Wight, over open sea – a long stretch of water from the coast of Southampton to the northern tip of Alderney and the Cherbourg peninsula. Close to ninety miles of open sea. James Taylor's body wouldn't be washing up on a beach anytime soon. If ever.

Almost gleefully he pressed the mic. 'Golf Alpha Victor Uniform Zulu, calling London one three three one eight zero for a radio check.'

98

'Oh Jesus!' Grace said.

Branson nodded, grimly.

'Could you go back and play again, please,' Grace asked the elegant, fair-haired woman seated in front of the screen in the airport management office, ten minutes later.

Hannah Thatcher stopped the clip and sped it back to the start of the segment. Moments later, the three of them again watched the footage, taken on a wide-angle lens, of the figure in a hard hat and hi-viz tabard. Grace and Branson could see immediately that it was Rorke. Carrying a large holdall in his left hand and a much smaller black bag in his right, he entered the hangar and looked furtively around. After a few seconds, either not spotting the CCTV camera or ignoring it, he hurried towards the Pilatus and around the port wing towards the back of the aircraft.

After looking around again, he tested the rear door, as if unsure whether it would be locked or not, lifted it up, looked around yet again, put the two bags in, clambered in, and immediately shut the door.

'The planes aren't locked, Hannah?' Branson asked.

'No, the hangar is locked at night so there's no need.'

Turning to Grace, Branson said, 'What's Rorke up to? Is the pilot knowingly smuggling him out of the country, or is he a stowaway? Has he got drugs in those bags? Or has he planted something and then left the plane before take-off?'

408

Grace asked Hannah Thatcher to play the footage again and watched it pensively. Then they jumped to the point where the Pilatus was towed out of the hangar. Rorke had not reappeared. Maybe he climbed out later, but Grace didn't think so. He thought about the strange activity of the aircraft they'd watched on the radar screen. Followed by the Mayday call. Then the anguished voice of the pilot saying, loudly, *Oh shit – no!*

Which didn't chime to Grace with the calm voice from the cockpit that followed.

He replied to his colleague. 'What we know about Rorke is that he is a qualified fixed wing and helicopter pilot. What we saw on the radar could be explained by a malfunction on the plane's autopilot. But the voice of the pilot shouting, *Oh shit – no!* is not in my opinion the same voice as the person who assured Air Traffic Control that all was now fine.'

Branson frowned. 'Meaning?'

'The pilot, James Taylor, who filed the flight plan, is no longer flying the aircraft. Rufus Rorke is.'

'Shit.'

Grace nodded. 'We do need the military up there to tell us what the hell's going on.' He picked up his phone and called Alan Moss in the tower.

Then they headed back up there. As they entered, a few minutes later, Moss said, 'The RAF have scrambled a Typhoon from Coningsby. The ETA to be alongside the Pilatus is ten minutes.'

99

A considerable distance off the coast, Rufus Rorke transferred from London Air Traffic Control to Jersey, enabling him to continue the flight into Channel Islands airspace.

Giving it a couple of minutes after the exchanges with Jersey, Rorke radioed, 'Jersey Control, this is Golf Alpha Victor Uniform Zulu.'

'Golf Alpha Victor Uniform Zulu, Jersey Control,' the controller said.

'We have an issue with pressurization. I need clearance to make an immediate descent.'

After a few moments, the Jersey controller responded. 'You are cleared to descend to maintain flight level one one zero. Maintain your current heading and advise the nature of your problem.'

'Roger,' Rorke responded, evading the request about what sort of problem.

Glancing over his shoulder to check on Taylor, who remained motionless, he began a rapid descent. In a few minutes they would be midway between the south coast of England and the island of Alderney. The perfect dumping spot for Taylor's body. He needed to descend to a height where pressurization in the cabin was not needed, so that he could open one of the doors without needing a portable oxygen mask – and without the risk of being sucked out.

He watched the large screen in front of him, the dials and

digital readouts giving him all the vital information he required as they steadily lost height. They were still in bright sunshine with the clouds a long way beneath them. And the English Channel was a long way beneath the clouds. The chances of Taylor hitting a ferry or a fishing boat were millions to one against. He'd hit the water, and if he wasn't already dead, the impact would finish him off. Hitting water from terminal velocity of 120mph would be no different to hitting concrete.

He levelled out at flight level one one zero and dutifully radioed Jersey Control to tell them.

They confirmed and gave him instructions to the Jersey landing runway.

Ending the radio comms, Rorke set the autopilot to maintain the Pilatus in level flight at 250 knots and checked his watch. *Time to say goodbye, Jamesy!*

As soon as he had dumped Taylor out of the aircraft, he would radio Jersey and inform them he was diverting to Brest on the French coast for *operational reasons*, where he could get engineering support. They would accept that without questioning him. Brest was one of the nearest major airports and would likely have engineering facilities for the Pilatus that Jersey did not.

Then, as soon as he had left Channel Islands airspace and entered French, he would turn his transponder and nav lights off and descend to 200 feet, below the level at which radar would pick him up, and be all but invisible. His destination was the island of Ouessant, off the coast of Brittany.

By the time he got there, which would be approaching 12 o'clock French time, he knew from past experience that the local Air Traffic Control would be off-duty and away from the tower for lunch. He would put the aircraft down and half an hour later be on the powerboat he had arranged to take him to Brest. And from there, the private jet to Malaga, where he would land well in time for cocktails tonight.

And perhaps a nice little goodbye night with Shannon.

It was great, he thought with a big smile, when a plan came together.

100

Taylor felt like his head had been split open. Pain seared through his skull. It took him some moments of confusion to work out where he was. And what had happened. And as his thoughts began to clarify and his memory came back, he realized the very real danger he was in.

He heard Rorke's request to Air Traffic Control to descend because of depressurization, and he had a pretty good idea why he wanted to do that. His former friend was bigger and stronger than him; his best – maybe only – hope would be to surprise him. And he would have just one chance to do that. From his position, on his back on the cabin floor, he could see the rear of Rorke's head, and headset.

His brain was muzzy, all shaken up, like it had been in a blender, but not so shaken up that he couldn't think increasingly clearly. If he could get to his feet without Rorke hearing, grab the fire extinguisher behind the right-hand pilot's seat, he'd whack him unconscious. He held his breath. This was his chance, now, while Rorke was still occupied with levelling out after the descent.

Then he heard a metallic click – snap.

Shit.

It was a sound he knew so well, from his years of flying this aircraft. It was the quality sound of a Pilatus seat buckle opening – exquisitely engineered like everything on this aircraft. It signified,

413

he figured, that Rorke had put the autopilot on and was now coming to deal with him.

He needed to play possum and bide his time. Holding his breath and closing his eyes, but not so tightly that he had no vision at all, he furtively watched Rufus Rorke glance down, briefly, at him. He saw a deep gash on his forehead and a trail of blood down his right cheek. Rorke stepped over him, wincing, walking with some difficulty. Good, at least throwing him around the plane had hurt him.

He heard the sound of a handle being moved, followed by a grunt of pain. Then a loud clunk followed by a hydraulic whine. Then a roaring sound and a sudden rush of freezing cold air that tore at his hair and his clothes.

The bastard had opened and lowered the front door, and was going to push him out. To fall to his death.

He felt a sudden moment of utter terror. Thought about Debbie. About how after all these past hellish years his life was finally coming good again with this gorgeous, sweet person.

You are not going to destroy this, Rufus. You are not.

But he had to bide his time. Surprise Rorke. One chance to do that. Just one chance. *Don't squander it.*

Rorke knelt, grabbed him under the arms and, grunting with pain again, hefted him a few feet back, towards the open, howling vortex. Then he did the same again. Taylor could feel the bottom lip of the doorway against the back of his neck. With the next shove his head would be out of the plane and battered by the brutal airstream. He had to make his move before that happened. He had to make his move *now*.

He waited briefly. Watching his enemy through the narrowest slit between his eyelids that he dared. Rorke's dyed hair was being batted around wildly by the icy wind.

Taylor had just one advantage over him at this moment, his knowledge of the cabin. In particular of the seats. There was an angled gap beneath them. He found the one under the nearest seat with his right foot, and quietly, trying not to move another part of his body, secured a toehold.

Still keeping up the pretence of being unconscious, he felt Rorke's hands grip his armpits again. Heard his voice, leering.

'Goodbye, Jamesy!'

Then, just as Rorke began to lift him, he struck out with a balled fist, landing a hard punch on the bridge of his nose.

Totally taken by surprise, Rorke howled in pain, jerked back and let go of him. As he did so, Taylor grabbed both of Rorke's wrists and, using the leverage of his foot hooked underneath the seat, pulled him forward with every ounce of strength in his body.

Like a circus acrobat, with strength he did not know he possessed, he raised Rorke up above him, and hurled him out into that swirling, mad vortex behind him.

And for an instant, his muzzy brain was surprised how weightless Rorke suddenly was.

Because he was no longer holding him, he realized.

He heard a terrified scream. It lasted no more than a fraction of a second.

Then there was just the banshee howl of the wind, the hiss of the slipstream and a fleeting pungent smell of exhaust fumes.

101

Taylor lay still for some moments, shaking in shock.

Rorke was gone.

Out of the cabin door. At eleven thousand feet.

He had just killed him.

He had just killed a man who had once, a long time ago, been a good friend. Like a best friend.

Somewhere, through the searing pain and the howling of the wind, a part of his brain was trying to make sense of this. Another part of his brain was telling him he was lying inches from the open door of a plane that was cruising at 11,000 feet, with no one in the cockpit.

First thing was to get safely away from the doorway. Still shaking badly, he wriggled forward into the centre of the cabin, behind the two rear-facing seats, safely away from the open door, then hauled himself onto his feet, staggered to the pilot's seat, sat down and checked the autopilot.

It all looked fine. They were flying at 11,000 feet across open sea on course for one of the main waypoints inbound to the Channel Islands. Their ETA was thirty-two minutes.

Rorke had set the autopilot properly.

Oh Jesus. He had just killed Rorke. Killed a human being. Killed his old friend. Oh shit, oh God. Oh my God.

He was so overwrought he was struggling again to think clearly. The door was open. In mid-air. It was hydraulically operated.

But he doubted it would close at an airspeed of 250 knots. He reduced the throttle, slowing the plane to 100 knots, just above the 67 knots stalling speed, then left his seat and carefully, unsteadily, holding on to anything that he could, struggled back around to the vortex of air and hit the button to close the door.

He heard the whirr. The door, with its built-in steps, rose and in less than a minute had closed with a reassuring thud.

Relief flooding through him, he made his way, still very unsteadily, the pain in his head feeling even worse now, back to the pilot's seat, sat and clicked himself into his harness. Then he pulled on the headset, trying to think clearly, all his pilot training and experience kicking in. He was about to tune the radio to 121.5 MHz to put out an emergency call to alert shipping in the area to be on the lookout for a body, when he was startled by a shadow to his right. At first, almost hallucinating, he thought it was an airborne great white shark. It morphed into a grey, sharply pointed nose cone. A glass bubble of a cockpit. A sideways fin.

A brief crackle through the headset, then a male voice. Crisp, calm, deadly serious. The voice of someone you didn't question, didn't mess with. 'Golf Alpha Victor Uniform Zulu?'

Taylor responded.

'I am the RAF Typhoon jet your right-hand side. Maintain your current height and heading.'

Now he could see the grey hull of the jet right alongside. Only yards away. The pilot was looking straight at him.

'Golf Alpha Victor Uniform Zulu, please identify the pilot who is currently flying your Pilatus then turn to face me.'

It felt, to his relief, like the cavalry had come.

'Golf Alpha Victor Uniform Zulu copy that. My name is James Taylor. I'm a private pilot working for Mr Thomas Towne who is based in Jersey. This is his aircraft.'

As he turned towards the Typhoon, Taylor saw a camera point at him.

The pilot's voice came through his headset again. 'Golf Uniform Zulu, we are informed there are two people on board your aircraft. Please confirm?'

Taylor pressed the mic. 'I can confirm there were two people on board this aircraft.'

The pilot's voice came back. 'Golf Uniform Zulu, did you say there *were* two of you on board your aircraft?'

'Copy that.'

'Golf Uniform Zulu, please clarify what you mean *were*?'

'Golf Uniform Zulu. There were two of us on board on take-off. But not any more. One of us is dead.'

102

The naked body was bloated and most of the skin was a hideous, mottled greenish black. Some of the extremities, including the tip of his nose, part of his lips and one eye had been nibbled away by fish and crustaceans. His head and three remaining limbs were at odd angles and the parts of his face that were still intact looked distorted.

Grace and Branson, gowned up and masked, stood well back from the post-mortem table, well back from the horrific smell. The attending coroner's officer was doing the same, although the CSI photographer, James Gartrell, seemed oblivious to it.

When a human body decomposes, methane, hydrogen sulphide and carbon dioxide build up within the body cavity. They make it increasingly buoyant so that eventually, anywhere from two to seven days after sinking to the seabed, the body will float to the surface and remain there for up to a week.

There was something ironic about Rufus Rorke's floating corpse being found by a fishing boat, Grace thought. Almost déjà vu. It had been caught yesterday in a trawl net, ten miles off the coast. A strong sou'westerly wind over the past few days had probably speeded up its passage.

'I don't think he's faking it this time,' Branson murmured.

'If he is, he deserves an Oscar,' Grace retorted, drily.

They'd watched Rorke's skull cap being sliced open at the base of his head, then peeled forward exposing his skull, which was a mosaic of cracks and was hanging over his face. His left leg was missing. There was a white plastic ID band around his left wrist and a white tag, labelled Brighton & Hove City Mortuary Service, tied to his right big toe with a piece of string. Under *Name or Description* was written *Rufus Rorke*. Under *Where Removed From* was written *English Channel*.

Grace looked at Rorke's bloated, partially eviscerated body. Luke Stanstead had helpfully provided him with the calculation that falling from an aircraft at 11,000 feet, it would have taken Rorke approximately sixty-six seconds to hit the water. *What was going through your mind in those sixty-six seconds, Rufus Rorke? Was it sixty-six seconds of utter stark terror? Or did you figure out you'd score 10 for a perfect dive and then swim to the shore and fool everyone yet again that you were dead?*

He doubted Rorke had spent it in prayer.

Branson moved closer to Grace. 'Sure this isn't another of Rorke's elaborate disguises?'

'I wouldn't put it past him.' Behind his mask, Grace was grinning.

Nadiuska, at the cutting table, was slicing through his liver, assisted by Cleo's deputy, Darren Wallace, who was standing by with a plastic water jug, sluicing away the excess blood at regular intervals. Without looking up she said, 'The liver has been ruptured – this is consistent with the blunt force trauma of striking the sea at terminal velocity. The density of water doesn't allow it to be moved out of the way quickly – so at this speed it's as hard as a tarmac road. You can see the multiple fractures to his skull, and I'm pretty sure his spine is broken too, along with every bone in his body – the ones that are still attached.'

'So it's fair to say he's not going to be doing a runner any time soon,' Branson remarked.

'Well, if he does,' Darren quipped, 'we'll call him Houdini.'

103

The two detectives entered the interview room at Brighton police station and sat down at the table, opposite the casually, but conservatively, dressed thirty-nine-year-old man. 'I'm Detective Superintendent Grace of the Surrey and Sussex Major Crime Team and this is my colleague, Detective Inspector Branson.'

'Nice to meet you, gentlemen,' Taylor replied with an authoritative, slightly combative tone, as if to show he was on equal terms with the police officers and wasn't about to be monkeyed around. Suddenly both of the officers appeared fuzzy, before coming back into focus. All kinds of shit had been going on inside his brain these past days. It was the result of his severe concussion, the consultant neurologist at Southampton Hospital had told him. He could expect his brain to play weird tricks on him for some while to come, until it settled back down. For that reason he was temporarily signed off from flying, and he'd also been advised not to drive until he felt fully recovered. Debbie had dropped him here and would drive him back home afterwards. Via somewhere nice for lunch.

Peering for some seconds at the swollen and badly bruised right-hand side of Taylor's forehead and face, Branson said, 'Looks like you took quite a whack. I understand you've been under observation in Southampton Hospital for the past week? I hope you're feeling better now, and recovering?'

Taylor nodded, grimly. 'Apart from a fractured skull, fractured orbital bone and a fractured cheek bone, I'm fine. Seems like Rufus Rorke had an interesting line in cabin baggage.'

Both detectives nodded. 'Yes,' Branson said. 'A holdall with three different passports and driving licences, four mobile phones and £250k in cash, as well as a knuckle duster.'

'Doesn't everyone?' Taylor said with a wry smile.

Smiling back, Grace said, 'I know you have already been interviewed by two of my colleagues, we just have a few more questions we'd like to ask you.'

'Am I under suspicion?' Taylor asked warily. 'Because if so I would like my solicitor present again – I'm using Paul Donnelley.'

The two detectives looked at each other at the mention of the solicitor's name. Donnelley was a particularly sharp and astute opponent – neither of them ever relished coming up against him. 'If you would be more comfortable,' Grace said. 'This is not a formal interview, and I can assure you that you are not under suspicion – we are only interested in understanding what happened on the morning of Tuesday, October the eighteenth and establishing the facts. OK?'

'OK,' Taylor consented, and then continued. 'If I'm not under suspicion, gentlemen, can you explain why, after my RAF escort saw me all the way to Jersey, the Pilatus I was flying has been impounded by the police as a crime scene, preventing it from having urgent repair work? I have one very pissed-off boss at this moment.'

'I appreciate that,' Grace said. 'But someone who was on your plane is dead, after exiting in mid-flight – as a result of actions you took in self-defence.' He raised a pacifying hand. 'I'll come on to that, but it's a necessary procedure for Jersey States Police, working in cooperation with us, to carry out a full forensic examination of the aircraft.'

'Forgive me if I've got this wrong, Mr Taylor,' Branson said. 'But your boss, Mr Towne, owns another aeroplane he could use?'

'He does, a Citation jet, but it's a long-range aircraft and it's not really economic to use it for the short-haul work we do most of the time.'

Branson gave him a bemused look. 'No disrespect, but isn't that rather a First World problem?'

Taylor granted him a small nod and a slightly reluctant smile.

'OK,' Grace said. 'Let's make something very clear, James – may we call you James?'

'It's my name,' he replied. 'Why not?' But his humour was lost on the detectives.

'The Pilatus you were flying was, as I'm sure you know, fitted with a factory optional extra of a voice and data recorder – which has a similar function to the Black Box recorders on all commercial aeroplanes,' Grace said. 'We've listened to the cockpit voice recording and had all the data analysed. Additionally, we have seen CCTV footage from Brighton City airport that shows Rufus Rorke surreptitiously entering your aircraft before it was towed from the hangar. I'd like to emphasize again that you are not a suspect in Mr Rorke's death. In the recordings we've heard, it is pretty clear you were the victim of Rorke's aggression.'

Taylor nodded. 'How much do you gentlemen know about him?'

Grace replied. 'Mr Rorke had been a person of interest to us for a very long time. Long before he "disappeared", as it were, off a yacht off the coast of Barbados.'

'He'd been of particular interest to me ever since I was certain I saw him at a funeral last month – September the twenty-third,' Taylor said.

'Why was that of *particular* interest to you?' Branson asked.

Taylor paused for a beat before replying. Then with a wry smile said, 'Well, because I'd delivered the eulogy at Rufus Rorke's funeral over two years ago. I think you guys would have been pretty interested in finding out if he was actually still alive, if that had been you, right?'

'There was no body at his funeral, I recall,' Grace quizzed.

'No, it was a slightly odd service.' Taylor frowned. 'You were there?'

'One of my team was.'

'Why?'

'Because we had been close to arresting Rufus Rorke on a series of very serious charges, and we think he was aware of that.'

'Is that why he disappeared?'

'It's one of our primary lines of enquiry.'

'So, James, after you were *certain* you saw Rorke at a funeral a month ago – did that have anything to do with your trip to Barbados?' Branson asked.

Taylor looked at him sharply, thrown by the question. And thrown by the detective's hard stare. He thought carefully before responding. 'I went there on holiday, to have a rest after running the Chicago Marathon. But yes, I was curious. I thought while I was there I'd try to talk to the fisherman who had apparently found Rufus's jacket – or part of it.'

'John Baker?' Branson said.

Taylor studied his face to see if there was anything in his expression that hinted of a trap. But all he saw was warmth and friendliness. An ally, perhaps. 'Yes, John Baker. Quite a character.'

The detective tilted his head to one side. 'Well, that's one way to describe him.'

'Meaning?' Taylor quizzed.

'When did you last speak to him?'

Taylor hesitated before replying. 'About a fortnight ago, when I was in Barbados. Why?'

'Did you believe what Baker told you?' Branson asked.

Taylor reflected for a moment. 'There was something he said that didn't ring true, so no, I didn't. And bear in mind, I was convinced Rufus was still alive, so I figured he had to be lying.'

'Was there a reason you didn't come to the police and report your suspicions?' Grace asked.

Taylor shrugged. 'I thought you'd probably think I was crazy. After I saw him in the church, at the funeral, I went to the vicar and asked to view all the CCTV footage of the mourners arriving and leaving the service. Rufus didn't show up on it. I then went to see his widow, Fiona. She seemed pretty convinced – and convincing – that he was dead.'

As he said this, Taylor noticed a strange glance between the two detectives. 'Have I missed something?' he asked.

Ignoring the question, Grace asked, 'Can you talk us through your flight from Brighton City airport on the morning of Tuesday, October the eighteenth, in as much detail as you can recall?'

Taylor looked at him for a moment, pensively. 'I'm not under caution, so I'm correct that nothing I say can be used against me in court?'

Grace nodded. 'That's correct, James. All we want to do is to confirm the facts leading up to Rufus Rorke's fall from your aircraft to his death.'

'I'll do a trade-off with you,' Taylor said. 'I'll talk you through everything I can remember from the time I arrived at Brighton City airport, if you can explain to me how the hell – if Rufus Rorke really did go off the back of a yacht, late at night, several miles off the coast of Barbados – he survived? Do we have a deal?'

Grace and Branson looked at each other. After a few moments they nodded. Grace turned to Taylor. 'I think we can accommodate that.'

104

Thursday 27 October 2022

'You are actually home in time to bath Molly and to read Noah a story – I can't believe it after the last few weeks!' Cleo said, beaming. Although Roy tried to ensure they shared care of the children equally, there were times – as just recently – when a case inevitably took over his life. But he always did his best to make up for it afterwards. Such as he was doing now.

'*And* I'm going to cook dinner!' he replied, striding over to the fridge followed by a very interested Humphrey, who then sat without being told and looked up expectantly.

Grace removed a cocktail sausage from the pack in there, held it towards Humphrey's mouth and said, 'Gentle, boy!'

Humphrey obediently did take the treat gently and trotted happily over to his basket with it. Smiling at the dog he loved so much, Roy picked up the small pile of post on the kitchen table and quickly looked through it.

'Still nothing from the new DNA test to confirm once and for all Pewe is not the father,' he said, placing it all back on the table.

'That result will come soon, we just have to be patient, Roy.'

'I know, but I just want to be sure that sneaky slimeball won't get a penny of Bruno's inheritance from Sandy.'

'Don't give him any more of your headspace, he's just not worth it.'

'Yep, I agree.'

He walked over to the cupboard under the stairs, rummaged

around for a few moments, then returned with a dusty bottle of red wine, holding it high. 'Remember that bottle your cousin gave us for a wedding present? He said to open it on a special occasion.'

Cleo frowned. Then smiled. 'I sort of remember.'

'Well, this is a special occasion.'

'What is?' She looked confused.

'I'm not sure how much credit I can really take for it, but we've finally nailed that bastard Rufus Rorke, bang to rights. Well – I guess a bit more than that . . .'

'The one in the mortuary yesterday? You attended his post-mortem.'

'I did.'

'He was the man who disappeared off a yacht somewhere off the coast of Barbados?'

'The very same. Didn't do such a good job of disappearing out of a plane off the south coast of England.'

'So how did he survive going off the boat in Barbados? It was late at night and the sea wasn't calm, you said.'

Grace nodded. 'It seems he had given a bung – a very big one – to a fisherman in Barbados, name of John Baker. Baker had to take a torn fragment of a white tuxedo, which had been immersed in seawater, and had some of Rorke's blood on it – which he'd given to him in a vial – to the local police. His brief was to tell them he'd found it wrapped around one of his net ropes, and that having seen a photograph of Rorke in that jacket, taken earlier the night he'd gone overboard, he just wondered if it could be from the same garment. The police swallowed it, hook, line and sinker.'

'Very appropriate choice of words, darling,' she teased with a grin.

He grinned back. 'So, when the Bajan police arrested Baker, not long after Glenn's visit to see him, he fessed up pretty quickly.

It had all been part of an elaborate deception – which Rorke's wife, Fiona, was a part of. She's been arrested and is currently out on police bail. Rorke had worn a transponder, which a colleague of this fisherman, John Baker, had been tracking via a drone with an infrared camera from another boat close by, with its lights and transponder off. Rorke was picked up and safely aboard the colleague's boat within ten minutes of jumping from his chartered yacht.'

'That's insane!' Cleo said. 'There's so much that could have gone wrong.'

Grace nodded. 'Sooner or later every smart criminal gets to the point where he or she thinks they're invincible. The longer they get away with their crimes, the bolder they become. Eventually they become reckless, and that's when they start to make mistakes. Luckily for us. And we've found pure gold – Rorke's laptop, concealed in a wine cellar at Fiona's home, well, the home they used to share; she told us where to find it.' He began to remove the foil from around the top of the bottle.

'I saw a documentary some years ago, about wars – battles. The thesis was that victors rarely win wars through their clever strategies, it's the other side that loses, through its mistakes.'

He picked up the corkscrew and began working it in. 'I can go along with that.'

'We were taught at school that we won the Battle of Agincourt because the English longbow was superior to the French crossbow. But the narrator in the documentary said that's not the reason we won. The French had chosen the battleground and it was a muddy field. There was torrential rain and their knights on horseback, and the infantry, got bogged down and were picked off easily by the English archers.'

'Yep,' Grace said. 'That chimes with so many cases. It's often not what we do, not our brilliance in solving a crime, it's the offenders making a basic mistake. Like Rufus Rorke coming back to Brighton and thinking he could get away with it without being recognized. Pure hubris.'

The cork slid out with a sharp *pop!*

'That's one of the nicest sounds in the world!' Cleo said.

'There's one other sound I like almost as much,' he replied, putting the bottle down.

'Which is?'

'The sound of a jury foreman's voice saying "guilty".'

'Well, your friend Rufus Rorke's death has deprived you of that satisfaction.'

'He must be feeling very smug,' Grace said, and sniffed the top of the bottle.

'Rorke?'

'He's cheated justice twice. The first time by faking his death. And now by actually dying.'

Cleo nodded vigorously. 'That explains it!'

Grace, reaching up to take two wine glasses from the Welsh dresser, frowned. 'Explains what?'

'When I was preparing him in the mortuary, he had this big rictus grin on his face!'

'Thanks a million, my darling. That's a great feeling, to be outwitted by a corpse.'

She walked over and put an arm around him. 'If it's any consolation, my love, he wasn't smiling quite so much at the end of his post-mortem.'

Grace shook his head, and he was grinning himself now as he poured some wine into each glass. 'Are we normal, do you think? Do other couples have conversations like this about corpses, around the kitchen table?'

She feigned a look of shock. 'Don't they?' She picked up her glass and held it out to his, looking him straight in the eye. 'If I'd thought for one moment you were *normal*, my darling, I'd never have married you.'

They clinked glasses. Grace looked her straight back in the eye. 'Touché!'

'Remember a few months back we were looking into getting a rescue dog through the RSPCA? As a companion for Humphrey – and maybe for the kids too?'

He nodded. 'The one we liked the look of – that was supposedly very good with kids – was rehomed before we got to see it.'

'They've just sent pics of another through.' She turned her phone towards him, so he could see. Then looked at him questioningly as he flicked through the photos. 'What do you think?'

'He's bloody adorable!'

'She's actually a *she*.'

'She's adorable too.'

Cleo grinned and gave him a kiss. 'So are you – sometimes.'

105

This time there was a coffin, and there was a body inside it. It looked cheap, cardboard with fake brass handles, and there were no flowers on top of it. As if this was Fiona Rorke's Parthian shot at the odious husband she had come to despise, and only been liberated from through his death. Although not as liberated as she thought, Taylor had learned from a slip of the tongue from detective Glenn Branson.

The coffin was carried by six pall bearers – almost as many employees of the funeral directors as there were mourners – into the South Chapel of Brighton's neo-Gothic Woodvale Crematorium.

The interior, with its wooden chairs and benches, red seat cushions and carpet, and vaulted ceiling, felt like being in a small church, which, Taylor, supposed, was the intention. He stood at the back accompanied by Debbie Martin, there to support him – and out of curiosity – as the service began. It was officiated by a celebrant, as Rorke's last 'funeral' had been – Fiona's one concession to his atheism.

The chapel could hold eighty people. It was less than a quarter full: Fiona, looking striking in widow's weeds, and their twin boys; a handful of other people, middle-aged and older, a sister, and some relatives whom Taylor vaguely recollected meeting at Rorke's previous funeral.

The celebrant clearly hadn't read the press release – nor the

431

press – or perhaps was choosing to ignore all of that, as she waxed almost lyrical about what a fine father and husband Rufus Rorke had been. And then, one small nod to his dubious past, by acknowledging that all humans made errors of judgement.

Murdering at least six people, as the two detectives had told him, off the record, constituted a bit more than *errors of judgement*, Taylor opined, not sure he could take much more of this sanctimonious crap about a man who had come within moments of murdering him too. But, as he turned to slip out of the service, gripping Debbie's hand, he noticed that both detectives, suited and booted, were standing just inside the doorway directly behind him.

He went over to them. Detective Superintendent Roy Grace was attired in a respectfully sombre suit. Detective Inspector Glenn Branson looked like he was dressed to brighten someone's day, with a tie that could have been seen from Mars. They both nodded at him in acknowledgement, and at his companion.

'You guys here to make sure he hasn't faked it again?' he asked quietly.

'Doesn't seem like he's being mourned by too many people,' Branson replied.

'Could that be because he's murdered – or tried to murder – all the people who might have grieved for him?' Taylor posited. 'When I gave the eulogy at his last funeral, the church was full.' He looked at the two detectives.

'You decided against giving Rufus Rorke's eulogy – again?' Grace asked.

Taylor smiled. 'He actually complimented me on it.'

'We heard, on the voice recording in the plane,' Branson said. 'He seemed genuinely pleased.'

'He did Rufus proud,' Debbie Martin interjected, keeping her voice low. 'Much more than he deserved.'

Grace looked at him. 'Sounds like you were a loyal friend to him. Too bad he had strange ideas about repaying loyalty. Listening to this celebrant, you'd think he was a saint.'

Taylor replied, still keeping his voice low, 'It makes you realize, doesn't it, how well do we really know anyone? Who would have thought that Rorke's girlfriend would end up helping to save my life? What's happened to her?'

'She was arrested and fully cooperated with the investigation. She is currently on bail while decisions are made as to what charges she may face, but her assistance will certainly help her outcome. And it certainly helped you!'

The celebrant finished her eulogy. A hymn struck up, chosen by Fiona. The meagre congregation sang, or mimed as best they could, to the words.

So I'll cherish the old rugged cross . . .
'Til my trophies at last I lay down.
I will cling to the old rugged cross.
And exchange it some day for a crown.

James Taylor, Debbie Martin and the two detectives did not join in.

When the organ stopped, the only sound was that that of the green curtain drawing slowly, with a slithering sound, until the coffin was no longer visible behind it.

Glenn Branson looked mischievously at Grace then at Taylor. 'I guess that's what they mean by *curtains.*'

Roy Grace gave him a sideways look, grinning. 'Let's hope he's not planning on reappearing for a second curtain call.'

As they walked out of the crematorium together, Grace said, 'How about we call the girls and take them and the kids out somewhere tonight for a celebratory meal. On me. What do you think?'

'Nice idea, except—'

'Except what?'

'After seeing Rorke's post-mortem – you know – all the bits that had been eaten – let's not go to a seafood restaurant.'

'Wuss!' Grace said.

GLOSSARY

ANPR – Automatic Number Plate Recognition. Roadside or mobile cameras that automatically capture the registration number of all cars that pass. It can be used to historically track which cars went past a certain camera, and can also create a signal for cars which are stolen, have no insurance or have an alert attached to them.

CID – Criminal Investigation Department. Usually refers to the divisional detectives rather than the specialist squads.

CPS – Crown Prosecution Service.

CSI – Crime Scene Investigators. Formerly SOCO (Scenes of Crime Officers). They are the people who attend crime scenes to search for fingerprints, DNA samples etc.

DIGITAL FORENSICS – The unit which examines and investigates computers and other digital devices.

FLO – Family Liaison Officer.

MO – Modus Operandi (method of operation). The manner by which the offender has committed the offence. Often this can reveal unique features which allow crimes to be linked or suspects to be identified.

SIO – Senior Investigating Officer. Usually a Detective Chief Inspector who is in overall charge of the investigation of a major crime such as murder, kidnap or rape.

CHART OF POLICE RANKS

Police ranks are consistent across all disciplines and the addition of prefixes such as 'detective' (e.g. detective constable) does not affect seniority relative to others of the same rank (e.g. police constable).

| Police Constable | Police Sergeant | Inspector | Chief Inspector |

| Superintendent | Chief Superintendent | Assistant Chief Constable | Deputy Chief Constable | Chief Constable |

ACKNOWLEDGEMENTS

'Where do you get your ideas from?' is the one question I get asked more than any other. And, more often than not, the truth is that many of the best ones just seem to find me. Which is how this novel came about.

It was an old friend who approached me, a couple of years back, saying, 'I have a story you are going to want to write.' I told him politely that someone actually says this to me about once a fortnight – usually it is a nice story, but not one that would make a compelling novel. He just shook his head and said firmly, 'You are going to want to write this.' And he was right.

The moment he told me the story, I was hooked. I knew then and there that it had the makings of a compelling Roy Grace novel, with all the ingredients I love, starting with a great mystery. The story he told me is pretty much Chapter 1 of this novel – and from there I was on my own. Writing this book has been quite a ride. I hope you've had as much fun reading it as I had researching and writing it.

There are so many people to thank, as always, for the research help they have so generously given me, starting with: Sussex Police; Surrey and Sussex Major Crime Team; Surrey and Sussex Police Forensic Investigations Department; and the Metropolitan Police Central Imaging Investigation Unit.

A very big thank you to Police and Crime Commissioner Katy Bourne, OBE, and to Chief Constable Jo Shiner and so many officers and support staff, as well as retirees, from Sussex and other forces. I've listed them in alphabetical order and beg forgiveness for any omissions, but first I'm singling out Detective Superintendent Andy Wolstenholme for the immense help he has given me, lending me hours of his private time.

Inspector Jo Atkinson; PC Katie Baldwin; retired Chief Superintendent Graham Bartlett; PC Jon Bennion-Jones; Inspector James Biggs; Chief Inspector Steve Biglands; PC Olli Brooks; Rob Cooke; Dr Peter Dean; Emily Denyer, Financial Investigator; APS Andy Eyles; CSI James Gartrell; CSI Chris Gee; Aiden Gilbert, Digital Forensics; DC Julian Harrison-Jones; Chief Inspector Johnny Hartley; PC JJ Jackson; DC Vicky Jones; Charlotte Mckee, Digital Forensics; Chief Inspector Michelle Palmer-Harris; Sgt Russell Philips; Jason Quigley, Digital Forensics; DC Simon Rideout, Forensic Collision Investigation Unit; Meagan Robinson; Detective Superintendent Nick Sloan; Robin Smith, Chief of Police, States of Jersey; James Stather, Forensic Investigations; Pauline Sweeney MCT; DS Mark Taylor; Julian Taylor, Senior Collision Investigator for Sussex; Detective Chief Superintendent Jason Tingley; PC Richard Trundle; Gabriella Weston, Digital Forensics; Chief Inspector Andrew Westwood; and finally Beth Durham, Suzanne Heard, Jill Pedersen and Katie Perkins, all of Sussex Police Corporate Communications.

Heartfelt thanks also to: Martin Allen, John Baker, Brighton City airport, Professor Alison Bruce, Charlie Cahill, Mike Canas, Rob Cooke, Sean Didcott, Sam Down, Geoff Duffield, Lorna Fairbairn, Dominic Fortnam, Darren Fry, Gemma Hawkes, Debra Humphris, Haydn Kelly, Rob Kempson, Joseph Langford, Richard Le Quesne, Rupert Maddox, Dr James Mair, David Martin, Chris Meredith, Marnie Middlemiss, Alan Moss, Dr Adrian Noon, Ray Packham, Thomas Paul, Richard Pedley, Alex Petrovic, Richard Price, Dr Graham Ramsden, Carl Read, Jack Roberts, Danny Robinson, Kit Robinson, Molly Robinson, Karina

Rodriguez Echavarria, Bob Ruffle, Alan Setterington, Bridget Short, Anthony Skeete, Reverend Ish Smale, Adam Stevens, John Stewart, Helen Touray, Dr Orlando Trujillo, Matt Wainwright, Emma Weir, Steven Willis, Dr David Wright, Joni Wood.

A massive thank you to my brilliant new publisher, Francesca Pathak, and the team at Pan Macmillan – to name just a few: Jonathan Atkins, Melissa Bond, Lara Borlenghi, Emily Bromfield, Sian Chilvers, Tom Clancy, Alex Coward, Stuart Dwyer, Claire Evans, Elle Gibbons, Lucy Hale, Hollie Iglesias, Daniel Jenkins, Christine Jones, Rebecca Kellaway, Neil Lang, Rebecca Lloyd, Sara Lloyd, James Long, Ellah Mwale, Rory O'Brien, Joanna Prior, Guy Raphael, Grace Rhodes, Laura Sherlock, Jade Tolley, super-star and recently retired Jeremy Trevathan, Charlotte Williams, Leanne Williams. And my brilliant freelancers Susan Opie and Fraser Crichton.

A huge thank you to my amazing literary agent, Isobel Dixon, and to everyone at my UK literary agency, Blake Friedmann: Sian Ellis-Martin, Nicole Etherington, Julian Friedmann, James Pusey, Daisy Way, Conrad Williams. And a big shoutout to my fabulously gifted UK PR team at Riot Communications: Caitlin Allen, Jules Barretto, Niamh Houston, Hedvig Lindstrom, Emily Souders.

I'm blessed with two incredibly talented and hardworking people in my life: my wife, Lara, and former Detective Chief Superintendent David Gaylor, both of whom head up Team James. David contributes so much to every aspect of my novels, both creatively and editorially, as well as, very crucially, to the authenticity of the police characters and scenes. He does the same with the stage plays and is a retained police adviser for the *Grace* TV series, also.

The other members of the team, each invaluable in their own way, are Chris Diplock, Jane Diplock, Martin Diplock, Dani Brown, Emma Gallichan, Lyn Gaylor, Sarah Middle, Amy Robinson, Mark Tuckwell and Chris Webb.

My most special thanks of all are reserved for Lara, who has the patience of a saint and so much wisdom. Lara is incredibly in tune with the beats and mood of our times and gives me invaluable help with the inner lives of my characters, as well as the storylines. She is equally invaluable when helping with the scripts and casting of the television series, *Grace*, and the stage plays.

A final shoutout to all the creatures in our ever-expanding menagerie, who enrich our lives in so many ways, as well as the sheer, non-judgemental love of so many of them helping to keep me grounded and sane! No matter how dark the morning's news might be, hand-feeding our pygmy goats popcorn and crackers, our guinea pigs carrots and dandelions, and our dogs their morning sausage treats never fails to put a smile on my face. Even the cats, who regard us as their servants, always make us laugh with their antics. Although we know that really they are judging us . . .

Something else that puts a huge smile on my face is to hear from you, my readers – I owe you so much for your support. Do keep your messages coming through any of the channels below.

Above all, stay safe and well.

Peter James

contact@peterjames.com
www.peterjames.com
 @peterjamesuk
 @peterjames.roygrace
 @peterjamesuk
 @thejerseyhomestead
 @mickeymagicandfriends
You Tube @PeterJamesPJTV
 @peterjamesauthor

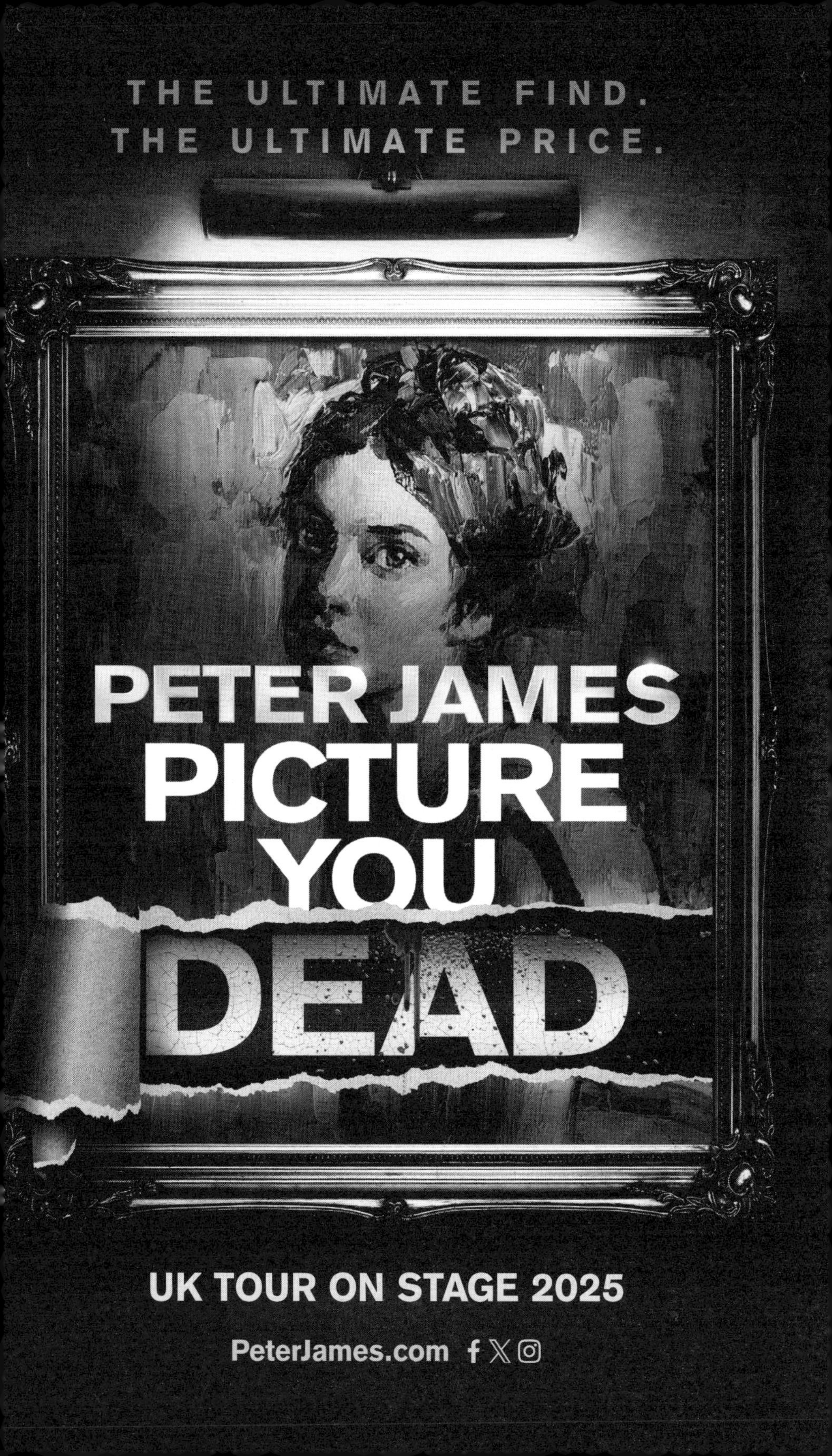

THE ULTIMATE FIND.
THE ULTIMATE PRICE.
PETER JAMES
PICTURE
YOU
DEAD
UK TOUR ON STAGE 2025
PeterJames.com

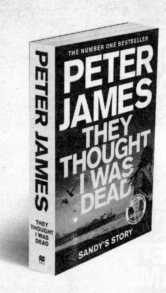

NOW A MAJOR ITV SERIES

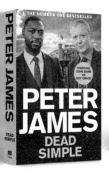 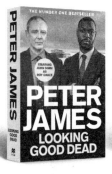 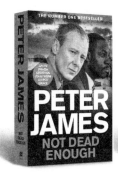 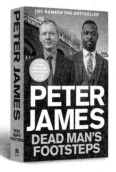

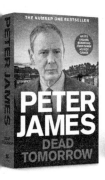 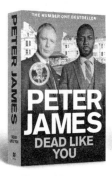 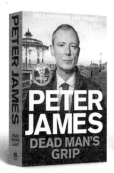 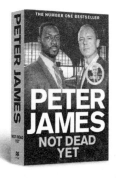

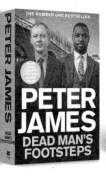 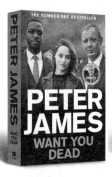 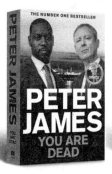 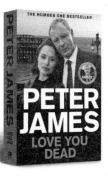

Peter James's first twelve books in the Detective
Superintendent Roy Grace series have been adapted
for television and star John Simm as Roy Grace.

Discover Peter James's books at
peterjames.com

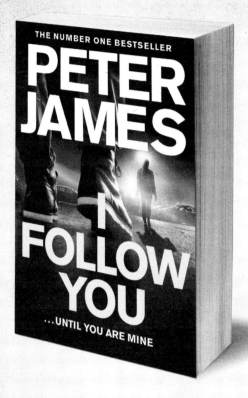

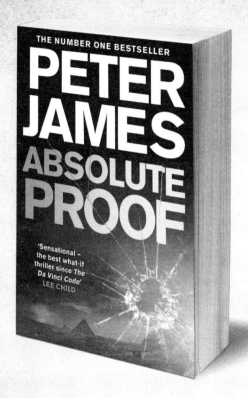

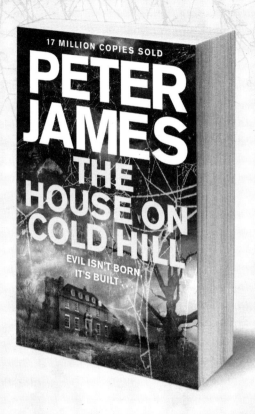

ABOUT THE AUTHOR

Peter James is a UK number one bestselling author, best known for his Detective Superintendent Roy Grace series, now a hit ITV drama starring John Simm as the troubled Brighton copper.

Much loved by crime and thriller fans for his fast-paced page-turners full of unexpected plot twists, sinister characters and accurate portrayals of modern-day policing, Peter has won over forty awards for his work, including the WHSmith Best Crime Author of All Time Award and the Crime Writers' Association Diamond Dagger. In 2024, it was announced that he is the creator of Her Majesty Queen Camilla's favourite fictional detective.

To date, Peter has written an impressive total of twenty *Sunday Times* number ones, has sold over 23 million copies worldwide and has been translated into thirty-eight languages. Six of his novels have been adapted into highly successful stage plays, grossing over £17 million at the UK box office alone, and his seventh play, based on his novel *Picture You Dead*, starts its national tour in early 2025.

www.peterjames.com
 @peterjamesuk
 @peterjames.roygrace
 @peterjamesuk
 @thejerseyhomestead
 @mickeymagicandfriends
You Tube @PeterJamesPJTV
 @peterjamesauthor